You Then, Me Now

ALSO BY NICK ALEXANDER

Things We Never Said

The Bottle of Tears

The Other Son

The Photographer's Wife

The Hannah Novels

The Half-Life of Hannah

Other Halves

The CC Novels

The Case of the Missing Boyfriend

The French House

The Fifty Reasons Series

50 Reasons to Say Goodbye

Sottopassaggio

Good Thing, Bad Thing

Better Than Easy

Sleight of Hand

13:55 Eastern Standard Time

You Then, Me Now

nick alexander

LAKE UNION
PUBLISHING

This is a work of fiction. Names, characters, organizations, places, events, and incidents are either products of the author's imagination or are used fictitiously. Any resemblance to actual persons, living or dead, or actual events is purely coincidental.

Published by Lake Union Publishing, Seattle

www.apub.com

ISBN-13: 9781503958623
ISBN-10: 1503958620

Cover design by Debbie Clement

Printed in the United States of America

You Then, Me Now

PROLOGUE

She is staring at her toes. Her legs are outstretched above the shimmering blue of the swimming pool and she's surprised at the lime-green gloss of her toenails – she doesn't remember painting them this colour. But it's pretty, she decides. And it contrasts particularly well with the sunlit mosaic of the pool. Perhaps, for summer at least, green is the new pink.

She closes her eyes and turns her face skywards. She can feel the hot sunlight on her eyelids. The world, momentarily, is red, and warm. She has never felt more relaxed.

A movement of air caresses her body, followed by a harsher, cooler gust of actual wind, so she opens her eyes and watches the leaves of the tree at the far end of the pool as they shimmer in the breeze, switching from light to dark and then back again, like pixels that can't make up their minds on a faulty television screen.

The wind blows again and she can feel goose pimples rise on her arms so, in search of a T-shirt, she turns just in time to see three sheets of paper from the table behind her rise and flutter into the water.

Her initial reaction is to laugh. *Sod's law*, she thinks. *They could have landed anywhere, but they landed in the pool.*

Leisurely, still amused, she stands and walks along the edge of the water until the sheets of now-soaked paperwork are within reach. She kneels – the hot concrete burns her knees – and by leaning out, manages to recover two of the pages. She lays them on the paving to dry, but the third, a flimsy slip of paper, is out of reach and sinking fast, rolling and twisting as it goes under, so she stands and dives in gracefully. It's cooler than she expected and the shock of cold makes her gasp.

She swims to the centre of the pool, takes a breath, and plunges. She's aware that the breath should have been deeper. It's as if she has a sense of déjà vu warning her of what's to come.

At first, the sunlight shimmers across her bare arms and she can still feel the warmth of it across her back. But as she swims ever deeper, chasing the elusive slip of paper, the light fades and the water changes from blue to green, and then, slowly, to inky black.

She starts to feel scared. The slip of paper is, she remembers, incredibly important (though she can't, strangely, remember why). But the pool is so deep and dark and cold, and some inexplicable undercurrent is sucking the prize ever deeper.

There are things down here, too – living things. She can sense them all around her so, suddenly fearful, she glances upwards to see the distant ripple of daylight far, far above.

She releases a bubble of air from her mouth and watches it shape-shift and break into smaller bubbles as it rises. When she looks down again, she can barely see the rectangle of paper, so fast is it descending.

Panicky now, she dives jerkily, urgently, but her lungs are bursting and though, when she tries really hard, when she gives it everything she's got, her fingers brush the edge of the paper, she fails every time to grasp it.

Something touches her leg and there's a clicking sound that makes her think of an octopus. Did she see a documentary about them? And was that not the sound they made?

But something is definitely wrapping around her leg; something that scares her, something that makes her gasp again, releasing precious air from her lungs. She twists her head upwards but the light has vanished and she's suddenly unsure of the right direction. *What if up is down now?* she wonders. Things can swap around in life, unpredictably, she knows this. Left can become right. Hope can become despair.

She kicks towards where the light should be but there's nothing there, just more inky, oily blackness. Full-blown panic starts to set in, and she thrusts with all her might, trying to escape whatever has a hold of her right foot as she begins, she can sense it, to drown.

She knows now. She knows as if she has always known it – that this is how she dies. This is where and when and how it happens. *She drowned in a pool*, she hears them saying. It seems such a pathetic way to go; almost laughable really.

But then a voice reaches her, distorted and filtered by its passage through the water. 'Mum,' it's calling. 'Mum! I know you're in there. MUM!'

She swims towards the noise, kicking hard to free her right leg and floundering with all her might so at least whoever is there will be aware of her presence, and just as she exhales the last snatch of stale air from her lungs, just as she knows that she has no choice but to let the liquid invade her body, she breaks the surface to find herself soaked in sweat, her leg wrapped in a sheet, and her spirit distraught, once again, at the loss of that damned slip of paper.

'Mum!' the voice calls out again. There's a rap-tap-tap on the window and she recognises the tapping, just for a moment, as the clicking noise a dream octopus might make, and feels scared all over again.

Laura opens her mouth to reply but no sound comes out, so she runs her tongue across her teeth, swallows with difficulty, and tries again.

'I'll be right there, Becky,' she croaks. Then again, louder, more successfully, 'I'll be right there! Just give me a minute.'

ONE

Becky

I invented my father when I was five years old.

He was a fireman and wore a stiff uniform with big brass buttons. He drove around in a shiny red fire engine with an extensible ladder on the roof.

Dad had many different jobs over the years: he was, as I say, a fireman but also a policeman, and a brain surgeon. He was even, briefly, the president of Norway.

That should have been a bit of a giveaway to my school friends actually, because there is no president of Norway. Norway, it turns out, is a monarchy. But of course no one knew that at Salmestone Junior School. If we're being completely honest here, I think half of the teachers would have struggled to point to Norway on a map.

Though, at school, I'd declare with unshakeable and apparently convincing certainty that my father was now at the pinnacle of this or that profession, at home he was always the Great Unmentionable Mystery.

He had died before I was born – this much I knew. But I didn't know who he had been or the details of how he had died, and I didn't know why I wasn't allowed to ask about him either.

For the most part, I didn't think about it that much, not about the reality of him as a specific person who had existed and who no longer existed. Perhaps that's just a concept that's too hard for a child to wrap her brain around.

I was generally pretty happy though: with Mum, with my life, and with my astronaut father (yes, that was another one). In fact I was happier about my make-believe dad than a number of my school friends were with their very real fathers.

'Does your dad smack you?' I remember a friend asking.

'Never!' I replied. 'But he always brings me chocolates when he comes back from the space station.'

My mother was undeniably real, so I couldn't pretend she didn't slap the backs of my legs when I came out of school with muddy knees, and I couldn't pretend she was anything other than an estate agent's secretary.

But I did have to invent what was going on in her head, because there was always something unknowable about Mum. She always looked as if she was keeping secrets from you, and as it turned out, of course, she was.

Mum was a nervous, skinny, rather pointy-faced woman with few real friends. She has rounded off with age, both physically and psychologically, but back then she wasn't an easy woman to feel close to, not even as her daughter. On the material side of things, though, she was an absolute ace.

It must have been really hard being a single mother but I never wanted for anything, and that certainly wasn't any thanks to Gran who, being a devout Catholic, was as furious with Mum for getting pregnant as she was with me for being an everlasting reminder of her daughter's sins.

Mum cried a fair bit when I was little. Actually, my earliest memory is of her crying. We were still living in that tiny bedsit by the station, so I must have been under five, because once I started school Mum got a job and we moved to a council flat. Anyway, I woke up and realised Mum was sobbing, so I crawled to the end of the bed. In my memory, that was quite a long crawl, so maybe I was even younger. I put my arms around her, just like Mum did when I cried, and asked her what was wrong.

She gestured at the room around us and said, 'Oh, it's nothing. It's just this place. It gets me down sometimes, that's all. But don't mind me, I'm just being a silly sausage.'

I remember picturing her as a sausage with a face, frying, crying. And then I looked around the room in puzzlement, trying to understand what was wrong. Because to me it looked perfect.

We had one of those mini-hob/oven combinations in the corner – a Baby Belling, I think it was called. There was a television that showed *Budgie the Little Helicopter*, and a wardrobe full of clothes and toys. We had a red velvet armchair from the previous tenants, with cigarette-burn holes I could stick my fingers through, and orange curtains with a swirly pattern that looked like lollipops. I honestly didn't understand what more anyone could want.

Looking back it must have been horrible, I suppose. And it must have been depressing beyond belief to bring a child up alone in a single room in a town where she knew virtually no one.

But me? I loved it. I liked the doll's-house nature of our accommodation and I liked the fact that we spent every possible moment alone together, invariably on the beach. I liked the flashing lights of the amusement arcades and the sound of the trains trundling past the end of the road. I liked being walked to town along the seafront and laughing at the wind, which was so strong sometimes that I had to hang on to Mum's hand really hard to avoid being, quite literally, blown away. So I struggled to understand why Mum was so sad.

Once I started school, things got slowly better for her, thank God. Mum got jobs – a brief stint in a taxi office and then the secretarial job at the estate agent where she was to work for fifteen years. And when I was ten, she met Brian.

I latched on to Brian like a limpet. I think I was genuinely afraid he'd just walk back out the door, but I'm told I had always been obsessive about men. I was forever walking up to them in the supermarket and taking their hands, just to see what it felt like. By the time I was eight, I was quite consciously trying to fix Mum up with my school friends' fathers or with the meter man, or even the guy who owned the sweet shop. 'What do you think about the man with the Labrador?' I would ask her, desperately looking for an opening while also trying to obtain more data so I could refine my search criteria. 'Do you think he's nice-looking?' But my search seemed hopeless and I suspected, even at an early age, that my mum was in some way broken and quite simply incapable of relationships.

So Brian was unexpected, to say the least. Being generous and funny and bald (the bald was a plus – I liked rubbing his shiny head), and incredibly relaxed in the face of what wasn't, looking back, a particularly relaxed relationship, he seemed heaven-sent.

He dumped Mum when I was eighteen, which was one of those surprises which turns out to be not so surprising after all. It always seemed to me, and no doubt to Brian, as if Mum was holding out on him, as if she was forever keeping something back – her joy, her sense of fun. Her love, ultimately.

I had known from the earliest age how it felt to be aware that you never quite knew someone, because that's how things were for me, too. Because the one subject I wasn't allowed to discuss was my father, I suspected Mum's aloofness, her brokenness, was linked to that.

Mostly, when I tried to discuss in my clumsy, childlike way who my father was or, more precisely, why I didn't have one, Mum would distract me by talking about something else. Other times she'd ward me off with a few sharp words or a sudden headache or simply silence, as if she hadn't heard my question at all. Only once, when I was about seven, I think, did I manage to force her to engage.

I had a perfectly calculated meltdown about it all. I stamped my little feet and demanded to know why, unlike all my school friends, I didn't have a father. Mum made a cup of tea – to give herself time to think, I reckon – and then she sat me down in the lounge. 'This is incredibly difficult for me to talk about,' she explained earnestly. 'So I only want to go over this once. Do you understand?'

I nodded that I did. I was trembling with excitement, as I recall, because I had never before got this far with her on the subject.

'Your father was a gorgeous, lovely man,' she said. 'He was very good-looking, just like you – in fact he looked a lot like you – and I loved him very much. But sadly, *very* sadly, he had an accident and died, just after I met him. I thought my heart was broken, but then you came along and mended it for me. OK? And now it's just the two of us.'

I nodded thoughtfully. 'But . . .' I started.

'How would you like to go and get a 99 ice cream on the seafront?' Mum asked.

'But . . .' I said, struggling as I spoke to resist caving in to the unusual and tempting offer, even as I understood it was pure bribery.

'You don't want an ice cream?' Mum asked. 'Oh, well . . .'

I knew from experience that that, as they say, was the end of that. I also knew that unless I shut up about the subject of my father sharpish, the ice cream offer would be withdrawn. And so I smiled and nodded, and ran to get my coat. As I pulled it on, I remember looking at myself in the hall mirror and trying, and failing, to imagine a man who looked like me.

If someone were to make a sort of colour chart of emotions, Mum would rarely have moved out of the zone that lies between 'normal' and 'sucking lemons'. That'll sound a bit harsh, but she really did always have this strange expression on her face. She always seemed to be squinting a little bit, as if whatever she was looking at was hurting her eyes, or as if, perhaps, she had the beginning of a toothache. I don't really know how fun-loving Brian managed to put up with it for eight whole years.

I loved – I love – my mother, though. Don't get me wrong. I love her like I love my right arm or my eyesight or my heart. She is and always has been the centre of my whole world. As humans, we're designed to be able to love people despite their imperfections, and that's just as well really, because as a race, we do seem to have so many of them. When you grow up with someone, those imperfections seem totally normal to you. I felt I knew Mum better than I knew myself, though of course, naming her quirks and understanding her in a conscious manner wouldn't come until much later; not until I had the necessary vocabulary to construct those thoughts. But on an unconscious level, I *got* her. I understood her, limitations and all. And so was unsurprised, as I said before, when Brian left.

I hated him for it, all the same. More specifically, I hated him for leaving *me*. Jenny, his new girlfriend, had a whole ready-made family for him to slot into, and I'm sure that having gone overnight from one child to five, Brian must suddenly have found himself very busy. But he basically never phoned me again, and that still strikes me as unforgivable. I mean, I know at eighteen I was a bit of a sarky, moody so-and-so, but all the same . . . a gift at Christmas, a phone call on a birthday – just something to say, 'You were *not* nothing to me.' I truly struggle to see what the cost of maintaining basic civilities would have been. Then again, maybe my need for a father had simply blinded me to the truth. Perhaps he was just a bit of a nob all along.

Anyway, I was angry with Brian for dumping me (that's how it felt to my eighteen-year-old self) but also angry at Mum for not loving him enough to make him want to stick around. And being off at college provided the perfect excuse to cut the umbilical cord linking me to the whole sorry mess.

I was living in a shared house in Bristol; I was going to parties and smoking joints; I was working my way through a whole string of unsuitable boyfriends. Visiting Mum felt like the most unappealing option out there. And so I shamefully abandoned her for a while.

In my final year, though, Gran died, and Mum was surprisingly upset about it. I mean, you could hardly say they were close. Mum had told me very little about her childhood with Granny Eiléan, but what I did know from the few stories she had told me – tales of evenings locked in her room without meals, and beatings and forced confessions of her sins – made my blood curdle.

All the same, Mum seemed to cry about Gran's death every time I phoned. A few months later, Right-House laid her off as well, just like that, after fifteen years – the bastards. So my anger shifted to concern, and I started to visit more often.

On one trip home, I found Prozac in her bathroom. On another, I found an empty blister pack of generic Valium in her bedside cabinet. Mum went quiet for a while as well. I'd catch her staring into the middle distance looking vacant, as if her soul had temporarily left her body. Whatever it was that had previously been broken within her seemed to have shattered, under stress, into a thousand tiny pieces, leaving her unable to even pretend any more that everything was OK.

So despite the ambiance at Mum's being pretty miserable, in my more optimistic moments, I started to envisage moving back once my course was over.

I was missing the sea breeze and the twinkling lights, I suppose. Plus, the town was purportedly going through a bit of a hipster revival. There were clearly worse places to live, I told myself.

And that's how I came to find the envelope.

TWO

Laura

No matter how you look at it, Conor changed my life.

I met him at a rave party in 1994. That seems such a ridiculous thing to say, especially coming from a sensible soul like myself, but it's true.

My mother was a deeply religious Catholic who for some reason seemed determined to inflict upon me the same sadistic upbringing her own parents had inflicted on her. And outside the home, my education had been assured by St Angela's Ursuline. Suffice to say, I hadn't had the wildest of childhoods, and I'd taken far longer than most kids to cut free. Mum continued to treat me like a child well beyond adolescence, giving me curfews, kicking off about where I went out and with whom, and it wasn't really until my mid-twenties that things loosened up a little.

Because my father, a rarely present merchant seaman, had left us when I was eight (to shack up with a woman he'd met in Denmark – oh, the sin!), I hadn't felt able to move out, as that would leave my mother *entirely* on her own. Plus, living in London, I would never have managed to pay the bills single-handed anyway. But when I was about twenty, Mum, who was a nurse, began to alternate between eight- and twelve-hour shifts with occasional sixteen-hour 'sleep-busters', as she called them. These sleep-busters, specifically, provided a window of opportunity that had never existed before. So though officially I was always at home tucked up in bed, I increasingly managed to cut loose from her terrifying iron rule.

Most of my friends came from similar backgrounds to mine, and they had definitely all suffered the same guilt-inducing education at St Angela's, so none of them were particularly crazy either. With one exception: Abby.

The first thing Abby ever said to me was, 'My dad says this is all bollocks.'

'I'm sorry?' I whispered. We were in a Bible study class.

'My dad says all this water-into-wine stuff is about as true as *Doctor Who*,' she explained confidentially.

I was ten years old, and coming from where I came from, no one had ever suggested any of this was open to debate, let alone 'bollocks'.

'Shh,' I said. 'That's blasphemy.' Blasphemy was severely punished in our house, often with physical violence.

But I had already decided to make Abby my new best friend.

By age twenty-five, we were still best friends, and Abby had well and truly broken free.

She was dating a beautiful black guy called Winston Harper. He looked a bit like Terrence Howard – he had the same beautiful eyes – but he was taller and more muscular.

Winston's best friend was a well-known DJ called Carl Fox, and that friendship opened the doors to just about every rave party in Britain. And in the early nineties there were a *lot* of raves in Britain. Almost every weekend Abby and Winston would head off to some muddy field or another to dance the night away.

Abby had been trying to convince me to go with them for years, but as I was of a less-than-adventurous nature, and because most of the music Winston favoured sounded like computer beeps, I'd resisted. I was terrified, too, of what my mother would do to me if she found out.

By 1994, though, it seemed the rave party thing was nearing its end. The newspapers were full of outraged reports about irresponsible youngsters leaving fields littered with beer cans, and the government was legislating to make all the 'orbital' parties around the M25 illegal. And I can only admit that this almost universal condemnation started to make them seem quite attractive to me. So finally, that August, I let Abby convince me.

'It's gonna be one of the biggest parties the country has ever seen,' she told me one evening. 'It's going to be like the Woodstock of dance music or whatever, and one day you'll have kids and you'll have to tell them you stayed home and watched it on the bloody news, Laura. Just think of the shame!'

'I can't, Mum would go crazy . . .' I said, starting to spout my usual fears. But then I remembered Mum was on a sleep-buster that weekend. 'Actually, she's got a double shift on Saturday,' I said. 'Would we be home for four a.m.?'

Abby shot a complex glance at Winston. 'Oh, of course,' he said. 'Absolutely.'

We travelled to Northampton in a Transit van. I was wedged in the back between boxes of Carl's records while Abby and Winston travelled up front. I felt sick at first – I couldn't see out of the windows – but I soon fell asleep, so was fine. When I woke up, we were at a racetrack and thousands of people were already milling around the open, grassy space in the centre.

We carried all the boxes of records on to the sound stage and I was finally introduced to Carl. He was already quite the star by then but he was very ordinary and friendly towards me. Next we went to a beer tent and drank pints of lager from plastic goblets. Everyone was smoking joints and I remember being shocked by the fact that there were no police to stop them. Both Abby and Winston tried for the umpteenth time to get me to smoke, but I refused. I have never smoked a single cigarette in my life. I have always found the idea utterly repulsive, and that's always struck me as rather lucky really.

The music started about nine, and what can I say? I didn't like it. I did my best to dance by emulating those around me, and just occasionally there would be a snatch of a tune I could latch on to, or a moment in a song when an actual human voice came through. But mostly it still sounded like random computer noise to me. I was always far more Britpop than techno.

By eleven, my feet were aching and I was feeling well and truly bored. I had lost track of Abby and Winston too, which made me want to cry. But then the music stopped and everyone cheered and there they were again, holding little bottles of water. 'Carl's on next,' Abby told me. 'You'll love it. Here.' She proffered one of the bottles and I frowned.

'Is that water?' I asked. I suspected she'd used the bottles to smuggle vodka in or something. Water seemed unlikely, to say the least.

'Of course it's water,' she laughed. 'Hydrate, dear. Hydrate!'

I shrugged, unscrewed the cap, and swigged. It was, to my disappointment, just water. 'Are we going soon?' I asked. It was almost midnight, and if we were going to be home by four we'd need, by my reckoning, to get going.

At that moment, Carl appeared on stage and people started to scream deafeningly. He began flicking through his records, propping specific ones up so they stuck out of the box.

'We're not going anywhere for hours,' Abby said. 'So take a chill pill.' She held out one hand and opened it, revealing a small yellow pill, printed with a smiley face. 'Here, take this,' she said.

'Why?' I asked.

'Because then you'll stop worrying about getting home.'

'And because if you take it you'll have a *really* good time,' Winston added.

'And if you don't, you'll just carry on being a bore,' Abby said. 'All right?'

'Is it drugs?' I asked.

Both Abby and Winston fell about laughing at this.

'But I don't want to take drugs,' I said, while trying to imagine what kind of punishment Mum would mete out if I did and she found out. Mum was still perfectly capable of slapping my face or sending me to my room without dinner. She might even phone the police and report me. Even at twenty-five, I still didn't have the faintest idea how to stand up to her.

'How long have we been friends?' Abby asked. 'Forever, yeah?'

'Well, yeah . . .' I conceded.

'Then trust me. It's just an E.'

'But I don't see the point.'

'Well, of course you don't,' Abby said. 'That's why you need it. Don't be such a bloody Virgin Valerie.'

Virgin Valerie had been the most unpleasant, pious member of our class. The comment cut me to the core. I reached out and took the pill between finger and thumb. 'You'll look after me if it makes me ill, right?'

Abby nodded. 'I'll look after you. But it won't. I promise.'

I moved the pill towards my lips, but then hesitated. 'And I won't end up addicted or anything?'

'It's an E,' Winston said. 'It's not bloody crack cocaine. Jesus!'

And because I felt like I was being unreasonably prim and proper, and because a few people were laughing at me by now, and because I'd spent half of my short life trying to shake off the various shackles of my upbringing, I took it.

'So, what happens now?' I asked, once I'd taken another swig of the water.

'Now, we *dance*!' Abby said theatrically. Carl had just put his first record on and the crowd had started to scream and throb and bop up and down. The excitement was palpable.

I forced myself to sway my hips to the music – at least Carl's stuff had a rhythm I could understand. But I still didn't like it much, I was desperately craving a bit of Blur or Oasis, and so I soon decided that the drug wasn't working, and that was fine by me.

Over the course of the next thirty or forty minutes, though, my fake dancing became more real, and I slowly, almost unnoticeably, ceased feeling bored. Then a further half an hour into Carl's set, something happened. I honestly couldn't tell you today if the music suddenly got better or whether the drug took effect, or whether perhaps it was a bit of both, but something amazing happened to me, something I can only describe as ecstatic.

The crowd had become ever more tightly packed until we were dancing as a sole organism. Your rhythm really had to match that of your immediate neighbours, otherwise you bumped elbows uncomfortably, and so gradually everyone had begun to groove together.

Carl was doing something clever with his music, too, something I didn't immediately understand. It seemed to build slowly, become denser, ever more complex, ever more compulsive. And then he would drag all of the bass out of the sound leaving you hungry, thirsty, craving for the rhythm . . . Somehow, almost undetectably, it would start to build again, hinting at something that was coming, at some brighter future just around the corner. And then with a flick of the wrist – from where we were dancing, you could see him do it – he'd whack some lever on his sound deck and the bass would come rushing back in, enveloping you, soaking you, rolling over you like a breaker and when this happened the hairs on the back of my neck would stand up and I'd smile uncontrollably and bounce up and down with the seven thousand people around me. There were so many of us that I swear I could feel the ground beneath us vibrating. If you've never danced to that kind of music then I can only really describe the force of that feeling by saying it was the closest thing I've ever felt to an orgasm – every part of me was tingling – and it happened over and over again.

I started to copy the various dances of the people around me. Abby swayed like bamboo in the breeze, looping and rolling her arms over each other while smiling beatifically. I had never seen her look so beautiful. Winston had an entirely different style of dance, barely moving his feet and chopping with his hands as if he were doing slow-motion karate moves. He danced as if he were in a Perspex tube limiting himself to the space within, or perhaps moving as if one of the laser beams that floated above our heads might chop off any limb that extended beyond the space he'd been allocated. At one point he put his arm around my shoulders and shouted, 'Are you having a good time?'

'I am!' I shouted back. 'I never liked this music before! Crazy!'

'It's the E,' Winston said. 'It's a decoder. It makes no sense otherwise.'

And then the music reached another one of its climaxes – it felt like each was more powerful than the last – and as it rolled over us all and the crowd went crazy, I pushed Winston laughingly away. I needed my space back so I could swim freely through the warm surge of sound enveloping me.

It was then that Conor appeared. I had closed my eyes for a moment, the better to concentrate on the overwhelming beauty of all these sound waves, and when I opened them, he was there, grinning at me, and I felt like I was in love with him instantly. I was in love with everyone around me at that precise moment, but because Conor was the closest, I was in love with him the most.

He was short, stocky, balding, bearded, red-headed, with brown eyes that were so dark, they looked almost black. He was wearing, somewhat incongruously, a shirt and a waistcoat with jeans, and there was something incredibly sexy, incredibly self-confident about him. And he was dancing the most brilliant dance. It was as if his lower half was dancing like Abby, swaying and rolling and grooving – he seemed to have the most amazingly mobile hips. Meanwhile, from the waist up, he was dancing like Winston, chopping and cutting, seemingly forming little boxes with his hands and, from time to time, outrageously spinning on one foot and then landing perfectly facing me all over again, a vast self-satisfied grin on his face.

I felt more drawn to him than I ever had to anyone in my entire life up until that moment. Which is a lesson for us all, is it not? Never choose a man while under the influence of chemicals that mess with your brain, my friends. Never.

We danced until three, but then a new DJ came on who favoured a really harsh, angular kind of techno that I was convinced was going to make my ears bleed.

Conor took my hand. 'Come,' he shouted in my ear. 'This is shite.'

So I let him lead me through the crowd.

We crossed to the furthest end of the track where a few hundred people were sitting or lying down. I sat and then rolled onto my back to look at the stars.

Conor sat beside me and then manoeuvred himself so my head was on his thigh.

'What a great bash!' he said, stroking my hair in a way that seemed entirely normal, entirely logical. His caresses felt like a thousand tiny electric shocks, which seemed to my addled brain to match the hundreds of stars above us.

'My first,' I said.

'I'm sorry?'

'My first-ever rave.'

'Really?' Conor asked.

I nodded. 'I'm a good Catholic girl, me.'

'Lucky for me,' Conor said.

'I'm sorry?'

'I *love* good Catholic girls. Because I'm a good Catholic boy, myself.'

'You're Irish,' I stated. I'd only just noticed his accent.

'Conor O'Leary at your service,' he said. 'And other than being the most beautiful girl here, you would be?'

'Laura. Laura Ryan,' I said. I could feel myself blushing. 'I'm half Irish too, as it happens. My Mum's Irish. Dad's name was Sturgis, but Mum went back to Ryan when he left, so I changed mine too. Mum preferred it that way, so . . . It's easier to just do what she says most of the time,' I explained, wondering why I was blathering in such a way.

'Pleased to meet you, Laura Ryan,' Conor said. And then he moved so his face was hovering just above mine. 'May I?' he asked.

'Oh, yes please,' I replied brazenly.

When he kissed me, I closed my eyes and all those stars I'd been looking at seemed to explode inside my head. And I remember thinking two thoughts simultaneously. *I love you, Conor O'Leary.* And, *I love this drug.*

I was still incredibly immature back then, and terribly inexperienced with men, too. I had slept with two boys in my entire life, one who, because he wanted to sleep with me, I had assumed was my boyfriend, but he dumped me about thirty seconds after it was over, and another who I suppose one could say I 'dated' for a few weeks when I was eighteen. Mum had put an end to that one, and because I was already realising I didn't much like him, I'd been relatively happy about her intervention. But since I was eighteen, there had been nothing. I had no idea what love actually was, and so chose to assume that this must be what it felt like.

Though the kiss felt heavenly, any thoughts of sex were a million miles away. Conor's mouth felt warm and magical, his embrace seemed in some way like home. I felt at one with everyone and everything and, sensing that warmth, that physical closeness, was simply part of the whole experience. It won't make much sense, but it felt like a God-given right. My right to be happy, perhaps. To feel loved. To be at one with this world; a world as soft and welcoming as marshmallow. Conor was just part of the bigger picture.

Despite the music, which even at this distance was deafening, we must have fallen asleep, because it was the sun on my face that woke me. Conor was behind, spooning me, his arms enveloping me against the cold. I lifted his heavy, hairy arm away and sat up and yawned. I still felt wonderful and I wondered if this feeling of being submerged by optimism might now be a permanent state. Perhaps a single pill had immunised me against the all-encompassing guilt of my upbringing once and for all. Wouldn't that be wonderful? Or perhaps it wasn't the pill at all. Maybe it was being in love that had changed everything.

It was almost eight thirty and the music, by now, had ceased. The sound stage was empty and only a few hundred people were left, milling around in a sea of Coke cans, plastic goblets and discarded water bottles.

'I need to find Abby,' I said quietly.

'Uh?' Conor asked, propping himself up on one elbow and rubbing his eyes.

'I need to find my friends. They're my lift home.'

'Right,' he said. 'Where do you live again?'

'Hornchurch,' I told him.

'London?'

'Yeah. East. Out by Upminster.'

'Well, I can take you to central London, if that helps. I've got to get to Harrow by lunchtime anyway, so . . .'

◆ ◆ ◆

We wandered around for a while, but though the Transit van was still parked behind the sound stage, there was no sign of Abby, nor Winston, nor Carl, so I found someone with a pen and left a note on the windscreen saying I'd got a lift home.

Conor's car was in a nearby car park. It was a big, rather flashy, white BMW. It looked a bit like a drug dealer's car. But the leather seats felt heavenly to my tired body, and I slipped into a sort of trance as Conor sped away and the world began to flash by.

'I want to see you again,' Conor said out of nowhere, as we were hurtling down the M1. He was holding my hand. Other than to change gear, I don't think he had let go of it since we'd left.

'Me too,' I said genuinely.

'Great. Well, I've a job in Wales starting tomorrow. Till the twenty-seventh. And after that I've promised myself a break in the sunshine somewhere – maybe a week, ten days – but we could meet up after that if you want.'

'Wow,' I said. 'That's a long way off.' I was struggling to even imagine letting go of Conor's hand at that moment, let alone a one-month break. I told him I was on holiday too. 'The last week of August, first week and a bit of September.'

'Interesting,' Conor said. 'Plans?'

I shrugged. 'I thought I might go to Ibiza,' I said. 'But I haven't decided yet.'

'Ibiza . . .' Conor repeated. 'Sounds like good craic.'

I sighed. 'Abby – my friend – and her boyfriend are going. They've invited me to tag along, but I'm not sure.' I wasn't that keen on the idea of playing gooseberry for two weeks, if the truth be told. Plus, Abby and Winston would be out dancing every night and I feared I'd come home more tired than before I left.

'Oh,' Conor said. 'Well, Ibiza's pretty cool, so they tell me. If you like to party.'

'It wouldn't have been my choice,' I said. 'But that's where they're going, so . . .'

'And where would your choice be?' Conor asked.

'Oh, Greece!' I said definitively. 'Santorini.'

'Because?'

I smiled at the fact that I'd spotted Conor's trait of asking one-word questions. It seemed somehow to be the first thing I actually knew about him. *This is how it starts*, I thought.

'I don't know, really,' I answered. And it was the truth. Other than the fact that I'd had a poster of Santorini on my bedroom wall for so long I couldn't even remember where it came from, and I'd woken up for twenty years looking at those blue-domed rooftops, at that rippling, sparkling sea, I knew nothing whatsoever about the place. 'It's just a sort of obsession, I suppose. A dream of mine.'

'Ibiza's gotta be more fun,' Conor said. 'Would you fancy it? With me?'

'Ibiza?' I said. 'Um, maybe . . . yes . . . Perhaps.' Though the ecstasy was still playing with my brain, still making everything sound wonderful, making the unlikely seem entirely possible, my normal, logical self was starting to wake up somewhere, deep within. And that tiny anaesthetised part of me was aware that planning to go on holiday with someone I had only just met wasn't necessarily a reasonable course of action, even if I was, perhaps, in love with him.

'We could go with Abby and Winston, I suppose,' I said, thinking I'd feel safer with them around. Was my subconscious already tuning in to unspoken clues Conor was sending out into the ether?

Conor frowned. 'I could take you to your Santa place,' he said. 'Realise that dream of yours. That'd be a great way for us to get to know each other, don't you think?'

I sat up straight and turned to look at him. 'Santorini?' I said. 'Are you serious?'

Conor shrugged. 'Why not?' he said. 'You only live once, right? It's hot, is it? They have beaches and shit, do they?'

'Oh, absolutely,' I said. 'And you're on holiday the same dates as me?' My excitement had provoked a fresh rush of drug-enhanced optimism. 'Last week of August, first week of September?'

'That's it,' Conor replied. 'Well, from the twenty-eighth to be precise.'

'Me too!' I laughed. 'The exact same dates. Well, I'm off from the Saturday before, but . . .'

'It's destiny,' Conor said, squeezing my hand. 'I'm your destiny.'

And I'm yours, I thought. But unlike Conor, I couldn't say such things.

'What do you do?' I asked, that little voice now reminding me I didn't know this man at all.

'Roofer,' Conor said.

I took in the drug-dealer opulence of the car again, of Conor's expensive shirt and waistcoat, his brogue shoes . . . 'You must be a very successful roofer,' I said.

Conor released my hand from his and returned it to the steering wheel. 'What the feck is that supposed to mean?' he asked, turning a little red in the face.

'Oh, I didn't mean . . .' I stumbled, realising I'd upset him by sounding suspicious. 'I was . . . It was supposed to be a compliment.'

'If a roofer's not good enough for you then maybe you should find yourself someone else to go to Santa-fecking-wherever,' Conor said, sounding almost as if he was joking, but not quite.

'I just meant that you look very successful,' I explained, tears unexpectedly threatening. I was so used to Mum flying off the handle at things I said that I still assumed, back then, that it must automatically be my fault.

Conor's nostrils flared as if he was going to explode but then, for a minute or so, he said nothing, visibly calming himself down. 'I do all right,' he finally mumbled, 'thank you very much.'

'I can see that,' I said. 'You have a lovely car. Lovely clothes . . .' I looked out of the side window and grimaced at the service station we were passing.

'And you?' Conor asked after a few minutes. 'What do you do?'

'Oh, nothing exciting,' I said, feeling like the cat who rolls over in submission before a dominant male. 'I'm just a secretary. In an accountant's office. Just a typist really.'

'Right,' Conor said, sounding reassured. 'Well, then.'

About a minute later, he squeezed my hand and added, 'It's good you have a job, though. I mean, you meet so many wasters at these things. I could tell you were a clever lass when I met you.'

He dropped me off on Edgware Road so I could get the District Line back home, but though he'd jotted my phone number down in his little diary, I honestly never thought I'd hear from him again.

As I trundled along on the Tube, my mood plummeted. The drug was wearing off and my absurd optimism was being replaced by a sense of inner emptiness and self-doubt. I'd said the wrong thing again. I'd upset him. I'd blown my chances. He was good-looking and well-dressed and funny, and I'd blown it. And now I had to go home alone and face Mum's anger. And even without her having any inkling of where I'd been and what I'd been up to, just the fact of my late arrival made that terrifying.

I'd slept at Abby's, I decided, trying to get my story straight. I glanced down at myself and noticed, for the first time, the grass burns down the side of my pink trousers and the mud on my white trainers.

Hopefully Mum would be asleep when I got in so I could slip them into the wash without her realising.

Yes, I'd slept at Abby's because . . . because we'd been to the cinema and . . . the film had been much longer than I expected. And I'd missed the last Tube home!

She'd still be furious, of course, but I'd make her lunch when she got up. I'd do the laundry (including my pink trousers) and even hoover. Mum hated hoovering. If I was lucky, I might get away with a mere telling-off and a few days of sulking.

And then, once she headed off to work, I'd sleep. Because I was suddenly feeling very, very tired.

Conor phoned me twice that week and, thank God, Mum was out at work both times.

He called once at eleven in the evening to (drunkenly) tell me he was in love with me – which was enough to set my heart beating all over again – and once in the morning, just as I was leaving for work, to ask me if I really wanted to go to 'Santa-whatever-the-fuck-it's-called' with him.

The drugs, of course, were a long-forgotten memory by then. If anything, the after-effects had left me feeling insecure and rather depressed about everything. Not so much about Conor, who I still remembered as being quite lovely, but about my own ability to seduce him. About my worthiness, perhaps, for his love. To convince me, Conor persuaded me to meet him in central London the following Saturday. The fact he was prepared to drive all the way in from Cardiff just to talk to me struck me as mad, but in a romantic kind of way. Maybe he really liked me!

We met up in Oxford Street at two o'clock in the afternoon. He was wearing a suit, an elegant blue-checked number, and a pink, rather dandy tie. He looked pretty damned gorgeous in it. We kissed and it seemed to me that his breath smelled vaguely of beer, which seemed unlikely for someone who had just driven from Wales, so I discounted it.

I nearly asked him how a roofer came to be so impeccably dressed, but remembered at the last minute how badly my remarks on this subject had backfired previously. So instead, I simply said, 'Wow! Look at you!'

Conor fiddled with his tie, straightened himself proudly and said, 'Yes. That is the general idea.'

We ducked into a coffee shop. I was feeling shy and uncertain of myself, so I let him do all the talking. He certainly had the gift of the gab.

He told me about the village near Cork where he came from, and a few anecdotes about the job he was working on, roofing an old church in Wales for a posh couple who were converting it. He told a few unsavoury jokes about the Welsh, too. They all involved the misuse and abuse of sheep. And then he ushered me outside and took my hand again.

It felt wonderful to be walking together, holding hands. I felt proud, if the truth be told, to be striding down the street with such a good-looking man. But it felt strange, too – incongruous, as if we were children dressed up as adults, merely playing at being a couple. But then, doesn't adulthood often feel like role play? Even these days, I sometimes feel like an imposter. Even now, I struggle to convince myself that I'm a fully grown adult, doing fully adult things. I'm not sure the ageing, wrinkled exterior ever quite convinces the innocent inner child that this is the real deal, that this is what's really happening.

'Here,' Conor said, as we walked in front of a travel agent. 'Let's pop in here.'

'Oh, no . . .' I said, pulling back.

'No?'

'I mean, I'm not sure. About the whole holiday thing.'

'It's just to see,' Conor told me. 'It's just to have a look. Where's the harm in that?'

◆ ◆ ◆

The woman – her name tag said 'Tracey' – was nice. She smiled at us the way people smile at babies, and I felt reassured. If we looked like a couple then that was a good sign, wasn't it?

She showed us various brochures of the Greek islands and of Santorini in particular, and in response to Conor's quite specific questions, consulted timetables and calculated costs. Eight days' holiday came to over four hundred pounds each, which was way beyond my budget.

'I can't afford it, sweetheart,' I said, surprised by my own use of that word. I asked myself why I, too, was now playing the role of a newlywed. 'I'm sorry, but I really can't.'

'You won't find a cheaper deal than this one,' Tracey informed us. 'Not at such a late stage.'

'But you'd like to go, would you not?' Conor asked.

'What I'd like is neither here nor there,' I told him, avoiding the question. 'Because I really can't afford it.'

'So you don't want to go with me, after all?' Conor said, his face reddening.

'It's not that. No, it's not that at all. Honestly, look . . . I'd love to,' I spluttered. 'But that's way too much money. There's no reason why we can't go away for a weekend or something though.' A weekend trip away would feel less of a commitment, I reckoned. A weekend trip where a simple train ticket would bring me home if Conor changed his mind about me was a far more reassuring option. My mother was also less likely to find out I was lying to her.

Conor suddenly sat up very straight in his chair. He tugged at his cuffs and rolled his shoulders. 'Ah, feck it,' he said. 'We'll take 'em.'

'That's great,' Tracey said, smiling at us again. 'And I'm sure you won't regret it.'

'But Conor,' I protested. 'I can't. It's too expensive.'

'I can,' Conor said, tipping his head from side to side to stretch his neck. 'Where do I sign?'

I felt physically sick as he signed the paperwork and handed over his Amex card to pay for it all. But I didn't say a word. There was something about his will that had simply overwritten my own surprisingly flaky sense of self-determination.

Outside the travel agent he pushed the pouch of tickets into my reluctant hands. 'You take care of those,' he said. 'I need to get back now. There's rain forecast and I've got a whole shitload of flashing to finish.'

'You're really going straight back?' I asked, flabbergasted. 'To Wales? But that's *madness*.'

Conor shrugged. 'Sorry, honey. But work calls. I'll see you on the twenty-eighth,' he said. 'Gatwick South. I'll call you so we can arrange it all.' And then he kissed me, straightened his tie again and strutted off, the leather soles of his shoes resounding along the pavement.

I spent two weeks worrying about what to do, changing my mind the entire time. I spent hours on the phone with Abby discussing it, having the same conversation over and over again. But Abby was no help at all.

'He does sound a bit mad,' she agreed. 'A bit too sure of himself.'

'That's exactly it,' I said. 'But he hardly knows me. What if he changes his mind, mid-holiday?'

'He seems pretty certain. I mean, he must really like you if he's taking you to Greece.'

'I suppose. But what if he's a serial killer?'

'You're right,' she said. 'He does have that kind of profile.'

'I cancel then? But how do I get his ticket back to him without having my throat slit?'

'But you'd be mad not to go,' Abby said. 'You've been banging on about Santorini as long as I've known you.'

'I know, but . . .'

'It's eight days. Eight sexy nights in Santorini with a hot Irishman.'

'I know.'

'He is hot, right? I mean, you do fancy him, yeah?' she asked me on one occasion.

'I do. He's gorgeous. It's just . . .'

'Yes?'

'There's something a bit mad about him. It's his eyes, I think . . . But, yes. He's incredibly sexy, too.'

'So, it's a week with a sexy guy in Santorini. Where's the problem with that?'

'With a sexy guy who may be a serial killer.'

'Well, yes. There is that potential downside.'

'I think I should go,' I told her. An image of Conor in swimming trunks had sprung into my mind's eye. 'No, I think I should cancel,' I added. 'Definitely.'

'What's the alternative?' Abby asked. 'I mean, you're way too late to come with us now.'

'I know.'

'So what will you do if you don't go?'

'Stay here, I suppose,' I said.

'With your mum?'

'Yes, with Mum.'

'So you're going to stay at home and get locked in your room for something or other, and stare at your Santorini poster?'

'Maybe,' I said.

Abby laughed. 'Look, I know you're going and you know you're going. So you can stop pretending to be all Virgin Valerie about it.'

'I'm really not being Virgin Valerie about anything,' I protested.

'No,' Abby said. 'But you are pretending you might not go, because that makes you less of a slut than if you just abandoned yourself straight off to the whole eight-days-of-sex-in-the-sun-with-a-stranger thing, aren't you?'

'Perhaps . . .' I admitted. 'Yes, maybe that's it. And it's not just . . . you know . . . the sex thing. I think I might be a bit in love with him.'

'Hmm,' Abby said doubtfully. 'That sounds premature. But you'll soon find out. If you go you will, at any rate. But more importantly, are you on the pill?'

'You know I'm not.'

'Then buy some condoms,' she said. 'Buy lots of condoms, and you'll be fine.'

I arrived late at Gatwick. I'd had a bit of a panic attack at the exact moment I was supposed to leave the house and had lost first my keys, then my flimsy one-year passport (which I'd had to hide so Mum wouldn't find it), then the tickets, and then my keys again. By the time I left the house my forehead was pearling with sweat.

Conor was at the arranged meeting place, the pub at Gatwick South. He was nursing the remains of what clearly wasn't his first pint of beer.

'Jaysus!' he exclaimed on seeing me. 'D'you want to give a man a heart attack? I thought you'd left me standing at the bleedin' altar here.'

He was wearing chinos and a tight, light-blue polo shirt. He had muscles and ugly tattoos, neither of which I had ever noticed before.

'Sorry,' I said. 'I lost my keys just as I was leaving. But we're still in time, aren't we? The take-off's not for another hour.'

Conor downed the remains of his beer in a single gulp and lurched into action, grabbing the handle of his wheeled suitcase with one hand and roughly taking my wrist with the other.

'It's a bit early for beer, isn't it?' I commented as I trotted along beside him.

'Well, if you hadn't taken such a bleeding long time getting here, I wouldn't have had to drink anything, now would I?' Conor said as he strode towards the check-in counter.

The girl on the British Airways desk checked Conor in first, and it crossed my mind, even at that late stage, that I could walk away. There were officials and policemen all over the place. Conor wouldn't be able to force me to go with him. And he wouldn't be able to prevent me from leaving either.

'Can I have your passport, please?' the girl asked, and as I opened my mouth to speak, I honestly didn't know whether I was going to say, 'Yes, here it is,' or, 'Sorry, but I've changed my mind.'

But Conor noticed something was up. He looked at me and frowned briefly before slipping into the broadest of grins. 'Hey,' he said. 'She's talking to you, pretty lady. It's passport time. We're gonna have such a good time, you and me.'

He winked at me and, as if I had momentarily stepped out of my body, I watched him pluck my passport from my hand and hand it over.

'Thank you,' the BA lady said.

'You're welcome,' Conor replied, apparently on my behalf.

THREE

Becky

I sat my finals in May, did a wicked round of goodbye partying, split up with Tom (we'd only been dating for a few weeks, but that was enough to know it wasn't going anywhere) and loaded my stuff into my hired Corsa.

Mum, as I said, had been having a horrid few years, what with Brian leaving her, Gran dying, and then losing her job. She had lost a fair bit of weight, which at first seemed an improvement but then, as the process continued, started to worry me more and more. She was looking a bit ghostly, a bit transparent, and far older than her forty-nine years. Yet, incongruously, she reminded me of when she was younger, too. Her sadness, her sense of resignation . . . it all felt familiar.

It was hard to leave my life in Bristol behind, though. I'd loved that city, and I'd had a great group of friends there. I felt transformed by my four years at college. But everyone else was moving on to fresh pastures – not one of my close friends was staying on. So Margate seemed as good a place as any from which to plan my next move.

There was more than a hint of selfishness in the decision as well, I suppose. I was two grand overdrawn at the bank (pretty modest compared with most of my peers, thanks to the various McJobs I had done to pay my way), and I had twenty-four thousand pounds of student loans to reimburse at some point in the future as well. Chez Mum, there would at least be no rent to pay.

Mum really perked up when I arrived, and I wondered if she hadn't simply been achingly lonely since Brian left. But even if it seemed to do her good, it was incredibly difficult for me to revert to childhood after my four-year foray into independence.

Suddenly, there I was, waking up in my old bedroom, Mr D, the stuffed donkey, sitting at the end of the bed staring at me with his one eye. I had to eat at six thirty, because that was the way Mum liked it, and she'd hassle me about eating more, or less, depending on the day of the week. She would nag me to tidy my room and tell me my skirt was too short. I felt real fear, as if she were nibbling away at my sense of self, slowly dissolving the bubble of adulthood I had so carefully constructed to protect myself.

If no one was there to perceive this new, witty, self-assured me – because Mum really did seem to look at me and still see the baby she had breastfed – did that person really exist at all?

You forget, when you leave, how many tiny decisions your parents took out of your hands as a child. What to wear. What to eat. How much to drink . . .

I'd slipped into a surprisingly hard-to-break habit of having a couple of large glasses of cheap wine with my evening meal. Mum, though, served wine by the thimbleful and then put the bottle back in the fridge immediately after she'd done so. She didn't actually put a padlock on the cork, but I just knew from her aura that a refill was out of the question. *I'm twenty-three!* I wanted to scream. *I can drink as much as I want!* But I didn't. I sipped and smiled and tried to convince myself I was still a grown woman.

As far as my ten-a-day smoking habit was concerned, I daren't even leave the packet in sight. Instead, I hid them at the back of the wardrobe. I smoked out of my bedroom window, exactly as I had done aged fifteen, and I ripped the cigarette butts to pieces and flushed them down the loo.

One Friday in late June, a Friday of the grey, drizzling variety, I began hunting for a box of matches. My degree results were to be published at twelve o'clock precisely, and my lighter had run out of gas. I'd tried lighting a sheet of paper from the glowing element of the toaster but had merely burned my fingers and set off the deafening smoke alarm.

Mum was at the supermarket and would be away for at least an hour, so my initially frantic search took on a leisurely, if not nosey, aspect.

I found old photos, which I studied, and prescription drugs, which I googled, and cheap jewellery I'd never seen before: necklaces and earrings that I tried on in front of Mum's mirror.

I was looking through her nightstand (Valium, cough pastels, some condoms with a 2012 expiry date . . .) when I found the envelope. Inside were return plane tickets for the end of August, destination Athens.

Now, without you knowing my mother, it's hard for me to explain quite how surprising plane tickets might be. But Mum, with the exception of our bizarre and entirely out-of-character holiday when I was seven, had never been *anywhere*. And I mean that quite literally. She'd never travelled, or been drunk, or smoked, or even gone to bed after midnight. She was the most predictable, sensible mum anyone could ever have had. In fact, I was so shocked, I read the name on the tickets over and over again.

Once I'd convinced myself that my eyes were not deceiving me, I put everything back exactly as it had been and, wondering how I could get her to tell me about the tickets without revealing that I'd been going through her bedside cabinet, I returned to the lounge to wait.

It will give you some idea how intrigued I was, perhaps, if I tell you that I'd momentarily forgotten not only my need for a ciggy, but also the imminent arrival of my degree results. I stared at the clock on the Virgin box for a few minutes, watching the digits change, and I wondered why Mum was going to Athens, and how on earth she could afford it, and why she hadn't told me.

It was only when the figures changed to 12:00 that I remembered, with a jolt, about my exam results. I grabbed my laptop and clicked manically, and yelped when I saw the outcome. I'd got a first-class degree!

This left me overjoyed, obviously. But it also gave me an idea.

I shouted out my news before Mum had fully opened the front door.

She dumped her Aldi bags on the sofa and hugged me. 'I knew you would,' she said. 'You always were a clever clogs. That's why I bought this.'

She reached into one of the bags and produced a bottle of dodgy fake champagne.

My attempt at wheedling the information from her did not go well. In fact, it proved to be another whiplash straight back to childhood.

We were sipping our glasses of Aldi's finest sparkling wine and nibbling at the anchovy olives Mum had bought to go with it, when I said, very casually I hoped, 'I was thinking, I mean, seeing as we've got something to celebrate and seeing as we're both free for the first time in ages . . . well . . . what would you say to planning a little getaway somewhere, Mum?'

'What, like a weekend break or something?' Mum asked.

'Yeah,' I said. 'Or even . . . maybe . . . a proper holiday. A bit of sunshine. Mother and daughter. It could be nice.'

'Right . . .' Mum said, sounding doubtful.

'Spain, I was thinking. Or Italy. Or even Greece.'

Mum put her glass down and stared at me piercingly. It was the same look she'd had when I was a child, the look she'd given me at the precise moment she'd spotted the broken vase hidden at the bottom of the dustbin. She ran her tongue around the inside of her cheek.

'What?' I asked. I laughed and could feel myself blushing.

'You tell me,' she said, raising one eyebrow.

I shrugged. 'I don't know what you're on about,' I said. 'I was just . . .' But my voice faded out. I could hear how unconvincing I sounded. Trying to pull one over on Mum was like trying to cheat the Gestapo.

'So?' Mum said.

I shrugged again. 'Maybe I stumbled upon some tickets?' I said as cutely as I could manage.

'You *stumbled* upon them?' Mum repeated, mocking laughter in her voice.

'I was looking for something,' I said.

'You were *looking* for something.'

'A lighter.'

'Oh, a lighter, was it?'

'Yes, I wanted to light that candle,' I said, nodding at the huge red candle on the windowsill. 'But I couldn't find matches or a lighter anywhere.'

'You wanted to light that candle,' Mum said.

'Can you stop repeating everything I say?'

'Do you actually think I don't know about your Camels hidden at the back of the wardrobe?' Mum asked. 'Do you think I can't smell it when you smoke out of your window?'

'Oh,' I said.

'Yes. Oh.'

'So you've been rummaging through my wardrobe?' I asked, unsure if I was feigning or actually feeling the beginnings of outrage.

'I don't think you want to go there, do you?' Mum said. 'Not after rummaging through my bedside cabinet while I was out buying you champagne.'

'No,' I said. 'Maybe not.'

'That's what I thought.'

'So, Athens?' I said. 'How come?'

Mum shrugged. 'Your granny left me some money. She had quite a stash, as it turns out. Actually, that's something we need to talk about at some point. I've reserved a chunk of it for you. But anyway, I thought, why the hell not? I haven't had a holiday for years. And I have the time at the moment, too.'

'But you didn't want to tell me?'

'Oh, don't be like that, sweetheart,' Mum said. 'I knew you wouldn't want to go away with an old fogey like me.'

'But what if I would?' I asked.

'You could at least have denied that I'm an old fogey,' Mum said, laughing. 'But you didn't, did you?'

'You're not even fifty, Mum.'

'Not until September,' she replied.

'Ahh, that's it. Your fiftieth!' I exclaimed. 'Of course. But you don't want to spend your birthday on your own, do you? Unless you're planning on doing a Shirley Valentine and hitching up with some big, hairy Greek bloke?'

Mum ignored this comment. 'Would you really want to come?'

'I might.'

'In August, September?' Mum asked. 'Don't you think you'll be sick of me by then?'

'Maybe,' I said. 'But, no, I don't think so. I think I'd love to go to Athens with you for your birthday. We've never been anywhere together, really, have we?'

'We went to Bergen.'

'I was six,' I said. 'Other than the fact that you kept trying to get me to eat seafood, I don't even remember it.'

'You were seven,' Mum corrected. 'But yes, I suppose it might be nice. It's not Athens, though, sweetheart. That's just where the boat goes from.'

'The boat?'

'Yes. The boat to Santorini.'

FOUR

Laura

Though these days you can fly direct from London to Santorini if you so wish, back in 1994, before the whole low-cost thing had really got going, the options were much more limited.

The best route the travel agent had been able to find for us was from London to Athens with BA, then from Athens to Mykonos with the Greek national airline, Aegean, and finally a short boat trip to Santorini.

Conor, who it unexpectedly transpired was a nervous flyer, drank continuously during the trip, and as he drank he became both more talkative and noisier. In doing so, he seemed to match less and less the polite, well-dressed man I had met back in England, and more and more the tattooed roofer I seemed to have sitting beside me.

By the time we reached Athens, I had learned not only far more than I'd ever wanted to know about roofing, but also that his parents had died when he was young and he had grown up, along with his only brother, in care. This last bit of information produced an inevitable wave of sympathy for both his drinking and the vulgarity it seemed to let loose. For what woman can resist an abandoned child doing his best to shake off the trauma of a dodgy upbringing? Certainly not someone with a childhood as traumatic as my own.

We negotiated Athens airport, essentially thanks to me – Conor was quite drunk by the time we landed – and boarded a much smaller propeller plane for the final flight.

If Conor had complained about the turbulence of the first flight – and he had – it was as nothing to the ups and downs and sudden sideways lurches of our little propeller plane, and though I discovered, to my surprise, that I actually enjoyed the craziness of the flight, just as I might enjoy a roller coaster, that the excitement and sense of danger made me feel light-hearted and alive, poor Conor was terrified. He actually reached for a sick bag at one point, but thankfully, unlike the elderly chap across the way, resisted.

As we stepped into the balmy heat of tiny Mykonos Airport, Conor announced, entirely devoid of any context, that in addition to being a roofer, he was a middleweight champion boxer.

He was clearly trying to compensate for having been such a wuss during the flight, but not only did I not believe him, I also thought the claim made his trembling and praying of a few minutes earlier seem just that little bit more ridiculous.

As arranged, a driver was there to meet us, holding up a placard with the name of our hotel. As the minibus lurched along the poorly lit, bumpy roads of Mykonos, it was my turn to feel scared.

'Don't worry,' Conor said, suddenly brave. 'It'll be fine. This guy drives these roads every day.' He put one heavy arm across my shoulders and looked out of the window before adding, 'Looks like a right shithole though, doesn't it?'

When we got to the hotel, an imposing blue-and-white building on the seafront, he cheered up. 'Now this is more like it,' he said.

Even though we didn't have a sea view, our room was lovely. It had a huge double bed (which scared me somewhat – I hadn't, after all, slept with Conor yet) and a dressing table and built-in cupboards with blue doors that looked like Parisian shutters.

'A shower, then food?' Conor suggested, dumping his suitcase on the bed.

I told him that sounded fine.

To avoid being in the tiny en-suite with him while he showered, I faffed around hanging up clothes that would only have to be repacked the next morning. Because of the prices, which were double those on Santorini, Conor had booked only a single night in Mykonos.

As soon as he came out of the bathroom, a towel wrapped around his waist, I ducked in and locked the door.

Because I was both terrified and excited by the idea that Conor might be lying naked, waiting for me on the bed, I took the longest shower I thought I could reasonably get away with. And my plan worked perfectly because, by the time I came out, the room was empty. I sat for a moment in the cool of the air conditioning and watched the steam drifting from the bathroom, and I wondered if I was relieved or disappointed.

I put on a brand-new pair of snow wash jeans I had bought for the trip and a pinkish Calvin Klein T-shirt, before – after a long hunt for the room key, which I finally found in a slot in the light switch – heading downstairs.

The hotel restaurant was on the ground floor at the front of the building, overlooking the beach. The huge glass windows along the front wall had been completely folded back, effectively turning the whole place into one vast, beachfront balcony. The tables had candles and starched, white tablecloths, and beyond the opening, the sea twinkled with the lights of the fishing boats that were moored there. Ceiling fans spun slowly above the diners' heads and plinky-plonky, minimalist Greek music was playing, the kind of thing they use to fill up those Buddha Bar compilation CDs. I think I'd been too tired and sweaty and scared when we had arrived to truly appreciate the beauty of the setting, but now, after a shower and a change of clothes, I saw it all and gasped.

Conor had secured a table right at the front. He was wearing jeans and a white shirt and looked really rather beautiful. He waved at me and smiled and I remember thinking, as I wove my way through the tables towards him, *This is going to be all right after all.* I kept changing my mind about everything, back and forth, back and forth, over and over again.

'Jaysus!' Conor said when I reached the table. 'I was about to give up on you and order. I could eat the bleedin' twelve Apostles, I'm that hungry.'

I fluttered my eyelids and slipped into my seat. 'It's beautiful here,' I said.

'Aye, it's a bit of all right, eh?' Conor said. 'You're looking pretty.'

'Thanks,' I replied, blushing. 'You don't look so bad yourself.'

'But I hope you have some skirts with you,' Conor continued. 'We can't be having you in jeans the whole time, now, can we?'

I frowned. I was used to my mother telling me my skirts were too short, but having a man tell me what to wear was a whole different thing. 'I do, but . . . I'm fine in jeans, thanks,' I said.

'Well, it'll do for now, I suppose,' Conor said. 'But tomorrow wear a dress, OK?'

I nodded vaguely. 'Maybe,' I said. 'We'll see.'

Conor sipped his beer. 'Yes, we *will* see,' he said, sounding a little menacing, but as ever I couldn't tell if he mightn't be joking. He smiled at me then, and because I didn't smile back, he added, 'You've got lovely legs, you have. We can't have you hiding them the whole time, now, can we? If you've got it, flaunt it, babe.'

I broke into a grin despite myself. My legs were one of the only parts of my body I didn't feel insecure about, and I was glad he'd noticed them.

He nodded behind me and said, 'Have you seen all the ponces here?'

'I'm sorry?' I said.

'Ponces. Poofs. Homos,' Conor said, too loudly for comfort. 'Whatever you care to call them. Look around.'

I now glanced around the restaurant and took in that at least half of the tables were indeed occupied by same-sex couples, and at least two of these were now glaring at us.

'Right,' I said. 'I think Mykonos is sort of their special place. It's known for being gay-friendly and all that. But that's OK, isn't it?'

Conor shrugged. 'I suppose,' he said. 'If you like that sort of thing.' He clicked his fingers surprisingly loudly, and shouted, 'Garçon! Can we get some service over here? Garçon!'

'I think that's French,' I said, blushing.

'Whatever,' Conor said. 'As long as it works, which it does . . .'

I watched as the small, nervous-looking waiter sped towards us, and I cringed.

'I'll have a beer,' Conor told him. 'A pint. And whatever my beautiful girlfriend here fancies for herself.'

Girlfriend, I thought, already forgiving him for being so brash. *He called me his girlfriend!*

Amongst the ups and downs that characterised spending time with Conor, the rest of dinner continued on an upswing. The service was perfect – fast, efficient, friendly – and the food, succulent calamari for me and a Greek version of fish and chips for Conor, was delicious. With some food inside him, Conor quietened down considerably and even asked me a little about myself, my mother, and my job.

The bill came to some crazy number of drachma – I think it was fifteen or twenty thousand – but Conor insisted this was just fine and with a flick of the wrist added it to the hotel tab. For all his other faults – and they were many – no one could ever have accused Conor of being tight.

We stepped outside and, along with tens of other couples, both gay and straight, we wandered along the beachfront. Conor took my hand and I started to feel really romantic again. It was about eleven at night by this time, but still incredibly warm, and I decided I would have been better in my denim skirt. Pleasing Conor on that front wasn't going to prove to be too much of a drag after all.

To our left were neon-lit bars alternating with more traditional-looking tavernas, and they all seemed to have their own sound systems fighting it out. To the right, the waves lapped against the thin strip of sandy beach. It was beautiful, but loud.

'Santorini will be a bit quieter, hopefully,' I said as we reached the intersection of two of the noisiest bars. From where we were standing, the music from their loudspeakers merged, producing an unrecognisable dirge and a level of decibels that was almost impossible to suffer without wincing.

'Well, I hope it's not too bleedin' quiet,' Conor said. 'This is good craic. Here, let's grab a bevvy and see what's happening.' He took my hand and tugged me towards the door of a bar called Babylon.

Inside, rhythmic electronic music was playing and on the small dance floor some twenty people were grooving, mostly individually.

Conor pushed through to the bar and ordered, without consultation, one of those massive German one-litre glasses of beer for himself and another glass of white wine for me. It was too loud to talk, so we stood at the edge of the dance floor and watched. The majority of the dancers, I now saw, looked as if they might be gay. They were too trendily dressed and danced a little too unreservedly to be straight, I thought.

I glanced at Conor to see if he'd noticed and saw that he was transfixed by a couple of rather beautiful women kissing in the corner. They were olive-skinned, dark-haired beauties, almost certainly Greek.

'Perhaps we should go somewhere else,' I shouted in Conor's ear. 'I think this is a gay place.'

Conor shrugged and grinned at me so I decided he wasn't homophobic after all. Perhaps it had just been his brash sense of humour that had given me that impression.

'Look at those two over there,' he said, nodding towards the two women. 'D'you think they'd let me watch?'

I exhaled deeply and raised my left hand to pinch the bridge of my nose. The pendulum had swung back the other way and yet again I was doubting if this could work out.

Conor put his arm around my waist and pulled me in tightly. 'Hey,' he said. 'I'm only ragging you. Don't take everything so seriously, girl. You know there's only one woman here I've got my eye on, and she's the prettiest woman in the room.'

I felt both flattered and unnerved, so I gulped at my wine and forced myself to sway a little with the music, and after a few minutes decided that whatever happened I was going to be with Conor for the duration of the holiday, so I might as well make the most of it.

'Are ya dancin'?' Conor asked me, once he'd downed his drink.

'Are you asking?' I replied.

'I'm asking,' he said, plucking my empty glass from my fingers and putting it on a table beside us.

As he pulled me to the centre of the dance floor, we stumbled on the slightly raised edge – we were both a little the worse for wear by this point. And, for fifteen minutes or so, we danced.

As I've said before, electronic music has never really been my thing, but as I'd met Conor at a rave party it seemed churlish to explain that right then, so I did my best to copy Conor's moves and when these became too outlandish, as they quickly did, I did my best to emulate a woman beside me who had a great little shimmy thing going on. I was quickly saved when a six-foot drag queen with glitter eyeliner and a Barry Humphries dress inserted herself between Conor and me.

Ever unpredictable, Conor played along, grooving with her expertly, even eliciting a few whoops from admirers when he performed his trademark spin. Then suddenly it was all over and Conor was barging his way to the door. Assuming he was feeling ill – I had no idea what else could have happened – I ran after him.

When I caught up with him on the promenade he said, almost shouted, 'Fucking freak!'

'Are you OK?' I asked. 'What happened?'

'He tried to grab me bollocks is what happened,' Conor replied. 'Put his dirty mitts on my packet, so he did. Thank Christ we're leaving tomorrow. It's fecking Sodom and Gomorrah round here.' It was a horrible thing to say, but sadly nothing my mother wouldn't have agreed with, so I was saddened rather than shocked.

We walked along the seafront in silence for a moment until we came to a bar playing REM's 'Losing My Religion'. It had been a hit a few years before, and I loved it.

'I love this song,' I told Conor. 'Can we go in and dance to this?'

'Nah,' Conor said. 'That's shite, so it is.'

We continued to walk in silence until we found ourselves back at the hotel. The decision to retire had seemingly been taken without a word being said. I was feeling exhausted and fairly squiffy, so decided the idea suited me fine as long as it was sleep that was on the menu. Another drink in the REM bar mightn't have been such a good idea, after all.

On arriving in the room, I took another shower. I was feeling sweaty and uncomfortable from the heat and the dancing, and I decided that if something were to happen at least not being sweaty was one less thing to worry about.

But by the time I came out of the shower, and I really wasn't in there long, Conor was fast asleep, snoring, sprawled across the middle of the bed, still fully clothed.

Not daring to wake him (let sleeping dogs lie and all that), I pulled on a T-shirt and slipped between the sheets in the thin strip of space that remained. I'd never slept with anyone who snored before, and I learned that night just how annoying it could be.

I slept badly until about three in the morning, when Conor finally rolled onto his side and fell silent, whereupon I slipped into the deepest of deep sleeps.

In the morning, I was dragged screaming and kicking from a beautiful dream in which I had been lying on a beach with the sea lapping between my legs. It had felt heavenly.

It was really hard to wake up – I honestly was a thousand leagues below – but I really *had* to, I had to make myself surface, because here in the real world, something wasn't right.

For a few seconds, maybe considerably longer, I couldn't distinguish dream from reality. But when I finally did grasp the fact that the beach was the dream and Conor's head between my legs the reality, and that the lapping sensation was *not* caused by waves, I gasped and sat up. 'Agh!' I cried out.

'That's my girl,' Conor said, briefly pausing to look up at me.

'Stop!' I gasped, my still-present sleepiness muting my attempt at expressing outrage.

'Aye, you're not with the poofs now!' Conor said. 'And don't tell me that it doesn't feel good. You were laughing in your sleep!'

He rose up on his arms and slid forward, pushing me back down so he was effectively performing a press-up over me.

'I . . . I was *asleep*!' I said. 'And you . . .'

'I know!' Conor laughed, lowering himself slowly so that his solid little body pressed against mine, then reaching below to position himself before, in a single, painful movement, he was inside me.

'Fuck!' I gasped, unable to believe what was happening. 'Conor!'

'That *is* the general idea,' Conor said, still amused despite my obvious outrage and discomfort.

'Stop!' I said again. Then, 'God! Your breath!'

I turned my face to the side to escape the foul stench of beer and morning breath coming from Conor's grinning mouth.

'Ah, shut the feck up will you, woman?' Conor said, still sounding as if this was all funny, as he started to move gently above me.

Though my mind was still utterly outraged, some other biological part of me began to respond to the sensation of his body upon me, to his chest hair rubbing against my breasts (he'd pushed my T-shirt up at some point) and to the undeniably agreeable sensations his back-and-forth movements were producing.

Gradually, my groans shifted from soft gasps of outrage to gasps of exertion, and finally to what were undeniably sighs of pleasure.

I explain all of this because consent, of course, is a huge and complex issue. And sex without consent is rape. But did Conor rape me that first time? I still struggle to decide.

Younger women than myself with more clearly defined boundaries tell me it's perfectly simple these days. If you say 'no' – in fact, if you haven't clearly said 'yes' – then it's rape. And I'm genuinely glad for them that things have moved on, that there's debate on these issues – that there's a concerted effort to define, clearly, for everyone concerned, exactly what consent means.

But for me, in my twenties, it all seemed far more complex. Sex had never been discussed in any way at home and the thorny issue of consent certainly hadn't been addressed. And yes, I'd gone away with Conor fully intending to sleep with him. And yes, I'd enjoyed being called his girlfriend, and had got into bed with him thinking it was going to happen at some point. And yes, my body had responded to his touch with pleasure, enough pleasure to momentarily override my outrage, so that by the end I can't deny that I was no longer saying 'no' but instead, saying, 'Yes, yes, yes!' I wonder what a judge would make of it all?

It was only once it was over, once I had seen Conor withdraw without a condom, that I thought of birth control.

He cuddled me for a while and his momentary gentleness allowed me to convince myself that everything was fine. I would never have had the nerve to make a move on him anyway, I told myself, as he kissed my forehead and vanished into the en-suite.

At least the deed was done and my status as girlfriend was confirmed, I thought. I would just have to find a chemist in Greece. I would have to source either a morning-after pill while on holiday, or, potentially, an abortion pill once home. I was pretty sure Abby had told me there was a pill you could use for weeks after the act. It all left me feeling suddenly terribly grown-up, which reveals more than anything how immature I still was.

We had breakfast in the hotel – they had laid on a luxurious buffet with everything from croissants to bacon and eggs to papaya . . . I was still watching Conor nervously from the corner of my eye, trying to make up my mind about him, but in our post-coital hunger we stuffed ourselves silly. Afterwards, we returned to the room to put on our swimmers and headed for the beach.

The water was crystal-clear and amazingly warm, and Conor was playful and funny, duck-diving (again) between my legs and play-wrestling me in the shallows. It was good, honest fun. As we were lying on our towels on the crowded beach, my head on Conor's chest gently rising and falling, he said quite casually, out of the blue, 'I was surprised you're not a virgin, though.'

'I'm *sorry*?' I said, sitting bolt upright.

'I was surprised you're not a virgin,' Conor said again, with the same mellow intonation, as if this was a perfectly normal thing to say. 'A supposedly good Catholic girl like yourself,' he added.

'Agh!' I spluttered, my anger rising. 'If I *had* been a virgin, Conor, I wouldn't be now. You bloody shagged me in my sleep, for Christ's sake!'

At this, Conor merely laughed. He stood, clipped my ear playfully and said, 'Last one in's a ninny,' and ran back into the sea.

He'd clearly intended the slap to be nothing more than a joke provocation but my ear was really stinging. His off-hand comment about my virginity, or lack of, had stung, too. So I did not run after him. Instead, I rubbed my ear and glared at him and ignored his calls to join in. Eventually, with a laugh and a shrug, he turned and started to swim in an efficient, apparently effortless crawl, cutting a line across the bay.

Suddenly I'd changed my mind about him, so I returned to the hotel and packed my suitcase. I had a brief fantasy of vanishing before he got back from the beach. But where would I go? I had a return ticket in a week's time, but from Santorini, not Mykonos. Perhaps if I got to Santorini I could, if things remained bad, change it and go home early. From Mykonos, it was almost certainly an impossibility.

I sat on the bed and stared at my suitcase and bit my fingernails, and I was still doing this when Conor returned, his beach bag over one shoulder and his towel around his neck.

'I found a lovely little shell,' he said, crouching before me and opening one hand to reveal a huge clamshell with a pearly pink and purple interior. 'Here, it's for you.'

'I don't want it,' I told him glumly.

'Look, I'm sorry,' he said, as destabilising as ever. 'I'm a bit of a prick sometimes. I know I am.' His breath smelled of alcohol.

'Have you been drinking again?' I asked, starting belatedly to pick up on a theme here. 'It's only ten thirty.'

'Just a pint,' Conor said. 'To get rid of the taste of the seawater. I swam through a bit of diesel from one of your motorboats out there and it tasted rank.'

He jiggled the shell in his hand again. 'Here,' he said. 'I've said sorry. You can take it now without losing face.'

I looked into his eyes. There was something hypnotic about them. He was smiling gently.

'Come on. You do still want to be my girlfriend, don't you?' he asked.

I shrugged and did my best not to cave in, but I could sense I was fighting a losing battle. There was always something irresistible about him when he turned the charm on.

'Come on,' Conor continued. 'You'll give yourself wrinkles if you carry on like that, and we can't have that, can we?' He reached out and stroked my cheek. 'I've said I'm sorry,' he said again. 'What more do you want me to say?'

Unable to maintain my sour expression, I relented and took the shell from his hand, but not without telling him, 'You *are* a prick. Sometimes, you really are.'

'Now tell me something I don't know,' Conor replied.

'It's half past ten,' I said. 'And the taxi's booked for eleven.'

'I suppose I'd better get me arse into gear then,' Conor said, straightening and heading for the bathroom.

The trip to Santorini was sublime. The ship, a largish ferry, took us to Paros and Naxos and Ios . . . weaving its way through a series of islands, stopping occasionally to pick up and drop off hordes of tourists dragging their wheeled suitcases behind them. Other islands we passed were so small they appeared to be completely wild.

The sun shone down and the sea breeze felt gentle and refreshing. The light was of a kind I had never seen before – sort of piercing, like a thousand halogen bulbs, it made everything seem brighter. The colours of people's clothes seemed to shimmer and zing against the all-encompassing blueness of it all.

Conor and I stood at the rear of the boat grasping the railings, watching the trail of churning water, the seagulls following in our wake and the pretty islands as they slipped by.

At one point, Conor kissed my cheek and I turned to look at him and tried to reappraise him once again. The breeze was ruffling his white shirt and blowing my hair into my eyes, and despite everything that had happened, I felt brave like an adventurer, and happy like a lover, and when he winked at me, maybe even beautiful, which was something that hadn't happened that often in my life.

From the port in Santorini we got a taxi to Oia where our hotel was located. Though there was a central hotel building with a bar and a restaurant, the rooms themselves were tiny, blindingly white, dome-topped houses, clinging to the hillside and linked by zigzagging steps in all directions.

While the porter opened our front door and showed Conor the bedroom and bathroom, I stood on the little terrace and stared. It was the most stunning view I had ever seen. In fact it's still probably the most stunning view I have ever seen – a vast 180-degree vista of gently curving Santorini.

The island, if you've never seen it, is in the shape of a backwards C with a few tiny islands nestling in the bay, protected by the curve, and around them the open, endless blue of the sea and sky. It's truly breathtaking.

The rocky faces of the cliffs were a deep grey, almost black in places, and the houses, without exception, were spotless white with deep-blue doors and window frames. A few, which I guessed were churches, were topped with blue domes like the photo I'd had in my bedroom all those years.

'Wow,' I said to myself.

When Conor returned to stand beside me, I said it again. 'Wow! Just wow.'

'It's pretty, all right,' Conor agreed. 'But feck knows where the beach is.' We were a few hundred yards above sea level.

'Closest beach is Baxedes,' the porter informed him. 'It's ten minutes.'

'By car or on foot?' Conor asked.

'I'm sorry?'

'Is it ten minutes in a car?' Conor repeated, speaking pedantically and mimicking driving. 'Or by foot . . .' His fingers made a little walking motion.

'By bus,' the porter said in perfect English. 'You can buy tickets in the lobby.'

As soon as he had left, Conor headed off to rent a car. He didn't, he explained in no uncertain terms, 'do' buses.

He was gone for over two hours but I didn't mind at all. I folded out one of the deckchairs the hotel had provided and opened up the parasol, then reclined and stared at the view. I watched the tiny ferries as they came and went far below. I watched fishing boats and spotted a man on a jet ski criss-crossing the sea with little white lines as if it were a vast blue canvas. I tracked the sun as it moved across the cloudless sky and thought, *Wow! A week here!*

I was already in love with Santorini, just as I had always known I would be. Conor's ups and downs were perhaps, I decided, just the price to be paid to experience it all.

It was almost four o'clock when he returned and, though I'd eaten a sandwich on the boat, I was feeling hungry. But Conor had already eaten.

'The feckers were closed until three,' he told me. 'But we're mobile now, so let's go before we miss the sun.'

He drove erratically across the peninsula and I wondered if he was struggling with the car – a dusty little red Fiat – or if he had been drinking again. But I didn't dare ask. I think that slowly, subconsciously, I was starting to feel afraid of him. Better late, I suppose, than never.

The beach was a vast swathe of deep-grey, gravelly sand. It was so hot that when your flip-flops sank into it, it burned the edges of your feet.

There was a small, private section, a simple one-deep row of crisp white parasols flapping in the breeze, and a friendly young guy who couldn't have been older than fourteen selling beer, Coke and peanuts.

'Is there anywhere to get food?' I asked him.

'Peanuts?' he repeated, pointing to his basket of goodies with a shrug.

So while Conor downed endless Greek beers, I made do with Coke and peanuts.

A couple of hours slipped by in a contented blur of dips in the sea (it was so warm, you didn't even sigh as you slipped beneath the waves) and sips of Coke, and tiny siestas where I'd fall asleep on my back and then wake myself up by snoring.

Eventually, Conor declared, out of nowhere, that he was bored. He sprang to his feet.

I tried for the first time to pay the bill, but Conor wouldn't hear of it.

As we set off across the beach, he said, 'It's bullshit here. We should have gone to Spain.'

'Really?' I asked, shocked that we could be experiencing such different things and wondering if he was being facetious. 'I think it's stunning.'

'Stunning but boring.'

'What else would you have done in Spain?' I asked him, trotting to keep up. 'Other than lie on a beach and swim in the sea?'

'I don't know,' Conor replied. 'All I know is that lying on that beach bored me silly.'

'I'll lend you one of my books,' I suggested. I had brought three of Mum's novels with me to read on the beach.

'Yeah,' Conor laughed. 'Yeah, that'll do the trick!' Again, I didn't know if he was being sarcastic or not.

Back in Oia, we parked up in a dusty car park and descended a hundred steps to our beautiful, hobbit-like abode.

Again, we showered, but this time when I came out of the shower Conor was there, waiting for me, his pride and joy clearly ready for another round.

'I've got a little problem here, so do you think you could see your way clear to coming and sitting on this for me?' Conor asked.

And because he was laughing and because I was loving Santorini, and indirectly Conor for bringing me here, and because after an afternoon on the beach I was feeling relaxed and yes, sexy, that's exactly what I did.

Afterwards, Conor said he was going to snooze for twenty minutes, and because I was too excited about our view, I showered again and crept outside to my deckchair.

I worried for a while about Conor and wondered again if it was all going pear-shaped and whether I was going to have to try to change my ticket. But I decided that if things carried on as they had been, it was probably going to be fine, and it was almost certainly easier to just put up with Conor's moods until we got home, whereupon I could take an informed decision based upon a sort of averaging-out of his erratic behaviour.

That might sound like a bad choice to some, and looking back that's almost certainly what it was. But as I said, I was incredibly inexperienced. I had no idea how sex, or even relationships, for that matter, were supposed to happen. I had no point of reference at all, and was about as naive as they come. I was also severely lacking confidence about things like trying to change air tickets in foreign countries . . . I had never travelled overseas before, after all.

I worried for a bit about the whole contraception business, too. But again, the idea of trying to get something from a Greek chemist scared me. Who knew what their attitudes to contraception were? My own mother had shouted and raged quite terrifyingly anytime anyone had even mentioned contraception on the television, so I knew people could react badly. Plus, it all seemed a bit of a moot point anyway. We'd already had unprotected sex twice, so I could hardly start asking Conor to use condoms now, could I? I decided to just deal with it once I got home.

I thought of Mum, of course, who believed I was in Cornwall camping with Abby, and wondered what she'd say if she knew what her daughter was up to, and felt a flash of pride at my recklessness, followed by a sharp rolling wave of Catholic guilt for my sinning, and then actual fear at the thought of what might happen if she did find out. But the view eventually calmed me. It stilled my thoughts and doused my worries and my fears.

The sun was heading inevitably towards the horizon and the sky was turning a deeper shade of blue. I sat and watched it change in what I suppose one might call a meditational state and observed my thoughts as they stilled. I surveyed my worries and imagined them drifting away, like clouds.

Along one side of our terrace was a little, irregular staircase, moulded from concrete and winding down the mountainside. Each step had been painstakingly bordered with white paint, presumably so you could see your footing better in the dark.

Occasionally people would pass by and at one point a tall, blond man of about my age, a sporty young hiker type in trousers with lots of pockets, wearing a backpack, passed by, and as he did so, he nodded and smiled. So I smiled back and asked him what was down there. I had been wondering about that for a while.

'A very small port,' he said in perfect English but with a strange accent I couldn't place. 'And a tiny beach.' He paused and dabbed at his forehead with a handkerchief from his pocket. 'It's just rocks, really,' he continued. 'But you can swim quite easy if you want to. And there is some small fish restaurants in addition. But they fish the fish – is that what you say? Yes? They fish the fish themselves.'

'That sounds lovely,' I told him. 'Maybe we'll go there tonight.'

'It is lovely,' he informed me, 'but about one million steps, so . . . Good day.' He tipped his blue baseball cap at me, in what seemed a strangely formal gesture in someone my age, and headed on, climbing the steps until he vanished behind our unit.

By the time Conor surfaced it was seven thirty and the sun was setting. The sky looked like a paint chart, with distinct bands of colour: a deep orange at the horizon, then yellow, then pink, and finally a stunning gradient of blue that went from turquoise at the base to a deep, star-studded inky black above our heads.

'Hello, sleepy head,' I said, without tearing my eyes from the mesmerising sunset.

'Will you look at that!' Conor exclaimed.

'I know,' I agreed. Then, only thinking it as I said it, I added, 'This is the first place I've ever been that makes you realise you're on a big lump of rock hurtling through outer space. Do you know what I mean?'

'Yeah,' Conor said vaguely, as he stepped to the edge of the terrace and looked out. 'It is pretty though.'

'Apparently there's a restaurant at the bottom of those steps,' I told him, pointing. 'It's supposed to be lovely. They do freshly caught fish from their own boat.'

'Says who?' Conor asked.

'Oh, just some guy who was walking past.'

'Some guy, huh?' Conor commented. 'So that's what you get up to when my back's turned!'

'I'm sorry?'

'Chatting up strangers, are we?'

As often, I couldn't tell if he was joking or not. I sometimes wondered if he knew himself.

'He was just a guy who was walking past, that's all. He said there are, like, a million steps to get down there though.'

'And a million steps back up again,' Conor said. 'Bollocks to that.'

'He said it was really lovely. He said it was worth it,' I added hopefully.

'Will you shut the feck up about your man?' Conor said. 'And get your arse into gear, will you? I'm starving.'

The hotel restaurant was lovely and in many ways similar to the one in Mykonos.

It had the same starched tablecloths, the same candles on the tables, and even similar minimalist music playing through the loudspeaker system. The only real difference was that here the folding windows opened not onto a beach but onto the incredible vista that is Santorini by night. For Santorini is just as beautiful once the sun goes down as it is by day. The moonlight shimmers across the deep, dark waters of the bay and the lights of a thousand dwellings, scattered across the rock face, twinkle at you, almost as beautiful as the stars above.

The menu was almost the same as in Mykonos, too, though Conor assured me the prices were considerably lower.

We ordered another vat of Mythos beer for Conor and a pretty little carafe of fruity white wine for me, and then Conor ordered a seafood platter while I plumped for moussaka. I was determined to order something different at every meal. I'd waited that long to be in Greece.

Conor seemed subdued so while we waited for our meals I asked if he was OK.

'I'm fine,' he said. 'You just let me sleep too long, so I'm a bit groggy.'

'OK,' I said, then as an afterthought, because I didn't really accept it was my fault, I added, 'Sorry, I didn't know . . .'

Conor shrugged. 'You're all right.'

'Isn't this the most beautiful place you've ever seen, though?'

Conor shrugged again. 'It's nice,' he said. 'The view's pretty good, it's true. But I think I prefer it when there's a beach and bars and shite. You know?'

'There's lots to see in Fira, in the middle of the island,' I said, pointing. 'Over there. I read it in the guide they left in the room. Perhaps we could go there after dinner. As long as you don't drink too much to drive.'

Conor laughed and took another swig of his beer. He was already half a litre into his first drink. 'I take it you can't drive?' he asked.

I shook my head. 'Sorry.'

'As usual, it's all down to Conor.'

'We could get a bus,' I suggested. 'They said they're every . . .'

'I told you,' Conor interrupted, sounding annoyed. 'I don't do buses.'

'Or a taxi,' I offered, thinking, *Or you could just not get drunk for once.*

'Jeez! I'm not made of money!' Conor said.

'I could pay,' I offered. 'I haven't paid for anything yet.'

'Are you *trying* to make me feel inadequate?' Conor asked. 'Are you doing it on purpose?'

'No . . .' I said, feeling suddenly tearful. 'No, I . . .'

Luckily, we were saved by the arrival of our food.

My moussaka was delicious, which was just as well because when I offered – thinking it was romantic – to swap a bit of my moussaka for a chunk of Conor's calamari, his response was a simple, 'Nope.'

'Nope?' I repeated, laughing, surprised.

'If you wanted calamari then you should have ordered bleedin' calamari,' Conor replied.

We finished our meal in silence.

I had already sensed the capacity for the evening to spin out of control. And I was also starting to realise, I think, that once it did so, there might be no turning back. So, thinking in terms of merely maintaining the peace as long as possible, I tried to bow out of the trip to Fira.

'I'm a bit tired,' I told Conor, as we walked towards the car. 'I think I might get an early night. But you go on and enjoy yourself.'

'Oh, just get yourself in the car, will you?' he said, taking my wrist and pulling me across the car park.

I sat silently beside him as he drove. I was scared now. I was scared of his driving, though in all fairness, he drove surprisingly well that evening, especially considering the fact that he had ingurgitated two litres of beer in the space of an hour. I was scared of him as well – scared in some undefined way about whatever was to come.

Once we got to Fira, things calmed down for a bit.

It was – still is – an incredibly beautiful town, comprising a maze of white, organic-looking buildings, clustered along the ridge and straggling randomly down the cliff face towards the sea.

Already, in 1994, it had a sophisticated St Tropez feel to it, and for an hour or so we wandered happily though the tiny streets, squeezing past other couples, pausing to look in a shop here or have another drink there. Under pressure from me, Conor switched to halves and, as during the drive, seemed surprisingly sober despite them. In one shop, he bought a funny T-shirt featuring a fluorescent cat with headphones on and in another, after some good-natured arguing, I let him buy me a cheap bracelet. 'Such beautiful hands require jewellery,' Conor insisted, and with my chrome and turquoise charms jingling on my wrist, I even let him take my hand again. It seemed mean, initially, to refuse, but after a few minutes I'd slipped back into enjoying the experience of actually having a boyfriend who wanted to hold my hand. I saw a young woman glance approvingly at Conor as she passed by, and felt proud, momentarily, that he was mine. I think, back then, I was pretty good at convincing myself that this was as good as things got.

As we headed towards the car, which we'd parked on the edge of town, the evening, it seemed, had against all odds been a success. I was feeling positively pleased with myself and actually quite besotted with Conor all over again.

But as we passed a taverna – one of those typical Greek places with vines overhead and blue-painted tables with plastic checkered tablecloths – a ripple of laughter reached our ears.

'Let's have one for the road,' Conor suggested, tugging on my hand in the same way I imagine the idea of a drink was tugging at him.

'One for the road is never a good idea,' I said, forcing myself to sound light-hearted. 'Especially on these roads. Have one back at the hotel, if you really want one.'

A voice rang out above the laughter – an English voice with an East End accent. 'I don't bleedin' know!' someone laughed. 'Ask Stavros over there!'

'Your countrymen,' Conor said, pulling harder, dragging me sideways. 'It'll be fun.'

Groaning internally, I followed him around the side of the building to where the voices were coming from. Bouzouki music was playing inside the restaurant and a group of a dozen or so Brits, both men and women, had pushed four tables together on the otherwise deserted terrace.

'Hello!' Conor said, once we reached the table. 'Do you mind if we join you? You look like you're having fun!'

A red-faced man in his fifties beckoned us in. 'Please!' he said, mocking Conor's Irish accent. 'Do get your good selves over here, will you not?'

Conor ordered the waiter – who was lingering – to bring fresh drinks for everyone, and once we had all introduced ourselves he squeezed in beside red-faced Mike, leaving me standing alone at the head of the table.

Sheila, a woman in the centre of a group at the far end, gestured to me and winked.

'Hello,' I said shyly, once I had pulled up a chair.

'Is that your bloke?' she asked. 'He seems quite a character.'

'He is,' I said. 'It's quite new, though . . . You know.'

'Holiday romance, is it?'

'Something like that. Are you here with someone?'

'Yeah,' she replied. 'Mike over there. Your Conor seems to be his new best friend.'

I looked over and saw Mike had his arm around Conor's shoulders. 'Yes,' I said dubiously.

'I hope your Conor knows what he's getting himself into,' Sheila said. This made both Mads, to her left, and Terri, to her right, snigger.

'I hope your Mike knows what *he's* letting himself in for,' I retorted, and everyone laughed.

We women chatted amongst ourselves for almost two hours. They were a friendly bunch and they'd had a few drinks too many as well, so the conversation flowed easily. Sheila and Mike lived in Southend and Mads was a Londoner, like me. This was the fourth island on their trip and their third visit to Santorini so they traded tips for the best restaurants, told me which brand of sun cream to buy if I didn't want to get 'burnt to a crisp', and, being amongst girls, laughingly informed me which beaches had the sexiest men.

At the other end of the table, the guys became more and more raucous, but because I was having such a nice time with Sheila, Mads and Terri, I didn't really notice how much they were drinking until the end. But about half past midnight, Conor stumbled off to the toilet and I suddenly took note of the tens and tens of empty bottles on the table.

'This is where we escape,' Sheila said, checking her watch and standing. 'And I suggest you do the same, darlin'.'

'Conor's driving,' I said. 'We're at the other end of the island.'

'Driving? Well, good luck with that,' Terri laughed. Then she, Sheila and Mads linked arms and headed off across the patio, leaving me feeling jealous of their sisterhood, and alone with the men.

Most of these now decided to leave, so by the time Conor returned only Mike and a Spanish guy, Pablo, remained.

Conor was paralytic. He bashed into three empty tables and almost fell over a chair just crossing the terrace to join us, and when he got close I saw that he'd had an accident. The front of his trousers was wet. I hoped it was only beer.

Taking my courage in hand, I stood to intercept him. 'Come on, Conor,' I said. 'It's time to get a taxi home.'

Without saying a word, Conor pushed me aside and managed, just about, to return to a chair opposite Mike.

'More beer?' Mike asked, his facial expressions grotesque and exaggerated due to his drunkenness.

'More beer!' Conor slurred, picking up an empty and turning it upside down to demonstrate. The dregs dribbled out over the table.

'Waiter!' Mike shouted, attempting to click his fingers, then, on failing, clapping his hands instead.

'Say "garçon",' Conor laughed. 'Apparently it annoys the shite out of them.'

'Garçon! Garçon!' Mike called out.

Pablo stood and, saying, 'Is enough. I am quite drunk!', he zigzagged off in the same direction the women had taken five minutes earlier.

I crossed to where Conor was sitting and crouched down beside him. 'Conor,' I said softly, putting one hand on his shoulder. 'Let's go home, eh?'

Without turning, he pointed at me with one thumb and, while visibly trying yet failing to focus on Mike's features opposite, he said, 'The woman actually thinks I'm going to go home now.'

Both men collapsed into laughter at this, and when he could speak again, Mike replied, looking glassy-eyed at me, 'She does. She really does, mate!'

'Conor!' I said more sharply now. I pulled a half-empty bottle he had found amongst the empties from his hand and raised it high above my shoulder, out of reach. 'You've *really* had enough. Come on. Please! Let's go!'

His hand flew so fast, there was no time to duck and no way to avoid the blow. It hit me squarely across the cheek, sending me flying into a tamarind tree in a pot behind me.

Just for a moment, Mike looked worried. Just for an instant, I saw his addled brain recognise that all was not well. But then Conor laughed and said, 'Now where was I before I was so *rudely* interrupted? Oh yes, beer, wasn't it? Garçon! We need more beer.' And I saw Mike choose to laugh. I saw him choose to forget about the woman lying on the floor.

I held it together quite well. A burst of adrenalin enabled me to leave the taverna and find a taxi and explain, after much pointing, where I was staying. I sat in the back and watched the dark roads whizz by and felt, just for a bit, quite pleased with myself.

I paid the driver – it was thousands of drachma and I had no idea whatsoever if he was ripping me off – then I crossed the road to the staircase that led to our hotel.

I had descended about twenty steps when I returned to myself. Whatever hormone had been seeing me through this ordeal now vanished and I realised that my elbow was bleeding where I had grazed it on the floor, and my cheek was stinging from where I'd been hit. I paused, staring out at the view, still so beautiful, and let myself realise: Conor had hit me. He really had. I managed another ten steps before the tears arrived and I sat on the step and cried. Childhood had rushed back up on me and I suddenly wanted to be home in my bed with Barney Bear. I wanted Abby, or even my mother, to look out for me, to tell me what to do. I felt scared and stranded and alone. And I didn't know how to deal with any of it.

'Excuse me?' The voice came from behind me so I wiped my face on my sleeve and turned to look. Two men were trying to pass me on the narrow staircase, no doubt to get to their rooms.

'I'm sorry,' I sniffed, shuffling to one side so they could pass.

'Oh, hello!' the thinner of the two men said. 'It's you. We met this mor—' But I had leapt to my feet and was already scuttling down the stairs, jerked out of my self-pity by sheer embarrassment.

When I reached my balcony, I realised I didn't have the door key. It was in Conor's pocket. So I dried my eyes on a towel we'd left on the back of a deckchair and, after a few panicky breaths, returned upstairs towards the hotel.

Two houses behind ours, sitting in his own identical chair, the young hiker guy was reclining, apparently enjoying the night-time vista.

'I don't have my key,' I explained when he nodded at me questioningly. He had a kind face. 'I'm hoping they keep a double in the hotel?'

'They do,' he said, then looking concerned, he added, 'Are you OK?'

I bit my lip against a fresh flood of tears. There's nothing worse when you're trying to keep it all buttoned up than someone being nice to you, is there?

He stood and crossed to where I was standing. He was much, much taller than me but because I was on the staircase, our eyes were almost level. 'You're not OK at all, are you?' he said, reaching out to gently touch my upper arm.

I shook my head and stared at the floor, squeezing my eyes shut as hard as I could. But it was too late. I'd been holding it all in for days, even though it was only now that I realised it. My tears were already dropping to the ground, staining the concrete where they fell.

FIVE

Becky

It was a good job, I reckon, that I found out about Mum's trip. I mean, I'm not saying she couldn't have managed to organise it all on her own, but I definitely think it would have been a challenge for her. As far as the holiday was concerned, Mum had booked plane tickets to Athens but that was about as far as she had got.

Despite her many years as a secretary, Mum had never been that good at all the online stuff. Oh, she could use her Internet bank to pay the electricity bill and she could even log in and choose a film on Netflix. But watching her do anything she hadn't done before – search for something on Google, for example, or research hotels or flights – made me want to pull my hair out. She forever seemed to be clicking on the least useful thing on the page. And I always, despite my best intentions, ended up elbowing her out of the way. 'You could have flown direct to Santorini, you know,' I told her, 'if that's where you want to go.'

'I know that,' she said. 'But I just thought a boat trip might be nice.' I wasn't sure I believed her.

The boat schedules were, Mum said, ever so complicated. And it turned out she was right about that. But together, over the next couple of weeks, we worked out a plan. We would spend one night in Athens (exciting!), travel to the tiny island of Serifos (a friend had told me it was amazing), then carry on to Santorini. Step by step we booked tickets and finally, after some argument about whether hotels were better or worse than self-catering apartments, we booked our accommodation as well. 'I just worry they're going to be dirty,' Mum kept saying.

We flew to Athens on the twenty-third of August. It was drizzling and fifteen degrees in London, but in Athens it was *scorchio*!

Mum seemed really nervous about our bags being lost, but they arrived quickly, jostling their way onto the carousel, so we headed towards the metro for the next phase of our carefully coordinated plan.

As we passed the taxi rank, Mum grabbed my arm. 'Shall we just get a taxi?' she asked.

'We decided to take the metro,' I reminded her. 'We planned the route and everything. It's cheaper and probably quicker, too.'

'But we won't see anything,' Mum argued. 'I mean . . . I'm in Athens, you know? I want to look out of the window and see, well, *Athens*.'

I agreed this was a good idea and though most of the journey was on the motorway, once we got into Athens proper I was glad we'd chosen not only a taxi but that precise taxi. Because the driver, a cute guy of about my age who spoke perfect English, gave us a running commentary as he drove, pointing out schools and parks and good areas for food, historical monuments, and occasionally the Acropolis, towering above it all.

We got into our little Airbnb just after four and thankfully it was spotless. We collapsed onto the big leather sofa. We'd been up since six.

'This is lovely,' Mum said. 'Good choice.'

'It is,' I agreed. 'Better than a hotel, eh?'

'Yes,' Mum said. 'OK. You were right.'

We showered and headed straight back out. We only had one night to explore Athens and were both too excited to rest. Our boat out was booked for the next day.

We walked through the streets for a while and, drawn almost magnetically, we started to head towards the Acropolis, only to quickly find ourselves distracted, if not actually lost, in a vast pedestrian zone en-route – a lovely maze of little streets and squares bordered with bars. All of the tables were full of pretty, young Athenians drinking and talking and laughing. The ambiance was magical.

'I expected it all to be a bit sadder, somehow,' Mum commented. 'What with the banking crisis and the bailouts and everything.'

'I know,' I agreed. 'I was thinking the same thing. But then I suppose it is the capital. I mean, if you go to central London you can almost see the money flowing down the streets. But the shops are all still boarded up in Margate High Street. I bet plenty of places in Greece look like that too.'

'It is terrible, isn't it?' Mum said. 'They really do need to do something about that high street.'

'What we *need*,' I told her, 'is a change of government.'

Mum gave me a thin-lipped shrug. She firmly believes that all politicians are the same, i.e. useless, whereas I obstinately cling to the hope that some are at least less useless than others.

We eventually chose a place that didn't look too touristy (almost everyone seemed to be Greek) but yet still had an English translation of the menu.

'Oh, we forgot about the Acropolis!' I suddenly realised.

'It's a bit hot for that, anyway, isn't it?' Mum said. 'Maybe tomorrow morning?'

'Sure,' I told her. 'This is lovely, anyway.'

'It is,' Mum agreed. 'I'm starting to feel like I'm on holiday.'

'You were going to do this on your own,' I said, looking around. 'I find that hard to believe now.'

'Me too,' Mum said. 'I'm so glad you came, chicken.'

Eventually, drinks arrived, misty glasses of white wine, and a bowl of olives and cubes of salty feta.

'Cheers,' I said. We clinked glasses and sipped. The wine was dry and chilled and lovely. I looked around again and noted how nearly everyone was smiling. 'It must be so much easier to live in a hot country,' I added.

'Yes,' Mum agreed. 'I always thought I might move somewhere hot, but it just never really happened.'

'Did you?' I asked. 'When?' I didn't really believe her on that one. Mum often seemed to say things that other people tended to say, whether they were true for her or not – it was just her way of making conversation. I was used to it.

'Oh, you know . . .' Mum said vaguely. 'Way back when. I thought about it a lot. Every time it rained, really.'

'I never knew that.'

'Well,' Mum said, 'although at your age it's hard to believe, there are plenty of things you don't know about me.'

I laughed. 'Like what?'

'Ahh,' Mum said, smiling. 'Now that would be telling.'

We ended up eating right where we were sitting – a salad for Mum, and a moussaka for me – after which our frantic day and early start caught up with us and we yawningly decided to head back to the flat.

As we left the restaurant, Mum said, 'Before the euro, there were thousands of whatever they were called – drachma, I think – to the pound. It's much easier now . . . Or so I imagine.'

'Yes,' I said. 'Italy was like that, too. We did it in economics. There were tens of thousands of lira to the pound at one point.'

Once I'd replied, however, something struck me as strange about her comment, though I couldn't for the life of me work out what it was. I glanced at her sideways as we walked along the street, and she smiled at me falsely, before turning away.

The following morning, we were both up early, so we packed up most of our things and headed off to check out the Acropolis.

We walked sportily through the early-morning streets, watching delivery men wheeling boxes around and seeing old Athenian ladies walking their dogs. It wasn't hard to find the Acropolis, in fact we didn't even need a map. Every time you went around a corner you could see it up there on the hill. As we approached the park surrounding it, the roads rose steeply and we both broke out in a sweat.

'It's boiling already!' Mum commented, pausing to wipe her brow.

'I saw a sign,' I told her. 'It said it's twenty-nine. In the shade!'

The park around the monument was scrubby but pretty and afforded some great views out over the city. We even came across a colony of tortoises, just roaming through the bushes, which got me unreasonably excited. I've always loved tortoises and if it hadn't become so difficult to buy one I would probably have one by now. The closest I ever got was a miniature turtle thing in a goldfish bowl, but I cuddled it one night and killed it. So it's probably a good thing that I never had a full-sized tortoise after all.

By the time we reached the gates to the monument itself, we were hot, thirsty and tired. The queue for the cashier was a snaking monstrosity and the cost of entry for two was forty euros. Our courage, at the last hurdle, failed us.

'I just feel like I'll spend my entire life telling people I *almost* saw the Acropolis but couldn't be bothered to queue,' I told Mum as we walked away.

'I won't tell anyone if you don't,' she replied, grinning slyly. 'Anyway, you can see it from here. Look.'

I paused and peered back up at the majestic columns, the birthplace of democracy, as the sign said, and sighed. 'God, I am such a heathen, but you know what? This really is close enough for me.'

'Like mother, like daughter,' Mum laughed. 'Now for more important things. We need to find some coffee!'

'Or even better, some of that chilled coffee they all seem to be drinking,' I said.

After lunch, we checked out of our lovely flat and took another taxi to the port, and this proved to have an unexpected queue-jumping advantage to it.

When we arrived on the quayside, there were thousands of people jostling for position, but our driver, Nick, squeezed right past everyone, almost squashing a dog in the process. He dropped us right at the front of the queue and as no one seemed to notice, or even less care, we just stayed there, albeit feeling guilty as hell.

The boarding process was stressful. Men blew whistles and shouted incomprehensible instructions and the crowd surged forward towards the gaping orifice at the rear of the boat. Someone dragged a suitcase over my toes, making me shriek.

The whole thing felt like some biblical exodus or a deportation or something. I wondered, for the first time, if certain things aren't scarier than they logically should be because we're tapping into a collective memory of the past. I felt scared that afternoon, as if I had already been there, as if I knew exactly what it meant when a thousand people ran for a boat while men with whistles shouted. And what it meant, my soul seemed to be telling me, was imminent, terrifying danger.

The interior of the boat was vast – rows and rows of comfortable cinema-like seats that in places were twenty or thirty wide. Mum was understandably disappointed that we couldn't go out on the deck but this was a high-speed jetfoil – the windows couldn't even be opened. Our seats were 26K and 26J, right in the middle of a boisterous Greek family, so we naughtily nabbed two empty window seats. It was Mum's idea and though I worried the whole time, no one ever did come to claim them, check our tickets or kick us out.

The sea was as smooth as a lake and the three-hour trip went by without a hitch. Mum snoozed and I watched through the salt-stained windows as Athens vanished behind us and the first islands slid into view.

Watching the passing scenery was hypnotic and I daydreamed, projecting the events of the past few days on the cinema screen in my head, until Mum's comment about me not knowing her as well as I thought I did came to mind. And that, obviously, got me to thinking about my father. Because as far as I knew, that was the only real gaping hole in my education.

When Mum woke up, I fetched gritty Greek coffees for us both – to butter her up, nothing ever worked better than coffee – and after a few deep breaths, I dived in. 'You know all those things I don't know about you?' I started.

Mum was sitting sideways with her legs hunched up. She peered over her coffee cup at me. 'I was only being silly,' she said. 'You know everything about me. We lived in each other's pockets for eighteen years. How could you not?'

'But before,' I said tentatively. 'I mean, I know you don't like talking about it, but I don't know anything about before.'

'Well, you knew Nanny Eiléan,' Mum said. 'You've stayed in the house where I grew up, too. I never met any of my grandparents. They were all dead before I was born. So you're already one up on me for family history.'

I looked into Mum's eyes and thought I could see that she knew exactly what I was alluding to but, as ever, didn't want to go there. She looked back at me with puzzlement, as if it was me that was speaking in tongues.

'But what about the other stuff?' I said as casually as I could manage. 'I don't know anything about that.'

'What other stuff?' Mum asked.

'The accident and everything,' I said. I still couldn't bring myself to say the forbidden words. Father. Dad. Progenitor. They had all been unmentionable for so long I couldn't even remember when I had first learned they were taboo.

'Oh, that,' Mum said. 'Well, there's really not much to tell. You know there isn't.'

I must have sighed in frustration at this because Mum went on, 'But there isn't! I . . . you know . . . I met a guy. We had a fling. And he died. I'm sorry, chicken. I know how . . . how . . . lacklustre that must sound but it's the truth. It's not very classy, but the truth is that I can barely even remember him myself.'

'Fine, Mum,' I said softly. 'Whatever.' I turned to look out of the window. We were passing another group of tiny islands, even closer this time, perhaps too close. I could see a man fishing from a rock and I wondered if that was OK.

'Look,' Mum said after a moment. 'I was on holiday with a girlfriend, OK? And I met a random guy. And I had a fling. Please don't sulk.'

'I'm not,' I said, turning back to face her. And it was true. I'd got so used to not talking about my father that not talking about him a little more barely caused a ripple these days. But because it was the first time she had ever volunteered any additional information, Mum had piqued my curiosity.

'A girlfriend?' I asked. 'Was that Aunt Abby?' Abby was one of Mum's oldest friends, not a real aunt at all. But she had visited us once or twice a year for as long as I could remember.

Mum nodded and licked her lips. 'And I met him . . . I mean . . . this will sound terrible to you, but remember I was only twenty-five . . .'

'Just a bit older than me.'

'Yes. But in my head, I was much younger than you, if that makes any sense. I hadn't been to college like you have. I hadn't known any boys – well, not many, anyway. I hadn't even had a proper boyfriend really. Your grandmother ran a tight ship. She ran a *very* tight ship.'

'Yeah, I know she did. So it was a holiday fling, nothing more?'

Mum nodded. 'But then he had . . . you know . . . the car accident. And that was that. I don't know if it would have gone any further, but we never had the chance to find out.'

'How soon afterwards was it?'

'A couple of days,' Mum said.

'After the holiday, or after you met?'

'Oh, we were still on holiday. It was awful really.'

'I can imagine,' I told her, but I couldn't. I had one of those powerful, fleeting realisations that my mother was this complex person who had lived through terrible things. Nothing bad had ever really happened to me. 'So you didn't know him at all really?'

'Not really, no. I mean, I knew him well enough to . . . you know . . . I mean, I didn't jump into bed with him the second I met him or anything. So I knew enough to know he was lovely. And I knew him well enough that . . . when I realised I was pregnant I knew you'd be lovely too. That's why I didn't . . . you know. But anyway, that's enough of that.'

'You considered an abortion?' I asked, a wave of existential shock rolling over me at the hard-to-grasp concept that I had almost never existed.

'No!' Mum said. 'Not once. My mother, your grandmother, she . . . Actually, never mind about that. But no. Not once. I knew you'd be lovely. And I wanted you. There was never any doubt.'

'Gran can't have been thrilled, though?'

'No,' Mum said. 'No, she wasn't. You know how religious she was.'

'She was ke-ra-zy religious,' I said. 'But what was he—'

'Now, do you think we could talk about something else for a bit?' Mum interrupted. 'Would that be OK? Because none of that was . . . Well, it wasn't much fun, really. And I am trying to enjoy my first holiday in decades, you know?'

And so, though every snippet of information I had gleaned made me want to ask another thousand questions, I let the subject drop. For now.

'Anyway, what about you?' Mum asked me. 'You never tell me anything about your personal life.'

'My personal life?' I said, feeling immediately queasy. Though Mum and I were close, we'd never had a girlfriend kind of relationship.

'Yes. You were dating someone when you came back at Easter. You kept sneaking off to phone him all the time. I'm not blind. Or deaf.'

'Hmm . . . OK. Well, that was Tom,' I replied thoughtfully.

'And what happened to Tom?'

I shrugged. 'He wasn't very nice in the end.'

'Right,' Mum said. 'Oh well. You have to kiss a lot of frogs before you find a prince.'

'Oh, he wasn't French,' I told her, straight-faced. 'He was Scottish.'

'I never said he was,' Mum said, looking confused. My humour, as so often, had gone whizzing over her head.

I turned back to look out of the window again. We were passing an arid red outcrop and I wondered if it might be Serifos. According to my watch we were due to disembark in twenty minutes. But the island passed by – it was completely uninhabited – and so I stared out at the vast blue sea, which again stretched to the horizon, and thought for a bit about Tom.

I wondered, as I had wondered a thousand times, if I should have made more of an effort to make things work with him. Because Tom, despite his faults, had been sexy, sporty and on his better days funny, too. Jen, my best friend from college, was of the opinion that if you had to struggle to make something work, it was doomed from the start. But it seemed more and more to me that the people around me at college who were in long-term relationships made constant and sometimes overwhelming sacrifices to stay in them. So I was beginning to doubt that such a thing as a carefree, effortless relationship existed. Not outside Hollywood, at any rate.

The red rocks hadn't been Serifos, but as our ship finally manoeuvred into port I could see that Serifos was made of the same stuff. It was a sprawling red rock almost entirely devoid of trees or greenery. It looked a bit like the upper edge of some vast asteroid that had landed in a deep, deep sea.

The owner of our holiday-let, an ageing farmer in dungarees, was at the port to meet us with his battered old Peugeot hatchback. He was holding a flapping piece of paper that said 'Mrs Laura & Mrs Robeeca'.

'*Mrs Robeeca*,' I said to Mum, pointing. 'That's me!'

'I don't speak English,' he said as we shook hands. And we quickly ascertained that he really didn't. But what he lacked in vocabulary, he made up for in smiles.

He drove us up and up the red hillside, along red roads, cut out of red rock. Even the dust that caked the car was red. When we reached the plateau at the top of the hill (a place where you could successfully film a fake Mars landing), the road turned and started, almost immediately, to zigzag back down the other side. Sitting in the back, I started to feel quite pukey.

As the car redescended (straight – hairpin bend – straight – hairpin bend . . .) we caught glimpses of the bay below: an incredible turquoise sea, a strip of orangey sand and then bushes, trees, crops . . . a vibrant oasis in the midst of the arid Martian desolation. There were even a few palm trees down there and the scene looked a bit biblical, like some ancient painting of Babylon.

The house was formed of a series of smooth-edged cubes, seemingly plonked on one another and painted in the obligatory blinding white. The farmer and his wife lived above – her huge knickers were pegged to a rotary washing line, flapping in the breeze – and our holiday flat was below. We had the entire ground floor.

The woman of the house spoke little more English than her husband, but had learned the names of the gifts they had left scattered around the house, so as she showed us proudly yet shyly around the rooms she would gesture theatrically at things and say, 'Bread – I make,' or 'Grape – we grow,' or 'Wine – from grape,' or 'Cheese – from Alpina, our goat.' Finally, bowing as if we were royalty, she backed out of the front door and left us to it.

'What an amazing place!' Mum said, once she had gone. The rooms were sparsely furnished but spotless, and cool despite the still-present heat of the day.

Outside, a goat bleated so I bowed and gestured towards the open door and said, 'Alpina – our goat!'

Mum frowned at me. 'Don't,' she said. 'I thought she was really lovely.'

'She was. They are,' I said, picking a grape from the bowl and feeling bad. I'd just been trying to make Mum laugh and I certainly hadn't intended to imply anything negative about our lovely, generous hosts.

We checked out the bedroom – it had two single beds with crisp, ironed sheets – and the bathroom, which had one of those wet-room shower affairs everyone is so into these days. You know, the ones where you can't shower without getting the bog roll wet . . .

And then we stepped outside to look at the view. We were halfway up the hillside, perhaps a few hundred yards from the water's edge. To the left, a red, rocky outcrop plunged into the sea, framing the view, and to the right were terraced hills covered in cultivated greenery. I guessed they were vines. In the middle, bang in front of us, nestled between the two hills, was the vibrant green oasis and, beyond that, the electric neon blue of the sea.

'It's stunning,' I commented.

'And did you see the beach as we were coming down?' Mum asked. From where we were standing, it was hidden behind the trees.

'I did,' I said. 'And I think it's just for us.'

Mum looked left and right. 'I don't see any other houses around, at any rate.'

'So, food, drink or a swim?' I asked.

Mum wrinkled her nose. 'I am a bit hungry,' she said. 'But I'm gagging to get in that water, too. We should have eaten something on the boat.'

'We could take the bread and cheese,' I suggested. 'We could picnic on the beach.'

Mum smiled and nodded. 'Yeah,' she said. 'Let's do that.'

Our two days in Serifos were paradisiacal.

Had we planned to stay longer (and I would have loved to, it was truly a wrench to leave) the absence of transport would have been a problem. But for two days, three nights, we were fine.

We'd get up, say hello to Alpina, give her some scraps from the previous evening's meal and then meander down to the beach where we'd swim in the warm waters of the bay, or snooze or read in the shade of the trees that overhung our private beach. Then we'd climb back up the hill to have lunch at the house with a random collection of cats around our feet.

Fresh gifts arrived constantly, basically any time we left the house. At lunchtime we discovered tomatoes and tiny red peppers. At dinner time a pot of home-made moussaka and some pungent yoghurt. At breakfast time a rather incongruous sponge cake appeared on the doorstep. It was so dry you had to wash it down with coffee for fear of choking. But even then, the intention to please was evident. And considering we'd paid only forty-five euros a night, we could barely believe our luck.

The wine was the only thing we honestly couldn't consume – boy, was it rough – and we discussed, endlessly, whether it was better to pour some of it away so they'd think we'd liked it, or leave it intact, as they clearly weren't wealthy people, and would probably frown at such waste.

In the end we decided to top it up with water (we'd barely touched the stuff). 'That way they'll think we're just teetotallers,' Mum said.

It was our final night in Serifos and as the sky turned deepest red, and as the husband fed the endlessly bleating Alpina on the terrace below, I got to thinking about Tom again.

'How do you know if someone's an alcoholic?' I asked Mum, a forkful of moussaka hovering.

'Why? Are you tempted by that paint-stripper wine of theirs?' Mum laughed.

'No,' I replied. 'No, I'm really not.'

'Then you're safe, I reckon.'

'I was thinking about Tom actually,' I told her. 'He was lovely when he was sober but pretty horrid when he'd had a drink.'

Mum sighed. 'Then you're well out of it, I would say.'

'You think so?'

'Most people drink to have a nice time,' she said. 'It's the ones who have a bad time but carry on drinking regardless you have to watch out for.'

'I keep wondering if I tried hard enough,' I said between mouthfuls. 'God, this moussaka is amazing, isn't it? It's even better than the one in that restaurant.'

'It is,' Mum said. 'And what do you mean by "tried hard enough"?'

'Well, he got drunk and lairy a few times and I just gave up really. I mean, it was the end of term and everything and we hadn't been going out for long, so . . . But I wonder if I shouldn't have tried harder – tried to get him to stop drinking or something?'

'Best thing you could have done, sweetheart,' Mum said. 'Run away quickly.'

'You sound like you're talking from experience.'

Mum shrugged.

'Are you?' I asked. 'Brian was OK when he drank, wasn't he?'

'Yeah,' she said. 'Yeah, Brian was fine. He just used to fall asleep. No, I saw a programme about it, that's all. And they said the only people who can help alcoholics are themselves. Everyone else just needs to save themselves.'

SIX

Laura

Other than the fact that I had argued with my boyfriend, I'd told the hiker guy virtually nothing. But as I had left – off to the hotel in search of a spare key – he'd said, 'If you have any problems just shout very loud, OK? I think we are close enough to hear.'

'I won't,' I'd told him, laughing falsely and wondering what kind of problem he was imagining. I'd said so little, after all. But the idea reassured me a tiny bit.

All the same, I barely slept at all that night and when I did manage to quit the misery of consciousness for twenty minutes or so, my sleep was so shallow I was hardly asleep at all.

Even with my friendly neighbour listening out, I was scared about Conor returning. I doubted that such a thing was possible. He'd been way too drunk to drive and almost certainly too drunk to organise a taxi or even remember where he was staying. But I was terrified all the same.

About seven, I finally gave up on sleep. The longer I lay in bed, the more the possibility of Conor getting home increased, and him finding me dozing would leave me feeling even more vulnerable.

So I forced myself up and showered and fixed up my face. I had only the slightest of bruises on my cheek, which I covered with foundation. My elbow was scabby from where I had fallen and I had a bruise on my back from the earthenware pot the tree had been in, but other than that, all things considered, I'd got off pretty lightly.

I hadn't decided what to do yet but I felt certain of one thing: it would involve a packed suitcase. So I set about making that happen. Afterwards, I sat outside and stared at the view as I tried to review my options. It was another beautiful day, but it brought no pleasure to me that morning. All I wanted was to escape.

I could get a taxi to the airport, I reckoned, and try to change my ticket there. But even in Mykonos the airport had been tiny and I hadn't seen an airline desk at all. The one in Santorini would probably be even smaller. Plus, I'd need to change not one but two plane tickets to get home: the Aegean one to Athens, and the BA ticket back home. It's silly, because it seems perfectly doable to me these days, but in my twenties the complexity of the whole thing just made me want to cry.

I could get a taxi and ask him to take me to a different hotel in a different town, and try to enjoy the rest of my holiday. But I wasn't even sure I could pay for it. I hadn't yet tested my debit card in Greece and the seventy pounds' worth of drachma I'd changed at the Post Office wouldn't get me very far. Plus, I'd inevitably have to face Conor for the flight home anyway.

I considered phoning Mum and asking her what to do, but knew she'd go ballistic, probably wouldn't have any answers I hadn't thought of already, and would punish me severely when I got home. I wished I could call Abby but she, of course, was in Ibiza. *Oh why, oh why hadn't I gone to Ibiza?*

'Good morning to you!'

I jerked from my reverie and turned to see Conor standing behind me. I'd be brave, I decided in that instant. I'd inform him of my decision and make him help me organise things. He owed me that at least. What a terrible feminist I was back then!

'Good morning,' I said coldly.

'I woke up on a bench,' Conor said, laughing as if this was funny. 'Totally shit-faced last night . . .'

'I know,' I said. 'I was there.'

'Have you eaten yet?' Conor asked, choosing to ignore my glare.

'Not hungry,' I replied.

'You're looking lovely,' Conor said.

I shrugged and turned back to look out to sea.

'Have you got the hump with me or something?' he asked.

I chewed my lip, trying to channel the anger rising within me into something concise and constructive. 'No, Conor,' I said icily, turning back to face him. 'No, I haven't got the *hump* with you. I'm . . . I'm . . . furious beyond belief. And I'm leaving. My bags are packed. I just need you to help me change my flights.'

'Oh,' Conor said, his stupid grin fading. 'You're leaving? May I ask why? I'm a little fuzzy on the details of last night.'

'You hit me, Conor,' I said. 'You whacked me in the face.'

'I did?'

'Yes.'

He peered at me to search for evidence of my accusation and shrugged.

'I covered the bruises with foundation,' I told him. 'One of the few advantages of being a woman.'

'Don't be daft,' Conor said. 'I didn't *hit* you. I'd never hit you.'

'Only you did. I tried to get you to stop drinking. And you punched me.'

Conor laughed sourly at this. 'I didn't *punch* you,' he said. 'If I'd punched you, you wouldn't have been able to cover it up with a bit of make-up, that's for sure.'

I thought about the truth of this and shuddered. 'Only you did,' I said coldly.

Conor wrinkled his nose. 'You're saying, like, accidentally?' he asked. The colour had drained from his cheeks. He was no longer finding this funny.

I shook my head. 'Look, I don't need to convince you, Conor,' I said. 'In fact, I don't give a shit if you remember at all. I just need to change my ticket so I can get out of here.'

Conor squinted at me and squatted down so he was at eye level. 'Let me get a shower, OK?' he asked softly. 'I'm feeling like shite here, so let me get a shower and we'll discuss this over breakfast.'

'I'm not going to discuss anything with you,' I told him. 'I want to go home.'

'OK,' Conor said. 'Then let me shower and change my clothes and we'll do anything you want, OK?' He sighed dolefully and reached out to stroke my cheek, but I flinched so, shaking his head, he stood and vanished into the interior.

'I'll wait for you in the restaurant,' I called out. Because suddenly I *was* hungry. I would also, I decided, feel safer with other people around.

I served myself two croissants and some orange juice and sat in the furthest corner of the restaurant, where people were less likely to overhear our conversation. The waiter came and filled my cup with coffee. 'It's a beautiful day,' he said, and momentarily I hated him for that.

The sun was already hot enough to prickle my skin and the sky above was a deep-space blue. But the horizon this morning was a misty, powdery colour, as beautiful as ever and constantly changing hue. I watched two ferries cross paths in the bay. A cat appeared from nowhere and, when I fed her a chunk of my croissant, two tiny white kittens appeared to join her.

After ten minutes or so, Conor appeared. He had changed into a baby-blue shirt the exact colour of the horizon. He pulled up a chair and said, sheepishly, 'So, I've been a bit of a prick, have I?' He winced as he said it as if his teeth ached.

'I really don't want to discuss it,' I said. 'But yes. In fact, *being a prick* doesn't even begin to cover it.'

Conor nodded and swallowed. He beckoned to the waiter and tried to order croissants, only for the waiter to remind him that the buffet was self-service.

'Are you eating that?' Conor asked, pointing at the half a croissant that remained on my plate. The thirty feet to the buffet were apparently too much for him this morning.

I blinked slowly and shook my head.

'Look, I'm sorry,' Conor said as he raised my leftovers to his mouth.

'Good,' I said. 'I'm glad you're sorry.'

'I'm really, really sorry.'

'Right,' I said. 'We've established that you're sorry.'

'So are we good?' Conor asked, raising his eyebrows hopefully.

I covered my eyes with my palms for a moment, then breathed into my hands before replying, 'No, we're not OK. We're not OK at all. You *hit* me, for fuck's sake.'

Conor looked nervously around and, following his gaze, I saw that a couple three tables away had turned to stare. I felt myself blush.

'Look,' Conor said quietly. 'I'm not saying that I didn't, OK? I'm not saying that I don't believe you . . .'

'Good,' I said, struggling to keep my voice level. 'I'm glad you're not saying that.'

'But it must have been an accident. It really must have been. I would never, you know . . . I would *never* hit a woman.'

'Only you did, Conor. Hit a woman is exactly what you did.'

'Then I'm sorry,' Conor said. 'What more can I say?'

'Unfortunately "sorry" doesn't work here,' I told him. 'Sorry's not enough. Not this time.'

'Then what?' Conor asked. 'Tell me what I have to do.'

I shook my head and looked into his eyes. I shrugged. 'I'm sorry,' I said. 'But I don't think there's—'

'I'll change your ticket for you, if you want. I'll go and do it now, if that's what you really need,' Conor said.

'It is.'

'But at least give me one more chance.'

'I can't,' I said. 'I'm sorry.'

'There's a beach,' Conor said. 'Your man, Mike, told me about it last night. It's half an hour's drive. It's beautiful. It's one of the most—'

'I can't, Conor,' I said again. 'You're not listening.'

'Let me take you there.' He reached for my hand across the table but I jerked it away. 'Give me one more chance to make it up to you. Let me give you the best day ever. What do you say? And then you can go.'

'But you're not listening,' I said. 'I can't.'

'Why not?' Conor asked. There was real desperation in his voice, genuine tears pooling in the corners of those big, brown eyes. I could sense my resolve faltering.

'Because I'm scared of you,' I said brutally. 'You change. When you drink. And I'm scared of you.'

'Well, that one's easily solved,' Conor said. 'I won't drink.'

I stared at him, flicking my gaze between one eye and the other as I tried to look into his soul. And I thought I saw a scared little boy hiding deep inside there. And I thought that was someone the scared little girl inside me seemed to recognise.

'Please,' Conor said again. 'You love it here. You've been dreaming of coming here for years, you told me so yourself. And I'm . . . I'm really into you, you know? I'll stay sober as a judge. I'll be on my best behaviour, I promise. Don't let a nob like myself ruin your holiday, for Christ's sake.'

I sighed deeply. 'Do you promise?' I asked. 'Do you promise you won't drink?'

'Yes,' Conor gushed. 'Yes, I promise. Jesus Mary, thank God for that.'

'And if I change my mind at any point, you'll help me change my ticket? No arguments.'

'If you change your mind at any point, I'll help you change your ticket,' Conor repeated, nodding eagerly. 'No arguments at all.'

I sighed deeply and shook my head – in sadness, I think, at the decisions I was watching myself make. 'This is the *absolute* last chance, Conor,' I said.

'I know that,' Conor replied. 'You know that I know that, right?'

As I unpacked my beach gear from my suitcase, I almost changed my mind. I froze for a moment, my sun cream in one hand and my bikini in another, and I thought, *You can still walk away from this. You can still just say 'no' and deal with this while Conor's in a good mood.*

But then Conor called out from the bathroom. 'This red beach is supposed to be incredible, you know?' He sounded youthful and excited – boyish, even. 'And the drive takes us right around the island.'

And like a gambler who can't stop gambling, like a gambler who pushes his chips back onto the board, I thought, *Oh, what the hell?*

It was true that I'd been wanting to come here for as long as I remembered. And it was true I wanted to see the red beach. I'd read about it in the Aegean Airlines magazine.

But what's perhaps hardest to admit is that my fragile ego, battered by the constant criticism dealt out by my mother, felt sated whenever Conor complimented me. And he complimented me almost constantly. I was enjoying the idea (if not the reality) of having a boyfriend. I was even enjoying, in a strange, rather perverse way, the unpredictability, the danger, the risk of it all . . . I felt excited to see if Conor would keep his word and how I'd deal with it if he didn't . . . That will all sound completely mad, I expect. But then, don't we all have moments of madness?

◆ ◆ ◆

The drive to the beach was incredible. It took us up into the hills and down to the coast, then up again, then down.

I stayed silent for the first half of the trip, partly because I was still genuinely wondering about my own mental processes and partly because I was determined to make Conor pay. It all seems childish looking back, but then I was pretty much still a child.

In the end, the scenery, which was stunning, and Conor's dogged good humour managed to grind me down. I asked him to pull over for a photograph and found myself laughing, despite everything, as he ran comically to join me while the self-timer on his camera beeped frantically.

We left the car in a dusty car park and clambered down the rocks to the beach. It was as beautiful as everyone said it was.

It wasn't called the red beach for no reason. The rock face, the sand, even the shallows were a deep-red ochre. Where the turquoise of the sea met the red of the beach, the outrageous colours seemed to shudder against each other.

We rented sunbeds and parasols and Conor ran into the sea. I started to wade in gingerly. Not only did I not want any horseplay in the shallows with him, but the sea was much colder today.

Conor swam back to encourage me. 'I'm counting to ten and then I'm gonna splash you!' he menaced.

I waved him away with one hand. 'Just go and . . . swim or something, will you?' I said, irritatedly.

'Still angry, huh?' Conor asked.

'Yep,' I told him, unflinching. 'Still angry.'

'Well, you'll have to forgive me eventually,' he said, then he laughed, turned, and swam efficiently out to sea.

By one o'clock, the sun was scorching and any part of my body that wasn't protected by the limited shade provided by the parasol seemed at risk, so I agreed with Conor that we should leave. As we clambered back over the rocks, I glanced back regretfully. It really was that beautiful.

We ate in Megalochori, a traditional hillside village made of another thousand hobbit houses and blue-domed churches.

The restaurant we chose was in a pretty little square, shaded by vines which had woven themselves around steel cables stretched between the buildings. Waistcoated waiters zipped in and out of the darkened interiors around the edges, bringing colourful Greek salads and pink carafes of wine – and then a prawn saganaki for me and ouzo-flambéed lobster for Conor. I debated with myself for a moment whether the ouzo in his meal violated the terms of our agreement but, because he requested a Coke to go with it, I decided to say nothing. When it came, my prawn saganaki – prawns steeped in a rich tomato sauce with lumps of melted feta – was delicious. Conor seemed pleased with his choice, too.

After a sweaty meander through the village, we drove to the eastern side of the island, to a vast expanse of almost-black sand called Perissa Beach. It was covered with wall-to-wall parasols. Once again we rented sunbeds and again Conor drank Coke.

'I know you haven't forgiven me properly yet,' Conor said on returning from a swim.

I glanced up at him over the top of the novel I was reading and did my best to look circumspect.

'But am I on the right track?' he asked.

'You're on the right track,' I said as flatly as I could manage. 'But you still have some way to go.' Was I starting to enjoy making him pay? Was I getting into the ever-shifting balance of who had the power? I think I probably was.

'Thank you,' Conor said. He leaned over me, dripping cold water from his swim, and kissed me on the cheek. I managed, just about, not to flinch. It was part of showing him that I still had the power.

We stayed there all afternoon and ate dinner in the beach's restaurant, our toes pushing into the sand. Conor remained good-tempered, sober, and drove calmly home. I told myself everything was going to be OK, even though, by now, I knew this wasn't true.

The sun had gone down by the time we got back; the last vestiges of red were draining from the sky.

'I don't suppose there's any chance of a bit of you-know-what?' Conor asked as he unlocked the front door.

I sank into the deckchair to look out, as ever, at the view. 'Any chance of a bit of wh— Oh!' I said. 'No! No chance of that whatsoever.'

'Right,' Conor said. 'Fair enough. I fancy a ciggy.'

'A cigarette?' I asked, surprised. I had never seen Conor smoke.

'Yeah, it grabs me from time to time,' Conor said. 'The idea of a ciggy. Especially if I can't drink. Shall I nip up to the hotel and see if they have some?'

I shrugged. 'Do whatever you want,' I said. 'I never smoke, so . . . But do whatever you want.'

'Right,' Conor said. 'Well, I won't be a tick.'

I watched the horizon until the final swathe of purple had vanished, until the sky was a deep uniform blue and the stars were twinkling above. And it was only then I realised that Conor wasn't coming back.

'What the fuck did you go and do that for?' It was his voice that had woken me with a start.

I sat up blinking at the bedroom light he'd switched on, then managed to focus on his face. He was sitting on the edge of the bed right beside me, staring at me crazily.

'You're drunk,' I said simply.

'You locked me out!' Conor replied, sounding outraged. 'Jesus!'

'I . . . I didn't think,' I lied. I had expected to be awoken by his knocking. I had wanted to be awake when he returned, that was all. 'I'm sorry. But you're drunk. You promised.'

Taking in the fact that I was still fully clothed – I'd prepared myself for precisely this – I edged across to the far side of the bed and stood up. I glanced at the clock on the bedside table. It was half past one in the morning.

Conor stood with difficulty and started to lumber around the bed to where I was standing. I backed towards the front door.

'You locked me out of my own fecking room,' Conor said again. 'I had to ask that wanker in the hotel for the key.'

'I'm sorry,' I said again. 'Now just calm down and—'

'Gimme a kiss and maybe I'll forgive you,' Conor slurred, stepping into my personal space. 'Just a kiss,' he added, 'because, unlike yourself, I'm a forgiving kind of guy.'

'I'm not kissing you,' I said, turning my face sideways. He stank of ouzo and cigarettes. I fumbled behind me to unlock the front door.

I wondered, momentarily, if this was a dream. Because it had all of the classic elements of a nightmare. The pursuer. The fear. The inability to escape. I looked around the room, checking for detail. I glanced at my open suitcase beside me hoping to spot something incongruous that might reveal this as a nightmare – something like, I don't know, a leopard in my suitcase, or a hand beckoning, or a secret door. But my case was exactly as I had left it. My clothes were neatly piled and stacked in the two open halves. My fingers had found the lever on the lock by now, but when I tried to pull it open, it wouldn't budge. It was locked and Conor had the key.

'You're not going anywhere,' Conor said, following my gaze to my suitcase. 'Not anywhere at all.'

'I wasn't even . . . I'm not . . .' I spluttered, hesitating between submission and anger as the best way out. 'Stop, Conor,' I pleaded. But it was too late. He had hurled my case across the room with ease. The contents were scattered across the floor.

I turned now to glance at the door lock but my fingers hadn't lied. The key was missing. 'Give me the key,' I said, turning back to find Conor mere inches away. 'Let me out.'

He grabbed my wrists and, using his hips, pushed me back against the door so hard that I hurt my back on the doorknob. I couldn't believe how strong his grip was. I worried he was going to break my wrists. 'A kiss,' he said in a mock-reasonable voice. 'Is that too much to ask?'

'Let me out,' I said again, struggling pathetically against his grasp.

'Kiss me,' Conor said, his head now too close to focus on. He reached and forcibly turned my head to face him, pressing his fingers into my chin and cheek as he did so. The doorknob was digging so hard into my back now that I could barely stand the pain.

'If you don't stop, I'll scream,' I threatened, thinking of the hiker and his friend, just two tiny houses behind us.

'You'll *scream*?' Conor repeated, laughing horribly. His mouth held a sneer and his eyes were so dark, they looked as if he were possessed. I know that's a thing people say quite a lot, but they really did. I looked into them and wondered if evil, if the devil himself, didn't exist after all. I had always assumed Abby was right and that these things were just metaphors.

'Get . . . off . . . me . . .' I said, starting to cry in despair.

'The *poor* little thing,' Conor said in a revolting tone of voice. 'She's *crying*.' He was undoing his belt now with one hand, so I tried to take advantage of the fact that he only had one hand to hold me. I tried to break away.

He yanked me back so fast and with such force that it left me breathless. He slammed me back against the door so hard that I wondered, just for a second, if he hadn't damaged my skull.

I went limp. Some instinct in me telling me to survive, to just stay alive, made me stop fighting. Men have a fight-or-flight response, they say. For women, it's fight or flight, or freeze. Because in the face of overpowering physical strength, our overriding instinct is to survive, to not die here. I went numb, suspending my consciousness. It was a technique I had perfected as a child during beatings.

All the same, I remember thinking both *This is how women get raped* and *This is where Conor rapes me*. Fight, or flight, or if all else fails, *freeze*.

He unbuttoned my jeans and pushed them down my legs. 'I'm gonna fuck you so hard, you won't be able to walk for a week,' he said.

'Conor,' I whimpered. 'Please don't . . .' I was trembling and crying. Snot was running from my nose.

Unexpectedly, Conor paused and looked down at himself, losing his balance and staggering backwards a few paces in the process. 'Aw Jesus,' he said, sinking back onto the bed behind him, his jeans still around his ankles. 'Now look what you've gone and done. You've put me right off my stride.'

It was then I realised that, for now, I'd escaped; he couldn't rape me, not tonight. He was too drunk for that.

He let himself flop backwards so he was looking at the ceiling and I slid silently down the door until I was out of his line of sight. Too scared to make a sound in case he remembered I was there, I sat on the cold, tiled floor and waited.

In less than a minute he started to snore.

I waited much longer, though. I waited until I felt certain he wasn't going to wake up, then I stood silently and pulled my jeans up before going in search of the room key. As I pulled it from his trouser pocket, Conor twitched his left foot and murmured, 'I'm sorry, sir. I'm sorry. I'll do it better next time.' I didn't know and didn't care what he might be dreaming about.

I wiped my face on a T-shirt from the floor, quietly opened the door and made my way up to the lobby where I rang the bell on the counter. A night porter appeared from a room behind the desk and smiled at me. I could hear the sounds of Greek television drifting through the open doorway – a shouting woman, a dog barking, canned laughter . . .

'Hello,' I said. 'I'm sorry to trouble you.'

'That's OK,' he replied, yawning. 'That's my job.'

'I need another room,' I explained, a pained expression on my face. 'Is that possible?'

'You don't like your room?'

'No, that's not it. I've had some problems with my . . . with the person I'm sharing my room with. He's . . . well . . . he's very drunk. And I need somewhere else to sleep. I know that's . . .'

'Room 43?' the man asked. His smile had already vanished.

I nodded and felt inexplicably ashamed.

'Your husband is very rude man,' he told me.

I nodded and bit my lip. 'I know,' I told him. 'But he's not my husband.' I could only imagine what kind of hell Conor had given the poor guy.

'I think is better if you leave the hotel,' the man said. 'Both of you. Tomorrow I talk to the boss man.'

'I understand, but really it's not my fault. He's nothing to do with me.'

'He paid for your room. You are together.'

'I know. I'm sorry. I know he's awful,' I said, fighting back tears. 'That's why I need another room.'

'It's impossible,' the man said. 'All rooms are busy. We are August, you know?'

I glanced around the lobby, wondering if there was anyone else who could help me. But the only people present were a young couple kissing on a sofa in the corner.

'Please,' I said again.

'I'm sorry.'

'Can I stay here?' I asked. I glanced at an empty sofa on the far side.

'No,' the man said. 'You cannot sleep in the lobby.'

'Can you lend me a blanket or something, then? I can probably sleep outside somewhere if I have a blanket.' Tears were now rolling down my cheeks.

'It's too cold. You should go back to your room,' the man said, his tone softening.

'I can't,' I snuffled. 'I'm scared.'

I often think that if men realised how much time you spend as a woman pleading with men – pleading with them to stop doing what they're doing, or pleading with them to let *you* do whatever needs to be done – they'd understand a lot more about what our lives are like.

The man chewed his top lip. 'I have one room,' he said, 'but it's dirty. The cleaning is tomorrow.'

'That's fine!' I told him, straightening my posture and swiping away the tears. 'I don't care. Please. That's absolutely fine.'

'I can give you some sheets. But it's all I can do.'

'That's fine,' I said again. 'Thank you. Thank you so much.'

He vanished into the back room and returned with a pile of sheets and a folded towel. Then he lifted a key from a hook and slipped out from behind his counter. 'Come,' he said simply.

To get to the room, we wove back down the staircase, past the tall man's room and on past our own.

The new room, number 73, was exactly three rows down from where Conor was sleeping, which was just far enough that my terrace was out of his line of sight. I was thankful it was further down as it seemed unlikely he'd pass by.

'Thank you,' I said again, as the man unlocked the door and handed me the pile of fresh laundry. 'Thank you; you're wonderful.' I was fighting back a fresh round of tears prompted by his kindness. 'And please, please don't tell him which room I'm in, OK?'

'Your husband?' he asked.

'He's *not* my husband.'

'No. Sorry. And no. I don't tell him anything. I don't like him so much, you know?'

'Thank you!' I said again as I turned to enter the room.

'He needs to stop drinking,' the man said, sounding severe, as if he was giving me a final telling-off, just in case I hadn't got the message.

'Yes,' I said quietly. 'Yes, I know that. Thank you.'

The room was visibly unmade. There was rubbish in the bin and toothpaste around the washbasin. The sheets were a tangled mess.

But my adrenalin was fading and it was as much as I could do to pull the dirty sheets from the bed and throw a clean one over the mattress.

I checked one last time that the door was locked. After a moment's reflection I returned and gave the key a half-turn in the lock, thinking that this way I'd be safer. Then I kicked off my jeans and crawled onto the bed. I was asleep within seconds.

I was awoken at half seven by someone noisily attempting (but failing) to unlock the door.

'Who is it?' I called out, when the noise showed no sign of abating.

'Cleaner!' a woman's voice said, so I steeled myself, opened the door and peered out.

'Sorry,' she said, a mop and bucket in one hand. 'No body, this room.'

'It was an emergency,' I told her. 'The night porter let me stay here.'

'OK,' she said, turning to leave. I could see she had no understanding of what I had said.

Worrying I was about to be kicked out, I showered and dressed quickly, putting back on yesterday's jeans and T-shirt. Then I sat in the doorway and looked out at the almost identical view to the one we had from our room and tried to decide what to do.

There was a cool sea breeze that morning, and the parasols were all aflutter. I was glad I hadn't had to sleep outside.

Taking stock of my body, I realised I was really quite hungry but I was too scared of bumping into Conor to dare eat breakfast in the restaurant. In fact, I was too scared to even pass by our room.

I was just trying to calculate the probability of Conor being up at eight when a voice said, 'You changed rooms?' I looked up to see the tall man smiling at me from the staircase. 'I snore too loud?' he asked, grinning at his own joke.

'Oh, hello,' I said.

'Good morning. New room,' he said again, indicating the room with his chin.

'Yes . . . I . . . we had some problems,' I told him. 'I had to change rooms.'

He nodded and smiled as if what I'd said enabled him to understand exactly what had happened. 'I go swimming,' he said, wiggling his eyebrows and tugging at the towel he had draped around his neck.

'Down there?' I asked, pointing.

He nodded. 'You should come,' he said. 'It is good for you.'

I wrinkled my nose and shook my head. 'No thanks,' I said. 'It's a bit cold for me this morning. And I need breakfast first.'

'Yes, cooler,' the man said. 'September comes, huh?'

'But enjoy your swim,' I told him.

'Thank you. Enjoy your breakfast,' he said. He gave me a shy little wave, and turned to continue his way, but I jumped up from my seat and called him back. I'd had an idea.

'Do they do breakfast down there?' I asked.

He frowned at me in confusion.

'Sorry,' I said. 'The restaurant you mentioned. At the bottom of the stairs. Do they do breakfast?'

He shook his head. 'Only coffee,' he said. 'And maybe some bread.'

'Can you wait for me?' I asked.

'Of course.'

'I just need to get a towel.'

It was only when I re-entered the room that I remembered I didn't have my swimming things with me. 'Actually, I'll just have some breakfast, I think,' I told him as I locked the door behind me. 'It really is too cold for swimming this morning.'

I followed him down the steep staircase, past another five rows of hotel rooms, on and on winding down the naked rock face. We crossed paths with a couple coming up and, as they paused for breath, the man shook the fingers of one hand back and forth in a gesture that I assumed was meant to convey the extreme effort of the return journey.

'*C'est dur*, huh?' the tall man said.

The man laughed and nodded.

'What language was that?' I asked, once we'd resumed our winding descent.

'French,' the tall man told me. 'They are very nice. They swim here every morning.'

The staircase eventually joined a wider zigzagging path down the hillside and we passed another couple riding on some long-suffering-looking donkeys.

'They chose the easy way,' I told him.

'Yes. But you have to really not like the animals to do that, huh?' he said.

The port at the bottom was beautiful: three closed restaurants right on the edge of the quayside and a tiny beach, just twenty or thirty feet wide. The coastline either side was grey, inaccessible rock, tumbling down into the sea. At the end of the quay was a small concrete jetty with a single, faded-green fishing boat tied up. And at the land end of the jetty was a tatty wooden shack with four plastic tables, each sprouting a sun-bleached Magnum parasol. This place, at least, appeared to be open.

'You're sure you don't swim?' the tall man asked. He was already kicking off his trainers and pulling his T-shirt over his head to reveal a long, pale, wiry body that seemed in some way to be the exact opposite of Conor's compact muscles.

I shook my head. 'I really do need coffee,' I said.

'I'll see you there, then,' he replied, nodding towards the shack.

I scrambled across the rocks and sat on the first chair I came to, and by the time I looked back out to sea he was already swimming badly and splashing around, yelping like a child.

The coffee, when it arrived, was so strong I could barely drink it. But I added plenty of sugar and did my best to strain it through my teeth.

The woman who served me, a woman in her late fifties or sixties, asked me something complicated in Greek but I had no idea what she was saying. It was only when she reappeared with a slice of sponge cake that I understood what she'd been trying to ask me.

I nodded gratefully. 'Thank you,' I said.

'*Parakalo*,' she replied with a gentle smile and a nod.

I sat for ten minutes watching the tall man duck-dive. I saw fish nibbling at algae on the jetty just below me. A small plane dragging an advert flew overhead. I tried to concentrate on the details of here and now. I was trying not to think about what to do next because thinking about my options made me feel panicky.

And then, the water droplets still pearling on his pale, hairless body, the tall man appeared at my side. He waved to the woman who ran the shack and pointed at my coffee cup before giving her a thumbs-up sign. 'Good coffee, huh?' he said, as he dried himself and sat down.

'It's strong,' I said. 'I'll give it that. But a bit gritty.'

'You have to leave it for a while. You have to let it . . .'

'Stand?' I offered. 'Let it settle?'

'Settle,' the man said. 'Yes. So, I am Leif.' He held out his hand.

I smiled at the awkwardness of the gesture. It seemed a little late for introductions. 'I'm Laura,' I said, taking his hand, still cold and damp from his swim. 'Is that Leaf, did you say? Like the leaf on a tree?'

'Something like that,' he said.

I broke off a chunk of the cake and fed it to my lips. 'It's a nice name,' I said. 'I like trees.'

Leif nodded. His face flushed red and I worried he thought I was trying to chat him up when I'd just said the first thing I could think of to fill the silence. 'So, you're here with a friend?' I blundered on. 'I think I saw you together the other day.'

'We are eight,' Leif said. 'Hillwalking party. From Norway.'

I nodded. The accent, the blond hair, the blue eyes; Norway made sense. 'I thought you were French at first. Because you spoke to those people . . .'

Leif shook his head and laughed. 'I know about one hundred words in French,' he said. 'That's all.'

'Your English is good, though,' I offered.

'It's not so bad as my French,' Leif said. 'Thank God.'

'So, hillwalking,' I commented, desperately trying to keep the conversation going, even though I didn't know why that seemed important. 'That must be lovely. Especially here.'

'It is,' Leif told me. 'But sometimes too hot. Not so many trees here.'

'No,' I said. 'That's true.'

The woman brought Leif his coffee. '*Efharisto*,' Leif said.

'*Parakalo*,' the woman replied.

'*Efharisto*,' I repeated, once she'd left. 'Is that, like, "thank you"?'

'You got it,' Leif told me. 'And *parakalo* is kind of . . . "for nothing".'

'For nothing?'

'You know . . . um . . . "you're welcome". "It's nothing", maybe.'

'Oh, right,' I said. '*Parakalo*. You're very good with languages.'

'It's rude not to try,' Leif said. 'This is their country, you know? We are the tourists.'

'That's true,' I said, thinking about the contrast with Conor's "Garçon!" 'It is.'

'So . . .' Leif said, sipping at his coffee.

'So . . .' I replied. I had run out of things to say.

'I saw your friend, as well,' Leif said. 'Last night.'

I studied his face but he wasn't giving anything away. 'Was it late?' I asked. 'Or early?'

'Late,' Leif said. 'About one.' Was that a brief tremor I'd seen in his eyebrow?

'Was he being horrible?' I asked.

'He was very drunk.'

'Oh God,' I said. 'Yes, I know. He argued with the people in the hotel.'

Leif nodded thoughtfully. 'I saw. I was there.'

'I'm sorry,' I said. 'Was it awful?'

'Awful, yes,' Leif told me. 'But not your fault.'

'No. He argued with me as well.'

Leif sighed. 'I just tell you this to be honest,' he said. 'I don't want to make you feel bad, but I don't want to pretend I don't see this either, you know?'

'No,' I said. 'No, of course not.'

'That way, if you want to talk, that's fine. And if you don't, well, that's fine too.'

I swallowed with difficulty. 'I'm not sure,' I said. 'But thanks.'

Leif shrugged and smiled again. 'Take your time,' he said. 'And try, you know, to breathe.'

'I am breathing!' I laughed. But once he'd said it, I noticed that I barely was. I tried now to take some deep, smooth breaths, but they came out all jagged.

Leif glanced at the big diver's watch he had strapped to his skinny wrist.

'Do you have to be somewhere?' I asked.

'I don't know,' Leif said. 'It depends.'

'You don't know?'

'Well, the meet for today is at nine,' he explained, glancing back up the path. 'Up there. So if I'm going, I need to be going.'

I nodded. I surprised myself with the realisation that I didn't want him to leave.

'But if you want me to stay, I can stay,' he continued, as if he'd been reading my thoughts.

I smiled sadly. 'I don't think so.' I said. 'I think I'm OK.'

'You *think* you're OK?' Leif repeated.

I frowned at him.

Leif scratched his head. 'I don't know,' he said. 'Just a feeling, maybe. I have a feeling that maybe you are needing to talk?'

I nodded and licked my lips. I was unexpectedly trying to hold back tears again. It felt like my head was swelling with the pressure. If I didn't let at least a couple out something was going to burst.

'Do you?' Leif asked.

'Do I what?'

'Do you need to talk? You look like you do.'

I bit my bottom lip to stop it trembling and nodded rapidly. 'I think so,' I said. 'Yes, I think I do.'

'OK,' Leif said, matter-of-factly. 'Then today, I am staying. And we will talk.'

It took me a while to get going, but once I'd started to tell Leif what had happened I found I couldn't stop. Later on, he would tell me that people often told him their problems, so perhaps he just had one of those faces. Actually, it wasn't his face, I don't think. It was his soul. He had one of those souls that makes you want to bare your own.

I jumped back and forth in my storytelling, filling in details of how Conor and I had met in an attempt at justifying my poor choices, then jumping back to my present lack of options in an attempt to explain why I was still here.

Leif smiled concernedly and nodded the whole way through. He didn't interrupt me and he didn't ask difficult questions. When I occasionally lost track of my own story or wondered which bit to tell next, he just sat placidly, with one hand placed upon the other, and waited for me to continue.

'And now here I am, telling you,' I said, when I finally reached the end.

'Wow,' Leif said.

'I'm so stupid.'

'You are strong,' Leif told me.

I laughed at that.

'No, really,' he insisted. 'I mean, some of these choices – they're not so good. But you're still here. You're still standing. I think you're doing OK.'

'Thank you,' I said, a lump forming in my throat at his kindness. It was exactly what I needed to hear at that moment.

'So what next?' Leif asked.

'More coffee?' I suggested lightly, playing, I think, for time.

'More coffee is probably a good idea,' Leif said. 'But I think you have bigger decisions to make.'

'I know,' I said. 'I do know that. It's just that I still can't see any options, really.'

'Well,' Leif said, leaning forwards. He straightened his back, visibly interrupting himself. 'Can I?' he asked.

'Please,' I said. 'Carry on.'

'Well, I think you should call your mother. At least, it's definitely what I would do. My mum is great for advice.'

'But your mother isn't *my* mother,' I said. 'Otherwise you might feel differently.'

'That's true,' Leif said thoughtfully. 'Only you can decide. But whatever she's like, I think she loves you, yes?'

I nodded.

'And I think you are going to need her help.'

'But how can she help me, Leif? She's hundreds of miles away.'

'Well, I'm guessing you're going to need money. You said you don't have too much, right?'

'That's right. I've got about seventy pounds in drachma left, and a few hundred in my bank, but I'm not even sure if my card works here.'

'If you need to change your flight and book another hotel, maybe your mother can help you.'

'Yes,' I said. 'Yes, I suppose that's true. Though I'm not sure how she'd get any money to me.'

'I'm sure,' Leif said, 'there are ways.'

'And you think I should change hotels.'

'Go to Fira, maybe. Oia is small. If you stay here then you will see him again.'

'He goes to Fira,' I explained. 'His drinking friends are in Fira. So I'd be scared in Fira, too.'

'Then maybe another town,' Leif said. 'You could try Megalochori. Or a beach place like Monolithos or somewhere.'

'I can't drive,' I pointed out. 'So it needs to be easy to get to. On a bus route or something.'

'I can take you,' Leif told me. 'If you need me to.'

'Oh, I couldn't . . .' I said.

Leif shrugged.

'I need to change my flight, too.'

'Do you?' Leif asked. 'If you stay in a different place, then . . .'

'But I'd still end up next to him for the flight home. I'd be terrified.'

'Ah, of course,' Leif said. 'Then we need to sort that out too.'

Tears welled up anew at his unexpected use of the word 'we'. Because that 'we' suddenly seemed to make it all seem possible. I'd been feeling so alone up until that moment.

'I'll need to get my stuff, too. It's all still in the room.'

'You have a key?' Leif asked.

I checked my pocket and nodded.

'Then I see when he is gone. I think the man in reception will help me if we need it. Then we move your stuff to my room. We go to Fira for the travel agency, and we try to change your ticket. And then . . . if you need to stay more nights we book a room in Monolithos. This way, you can walk to the beach. You can still have a holiday, yes?'

I nodded. I was shocked by how wise he seemed and wondered if he wasn't perhaps older than he looked. 'Are you sure you don't mind helping me with all of this? It seems ever such a lot of bother.'

'Not at all,' Leif said.

'But what about your hillwalking?'

He glanced at his chunky watch again. 'It's gone nine,' he said. 'The walk is started. So I'm free all day.'

'I'm sorry,' I said. 'I'm ruining your holiday.'

'Rubbish,' Leif said. 'It's like an adventure for me, yes? Like in a children's book or something. I'm sorry. I don't mean to . . . It's all very serious for you, of course. It's just that, me? I don't mind. I like helping you.'

'Thank you,' I said, struggling against tears yet again. 'I don't know what I'd do other—' My voice gave out on me.

'Stop,' Leif said, reaching across the table to rest his fingertips on my forearm. 'It's OK. It's all going to be OK, right?'

I nodded weakly.

We had another round of coffees and Leif, thankfully, paid. In my distress, I hadn't thought about the fact my money was still in the room. We climbed silently back up the path. It was so steep that talking and walking were impossible to do at the same time.

The room I had slept in that night had been cleaned. The bed had been made and the floor glistened. A mop was propped diagonally across the doorway, barring me from entering. So I sat on the little wall and waited.

Leif returned almost immediately. 'He is there,' he said. 'He was angry I woke him up, but he's there.'

'What did you say?' I asked him.

'I said I had the wrong room. They all look the same anyway. He believes me.'

'Well done,' I said. 'What now?'

'You should wait in our room, I think,' he suggested. 'Olav, my friend, is walking, so the room is empty. I can sit on the balcony and read. That way, if he leaves I will see. And then we can go and get your suitcase.'

I nodded.

'It's a good plan, yes?'

I nodded again. 'It's a very good plan. Thank you.'

'So, come quickly. Before he gets up.'

My heart raced as we climbed the stairs. If Conor appeared, I decided, I'd just sprint up to the hotel – to safety. In the end, even though there was no sign of him at all, I put Leif's towel over my head and ran as fast as I could.

Leif let me into his room. It was identical to ours, just with the twin beds pushed to opposite walls where ours had been together to form a double. Though I insisted it was all fine, he ran around tidying up, which struck me as infinitely sweet. When he'd finished, he picked up a book and moved to the doorway. 'You can lock this if it makes you feel safe,' he said.

'It's fine,' I replied. 'He'll never guess I'm here.'

Leif nodded and silently vanished into the brightness, closing the door behind him.

I sat on his bed for a moment waiting for my eyes to adjust, then stood and wandered around the room.

There was a pile of books on the bedside table, all written in an incomprehensible language I assumed must be Norwegian. There was a map and a compass and a tiny portable CD player with a stack of five or six CDs. Some of these looked Norwegian, but he also had a George Michael album and REM's *Out of Time*. I remember those two because I had them at home.

Eventually I sat back on Leif's bed and lay back to stare at the pattern of light the shutters cast upon the ceiling. My wrists hurt and I noticed only now how badly bruised they were.

I thought about how strange it was to be lying on a stranger's bed. I noticed the soft musky scent of whatever deodorant Leif wore, drifting from the sheets.

I felt safe, for the moment at least. Though Conor was just yards away, I was hidden in the shadows and Leif was on guard outside. And I wondered at how unexpected it was to be feeling so safe in his company when the presence of the person I'd come away with made me feel so afraid. And then I must have fallen asleep.

SEVEN

Becky

Our ferry was at nine in the morning, so we got up just before seven.

Alpina was bleating, and the farmer, who would drive us to the port, was already out tending his garden. It was quite cool this morning but the air held a promise of heat to come. We ran down to the beach for a final swim, then showered and packed our suitcases. I actually felt quite tearful as we put them in the car. I could have happily stayed there forever.

The manic boarding process felt stressful again, though not quite as bad as the first time. We were getting used to it, I suppose. The engines shuddered and the quay started to slip away and I felt as excited as I have ever felt. There's something wonderful about that moment when a ship leaves the port, isn't there?

This time, the ferry had a tiny deck area at the rear so we left our suitcases in the care of our elderly neighbours and jostled our way outside. Other than popping back for food, I stayed there the entire four and a half hours.

The ferry stopped at Sifnos and Folegandros, both of which, seen from the port at least, looked almost identical to Serifos. Only the colour of the rock seemed to change, a deep grey for Sifnos and a lighter beige colour for Folegandros. It seemed a shame to be visiting them without getting off the boat. I couldn't help but think of all the beaches and kittens and goats we were missing out on.

'We should have gone to more islands,' I eventually commented, just as Folegandros was vanishing into the haze.

'Why?' Mum asked.

I shrugged. 'Why not? I mean, we're stopping at them all anyway. We could have spent two nights on each of them.'

Mum pulled a face. 'It's very tiring moving all the time, I think,' she said. 'And I'm sure you'll like Santorini.'

'I just keep thinking of all the things we won't see. All the adventures we've almost had, do you know what I mean?'

Mum nodded. 'Well, I'm sure you'll like Santorini. I mean, everyone says it's lovely, don't they?'

There was something fake about her voice. I knew her so well and I'd always felt I could sense it in the ether when something had been left unsaid. I glanced at her sideways and I think she saw that I had noticed. 'I'm going to nip to the loo,' she said, turning away. And I remembered the conversation about drachma and how she'd avoided looking at me in exactly the same way. 'Will you guard these spaces with your life?' Space on the rear deck was in great demand and short supply.

'I will,' I told her.

By the time she got back, I'd worked it out. Or at least, I thought I had. 'Have you been here before?' I asked, the second she returned.

Mum handed me a plastic beaker of tea. 'Here?' she said obtusely, as if I might mean here on this boat in the middle of the Aegean.

'Santorini,' I told her. 'You have, haven't you? You've been here before.'

Mum sipped her tea. She was buying time. 'I told you,' she said. 'I was here with your Aunt Abby.'

'You never said it was Santorini,' I said. 'Or Greece. You've never mentioned it once. Not in my entire life.'

Mum nodded and sighed. 'Oh, I expect I did at some point,' she said vaguely. 'You probably just weren't listening.'

'Never,' I said definitively. 'Not once.'

'Well, I just have. So you know, don't you? Now, I think I might go inside for a sit-down. How long have we got?'

I glanced at my phone. 'Another hour and a half, I think.'

'Are you coming?' Mum asked.

I wrinkled my nose. 'No, I think I'll stay here for a while.'

I watched Mum leave then turned back to stare at the sea. I sipped my tea and thought about the fact that Santorini was apparently where I'd been conceived. And now we were travelling back here and there had to be a reason why. Was this some sort of pilgrimage, I wondered? A trip to my father's grave?

'Do you have a light?'

I turned to see an incredibly attractive man standing beside me. He was tall and dark with olive skin and hazel eyes. He had the most lustrous hair I had ever seen on a man, at least, outside a shampoo commercial. I suddenly realised that all of this sun and sea, all this relaxation, was making me feel a bit romantic. It had been months since Tom, after all.

'Sure,' I said. 'Can you hold this?' I handed him my tea and rummaged in my handbag until I found my lighter and cigarettes.

'It's beautiful, huh?' he asked, once we had both lit our cigarettes. 'And the air is so fresh and salty, you know?'

I nodded. 'Well, except for all that diesel.' I pointed to a ferry passing by in the other direction, a long, black vapour trail of smoke rising from its funnel.

'Huh,' the man said.

'You're American?' I asked.

'Canadian.'

'Sorry.'

The man shrugged. 'It doesn't matter,' he said. 'Except that Donald Trump is *not* my president.'

'There are so many islands,' I commented. We were zipping past another one. 'I had no idea.'

'I know,' he said. 'It makes you want to visit them all, right?'

'Absolutely. Are you going to Santorini, too?' I asked, I'll admit, not without hope.

The man shook his head. 'Mykonos,' he said. 'With my partner.' He nodded towards the interior. 'He's inside feeling seasick.'

'Right,' I said, trying to keep the disappointment from my voice. 'Of course.'

The port of Santorini was quite different from all of the others. The hills behind the port – perhaps they should be called mountains, really – rose steeply, and whereas on the other islands towns had sprung up around the ports, here there was nothing but a jetty and a zigzagging road up the cliff face. And the town, instead, had been sprinkled along the top. From a distance the white houses looked like snow on a mountaintop or icing on a cake.

With a hundred other travellers, we trundled our cases along the jetty and then waited for our taxi to Oia.

Bits and bobs of conversations I'd had with Mum were suddenly starting to make sense for the first time. 'Were you in Oia before?' I asked, once I'd shown the driver our address on my iPhone and our taxi had lurched away.

Mum turned from the window and nodded. 'It was nicer, as I recall, although the main town seemed a bit full-on even back then.'

We'd been given a number to call on arrival but Baruch, our contact, wasn't answering, so we followed his incredibly detailed instructions and descended exactly seventy-seven steps from the minimart.

And there, as in the photo, was our cave house. The door was wide open and the key was in the lock.

The rooms had been carved into the mountainside and had rounded ceilings with bumps and irregularities. Each room led to the next slightly smaller room, in an unusual sort of daisy chain, until finally, deep within the mountain, we arrived at a tiny blue-tiled bathroom. All of the furnishings – the shower cubicle, the washbasin, the shelves – had been carved from the rock face. Only the toilet was made of traditional ceramic. It was a bit like being in a *Flintstones* house, only designed by Martha Stewart. I loved it.

'I didn't realise you'd have to go through one bedroom to get to the other,' Mum commented, hesitating between the two.

'Me neither,' I said. 'But it doesn't matter, does it? You should have the bigger one, because you get up first.'

'But I'll wake you up if I need the bathroom,' Mum said.

'Nothing wakes me up,' I told her. 'You know that.'

We dumped our cases on our beds and, drawn by the view, headed back outside. There were two folding chairs which we set up so we could sit and stare at the sea. Looking out over the bay to a series of ragged outcrops and islands was pretty damned amazing.

'Now *there's* a view,' I commented.

'I knew you'd like it,' Mum said. 'Incredible, isn't it?'

I nodded. 'Is this where you stayed with Aunt Abby? Is this the same hotel, I mean?'

'Not quite,' Mum said. 'We were a little bit further round that way, I think.' She pointed to the left.

'Will you show me?' I asked. 'Not now, but at some point.'

Mum nodded. 'If it's still there. There was a staircase down to the sea, if I remember correctly. We could try to find that. It's only a tiny beach but it's big enough to swim.'

'There are proper beaches here, too,' I said. 'Huge beaches. I saw them in the guide.'

'But you need transport to get to the other ones,' Mum said. 'I suppose there might be a bus.'

'You could rent a car,' I suggested.

'I'm not sure I'd want to drive in Greece!'

'Or we could rent one of those mopeds,' I said. They were buzzing all over the island.

'I definitely can't drive a moped.'

'I can,' I said. 'No problem.'

Mum laughed. 'No, I don't think so,' she said, as if this was the silliest thing anyone had ever suggested.

Deciding to save that battle for later, I got up and headed inside. I peered into the fridge but it was totally empty.

'Do we need supplies?' Mum asked. She had followed me and was standing in the doorway.

'I fancied a cup of tea, that's all,' I said. 'But there's not even a tea-bag. I might nip up to that shop.'

Mum nodded. 'Are you OK on your own? It's just I'd better wait here in case Barak, or whatever his name is, comes.'

'Baruch, I think,' I said, checking the sheet of paper on which I'd printed the instructions. 'Yes, Baruch, spelt with U-C-H at the end. Do you need anything?'

'No, no,' Mum said. 'Just tea and milk.' She'd seemed deflated since we'd arrived here. I guessed she needed some time alone to think about her holiday here all those years ago.

'OK, just tea and milk?'

'Get some toothpaste too, could you?' Mum said.

'Tea, milk and toothpaste.'

'And some bread and cheese perhaps. Or some crisps or something. Just a snacky thing – in case we get peckish.'

I groaned. Never-ending shopping lists were one of Mum's specialities. 'Tea, milk, toothpaste, bread and cheese, then?' I said.

'And some chocolate. And some wine? Oh, and coffee, of course.'

'Hold it there,' I said, pulling my phone from my pocket. 'Now, start again, could you?'

Once I had typed the list on my phone, I started to climb the stairs. I was feeling a tiny bit disappointed with Santorini, if I'm honest. It's not that the view wasn't wonderful, but I'd been in love with our beach in Serifos. I'd just have to convince Mum about the transport business, I supposed.

I wondered again why we were here. The choice of Santorini, of Oia, was no accident. That much was obvious. Perhaps, just perhaps, Mum had brought me here to tell me about my father. If so, it was about bloody time.

The minimart was open but deserted. There wasn't even anyone behind the till. So I made my way up and down the aisles, filling my basket with things that looked like they were probably toothpaste and chocolate and tea. Most of the labels were written in Greek so it was hard to be totally sure.

There was still no one there when I reached the checkout. I thought, *Wow, what a trusting culture!* A boy of about eight stuck his head around the door and said, 'Wait! I get Baruch.'

After a minute or so, when no one had appeared, I took another meander around the shop just in case I'd forgotten something, and by the time I got back, he was there, seated behind the till as if he had never been away.

'Hello,' he said, flashing his white teeth at me. 'You're Becky, yes?'

I opened my mouth to respond but for a few seconds my voice failed me. Because Baruch was so, *so* beautiful, I could hardly believe my eyes. He was like a blue-eyed version of the guy I'd seen on the boat, only with a deeper tan, and less gel in his hair. He was also, hopefully, straight. 'Um, yes,' I finally managed.

'I went to meet your mother,' Baruch told me. 'It's why I wasn't here.'

'Of course,' I said. I could feel myself blushing.

'Welcome to Santorini,' Baruch said. 'Did you find everything you need?' He reached for the first item in my basket.

'Oh yes,' I told him. 'Yes, I found *everything* I need.'

By the time I left, I was already trying to think what other things I could buy . . . what other excuses I could find to return and speak to Baruch.

'I take it you met the lovely Baruch,' Mum called out as soon as I had stepped back in the door. Her voice was coming from the bedroom.

I put the bags down on the countertop and peered in through the open doorway. 'I did!' I said.

'He's a pretty one, huh?' Mum laughed, rolling onto her side to look at me.

'He is!'

'I thought you'd like him,' she said, 'the minute I saw him.'

'He's like a young Javier Bardem,' I said.

'Was he the guy in *Grey's Anatomy*?' Mum asked. 'Denny, wasn't it?'

'No,' I said. 'But you're right. He looks like him, too. So, are you OK?'

'Me?' Mum said. 'Oh . . . Yes . . . I'm fine. I think all the travelling caught up with me a bit. I need half an hour's snooze, that's all.'

'Fair enough,' I told her. 'Me too. I'll be just outside in the shade.'

Mum slept for over an hour but though I only really dozed myself, I resisted the desire to go shopping again. I was being silly and I knew it. Baruch probably had hundreds of women fawning over him every season, and even if that wasn't the case there was no real point to it. We were leaving in less than a week. And what could I possibly have in common with a Greek minimart cashier? But for all my arguing with myself, I couldn't, if I'm honest, push the idea of a holiday romance from my mind. And I couldn't help but wonder if that's how things had been for Mum all those years ago.

Just after five, we went for a wander around town. Everything was spotless, the buildings all whiter than white. Expensive boutiques lined the streets. 'Was it the same when you were here before?' I asked. After Serifos, I was a bit surprised by the opulence.

'Oh, no,' Mum said. 'No, it's much posher now. I mean, it was nice even back in '94, but it's definitely more touristy now. More upmarket, too.'

The streets, all the same, were pretty. And the views, which were everywhere, were incredible.

'You know, I thought when I was here before,' Mum said, pausing to take a photograph out over the bay, 'that this was the prettiest place on the planet.'

I nodded. 'It is very lovely.'

'Yes, I still think that's true,' Mum said, lowering her phone and appraising the view again. 'I've never been anywhere nicer, anyway. Not that that means much.'

We had cappuccino freddos in one place and creamy ice creams in another. 'London prices,' I commented as I paid for the latter.

Mum nodded. 'Yes, that's changed too,' she said. 'Although, to be honest, everything was so many thousands of drachma that I had no idea what I was spending.'

'So that's why you mentioned it,' I said.

Mum nodded and wobbled her head from side to side in a way that meant, *Apparently so.*

'Gosh, it's getting crowded,' I said, as we struggled to squeeze through a group of German tourists.

'Yes, people come for the sunset,' Mum told me. 'They come from all over the island. I'd forgotten about that. It's supposed to be the best sunset on Earth. They organise buses to come and see it and everything.'

'And is it?'

'Is it what?'

'The best sunset on Earth?'

'It's pretty good,' Mum said, 'as far as I can remember.'

Despite the fact that my instinct is generally to go in the opposite direction to the crowds, we decided it was best if we tagged along. I was still hoping to visit another part of the island the next day, hopefully somewhere with a beach, so it seemed like a good idea to make the most of being here. It seemed best to get the Santorini sunset over and done with, otherwise I could see myself adding it, beneath the Acropolis, to the list of things I'd only nearly done.

We squeezed our way through the tiny streets with hundreds of other sunset-viewers until we arrived at the western tip of Oia. And I have to admit that despite the crowds, or maybe even because of them, the whole thing was really quite moving.

The sky put on a technicolour display that seemed to use every colour in the spectrum. There were wispy orange highlights below the clouds on the horizon and flecks of purple on the upper edges. There was a band of turquoise blue and swathes of yellow and red. There was even a splodge of grey-green cloud to the east and everywhere else the deep, endless blue of the sky above.

We spectators, here for this event that happens everywhere on the planet every day but which we so often forget about entirely, were bathed in the golden light. We looked, we smiled at the ball of fire and we said pointless mundane things like, 'Gosh! That's pretty,' in a whole raft of different languages.

Whether it was out of reverence at the light show or respect for the others, everyone spoke softly and the resulting hubbub felt warm and friendly and safe. It was a shared moment of happiness with strangers, and I loved every minute of it.

'Food?' Mum asked, once the last snatch of sun had slipped behind a distant island. Everyone was on the move.

'Definitely,' I said. 'Do you remember any good places?'

Mum shook her head. 'Even if I did, I don't think they'd be there now.'

'You never know . . .' I replied. 'Do you want me to look on TripAdvisor or something?'

Mum shook her head. 'Let's just take a lucky dip, shall we?'

'OK,' I agreed. 'Let's do that.'

We followed the herd into town and, seeing that all of the restaurants on the main strip already had queues outside, we headed into the maze of side roads until we came upon a beautiful little restaurant in an open-air, candle-lit courtyard.

'Here?' Mum asked.

'It looks expensive,' I said, peering at the menu.

'It's our first night in Oia,' Mum said. 'Anyway, Granny is paying for this one.'

'Table for two?' a voice asked and I turned from the menu to see Baruch's smiling face.

'Oh, hello!' Mum said. 'You're everywhere! Not that we're complaining . . .'

Baruch laughed. 'My aunt's place,' he said, gesturing. 'My uncle's ill, so . . .'

'As long as he doesn't have food poisoning,' Mum said, cracking one of her rare jokes.

'Food p—? Oh, no!' Baruch said, glancing around nervously in case anyone had overheard. 'No, it's his knee. It hurts him sometimes. So . . .'

As he led us through the tables, he said, 'I have only this table left. The others, I'm afraid, are reserved.'

'You're bright red,' Mum said, once we were sitting. 'Are you OK?'

I nodded and did my best to hide myself behind the menu.

'Oh, are you . . . ? You are! You're blushing!' Mum said, leaning over and pulling the menu away from my face. 'I thought you were just hot but you're *blushing*.'

I rolled my eyes. 'Cheers, Mum,' I said. 'It always helps to have that pointed out.'

'Is it because of him?' Mum asked, nodding sideways towards Baruch. 'Have you got a crush on him or something?'

'Stop it, Mum,' I said. 'Jesus!'

'Well now, there's a thing!' Mum said. She glanced over at Baruch who was showing a group of people to the reserved tables. 'He is very pretty,' she said. 'And he has a lovely booty in those jeans, I'll give you that. It's just that—'

'Stop! Please!' I said.

'Oh Lord,' Mum said. 'Then it's serious.'

'You're impossible, you know that?' I told her.

'Yeah, but you love it really,' Mum said. 'Don't you?'

'No,' I said. 'No, I don't.'

'Yeah,' Mum said. 'I think you'll find that you do.'

In the hotel restaurant the next morning, over breakfast, I again tried to convince Mum to let me rent a scooter. 'I had one for a whole year in Bristol,' I told her. 'It isn't as dangerous as you think.'

'Only there aren't so many Greek drivers in Bristol, are there?' Mum retorted.

'I want to get around,' I told her. 'I want to see the rest of the island. I want to go to the beach.'

'Well, there's a beach here,' Mum said, finishing her coffee and standing. 'If that's all you're worried about, we can go now. I'll go and get my beach stuff together.'

I watched her head down towards the room and sighed. I would get my way in the end, I knew I would. But I had to let Mum work through all the other options first. It had always been thus.

Baruch passed by at that moment. He gave me a little wave and I nodded sedately back. I was feeling, rather ridiculously, as if I had been jilted the previous night. Oh, he'd been perfectly pleasant to me, even flirty and funny. But really no nicer than he had been to anyone else. And I'd come to see that he was just one of those people who charms everyone – one of those people who makes everyone feel as if they have a special connection with him. Perfect waiter material!

As if to prove the point, a girl at the next table – she was having breakfast with her parents and can't have been more than thirteen – waved her fingertips at Baruch. She clearly thought he'd been waving at her, and she was very possibly right.

The walk down to the 'beach' – and I use those inverted commas for a reason – involved climbing back up to street level, heading a couple of hundred yards to the right and turning down another almost identical staircase.

'Are you sure about this?' I asked. I was scared we'd go down a thousand steps only to have to turn back.

'Totally,' Mum said. 'I stayed in one of these way back when.'

'Which one?' I asked, hoping to catch a glimpse of the room I'd been conceived in.

Mum paused to consider the question. 'I'm not sure,' she said eventually. 'It was a long time ago.' For some reason, I didn't believe her.

The steps led down and down, past the end of the buildings and on down the sheer rock face. Even descending, I was breaking out in a sweat. The temperature was already in the high twenties and the sun was so strong it felt as if it were frying my skin, despite my factor fifty. Eventually our path joined a wider one. Some knackered-looking donkeys were being whipped up the hillside by a wrinkled old Greek farmer-type. On their backs sat two obese Americans who were complaining about the heat.

'Poor donkeys,' I said, once we were past.

'I know,' Mum replied. 'I was tempted to yank that whip from his hand and whip *his* arse instead. You have to really not care about animals to do that.'

At the base of the track was a pretty little bay with a small concrete quay on which were crammed five small restaurants. The 'beach' consisted of a two-metre stretch of rocks at one end of the quay. 'Oh,' Mum said when it came into view. 'The beach used to be bigger.'

'Right,' I said. 'Oh well, never mind. We can still have a dip, can't we?' I was feeling quite joyous about the size of the beach, to be honest. I could sense my moped moving from possibility to the realms of probability.

The water, all the same, was lovely. It was warm enough that you could wade in without thinking about it, and crystal-clear and stuffed with crazy-looking fish. It was like swimming in an aquarium.

Afterwards, we sat in one of the restaurants and drank chilled coffees. Neither of us were in any great hurry to attack the climb back up.

'I suppose if you went really slowly,' Mum said out of nowhere.

'I'm sorry?'

'I suppose we could get a little one. Nothing too powerful. As long as you promise to drive slowly.'

'It'll be fine, Mum,' I told her. 'It'll be fun, you'll see. And if you've never been on a bike before . . .'

'I have,' Mum said. 'I've been on one right here. And that's why you need to listen to me about those Greek drivers.'

EIGHT

LAURA

I was on the verge of dozing off when Leif woke me from the halfway land between waking and sleep. I usually enjoy that floating state but that day I think my thoughts were too troubled for it to have been pleasant in any way.

'Wake up,' Leif whispered. He was crouching to the right of the bed. 'He's gone.'

'Is he nearby?' I asked softly. 'Why are you whispering?'

He shrugged and grinned. 'No,' he said. 'No, he's gone. And I don't know why I am whispering.'

I swung my legs over the edge of the bed and yawned. I splashed water on my face in the bathroom then walked to the door. 'He's definitely gone?' I asked, peering out at the shimmering heat of the day.

'Yes. I watched him leave,' Leif said.

'But what if he's just having breakfast? Or lunch or whatever. What if he's forgotten his wallet and comes back?' My voice was taking on a brittle, hysterical quality that I decided I needed to get a grip on.

'He took his car,' Leif said. 'I followed him all the way to the top and he took his car. So it's OK.'

Still nervous, I stepped outside and looked left and right.

'Do you want me to go first?' Leif asked, one hand upon the doorjamb.

'No,' I told him, steeling myself. 'No, I'm fine.'

We descended two flights of stairs and I unlocked Conor's front door.

'Shall I stay here?' Leif asked. 'To keep watch?'

'Yes,' I said. 'Actually, go up a flight of stairs so you can see the whole staircase. And if you see him, call out as if you were calling for a friend. Shout "Mary" or something.'

'Mary?' Leif repeated, looking confused.

'Anything,' I said. 'Just not Laura and not Conor.'

'Ah, OK,' Leif said, looking vaguely excited. 'Like a code word.'

'Yes,' I told him. 'If you like.'

'I will say "Mary", then,' he said.

'Fine,' I told him, impatiently. 'Mary is fine.'

Even with the lights on, it was hard to see at first. All that white paint outside was so blinding that my dazzled eyes took ages to adjust to the darkness of the interior. But slowly everything came into view: the dishevelled sheets; my clothes, still scattered across the floor; my suitcase in the corner . . . There was an empty ouzo bottle too, I noticed, lying on the bedside table. I hadn't seen it the previous night.

I gathered everything up as fast as I could and stuffed it all in my suitcase. And, after a last run around the bedroom and bathroom, I wheeled it out into the sunshine.

'You have everything?' Leif asked, once I'd joined him.

'I think so,' I said.

'Check again, maybe?' he suggested. 'You don't want to have to come back.'

So, leaving him with the suitcase, I popped back to give the room a final once-over. I couldn't see anything else.

Back in Leif's room, I unpacked my suitcase on his bed and started to fold everything properly. It was then I realised something was missing. Something essential.

'My bumbag,' I said, rifling through my case. 'Shit, my bumbag's not here.'

'It's important?' Leif asked.

I nodded gravely. 'Yeah,' I explained. 'It's got my money in it. And my bank card. *And* my passport. Jesus!'

Adrenalin pumping all over again, I returned to the room. I was meticulous this time, checking drawers and cupboards, checking Conor's own case and even his pockets. 'The fucker!' I finally exclaimed, my hands on my hips as I scanned the room for any remaining unexplored spaces.

Leif, who'd come to help me look, seemed a little shocked so I apologised.

'There is no need to apologise,' he said in that funny up-and-down accent he had. 'A fucker is a very good description of this man, I am thinking.'

We returned to Leif's room and debated what to do for some time.

'I don't have any money,' I explained. 'I don't even have a card to get any money out with.'

'Without ID your mother can't even wire it to you, I think,' Leif said.

'No,' I conceded. 'No, I'm stuffed, aren't I?'

'Well, the money is not a problem,' Leif told me, matter-of-factly. 'I will lend you some money and . . .' He raised one hand to interrupt my protests. 'I will lend you some money, whatever you need, and you will repay me when you get home. This much is easy. We need to worry only about the passport.'

Leif had a brief, hopeful idea that Conor might have left my passport at reception. He'd had to leave his own passport there, after all.

But the man on reception – the same guy who had fixed me up with a room – shook his head. 'No, we only need one,' he said. 'We have your husband's.'

'Do you know where he is?' I asked, ignoring the husband reference for the simple reason I'd become bored with correcting him.

He shrugged. 'Why? You are friends again?' he asked.

'No,' I replied. 'No, not really. Not at all.'

He shrugged again. 'A friend phoned for him. A man called Mac? English.'

'Mike?' I suggested.

The man nodded.

'So Conor won't be back till late.'

'He says he will be here for dinner,' the man said. 'He reserved a table for two at the front. Do you want me to give him a message?'

I glanced at Leif who shook his head almost imperceptibly.

We sat in the hotel restaurant and tried to come up with a fresh plan over lunch. Leif ate some fish baked in tomato sauce while I nibbled at a salad. I had pretty much lost my appetite.

There seemed to be no point changing my flight home to an earlier one until I'd got my passport back and, until I had got it back, I didn't dare move to another hotel, let alone another town. Leif sat and chewed at a fingernail while I tried to think. But my mind remained totally blank. I seemed to have run out of options.

'I'm sorry,' I said eventually, 'but I can't think of any ideas at all.'

Leif nodded. 'I'm sorry,' he said. 'Me neither. Me *either*?'

'Neither,' I said. 'You were right the first time.'

'Are you sure you don't want to phone your mother?'

'I don't know,' I said, tearing up just at the thought of it. 'Maybe.' When all else fails . . .

We walked up to street level and about a quarter of a mile to a phone booth. Leif had a calling card that he said was cheaper than the hotel phone.

Though it was by far the most likely possibility, it hadn't even crossed my mind that Mum might be out. I suppose I was so wrapped up in what I was going to tell her and how she might respond that the most obvious outcome escaped me.

Afterwards, it took me a few seconds to spot Leif. He was seated at a respectful distance on a wall, looking out to sea. 'That was quick,' he said, when I climbed over and sat next to him.

'She wasn't there,' I explained, handing back the calling card. And then tears, more damned tears, started to flow. I couldn't tell you if they were tears of relief because I hadn't had to explain to Mum that I wasn't in Cornwall with Abby, but in Greece with a man – a monster – or whether it was because the fact of not being able to speak to her had left me feeling even more alone than before. It was probably a mixture of both of those, actually. Because there were certainly plenty of tears.

Leif wrapped one arm awkwardly around my shoulder. 'It's going to be OK,' he said, over and over. 'Hey, it's going to be OK. Leif is with you. Leif is here.'

Once my tears had subsided, Leif asked me what I wanted to do. I replied that I didn't know. My brain seemed to have ceased to function.

'Maybe we should go to a beach,' he suggested. 'I've been walking so much, but not too much swimming. Not so much beach.'

'But what if we miss Conor?' I asked.

'He'll be back tonight. He has a table booked. We have six hours. Swimming is better than sitting, no?'

'Sure,' I said, though I wasn't sure this was true. 'Have you got a car to get to the beach with, or is there a bus?'

'A bike,' Leif said. 'It's *craysee* fun. You'll see.' I liked the strange way he'd pronounced 'crazy'.

We stood and started back towards the hotel. 'There is a red beach I heard about,' Leif told me. 'We could go there. It is very beautiful, I think.'

'It is,' I told him. 'I've been there.'

'Then a different one,' Leif said. 'There are many. I will ask at the hotel.'

Leif's bike was a dusty green scooter. He gave me the crash helmet and wore wrap-around sunglasses to protect his own eyes. Hardly anyone we saw wore their crash helmets but I was too scared to go without.

I had to put my arms around Leif's waist as there was nothing else to hold on to. And this felt incredibly awkward at first – overly intimate really. But as he banked around the corners and up and down all the hills I got used to it. He'd been so very, very kind to me that I was starting to love him in a way. I wasn't *in love* with him. Though I'd come to understand, belatedly, that my attraction to Conor hadn't been love, I still had no idea what the real thing was supposed to look like. But Leif was cute and funny. He smiled all the time. He made everything seem easier and had been incredibly nice to me. So he was kind of hard not to love, really. I wondered why I'd come away with Conor. Why couldn't I have met someone who was actually nice, like Leif, instead?

My mind was obsessing about Conor and my passport and my bank card, and then Conor again, in an endless, messy loop. But as the scenery buzzed by, I managed brief snatches of presence, tiny bursts of awareness of where I was and how nice it still was to be whizzing around Santorini's dusty roads on a scooter.

We parked at the top of a dirt road and walked for ten minutes down the track to Caldera Beach. It was another little bay bordered by reddish rocks. The sand this time was almost black.

There were parasols and sunbeds available but Leif didn't seem to consider them and, seeing as I had no money, it certainly wasn't going to be my suggestion. Instead, we chose the far end of the beach where the rock face provided some shadow and we spread our towels out on the scorching sand.

'Do you swim?' Leif asked, pulling a bottle of water from his bag and offering it to me.

I nodded and took it. 'Not brilliantly,' I said. 'But I float quite well.'

'I'm not so good, either,' Leif told me.

'I know,' I told him. 'I saw!'

We paddled around in the shallows and let tiny fish nibble at our toes. We swam (badly) and wove in and out of the little fishing boats that were moored there. Later we lay at the water's edge with the tiny waves rippling around our feet.

'Tell me about Laura,' Leif said eventually. 'I don't know anything about you.'

I told him I was a secretary. And I told him I lived with my mother.

'OK,' Leif said. 'But that's just what you do. It's just where you live. What about *you*?'

'I'm not sure I understand.'

'OK,' Leif said. 'What food do you like?'

'Oh, that's easy,' I told him. 'Seafood: prawns, calamari, scallops, cockles, whelks. Anything that comes from the sea.'

'The calamari is amazing in Greece,' Leif said. 'The best, I think, in the world. And what music do you like?'

'Britpop mainly,' I said.

'This is Blur. Oasis . . .'

'Yes. I'm more Blur than Oasis,' I told him. You had to be one or the other in the nineties. 'The Verve. The Stone Roses . . .'

'I like these too,' Leif told me. 'And Radiohead. You know Radiohead?'

'"Creep" is an amazing song,' I said.

'Yes, amazing.'

'I have your George Michael album too,' I told him. 'The one you have in the room.'

'*Listen Without Prejudice*? It's Olav's actually. But I like it.'

'The one I can't get out of my head at the moment is that Blur song,' I told him. 'They're playing it everywhere here. I think Greece must be a bit behind.'

'"Girls and Boys"?' Leif asked.

I nodded.

'I love that song,' he said. 'It makes me want to jump around and go crazy, you know?' He had pronounced the Z of 'crazy' like an S, once again.

I sang the first few bars and Leif laughed. 'You even do the good accent,' he said.

'Ah, well, it's Essex innit, mate,' I mugged. 'It's a bit like the accent in East London where I come from.'

'You have a very nice voice when you sing. I sing like a . . . I don't know . . . like *The Scream*,' Leif said.

'The Scream?'

'It's a painting. By Edvard Munch. It's quite famous. Like this.' He sat up and clamped his hands to his ears and pulled a grotesque face.

I laughed for the first time in what felt like days. 'I know it,' I said. 'I actually know the one you mean.'

'Well, that's how I sing,' Leif grinned. 'Or maybe this is what other people do when I sing.'

We were back at the hotel by seven. When the concierge confirmed that Conor was still out, we had a drink in the restaurant and waited.

'What will you do?' Leif asked. The concierge had told me that there were definitively no spare rooms this evening. Not even dirty ones.

'I don't know,' I told him. 'I need to think.'

One of the tables in the restaurant had a reserved notice on it and I wondered if it was Conor's. Did he really imagine we would sit together for a candlelit dinner? Knowing him, he probably did. He probably thought he could talk his way out of the whole thing with that golden tongue of his. Plus, he had taken my passport hostage, of course.

Though Conor's table remained quite empty, we didn't dare leave in case we missed him. So we took a spare table at the back, and ordered food for ourselves.

Leif had mussels in saganaki sauce and I plumped for the calamari – I'd been thinking about it all day.

The waiter came back to offer us Conor's table, which had a far nicer view, but after a moment's reflection, I declined. I feared that he would see Leif's presence as provocation – especially if he was sitting with me. And I worried that Conor would punch skinny Leif out cold.

Other than an offer – accepted – to taste each other's food, we spoke very little over dinner. We were both, I think, too nervous about the upcoming confrontation.

As we finally moved on to coffee and dessert, and as the night grew darker and the temperature fell, the likelihood of Conor's arrival seemed to fade, so I worried instead about where to sleep.

I still had the key to our room, of course; I just felt too scared to use it. But after a couple of glasses of wine and in the absence of other options, I decided I'd have to be brave. If I turned the key in the lock at least Conor couldn't get in.

At the end of the meal, I discovered I could add it to 'our' hotel bill. So that is exactly what I chose to do.

Leif insisted he wasn't comfortable with this but I reminded him that Conor had stolen all my money. 'It's me inviting you, not him,' I told him. 'It's the least I can do.'

'OK,' Leif said. 'If you must.'

At eleven, Leif bravely rapped on our door. When it became evident that he really wasn't there, I checked the room once again to see if my bumbag had magically reappeared during our absence. It hadn't.

I stepped back out into the moonlight, to where Leif was keeping watch. 'I'm going to sleep here, I think,' I told him.

'You're staying *here*?!' Leif asked, apparently astonished.

'I can't see I have other choices,' I said. 'You heard what the man in the hotel said.'

'You're not scared?' Leif asked.

I nodded quickly and swallowed with difficulty. 'But I'll turn the key. He won't be able to get in. And if I scream, you and Olav will come to help me, right?'

Leif scratched behind his ear. 'No,' he said simply. 'No, I don't think so.'

'You *won't* come if I need you?'

'No, I don't think you can stay here.'

'I'll be fine. If I turn the key . . .' I started again.

'He will break a window,' Leif said. 'Or kick the door. I saw what he was like. It's too dangerous.'

'I'll be fine, Leif,' I insisted. 'He'll . . .' But my voice failed me. Because I knew Leif was right. Break down the door was exactly what Conor would do if he came back drunk and couldn't get into his room again.

'Come,' Leif said, holding out one hand.

'Come where?' I asked.

'We need to talk to Olav.'

We found Olav in the room. He was listening to music on his headphones and smoking a joint in the dark.

Leif spoke rapidly in Norwegian and waved his hands around in the clouds of smoke until Olav, looking bemused, stubbed the joint out and opened the windows and doors.

'I don't mind the smoke,' I told Leif.

'I do,' he said. 'I really do. This is my bedroom.'

Once the windows were open, Olav, a huge Viking of a man, came back to face me.

'This is Laura,' Leif said. 'Olav.'

We shook hands and said shy hellos.

Leif carried on in Norwegian and as the conversation went on, it got faster, then louder, and even what people might call animated. It went on for so long that in the end I sank into the armchair. I tried to interrupt them once or twice to find out if they were arguing about me. But Leif brushed my interventions away with one hand. 'Just hang on,' he said. 'Please.' And in the end things calmed down again. Some kind of truce appeared to have been negotiated.

'It's decided,' Leif finally announced.

'What is?'

'You're in my bed. And I will share with Olav.'

I protested. As much as anything else, I couldn't see how two six-foot men, one of whom was the size of a small mountain, could possibly share a single bed. But the men, apparently, had made their minds up.

'Please,' Olav said. 'I don't want to talk about it any more. It's decided.'

'I can sleep in the armchair,' I offered, my final attempt.

'You will sleep in Leif's bed,' Olav said. 'There is no more discussion now, please!'

And because my attempts at being nice seemed to be making him angry, and because other people's anger right then made me feel scared, I caved in to what seemed inevitable. 'OK, thank you,' I said. 'That's very, very kind.'

The two men top-and-tailed it and this apparently made them laugh. Which lightened the mood dramatically.

'What are you laughing about?' I asked.

'I can't tell you,' Leif said. You could hear the smile in his voice. 'It's too rude.'

'Oh, please,' I insisted. 'I don't mind.'

Through laughter, Olav said, 'Leif says my feet are too big. He says they touch his nose. I told him that's not my feet. It's my d—'

'Olav!' Leif interrupted. '*Please.*'

'It's OK, Olav,' I laughed. 'I get it.'

'I'm sorry,' Leif said. 'Now you know why I don't translate the words of Olav the poet.'

Olav said something softly. It sounded rhythmic and rather pretty.

'What was that?' I asked.

'You really don't want to know,' Leif said.

This made Olav guffaw heartily. 'Hey, at least it rhymes,' he said.

'Yes, but she doesn't need a translation.'

'I'll take your word on that one,' I said. 'Goodnight boys.'

'Goodnight, John boy,' Leif said.

I lay there for a while listening to the men's breathing and marvelled at the fact that they had *The Waltons* in Norway. As someone started to snore, I began to listen for Conor's return and wondered if he'd give me my passport back in the morning. I reckoned Olav could probably find a way to persuade him. Then I thought about the fact that the concierge might tell him I was with Leif, about the fact that he could still turn up raging drunk, and felt suddenly terribly awake. It was going to be a long night.

NINE

Becky

The next morning, I was up extra early. We'd spent a nice enough day chilling out in Oia, but the most exciting thing for me was that Mum had caved in about the bike. I was itching to get up to street level to rent one. It was only eight o'clock when I stepped outside, but Mum was already up, sitting on our little terrace looking out to sea.

'A penny for your thoughts,' I said, making her visibly jump.

'Oh, you know,' Mum said. 'This and that. Actually, I'm not really thinking at all. I'm just trying to wake up.'

'It feels cooler this morning,' I said, crossing the terrace and resting one hand on her shoulder. She seemed to be radiating melancholy. It was a mood that had frequently occurred during my upbringing, but one for which I'd only rarely been able to identify a cause.

She reached up and patted my hand. 'No, it's this temperature every morning,' she said. 'It starts to heat up about now.'

After we'd had breakfast in the hotel, I went up to discuss scooters with Baruch.

He was on fine form that morning. Like Mum, he warned me to be careful of Greek drivers. He told me which beach was his favourite and gave me a business card advertising 'Nick's Bikes'.

'Is everyone in Greece called Nick?' I asked. So far, we'd met a farmer, two taxi drivers and now a bike rental agent, all called Nick.

'Not everyone,' Baruch quipped. 'Just most.'

I took the card from his fingertips, thanked him and turned to leave. I was feeling pleased with myself for having remained calm in his presence. I felt I had finally managed to put him in a box marked 'Extremely cute minimart cashier'. Nothing more, nothing less.

But as I reached the doorway he called out, 'I wish I could come with you to the beach.'

I paused and looked back. I studied his features and tried to decide if his words actually meant anything or whether he simply couldn't resist being charming.

He shrugged cutely. 'Damned shop,' he said, gesturing at the aisles.

'Close it for the day,' I told him, trying to sound cool. 'Come!'

Baruch grinned. 'My uncle would kill me,' he said.

'Oh well,' I laughed, starting again towards the door.

'Tomorrow,' Baruch said. I wasn't sure if it was a question or not.

I froze and turned back once again. 'Tomorrow what?' I asked. Something fluttered deep inside my chest.

'Tomorrow I finish at eleven.'

We stared at each other for a moment. I wasn't sure what I was supposed to say to that.

At that moment, a bright-red Englishman arrived at the checkout with a basket of goods. On the top was a bottle of factor-seven sun cream. Judging by the state of his face, I thought he needed at least a factor fifty. The man looked at Baruch, I think to try to understand why nothing was happening, and then he followed his gaze to look at me.

Baruch snapped out of it and, seeming embarrassed, started to ring up the man's purchases. 'Have a great day,' he said flatly, without even looking up at me. 'You can tell me about it tomorrow maybe.'

So I gave him a little wave and stepped outside. 'Wow,' I said quietly. 'Just, wow!'

Nick had only one bike left, a knackered-looking Honda C90 with battered white fairings that were presumably designed to protect your legs from rain. I wondered if they ever actually had rain in Santorini.

I rode it once up and down the dusty street but was dubious. It had weird gears that lurched when they changed and a back brake you had to press with your foot. But Nick insisted that it was far better for two people than the aerodynamic-looking scooters I'd seen everywhere. It was something to do with it being a four-stroke, he said. I had no idea what that meant, but in the end, when he gave me 10 per cent off, I caved in and, despite being under the distinct impression I was being ripped off, I signed the paperwork and handed over my cash.

As it turned out, I think Nick was right. Once Mum and I had thrown our beach towels in the top case, the ancient little Honda carried us with ease up and down the hills. We regularly overtook couples on their pretty but noisy modern scooters.

We got lost a couple of times leaving Oia as the road signs weren't so good, but eventually we found ourselves on the long straight road towards Fira.

'Don't go so fast,' Mum said almost immediately.

'I'm not!' I shouted back.

'You're doing fifty,' Mum said. 'That's too fast.'

'They're kilometres, Mum! Not miles! We're doing, like, thirty miles an hour!'

We'd chosen Baruch's favourite beach as our destination. Its major attraction was that it was at the exact opposite end of the island. Plus Mum had never been there. The road took us through Fira, which was just crazy with tourists (they even had a traffic jam), then on to Megalochori, which we promised to stop at on the way home. And finally through Emporio and down to Perivolos Beach itself.

We rode through dusty, scrubby villages where goats limped across the road. They all seemed to have two feet tied together to stop them going too far or too fast. That seemed so cruel that I seriously considered stopping to untie them. But I didn't dare. Instead, I did my best to convince myself that they were probably happier limping painfully through the Santorini countryside than locked in a dingy factory-farm building like most dairy cows back home.

In places, we rose over desolate rock formations and as the road redescended, the views were quite unbelievable – wall-to-wall blue sky and sea with tiny islands floating in the mist. We stopped so many times for selfies that the journey took us two hours instead of the forty-five minutes Baruch had predicted. It was all really good fun.

As we pulled up in the sandy car park of Perivolos Beach, I knew Baruch's advice had been sound. Because with its enormous swathe of soft, black sand, rows of pretty thatched parasols and its sparkling turquoise sea, Perivolos looked, to my eye, like paradise.

We pulled off our crash helmets and popped them in the top case. Mum's cheeks were streaked with tears.

'Ha! You look like you've been crying,' I laughed, as she brushed them away with one hand.

'Don't be silly,' Mum said. 'It's just the wind.' Something in her voice made me wonder if that was really true.

We took off our shoes and walked along the water's edge to the furthest end of the beach. It was here that the sunbeds were widely spaced and the ambiance was the most chilled. Having chosen our spot – two beds at the water's edge – we paused.

'How does this work, do you think?' I asked Mum. 'Do you have to pay first? Do you remember?'

'I think you just sit down,' Mum said, 'and they come to you.'

A smiling youngster was jogging towards us. 'Sit anywhere,' he said on arrival. 'It's free.'

'Free as in nothing to pay?' I asked, suspicious as ever. For some reason, I always expected the Greeks to try to scam me but it never happened once.

He nodded. 'If you drink something I'll be happy. But even if you don't, it's free.'

'God, I love it here,' I said. I'd just got back from a swim and the salt water was still trickling down my back. It was almost midday and the sun was so strong that the air above the sand seemed to shimmer in the heat.

Mum looked up from the novel she was reading. 'It's gorgeous, isn't it?'

'Totally gorgeous,' I confirmed. 'It's like those photos you get in holiday brochures, only you never think they really exist. You always assume they've been Photoshopped, you know?'

Mum winked at me. 'Well, I'm glad you're liking it,' she said.

'You know when we went to Bergen?' I asked. I'd been thinking about Bergen during my swim for some reason.

Mum laid her novel across her chest. She looked puzzled. 'I thought you didn't remember that,' she said. 'You're forever saying you don't.'

'Well, other than you forcing me to eat prawns,' I told her, 'I don't much. I was just wondering why.'

'Why I made you eat prawns?'

'No, silly. Why you chose Bergen. I mean, it can't have been cheap.'

'No. No, it was very expensive.'

'Then we could have gone anywhere. We could have come here instead.'

'I suppose so.'

'So why Bergen?'

Mum shrugged. 'I thought it would make a change, I suppose.'

'From all of those lovely sunny holidays we weren't having?'

'Look, I'm sorry if you didn't like—'

'That's not what I meant,' I interrupted. 'I'm sorry. That came out wrong. I just mean, well . . . what did you do? Cover your eyes and stick your finger on a map or something? Because I've never met anyone who's been to Bergen.'

'I had a photo of it on my bedroom wall when I was a girl, if you must know. It's very famous for its fjords. And you know how I love a fjord.'

'I didn't know that actually. Was it pretty?'

'Yeah . . .' Mum said unconvincingly. 'It rained rather a lot unfortunately. In fact it rained the whole damned time. But yes, it was very pretty.'

'Did you buy me a plastic mac?' I asked. The physical sensation of sweaty polythene had just sprung into my mind as if from nowhere.

Mum nodded. 'And one of those see-through umbrellas. You loved that umbrella. You cried like crazy when it didn't fit in the suitcase on the way home.'

'I wish I remembered more of it,' I said. 'It seems like a waste, really.'

'Well, like I said, it rained pretty much the whole week. So I'm not surprised you don't remember it. Other than the hotel room and a few walks in the rain, there wasn't that much to remember.'

'Did you regret it, then?' I asked. 'I mean, it was the only holiday we ever had, wasn't it? Did you regret not coming back here instead?'

'Oh, I try not to regret things too much,' Mum said. 'Unless you're God and you know everything, including the past and the future, most of life is pretty much a question of closing your eyes and stabbing at a map. You have to try not to give yourself a hard time when things turn out to be not as good as you'd hoped.'

I sighed. 'Yes, I suppose that's true really. That's quite wise.'

'Can I get you ladies something to eat?' Our beach guy had returned and was standing right behind us. 'Would you like to see a menu?'

Mum shifted in her seat and looked back at the restaurant part of the beach where people were seated, dining. 'Do we have to go over there?' she asked. 'Or can we eat right here?'

'Oh, you can eat anywhere you want,' the man said.

Mum turned to me. 'That would be quite . . . what's the word I'm looking for?'

'Extravagant?' I offered. 'Lazy?'

'*Opulent*,' Mum said deliciously. 'Service on the beach . . . Yeah, let's do it.'

TEN

Laura

I woke up in the morning feeling dreadful. Though I had managed at some point to fall asleep, I'd slept so badly that I didn't feel refreshed at all. I crept to the bathroom where one glance at the mirror confirmed that this was not a mere impression. I looked no better than I felt.

On returning to the bedroom for my make-up and clothes, I was surprised to see that Olav's bed was empty. I had assumed the boys were still asleep.

Though I clearly needed to see Conor to get my stuff back, I was equally terrified of seeing him, especially alone. So as I nervously climbed the stairs to the hotel, I really couldn't decide if I wanted to bump into him or not. But he wasn't on the stairs and he wasn't in the restaurant either. I did spot Leif however, on the far side of the room, so I wove my way through the tables to join him.

'Hello!' he said. 'You find me! I was wanting to leave you a note but I couldn't find a pen in the dark.'

'It's fine,' I said, glancing nervously around the restaurant again.

'He's not here,' Leif said, picking up on my stress. 'I ask at reception and he didn't come home.'

I fetched croissants and a yoghurt and returned to the table. A waiter filled my cup with coffee. Leif was eating a selection of cheeses and some smoked salmon, which struck me as a strange kind of breakfast, but when I asked him he said it was perfectly normal where he came from.

'Where's Olav?' I asked, once I'd sipped at my coffee and decided that it was too hot. 'Walking already?'

Leif nodded. 'They are walking from Perissa to Megalochori, today,' he said. 'A big walk. But a good one.'

'You sound sad,' I told him. 'Is looking after me driving you insane?'

'No, I'm just tired,' Leif said. 'I didn't sleep so well.'

'Olav's snoring?' I asked.

He nodded and shrugged at the same time. 'He kept kicking me,' he said. 'In the face.'

'I'm so sorry,' I told him. 'It won't happen again. We'll sort something else out by tonight. But you really could have gone walking, you know. You don't have to stay with me all day.'

'Today we will get your passport back,' Leif said. 'And tomorrow I will walk.'

'I might even come with you,' I said. 'If you're not sick of me by then.'

'That,' Leif said, 'I don't think is possible.'

I wasn't sure whether he meant that it wasn't possible to be sick of me or whether it wasn't possible for me to walk with them. But I was too embarrassed to ask.

After a leisurely breakfast we returned to Leif's terrace where we sat in the shade of the parasol and chatted. It was windy that morning and considerably cooler than it had been. The parasol flapped in the wind and almost blew away once or twice.

Leif told me a little about himself. He said he was studying to be an engineer. 'I'm a bit of a geek really,' he said. 'You know, computers and physics and stuff.'

He told me a little about Bergen in Norway, where he lived, too. He said it was very beautiful.

When the conversation ran out, Leif retrieved a book he was reading from indoors. I asked him to read to me in Norwegian and laughed quite uncontrollably when he did.

'It sounds that funny, huh?' he said.

'I'm sorry,' I said, 'but yes. It sort of does. You sound like the Swedish chef in *The Muppets*.'

His book, he explained, was a history book. It told the story of Greece during the Second World War. 'They had a terrible time here,' he told me.

'I think everyone had a terrible time,' I said.

'Yes, but here, in these islands, they had a *really* terrible time. The Greeks were very resistant, you know? And the Germans killed many, many Greeks.'

I nodded. I tried to imagine these beautiful islands in wartime and failed.

I fetched my own novel and, until lunchtime, we simply read side by side. Occasionally Leif would look up at me and if I paused reading and looked back – when I wasn't too engrossed – he would tell me something from his book: facts about how Churchill promised to defend Greece but was overruled by Roosevelt, or how the Germans had rounded people up and shot them in retaliation for a British landing on Santorini.

I'd sit and imagine all of this for a moment before, feeling strangely comfortable, as if we were an old couple in armchairs by the fireside rather than strangers on a remote Greek island with a bloody past, returning to my book.

Conor never did come back that day, and by evening I was biting my nails and obsessing that I was never going to get my passport back. Leif refused to discuss what would happen if I couldn't get it before I had to travel home. He continued to insist that everything would be fine. 'He has to come back to the hotel,' he told me. 'Even if it's just to get his own passport back – even if it's just to pay the bill and get his stuff. He *must* come back.'

But I was terrified we would miss him – that one morning the concierge would announce that he had been and gone, and had taken my passport with him.

Leif convinced me that it was not such a good idea to add any more meals for two to Conor's bill, and even though I was angry, I understood that he was right. There was no point in provoking the guy when I needed something essential from him.

So, under pressure from me (because I was feeling bad about the cost), we picnicked on Leif's terrace for both lunch and dinner. And again, popping up to the little shop together, rinsing salad leaves and slicing tomatoes side by side . . . it all felt strangely domestic. I was starting to feel as if I had known him forever.

When Olav got back at eleven and collapsed without saying a word (or even taking a shower) on his bed, I insisted I'd sleep on the armchair with a blanket. And after a brief tussle, Leif caved in and let me do so.

By the following morning I was feeling quite ill. My head seemed to spin whenever I stood or sat down, or bent over. I had dark rings under my eyes that even my make-up struggled to cover.

'This Mike guy,' Olav asked over breakfast, 'where is he?'

'He's in Fira,' I explained. 'I know where he drinks, but I don't know where he's staying.'

Olaf nodded.

'You think Conor's still with him?' I asked.

Olav shrugged and wrinkled his nose. 'Maybe he knows where to find him,' he said. 'Because waiting here doesn't seem to be working.' He sounded annoyed and I guessed he was becoming frustrated that I was taking up all of Leif's time. It suddenly crossed my mind, for the first time ever, that perhaps Leif and Olav were gay. Perhaps they were a couple. But then why would they top and tail it? Just for my benefit? But that would be crazy, wouldn't it?

'Where do you live, Olav?' I asked, trying to explore my theory.

'I'm sorry?' he said, apparently confused by the conversational jump.

'I was just wondering where you live,' I said.

'In Bergen with Leif!' he told me, as if this was utterly obvious.

'Right,' I said. 'Sorry.'

◆ ◆ ◆

Once we'd waved Olav on his way – he was walking from Emporio to Kamari – Leif said, 'We give him until lunchtime and then we try Fira, OK?'

I nodded. My ticket home was in less than four days, and I was starting to get nervous enough that I was becoming selfish. I didn't try to persuade Leif to go walking. I couldn't find it in me to even pretend I didn't need his help that day.

We left the hotel at one thirty. It seemed obvious that Conor wasn't coming home for lunch and I thought we might just catch him at the taverna if we didn't hang around too long. So I climbed, once again, onto Leif's little scooter and we went whizzing off along the mountain-top. The gusts of wind blew our little bike from side to side and I think I must have shrieked more than once.

The taverna in Fira was packed solid but neither Conor nor Mike was there.

I went inside to see if I could find the waiter who had served us but he wasn't there either. I attempted to ask the elderly man at the cash till if he remembered me or Conor, but he just looked at me blankly. I wasn't even sure he understood what I was saying.

As we walked back towards Leif's scooter, he asked me what I wanted to do next. Just then, a man caught my attention and as he passed I turned back to look at him and saw that he was doing the same.

'Don't I . . . ?' I said. Then, more loudly, running to catch up with him, 'Excuse me! Don't I know you?'

'Yes?'

'Didn't I see you the other night?' I asked, once he'd stopped walking away. 'Weren't you with Mike?'

'Huh,' the man said, wobbling his head from side to side in a strange manner. 'Not *with* Mike, no.'

'But you're Paolo, aren't you?'

'Pablo,' he said.

'I'm sorry. Um, do you know where Mike is, Pablo? Or Conor? We've been looking for them but they haven't seen them.' I gestured towards the restaurant.

Pablo raised an eyebrow. 'I'm not surprised,' he said. 'They're not allowed in there any more.'

'They're not allowed in the restaurant?'

Pablo shook his head. 'A fight,' he said. 'Mike hit a man with a chair. And Conor broke someone's nose.'

'God,' I said. 'When? When did this happen?'

'Last night,' Pablo said. 'Well, this morning really.'

Leif had appeared at my side and when Pablo gave him a quizzical glance, Leif reached out and shook his hand. 'Leif,' he said.

'This is Pablo,' I explained. 'He was there with Conor and me the other night.'

'Do you know where this Mike guy is staying?' Leif asked.

Pablo almost-imperceptibly shook his head. 'Down that way, somewhere,' he said, gesturing vaguely in the direction the women had gone at the end of the evening. 'It's all I know. He's not my friend, you know?'

'No,' I said. 'No, he's not mine either. Have you seen any of them? Sheila, maybe? His wife?'

Again Pablo shook his head. 'They've left,' he said. 'To Mykonos, I think.'

'But Conor and Mike are still here?'

Pablo shrugged. 'They were here last night.'

I sighed deeply.

'Was anyone else there?' Leif asked. 'Anyone we could ask?'

Pablo cleared his throat. He shuffled awkwardly from foot to foot. 'Not really,' he said.

'Not really?'

'Please,' Leif said. Like me he had picked up on the fact that something remained unsaid.

'Two . . . women,' Pablo told us. 'Two . . . girls.'

'Two girls?'

'I'm sorry,' Pablo said.

'Do you know their names?' I asked. 'Where they live? Anything?'

'Candy?' Pablo said, as if it was a question. 'Candy was the blond one. The other one . . . Althea or Anthea or something like this.'

I nodded slowly, taking this in.

'I'm sorry but I think they are . . . *puta* . . .' Pablo said, glancing at his feet.

'*Puta*?' I repeated.

'Prostitutes,' Leif translated. 'That is right, yes?'

'Yes, maybe,' Pablo said. 'Yes, I'm sorry but, yes, I think so.'

After we had said goodbye to Pablo, we walked along the main street leading from one end of Fira to the other. It's a pretty, if touristy, town and there's plenty to see, but though we walked for a good half an hour, I don't remember much of it. I was too busy searching for Conor's face amongst the crowds.

When we got back to Leif's bike, I suggested we eat in the taverna in the hope that we'd see Conor there. But Leif quickly pointed out that I wasn't thinking straight. Because if Conor had been in a fight there the previous night, it was the last place he'd show his face.

'He's probably holed up somewhere with Candy,' I said bitterly.

Leif grimaced but notably didn't dispute this. Instead, he told me his walking group were meeting in Exo Gonia for lunch and suggested we join them.

I was about to say 'no' – I really wasn't feeling that sociable – when I realised that it was Leif who wanted to see his friends. I'd been ruining his walking holiday and isolating him from his group. Having lunch with them seemed the least I could do.

The bike ride wove back and forth up the hillside, and the wind in my face and the stunning views, plus the sensation of hanging on to Leif as he cranked the little scooter around the bends, blew some of the cobwebs from my mind. I started to feel a little better again.

The town was high up in the hills, with gorgeous views out over green valleys and, in the distance, the blue sea and sky of the horizon. One side was flanked by an even-higher point – Pyrgos, the highest village on the island.

As we locked my crash helmet in the top case, Leif pointed to Pyrgos and asked, 'How do you fancy a walk after lunch?'

'Up there?' I asked incredulously.

'Yeah,' Leif said. 'I bet the view is amazing.'

'Oh, absolutely,' I laughed, assuming he must be joking. 'I can't think of anything I'd rather do.'

We wandered through the pretty streets of Exo Gonia for twenty minutes or so. The town was much calmer and far less spoilt by tourism than anywhere else I had been. But though it was small, we failed to find Leif's group of walkers. So eventually we sat in a taverna to eat.

Leif had some kind of lamb stew, I think, while I had a pomegranate salad. I remember that clearly because I had never eaten a pomegranate before and I wasn't entirely impressed by all the pips. For dessert we shared an amazingly sweet dish that tasted like a cheese-stuffed baklava. This came with a fresh batch of pips in the form of pomegranate jam, and by the time we had finished I felt pipped out for life.

After lunch, we walked back towards the bike. Leif was still scanning the hills for his friends and I felt bad that we hadn't been able to find them. When we reached the bike, however, Leif didn't pause. He simply carried on walking.

'Leif!' I said, pointing. 'The bike's there!'

'Um?' he replied, absent-mindedly. 'Oh, I know. But we're going up there first, aren't we?'

'Oh,' I said, taking in the fact that he hadn't been joking earlier after all. 'Isn't it a bit hot for that sort of thing?' Though there was quite a breeze blowing, the temperature was in the high twenties.

'No,' Leif said, increasing his stride. 'It will be fine.' And because he'd done so much for me these last few days and because we hadn't been able to find his friends, I didn't say a word.

For the first fifteen minutes I hated it. I really hated it. I was still such a kid in so many ways and one of those was that I still hadn't realised that any kind of exercise might be pleasurable. If you're not a sporty kid it can take a very long time to find that out, and as far as I was concerned the only reason to walk anywhere ever was if there was no bus service.

But as I trotted along beside Leif that day, past farmhouses and goats, past some children playing in a garden and a woman watering her plants, and as the road rose higher and the views became more impressive, I started, just about, to get the point. Because yes, I was sweaty, and yes, walking up here in the heat of the day would not have been my choice. But my mind, which had been obsessing about Conor and my passport almost constantly, began to clear just enough for me to feel vaguely present again. I began to appreciate, albeit momentarily, that I was here at the top of a beautiful Greek island with sporty, easy-going Leif.

Pyrgos was simply gorgeous – a labyrinth of medieval streets which, when occasionally they opened out, provided breathtaking views over the whole of Santorini.

There was a beautiful domed church, which we visited, talking in quiet whispers while we looked around, and at the highest point, the ruins of a castle which, Leif informed me, dated from the fifteenth century. We paused in a café, gulped down glasses of Coke, then continued to the top to explore it.

Afterwards we walked around the outside walls, pausing to take photos of each other in front of the views with Leif's camera. When he suggested we leave, I found myself strangely reluctant to do so.

'But your passport,' Leif said. 'We need to get it, yes?'

I sighed. Today did not feel like the right day to tackle that particular monster and I wasn't quite sure why. Perhaps I was just fed up with trying to get it, or perhaps I had some inkling of what was to come. Maybe I'd just been enjoying thinking about something else for a bit.

'It's easy,' Leif said, mistaking my reluctance for laziness. 'It's downhill.'

'I can't bring myself to leave,' I said. 'It's just so peaceful up here.'

We were standing looking out to a distant island floating on the horizon in a sea of wispy blue. Above our heads, a Greek flag was flapping from a pole.

'Then let's stay for a while,' Leif said, sinking down to sit with his back to the castle wall.

'Everything's so simple with you, isn't it?' I said, looking down at his smiling face.

He pulled a puzzled expression. 'You think too much,' he said. 'You want to stay some more, we stay some more. No?'

I laughed and, saying, 'I think you're right, I do overthink things,' I sank to the grass beside him.

After a minute or so, I was suddenly overcome with fatigue. I'd barely slept for two nights, after all. When I shuffled forwards and stretched out across the grass, Leif quickly followed suit.

'Here,' he said, pushing his backpack towards me. 'For a pillow.'

'No, you have it,' I told him.

'No, you.'

'Please,' I insisted, and so Leif gave in and pushed it beneath his head.

'You can put your head on me, if you want,' he said. 'You can use me as a pillow.'

'No thanks. I'm fine.'

It took me less than a minute to overcome my shyness about that one. Because I wasn't fine at all. The ground was rough and stony. 'Are you sure you don't mind?' I asked, as I shuffled around.

'Not at all,' Leif said. 'I think I am sleeping, anyway.'

'Me too,' I said. 'I'm shattered.'

I closed my eyes and listened to the sound of the flag flapping in the breeze above us and to the tweeting of a nearby bird and the occasional whistle of the wind around the flagpole until finally, soothed by the rise and fall of Leif's chest, I fell into a surprisingly deep sleep.

I woke up with a start. The sun had moved around far enough that we were no longer in the shade but were warmed, instead, by the early-evening sun.

'Are you awake?' I asked gently.

'Yes,' Leif said, his voice resonating through his chest to the back of my head.

I sat up. 'I think I just realised something in my sleep.'

'In your sleep?' Leif asked. He was chewing a blade of grass and it bobbed up and down when he spoke. He rolled onto his side to look at me quizzically.

'Is it the first, today, or the second?' I asked.

'The second,' Leif said. 'The second of September. Why?'

'Are you sure?'

'Yes. It's the second. Why, what's wrong?'

I laughed. 'It's my birthday,' I said. 'And I forgot. How crazy is that?'

'It's your birthday?' Leif repeated.

I nodded. 'Twenty-six today.'

'Huh,' Leif said. 'You caught up with me, then.'

'You're twenty-six as well?'

Leif nodded. 'But twenty-seven soon.'

'I was looking forward to celebrating it here in Santorini,' I said, thoughtfully. 'I don't suppose Conor has even remembered. He's too busy with Candy.'

'Huh,' Leif said, sitting up. 'Now we have to do something for your birthday.'

I laughed lightly. 'No. No we don't. But for some reason, I really think I'd rather try to deal with Conor tomorrow.'

'He's probably not there anyway,' Leif said. 'So today we do something special. I have an idea. If you agree.'

'If it's an idea that doesn't involve Conor,' I said, 'then yes, I agree.'

'It doesn't.' Leif got to his feet. 'It really doesn't.' He reached out to help me up. 'Come on. You'll like this idea. Let's go.'

If the walk up had been challenging, the trip back down was pure joy. It was effortless of course, but something else had changed, too – something indefinable. Perhaps it was the fact that we'd both had a sleep or maybe it had more to do with the fact I'd decided not to see Conor that day. Whatever it was, my mood lifted and I experienced a rare moment of exaltation, of feeling quite simply happy.

Leif, who seemed to sense it too, sang 'Happy Birthday' to me, first in English and then in Norwegian. 'You don't do this?' he asked afterwards, miming once again *The Scream*.

'Oh, your voice isn't *that* bad,' I laughed, though in fact it really was.

Then, presumably because my ears weren't actually bleeding yet, he attempted not only to sing Blur's 'Girls and Boys' but to sing it with an Essex accent.

'It's *followin*',' I explained, 'not following. And *jungaw*, not jungle.' And so he tried again.

Once he felt he'd grasped the essentials of Damon Albarn's accent, we sang it again together. We were passing a woman who was busy pegging out her washing, and when she looked at us as if we were certifiably insane it only made us sing more loudly.

I remember glancing across at Leif as we walked, laughing and singing, and noticing for the first time just how good-looking he was. He didn't have the same kind of macho good looks or cocky charm that Conor had. He didn't turn people's heads in the street in the same way, and it was perhaps partly for this reason that I hadn't really noticed before. Rather, there was something warm and wholesome about him, something that seemed to shine out the more you got to know him. Singing badly and laughing loudly, he really looked quite beautiful.

We had to return to the hotel for our swimming things. That was my first clue to whatever Leif's surprise entailed. He grabbed a torch, too – one of those little ones you can strap to your forehead. 'It's just in case we are late,' he explained.

Now we were back at the hotel, the potential proximity of Conor and my passport became too much for me so, with Leif in the role of backup, we steeled ourselves and knocked on Conor's door. Once again there was no answer, so I let myself inside and checked the interior. Not only was my bag not there but there was no visible sign that Conor had been home at all. The room was in the exact state I had left it in.

Once our rolled towels had been stuffed into Leif's top case, he started up the engine again.

'Where are we going?' I asked as I strapped on my crash helmet.

'You'll see,' he said with a wink. 'Get on!'

ELEVEN

Becky

I didn't sleep well that night. I was too excited about seeing beautiful Baruch the next day.

By the time we'd got back, the minimart was closed, which left me feeling panicky about the next day's arrangements. Because if for some reason Baruch was not in the shop the next day I had no real way of finding him.

Mum, who had picked up on the unusual buzz in my mood, asked me a few times if I was all right. Once or twice I was tempted to tell her. But worrying that if it all fell through I'd look a fool, I didn't, in the end, say a word.

The next morning, I was up just after eight. Mum, as every morning, was sitting outside drinking tea.

'You're up early,' she said.

'I know,' I replied. 'Hunger woke me up. I'm starving. I'm just going to nip up to the minimart. Do you want anything?'

Mum shook her head. 'We've got bread and marmalade, or that muesli stuff you bought.'

I was trying to think of some other breakfast food I could reasonably need to buy when Mum's phone started to ring. She lifted it from the table and checked the screen before putting it down again.

'Who is it?' I asked. I was only now remembering that she had called Baruch when we arrived – that she had his number and therefore he had ours, too.

Mum shrugged. 'Some foreign number,' she said. 'No one I know.'

'Greek?' I asked.

'I don't know.'

I lurched for the phone and swiped at the screen. 'Hello?'

'Is this Becky?' It was Baruch's voice.

'Yeah,' I said, doing my best to sound cool.

'Are you still OK to do something together?'

'Uh-huh,' I said. I raised one finger to ask Mum to hold on for a few seconds more. She was on the verge of asking me who was calling.

'So, I'll meet you at the minimart,' Baruch said. 'At eleven, OK?'

'OK,' I said. 'That sounds great. Are we—?' But the line had already gone dead.

'Who the hell was that?' Mum asked, once I'd handed back her phone.

'That,' I told her theatrically, 'was the lovely Baruch. He's asked me to go to the beach with some friends. Do you mind?'

Mum rolled her eyes and sighed. 'Would it matter if I did?' she asked.

'Oh, come on, Mum. It's just for the afternoon. It's just a bit of time with some people my age. I can find out what real Greek people are like. You'll be OK for one afternoon, won't you?'

'Yes,' Mum said in a resigned voice. 'Yes, I'm sure I'll be fine.'

'Thanks.'

'But I'll tell you one thing,' she said.

'Yes?'

'You're lucky you got to that phone first.'

'Why?' I asked. 'Would you have said "no" on my behalf?'

'No,' Mum laughed. 'No, I'd have said "yes" on *my* behalf.'

I laughed. 'That would have given him a shock. My old mum turning up for a date.'

'Hey,' Mum said. 'Less of the old, you! And it's a date now, is it?'

'No,' I told her. 'No, it's like I said. It's just a trip to the beach. A beach-date, if you like.'

'Well, just you be careful. Don't do anything I wouldn't. And don't let him drink and drive.'

'No,' I said. 'No, of course not.'

It was five to eleven when I got up to street level, and Baruch was already there chatting to his replacement in the minimart. She was a pretty woman in her fifties who desperately needed to re-bleach her dark roots. She gave me a studious once-over and, looking as if she was suppressing a grin, waved us on our way.

As we crossed the road, I asked Baruch who she was. I was assuming that she was another member of his extended family.

'Cora,' he replied. 'She's just someone who works the days when I am off.'

Baruch had an old but powerful Yamaha trial bike. He climbed onto it and looked at me questioningly.

'Um, crash helmet?' I prompted.

This made him laugh for some reason. 'Really?' he said, when he finally realised I was being serious.

'My mum will kill me if she sees me without it,' I offered by way of excuse. I was apparently, in Greek eyes, being a wimp by wanting to stay alive.

Baruch shrugged and climbed back off the bike so he could retrieve a crash helmet from the top case. It was a battered, open-face affair that was at least two sizes too big for me and I wondered if I should go all the way downstairs to get the keys for the scooter so I could recover my own. I felt doubtful that this one was going to offer much protection, other than against Mum's wrath.

'It's a bit big,' I said, demonstrating how it wobbled from side to side.

But Baruch was already reseated and starting up the engine so I climbed on and, as we lurched off down the street, proceeded to fall backwards, whack my back on the top case and kick both legs up in the air comically.

'Jesus!' I exclaimed when he slowed down and looked back at me doubtfully.

'You need to hold on,' he said, taking one of my hands and pulling it to his waist.

He drove the exact route I had taken the day before, only ten times faster. It was all quite exhilarating. I quickly came to suspect that he was taking me to the very same beach. This was unsurprising really, as the beach had been Baruch's suggestion in the first place, but I didn't really mind at all.

Riding pillion felt lovely. The countryside sped by, the bike throbbed beneath us, and being seated so high up, the views were even better than before.

When we got to Perivolos Beach, Baruch led me to the grandest of the beach bars. It was the exact opposite of the choice I had made with Mum the previous day but it turned out to be great fun.

It had these huge four-poster bed affairs – like king-sized beds for giants, with suspended, flapping canopies to filter out the sun. Smooth electro beats were wafting from a sumptuous sound system.

Some friends spotted Baruch and beckoned us over, so we joined them on their 'bed' and propped ourselves up on the oversized pillows that were scattered around. I was impressed with the accuracy of the lie I had invented for Mum's benefit. For we were doing exactly what I had told her.

Baruch's friends – two pretty girls named Iona and Agatha plus a podgy young man called Damon – were instantly welcoming towards me. No one asked why I was there or where Baruch had dug me up. I suppose that with Santorini being tourist central they were simply used to such random appearances.

Damon produced a joint, which I must say shocked me a little as he didn't really look old enough to even buy cigarettes, and we all ordered drinks from the bare-chested waiter. I was surprised to be the only person ordering alcohol – the Greeks all chose chilled coffees – but when I asked Baruch about this he told me they simply couldn't afford anything else. 'We're on Greek wages, here,' he said. He nodded at my pina colada and said, 'That cost what I earn.' I wasn't sure if he meant per hour, per day or per week but, feeling guilty for my extravagance, I vowed to buy them all a drink before leaving.

The day slipped by gorgeously. We smoked, we drank, we chatted (they all spoke perfect English) and we ate snacks that Baruch had brought from the minimart – packets of crisps and out-of-date sandwiches, because once again the beach food was simply too expensive.

Whenever we got too hot, we swam. And it was after one of these swims that Baruch and I ended up sitting side by side at the water's edge.

'So, do you like Santorini?' Baruch asked. He was sifting the wet black sand through his fingertips and letting it drop onto his beautiful feet. It had turned out, now Baruch was in swimming trunks, that there was nothing disappointing about any part of him.

'Oh, I do!' I told him. 'It's beautiful. You're so lucky to live here.'

Baruch laughed. 'I live in Athens,' he explained. 'I only come here for the summer. To work for my uncle.'

'Ah,' I said. 'Well, you're very lucky to live here in the summer. What do you do in Athens?'

He shrugged. 'Anything,' he said. 'Whatever I can find. Things are hard at the moment, you know? So I've been a delivery guy, a motorcycle delivery guy, taxi driver . . . I finished my philosophy degree last year but there aren't so many jobs for philosophers these days.'

I nodded. 'Gosh,' I said. 'That must be a bit hard to deal with.'

Baruch shrugged. 'I'm philosophical about it,' he said.

I laughed. 'Very good! So, do you think things will get better? Now the bailout has ended and everything.'

'Who knows?' Baruch said.

We sat in silence for a moment and it made me wonder if I had said something wrong. But then he asked, 'Is it your first time on the island?'

'Yes,' I said. 'Well, sort of.'

'Sort of?'

'I was conceived here, in Oia,' I told him, wiggling an eyebrow suggestively. 'My mum had a holiday romance here twenty-four years ago and got pregnant. So in a way, I suppose I *have* been here before. I just wasn't born yet.' I was trying to get the concept of a holiday romance into Baruch's thoughts, I think. So far, the day had been lovely but entirely platonic.

'Wow,' Baruch told me. 'And your father?'

'I don't know,' I said. 'Maybe just some local guy. I don't know the details, really.'

Baruch grinned.

'What?' I asked.

'My uncle could be your father,' he said. 'He was, you know . . . how do you say this? He liked the girls. You know?'

'A bit of a Romeo?'

Baruch laughed. 'Yes. Yes, a bit of a Romeo.'

'But no,' I explained. 'Unfortunately not. He died. Whoever my father was, he died just after they met. In some kind of car crash, I think, while they were still here in Santorini. So we're definitely not related.' I wanted to get that one out of the way. I couldn't have him thinking we were cousins.

'God,' Baruch said, his smile fading. 'That's a sad story.'

I shrugged. 'I'm philosophical about it.'

He laid one arm across my shoulders and because it felt good, and because it was the first time he had touched me that day, I bit my bottom lip and nodded dolefully. It felt a bit naughty to be exploiting such a subject but it's not as if there are that many advantages to having a dead father. If I thought I could get a cuddle out of it I was certainly going to try.

My acting seemed to do the trick, because he pulled me in towards him so I could rest my head against his shoulder. His hand gently caressed my bare arm. He sighed gently. 'You know . . .' he said.

'Yes?' I asked.

He cleared his throat. 'I think . . .' he started.

And at that precise instant we were showered with water. Baruch jumped up immediately and sprinted athletically across the beach to catch and dunk the culprit. It was Damon. He was laughing like a hyena.

'Damn you, Damon,' I mumbled.

By the time we left the beach at five, I'd got no further with Project Snog. With Baruch's friends constantly present there hadn't been any opportunities to make such a thing happen. But I was sure, at least, that I wanted to try. He'd been friendly and funny and considerate all day. And if anything I now found him even easier on the eye than at first glance, which, in my case at least, is quite a rare thing. So often the cute ones seem to become less and less cute the more you get to know them.

Baruch had explained that he needed to get back early to take his grandmother to the doctor. Though this said something reassuring about his values, I felt gutted to find myself back outside the minimart at six in the evening.

'So, when are you off next?' I asked him, handing back the crash helmet.

'In a week,' Baruch said. 'Just one day a week, I'm afraid.'

'But I'll be gone in a week,' I moaned, sounding uncomfortably like a whiny child.

Baruch shrugged. 'That's life, huh?' he said.

I looked into his eyes. I did my best to beam the image of what I was hoping for from my brain into his. And this apparently seemed to work because he said, 'I could come around to yours later. At ten o'clock or something?'

'Mum will be there,' I reminded him.

'Of course.'

'And yours?'

'Here in Santorini I stay with my uncle,' he explained. 'In Athens I have a place, but here I live with my uncle. And his wife. And their kids.'

'Right,' I said.

'Tomorrow I can get off a bit early. We could go for ice cream if you want?'

'Ice cream?'

'Yeah. You don't like ice cream?'

'Sure,' I said. 'Sure, I love ice cream.'

'About eight?' Baruch asked.

'Yes,' I said. 'Maybe nine? So I can eat with Mum? Otherwise she'll feel abandoned.'

'Nine, then,' Baruch said. 'Meet me here?' He leaned in to kiss me. It was just a peck on the lips but his grin seemed to promise so much more. 'OK,' he said, glancing at his watch. 'Now I really have to go or she'll miss her appointment. We have to be in Fira by six thirty.'

'You're not taking her on that thing, are you?' I asked, nodding in the direction of the bike.

'Sure,' Baruch said. 'Why not?'

As I zigzagged down to our room, I asked myself for the first time just what I thought I was up to. Because there was clearly no future to be had with Baruch. Not when I was returning home to Margate and he to Athens. Was I being slutty, I wondered, for wanting to have a holiday fling? Or liberated? Or stupid? Was I following some genetic predisposition: the same thing that had led to my conception? Was I somehow trying simply to understand what had happened – using the idea of a holiday romance with Baruch to work out by what process I had come into being? Or was it more simple? Was it just that he was so very, very good-looking?

One thing was for sure, my desire for him wasn't fading. He was starting to make me go quite weak at the knees.

When I reached our room it was all locked up. I opened the door with my key and found a note from Mum saying she was down at the bottom of the 'Dreaded Steps' having a swim, and that I should come and join her if I got home early. So I picked up my bag again, and headed straight back out.

TWELVE

Laura

As we rode down the western side of the island, around craggy headlands and on further south, I wondered what Leif had in mind for my birthday. When we came to a tatty sign indicating a bar/restaurant, Leif took the turning, and rode along the gravelly dirt track until we came to an ad hoc car park. He locked the bike and led the way down a coastal staircase.

The bar had been built on what appeared to be a natural balcony, a flat expanse set in the middle of the cliff face. There were only three people in the bar when we got there, and even these people turned out to be employees. They all jumped up when we arrived.

Still uncomfortably aware that, birthday or not, I had no money, I ordered a single Mythos beer and Leif followed suit.

'It's lovely here,' I told him. 'How did you find out about this place?'

'Olav told me,' he said. 'They came here the other night.'

I leaned over the balcony and watched the sea as it lapped against the rocks below, and then, when my beer arrived, I sank back into my canvas chair and looked out at the view. The sun was heading towards the horizon and the sky was beginning to flame red.

The waiter brought us a dish of olives and some incredibly salty peanuts, and for an hour we nibbled at these and sipped very slowly at our beers as we talked.

'Do you know which island that is?' I asked Leif at one point, indicating a land mass to our left.

'I think it's Ios,' he said. 'But I'm not that sure, to be honest. Olav is better with that stuff, though only because he's the one with the compass.'

'I'm so sorry about spoiling your holiday,' I said again.

Leif laughed. 'Do I look as if I'm having a bad holiday?' he asked.

I wrinkled my nose. 'No,' I admitted. 'But all the same.'

Leif pointed to a house in the distance. Like the bar, it looked as if it had grown organically from the rock face. 'Imagine living there,' he said.

'Yes,' I agreed. 'It makes you want to never go home, doesn't it? It makes you wonder why you actually live where you do.'

Other people started to arrive: a young Italian-sounding couple and two American women. And as the food they ordered began to appear, food that looked delicious, Leif started trying to convince me that we should eat there as well.

Because the money issue was playing heavily on my mind, I resisted this idea for some time, but eventually Leif pulled the trump card that it was, after all, my birthday – and so, still hoping I could pay him back at some future date, I caved in and let him order what the menu rather quaintly called 'Grandmummy's Plate For Two'.

It was enormous, when it arrived, and delicious. It consisted of rice-stuffed vine leaves and cheese-stuffed tomatoes. There were also deep-fried cheese croquettes, calamari in olive oil, aubergine caviar, and sardines and fried okra . . . It was, without a doubt, the tastiest meal I had ever eaten. In fact, I'd go as far as to say that, to this day, it's still up there, still probably in my top three meals ever.

With nothing between us and the horizon, the sunset was spectacular, and by the end of the meal I was feeling almost tearful at how Leif had managed to turn the day, which had begun so inauspiciously, into such a beautiful moment. I hadn't had that many beautiful moments in my life until then.

Leif paid the bill, which he insisted wasn't in the least expensive, and we began to climb back up to the car park.

'That was the best birthday surprise ever,' I told him. 'Thank you!'

Leif laughed. 'This was not the surprise,' he said. 'The surprise is where we go next.'

At the top, we climbed back onto the scooter and bumped off along the winding coastline. The wind had died completely by now and even in shorts I didn't feel cold.

Eventually, Leif pulled off onto another dirt road and we followed it as far as it went.

'Now we have to walk a bit,' Leif said, handing me my bag from the top case.

We walked for about ten minutes along the ragged coast. The sun, by this time, had vanished beneath the horizon, but the red sky still lit the path just enough to see where I was putting my feet.

Some nesting birds squawked and took to the air as we passed them, startling me, and when I yelped Leif briefly took my hand.

After a few more minutes, we clambered down onto a tiny secluded beach.

There were no bars or restaurants here. There were no other people, either. And the only light on the long, smooth beach was from the just-rising moon, a distant streetlamp way up on the clifftop, and the final vestiges of the day, which were still illuminating the horizon with a vague honey-coloured band of light.

'I've never been swimming at night before,' I told Leif as we pulled off our shoes and began to cross the beach.

'This is good,' he said. 'You will like it.'

Back to back, we changed into our bathers and then, crossing the wet sand, I joined Leif at the water's edge. I glanced back at where our footprints mingled in the sand and turned to face out to sea. There were no waves at all and the surface was like a gently undulating mirror. It looked viscous, as if it was made of something much thicker than water, and because of the reflection of the strange sky it crossed my mind for an instant that it looked like it was made of honey.

'It's so pretty,' I said quietly.

'The stars,' Leif said, pointing upwards.

I leaned my head back to look up at them. 'Gosh, yes,' I said. 'How amazing.'

'Come,' Leif said, striding forwards into the darkness.

'I'm scared,' I admitted. 'I'm scared there are monsters in there.'

Leif laughed heartily. 'No monsters,' he said, 'only fish.'

'Fish that bite?'

'No. But they might give your toes a bit of a suck,' Leif said.

He reached back for my hand and I let him take it and slowly we edged our way in. The sea was warm and, because the day was now cooling, it felt even warmer than the air. Thinking that I was still scared, Leif tugged at my hand again, urging me to go deeper, but in truth I was just mesmerised by the ripples emanating out from my knees and the way they reflected the night sky.

'Wait,' I said. 'I'll be in in a minute. I just want a moment to look.'

'Sure.' Leif let himself fall to one side and slip beneath the surface of the water.

I waited, motionless, until he had swum away, until the sea had returned to its undulating smoothness. I looked out at the horizon, which by now was almost black with just a hint of sapphire blue remaining.

I listened to the silence of the night surrounding me and discovered that it wasn't silent at all. In addition to my own breath I could hear the lapping of the tiny wavelets on the beach. I could hear some chicks somewhere in the distance clamouring for their mother, and I could hear the rhythmic splash-splash-splash of Leif's inelegant crawl.

Somewhere to my right a fish briefly surfaced with a *plop* then vanished into the depths.

'Come on!' Leif called. 'It's lovely.' I could barely see his head by now, bobbing in the distance.

'Hold on,' I said. 'I'm just . . .'

'Just what?' he asked.

'Just . . . taking it in,' I said.

I couldn't think quite how to explain what was happening. Because something was breaking. And something else was beginning. I felt as vulnerable beneath the night sky as those chicks alone in their nest, but also there were stirrings of something like optimism deep within me, perhaps for the first time in my life.

I looked down at my knees again and felt the softness of the sand beneath my toes and the silky water nudging against my legs. And when I looked up and out, once more, the feeling, still nameless, washed over me.

It was as if I had been living in my head ever since I was born; as if I had been this little person sitting in a control seat, looking out at my life rather than actually inhabiting my body. I had been experiencing my life as a series of thoughts and fears and expectations. I'd been worrying about my mother and sin and my career and paying bills, and Conor and my passport . . . The list went on and on.

But suddenly, standing in the seemingly infinite sea of Santorini and beneath that quite-literally infinite sky, it all fell away, leaving me feeling fragile and raw, and scared, and ecstatically in love with everything and everyone – with the essence of life itself.

Conor, I suddenly saw, didn't matter. My passport didn't matter. My money didn't matter.

In that instant, I was a tiny grain of life gifted with being able to observe the inexplicable vastness of the universe, and the only thing that mattered was the excruciating beauty of being there. Of being there to experience it all.

I was fully present in that moment for the first time ever, and it felt beautiful and monumental, and really rather terrifying. I had a sense of belonging right where I was that felt new and exciting and moving. The moment was extraordinary.

I gasped suddenly. I had been holding my breath at the shock of it all. And just as I did so, Leif surfaced right in front of me. He stood, the water trickling from his smooth skin in the moonlight. He smiled.

'Oh . . . Leif . . .' I breathed, unable to even begin to explain what I was feeling.

'You're crying,' he said flatly.

'It's all so big,' I told him incomprehensibly. 'It's all just so big.'

He turned so that he was facing the same way as me, so he could see what I was seeing, and looked out with me at the vastness of the sea, at the panoramic infinity of the star-filled sky. 'I know,' he said. 'It's why we're here.' And I wasn't sure if he meant that it was why he had brought me here, or that it was the reason we were here, on this planet – to observe all this beauty. Perhaps he meant both.

He reached for my hand, and that sensation of being anchored felt good. I'd been feeling scared that I might perhaps drift away, that I might just disintegrate with the emotion of it all and float away as space dust.

'Can you hold me?' I heard myself ask before I even knew I was going to do so. 'Would that be OK?'

Without a word, Leif turned to me and wrapped me in his cool, wet arms.

'I'm *here*,' I said tearfully, still looking out over his shoulder, still unable to string anything together that might approximate a meaningful sentence. 'I'm right here, looking at all of this.'

But incredibly Leif got it. 'I know,' he said. 'I'm here too. It's amazing.'

◆ ◆ ◆

We swam for half an hour, diving into the viscous darkness and then surfacing into the rapidly cooling night air. I floated on my back and looked at the stars above me, and shrieked and laughed when, as predicted by Leif, a fish sucked at my big toe.

When we were too cold to continue, we climbed out and dried ourselves off.

We sat at the water's edge in silence for a while, both staring at the immensity of the night and both thinking, I reckon, about the fact that something else was happening here. I felt reluctant to name it or even think about it with any kind of precision. Perhaps I feared that trying to label it might kill it off.

'We should go,' Leif eventually said, prompted by the fact that I had shivered. 'It is cold.'

'I know,' I agreed. 'But I don't really want to. It's so lovely here.'

'But I think it is too cold now to sleep on the beach,' Leif said. 'If we had sleeping bags, but . . .'

In unspoken agreement, we stood and shyly, back to back once again, changed into our dry clothes.

As we walked across the beach, I felt an almost overwhelming desire to take his hand but resisted. We weren't there quite yet. I wasn't sure where we were, really, but we definitely weren't quite *there*.

Leif strapped his lamp onto his forehead and led the way back up the rock face and along the top of the cliffs to where we had left the bike. In silence, we climbed back on and started off along the bumpy road.

The night was growing cooler rapidly and a breeze was rising, so I hugged Leif's warm back and turned my head to look at the moon, which had now risen and was mirrored beautifully in the surface of the sea.

I remember thinking it was the best birthday ever and that I would never forget my twenty-sixth. And I think that was the moment I let myself become aware of what was really going on.

Did my feelings blossom that night because of the magical moment I had experienced on the beach or was it the other way around? Did the magic of the beach happen because of whatever was developing with Leif? I like to think it was both, that in some way everything that happened was the product of everything else, like some magical, mystical multiplication.

I like to believe that for the first time in my life I had found myself (due to the most unlikely circumstances) in exactly the right place at exactly the right time with exactly the right person. That's how things felt in that moment, anyway – as if everything, as awful as it had all been, had happened for a reason. And the reason was to bring me to this exact spot at this exact moment with this specific person.

I was still clamped to Leif's back, still smiling at the moon, when he pulled sharply off the road.

'What's happening?' I asked, but he didn't reply. I was momentarily scared as he wobbled down a gravelly track, but then we pulled up outside a big white house. The wooden plaque on the letterbox read, 'Lena's Rooms'.

'What are you doing?' I asked.

'Just wait,' Leif said. 'I have an idea. Stay with the bike. I won't be a minute.'

He was gone not one minute but ten, and when he finally reappeared he was grinning and dangling a key from one hand. 'The final birthday surprise,' he said. 'Come.'

I followed him across Lena's scrappy garden. The path wove around a few cacti and a tamarind tree to a small white-stucco building on the cliff edge. It was about the size of a large shed.

Leif unlocked the door and switched on the harsh centre light. 'Ta-da!' he said.

'God, Leif,' I said. 'Have you rented this for us?'

He nodded.

'Did you plan this all?'

'No,' Leif replied. 'I just saw the sign and we are lucky. She had only this one free.'

I stepped into the room and looked around. It was sparsely but cleanly furnished. It had two widely spaced single beds with white sheets. On the chest of drawers were two folded blue blankets.

I crossed to the window and threw back the shutters. Outside, the sea shimmered in the moonlight. 'Wow,' I said. 'Look at that for a sea view. Was it expensive?'

'Not even,' Leif said. 'We are in September now, so . . .'

I leaned on the windowsill and saw there was a small wooden balcony accessible from the side of the building, and then I lifted my gaze to look again at the mesmerising moon.

'This is a good idea?' Leif asked, joining me at the open window and leaning, like me, on the sill. 'You don't mind?'

I snorted and turned to face him. 'Mind?' I said. 'Are you crazy?' I had been feeling sick about returning to the hotel all evening.

'Just a bit,' Leif answered. 'Just enough crazy, I think. No?'

We returned to the front door and rounded the building to the balcony, where we sat at the little table and chairs. Leif produced a bar of chocolate, which we ate slowly, rationing ourselves to make it last. 'If I had planned this, I would have champagne,' Leif told me.

'We don't need champagne,' I told him. 'This is perfect.'

The wind returned as the evening progressed and quite early, about ten thirty I think, we were forced back indoors by the cold. I was yawning crazily anyway. It had been an emotional day.

Shyly, separately, we showered in the en-suite to get rid of the sand. And by the time I came out, Leif was already tucked up in bed.

My traumatic experiences with Conor had left me a bit scared of men, I think, so I was actually grateful that Leif wasn't going to try to seduce me.

I climbed into my bed and said, 'Goodnight, Leif. And thank you so much. It's been perfect.'

'You're welcome,' Leif replied through a yawn. 'Goodnight. And happy birthday again.'

He clicked off the bedside light and I lay looking at the room in the strange moonlight.

The night seemed silent at first, but as my ears adjusted I could hear both Leif's breathing and the sound of the waves landing on the beach below – they made surprisingly similar sounds. The wind, too, began to whistle sporadically through the shutters.

The day had been sumptuous and for ten minutes I lay in the crisp white sheets, feeling optimistic and sated by everything that had happened. But the wind continued to rise and an animal in the distance shrieked horribly – it sounded as if it was being killed – and unexpectedly the night began to change quality, feeling less welcoming and more lonely. *The day might be beautiful*, the wind seemed to be saying, *but at night you're all alone.*

I opened my mouth three or four times before I finally managed to speak. 'Are you asleep?' I whispered.

'No,' Leif said. 'I'm a bit cold. I think I will close the window. And get a blanket.'

I listened to him climb out of bed. I heard the slap of his big feet on the tiled floor as he closed the window and crossed the room to the dresser.

'I'm a bit cold too,' I said.

'Yes? You want I get your blanket?'

'I . . .' I said.

'Yes?'

I heard his footsteps approach. His face appeared in front of me as he crouched down by the bedside. Like me, he was wearing his T-shirt and underwear. 'Are you OK?' he asked.

'Yes . . . I . . .' I said.

'I'll get you a blanket,' Leif said.

'Oh, just get in, will you?' I told him, sounding unintentionally irritable. 'If that's OK?' I added, trying to soften the invitation. My irritation, I knew, was entirely caused by my own inability to say, to admit to myself even, what I wanted.

Leif smiled quizzically. 'You want that I get in with you?' he asked.

'*Yes!* If you don't mind?'

Leif's teeth flashed at me in the moonlight. His face was split in two by his grin. 'Thank God,' he said, pulling back the covers and sliding in beside me. 'I thought you were never asking.'

We lay side by side in silence, as rigid as two planks, for at least ten minutes. The only points of contact were Leif's shoulder and my own, a reassuring sensation of bodily warmth gently making its way through two layers of clothing.

'So what now?' Leif asked eventually.

'Can we just sleep like this?' I asked, even though every cell in my body seemed to be begging that I maximise the areas of skin contact between us. 'Would that be OK?'

'Of course,' Leif said matter-of-factly. But his feelings about this were belied by the deep sigh he emitted as he rolled onto his side away from me.

I followed suit by rolling towards him – I've never been able to sleep on my back – but in the single bed it was all but impossible to avoid touching Leif's back.

As neither of the other two options – asking him to return to his own bed or turning the other way and sleeping facing away from each other – seemed desirable, I caved in to the inevitable and shuffled towards him, laying one arm over his hips and spooning against him. 'Is this OK?' I asked.

Leif reached for my arm and pulled it tighter. 'This is *very* OK,' he said.

◆ ◆ ◆

I did not sleep well that night. Desire made my breath quicken, my heart race and my body tingle, and none of these were conducive to sleep. On top of this, my mind was racing about what was going to happen next – about what was going to happen in bed, in my life, and with Conor. But I must at some point have managed to drift off, because when I woke in the morning I discovered, to my dismay, that Leif had found his way back to his own bed.

I crept as quietly as I could to the en-suite where I went to the loo and brushed my teeth. As I returned, I saw that Leif's eyes were open. He was looking at me, albeit sleepily.

'Are you all right?' I asked, and he smiled at me gently.

'Better than all right,' he said, looking positively radiant.

'But you're back in your bed,' I commented. 'Couldn't you sleep? I didn't snore, did I?'

Leif rolled onto his back and propped himself up on pillows so he could look at me properly. 'It's hard for a guy,' he said. 'To sleep, when . . .'

I laughed. 'When what?' I asked, even though I knew exactly what he was referring to.

'When you want to . . . to kiss someone that much,' he said sweetly.

I stared at him, peering deep into his blue eyes. I bit my bottom lip.

'I'm sorry,' Leif said. 'I shouldn't have said this.'

'No,' I told him. 'No, it's fine. I . . . I feel the same really. I didn't sleep much either.'

'It's true?' Leif asked.

'Yes.'

'Please come here,' he said. He patted the bed beside him.

I nodded nervously. I had butterflies in my stomach. Something about Leif's approach made me feel unexpectedly embarrassed. It made me feel, for some reason, as if I was preparing for my first-ever kiss with a boy, as if I didn't know how to do this.

The few boys I had slept with, or even kissed, had come at me like freight trains, so all I ever had to do was acquiesce, to simply not resist. With Leif, it seemed I had to actively decide this was what I wanted and, though that felt empowering and really rather lovely, and though it made me only want him more, it didn't seem to make getting there any easier.

I moved towards him and perched on the edge of his bed with my back to him. He reached out to stroke my shoulders.

'You're not ready,' he said. 'It's too soon after . . . But that's OK.'

I shrugged. 'I think I am,' I said, swallowing with difficulty as I tried to pluck up the courage. 'I just don't know how to get there.'

Leif applied gentle pressure to my side and so I turned and lay back beside him.

'We don't have to do anything you don't . . .' he started.

But I had rolled to my side and pressed a finger to his lips, effectively silencing him. 'Just kiss me now,' I instructed. 'Before I change my mind.' And I could sense, through my fingertips, that he was struggling not to grin.

We kissed chastely to start with and then, as slowly we dared to let our fingertips explore each other's bodies, more passionately. Leif was grinning at me like the proverbial Cheshire cat and I found myself smiling stupidly back at him.

Leif's skin, I discovered, was cooler than my own and it felt unexpectedly soft, as though it had been powdered with talc. The whole thing was as gentle and respectful as things with Conor had been arrogant and brutal. Leif seemed like a custom-built antidote designed to restore my faith in men.

When my ever-increasing desire for more finally submerged my fears, I rolled to my back and attempted to pull Leif on top of me. Unexpectedly, he resisted.

'What's wrong?' I asked.

'We can't.'

'Why not?' I asked, fearing he was going to drop a sudden bombshell on me – that he was married or ill, or that he simply didn't feel for me in that way.

'I don't have . . . you know . . .' he said. 'I don't have any johnnies.'

I burst out laughing. I hadn't heard anyone refer to a condom as a johnny since Abby had shown me one at school when I was thirteen.

'Why are you laughing?' Leif asked, sounding offended and visibly peeling away from me.

'It's not . . .' I stumbled, still sniggering. 'It's just that word. Johnny. I'm sorry.'

'This is not the word?'

'It's just old-fashioned,' I told him. 'People call them condoms nowadays. The Americans say rubbers, I think.'

'Right,' Leif said, sounding only partially mollified. 'Well, I haven't got any anyway, so . . .'

I thought about this for a moment. I thought about the fact that I'd had sex with Conor already and would have to deal with the aftermath on my return anyway. I contrasted Leif's sweet concern against Conor's perverse narcissism and asked myself if I was really going to refuse Leif when I hadn't refused Conor. I took an instant to catalogue the level of desire my body was experiencing. Because even though our bodies had been pressed together, the overriding sensation was that it simply wasn't enough.

I reached down to touch Leif below the waterline and what I found there made me shudder with desire. 'It's OK,' I told him, pulling him towards me again. 'Please . . . just . . .'

Again, his face seemed to crack open with that toothy smile of his. 'Are you sure?' he asked. But he was already pushing at the gate.

We made love twice that morning, and it was everything I had ever imagined sex would be, and everything it had never been to date.

Leif was the sweetest, most attentive, generous lover I had experienced by a long, long stretch and I remember thinking, once it was over for the second time, when we were lying side by side, that this was why they called it making love. Because though I had perhaps accepted I was falling in love with Leif, by the time it was over, I was so deep in that I knew I would never get out alive.

We were interrupted by a knock on the door.

'Shit,' Leif said, grabbing his watch from the bedside table to check the time. 'It's gone eleven.'

'What happens at eleven?' I asked, stretching like a cat in the sunshine as Leif hopped comically into his shorts.

'We have to quit the room at eleven,' Leif said. 'That's what happens.'

THIRTEEN

Becky

The next morning, Mum and I chugged the full length of the island on our little C90 to Akrotiri, a Bronze Age settlement that had been destroyed by a volcano in 1627 BC. It had been Damon's suggestion to go there and because both Mum and I were feeling a little beached-out (I wasn't sure my pale skin could take much more sun, even with the factor fifty I had been slapping on prodigiously) and because we were both feeling guilty about the Acropolis, we decided that a bit of history was probably overdue.

It cost twenty-four euros for us both to get in and, even at ten thirty in the morning, the heat was unbearable. I really do think that if it hadn't been for the Acropolis factor, both of us would have happily carried on to a beach. But as it was, neither of us was prepared to admit this so we handed over our cash and made our way inside.

In the end, we were glad we'd been brave. Because walking through streets, visiting bedrooms and kitchens and bathrooms that had last been inhabited in the seventeenth century BC turned out to feel strangely moving.

'I wouldn't do it again,' was Mum's verdict when we finally stepped back outside. 'But I'm glad we came.'

'I just can't get my head around how old it all is,' I said. 'I'm still struggling with the fact that people made those beautiful pots more than three thousand years ago. I mean, they were really pretty. People were making *art* three thousand seven hundred years ago!'

'I suppose it's because our calendar begins at the birth of Christ,' Mum said. 'So we tend to think that's when everything started. But it didn't at all, did it?'

'No,' I agreed. 'No, it's weird.'

'Does everyone use the same, you know, start date as us? I mean, what about Muslims and Buddhists and what have you?' Mum asked. 'They don't count their years from the birth of Christ, do they?'

'No, there are others. I read a thing about it,' I told her. 'There's a Sanskrit one that begins three thousand years before Christ. And I think the Islamic one actually starts later.'

'Gosh,' Mum said. 'You're a clever little sausage, aren't you?'

'Not really,' I laughed. 'I just read a thing about it online.'

We ate a couple of rather average salads in Akrotiri whilst being harassed by a group of beautiful but hungry kittens, then, unable to think of any other way to survive the heat, we decided to head for the sea. A quick glance at the map revealed there was a famous red beach just ten minutes away and, as this was impressive enough that Mum remembered it from twenty-odd years earlier, we decided that's where we would go.

Riding at midday was like pointing a massive hairdryer at your body, and the car park, when we got there, was a shimmering mirage of pure heat. We parked up the bike and, sweating profusely, clambered across some rocks until the beach came into view.

I could understand why Mum remembered it. The sand was a crazy red ochre colour and the sea crystal-clear and tinted with turquoise. The contrast between the two colours side by side seemed almost unreasonable. We paid for a parasol, but because even in the shade the day felt parching, we changed and ran into the sea.

Other than asking if I'd had a nice time, Mum had been pretty discreet about Baruch. We'd never really had much vocabulary for talking about anything that was intimate, so that didn't really surprise me. But I'd been hoping she would ask because I'd worked out a way that I could use it to lead to discussing my father.

Eventually, sitting at the water's edge with our feet in the sea, her curiosity got the better of her. 'So how was yesterday?' she asked. 'You haven't said much about it.'

'Like I said,' I told her. 'It was nice.'

'And that's it, is it?' she asked, picking up a pebble and tossing it. 'Nice?'

I proceeded to tell her, pretty much verbatim, everything that had happened. There wasn't really anything to hide, after all.

I told her who had been there and the things we had talked about. We debated, for a bit, how low the Greek minimum wage might be. And as we were reaching the logical end of the conversation, I added, 'You know, Baruch said his uncle used to be a real Romeo character. Seducing all the ladies. The holidaymakers, I mean.'

'That doesn't surprise me,' Mum said.

'Meaning?' I asked.

'I just mean that if he looked anything like your Baruch, that wouldn't have been too difficult.'

'Oh, right,' I said. 'Well, he isn't *my* Baruch.'

'Isn't he?'

'Nope,' I said. 'Anyway, that left me wondering . . . was my father Greek?' The question had been on the tip of my tongue all afternoon but I'd been too scared to ask it. Now I had done so, I felt as if I had lobbed a grenade along the beach. I wanted to cover my head with my hands in case it exploded.

Mum frowned deeply and sighed. She pushed her toes into the wet sand. 'Why would you ask that?' she said.

I shrugged. 'It's not that unusual a thing to want to know, is it? What nationality your father is. *Was*.'

'It's just that it's never interested you before,' Mum said.

'Never interested me?' I repeated, a sense of outrage swelling within me.

'I mean, you've never asked me anything like that before,' Mum said.

'The fact that I've never dared ask it hardly means it doesn't interest me,' I told her. 'Like I said, it's not exactly an unusual thing to want to know.'

'Well, maybe . . .' Mum said, starting to sound angry, 'I don't want to talk about it. Maybe that isn't such an unusual thing to happen either.'

I realised in that instant that this was what she had always done. She had trained me from the earliest age that it was not OK to talk about this. And by teaching me that mentioning my father would cause a spike of discomfort, she had effectively stopped me from doing so.

'So was he Greek?' I now asked, clenching my fists at the effort required to resist dropping the subject as I had every other time in the face of Mum's malaise. 'Could my father have been Baruch's uncle, for example?'

'What?' Mum whistled, suddenly angry. 'What a ridiculous thing to ask! You know full well he died.'

'Yes, but . . .'

'So how could he be Baruch's uncle?'

I shrugged. 'Baruch's uncle might be dead,' I lied. 'I don't know. I didn't ask.'

'You didn't ask . . .' Mum repeated mockingly.

'But why not just answer the question?' I said, thinking that seeing as we had got this far, it would be a shame to give in now. 'Why not just tell me where he came from? What could possibly be so complicated about that?'

Mum stood. 'I knew I shouldn't have brought you with me,' she said meanly, avoiding eye contact. And without another word, she strutted off along the shoreline.

The day was ruined, of course. And I was in no doubt this was all my fault. I understood perfectly that this was my punishment for having asked directly about my father.

She walked to the end of the beach and sat upon a rock looking out to sea. It was more than an hour before she returned and dived straight into her book.

I was pretending to read mine as well, but I couldn't really concentrate. I was too busy feeling angry. I was too busy thinking about the fact that she had said she wished she hadn't brought me here, running the phrase over and over, rubbing salt into the wound. And I was too busy wondering how such a simple thing could be so damned complicated that she would prefer all this drama rather than simply answering the question.

We barely exchanged a word for the rest of the afternoon, so as soon as we got home I phoned Baruch to tell him I could meet him earlier than planned.

He told me to be at the minimart at eight and I wondered how I was going to survive another hour in the company of my petulant, sulking mother. But by the time I had finished my phone call, she was gone.

Mum did not return, and when the time came for me to lock up the room, she wasn't answering her phone either. Though we'd had far worse arguments in the past (especially when I was in my teens), I felt surprisingly upset about this one as I climbed the stairs to meet Baruch.

But call me shallow, because one look at his tanned face was enough to cheer me up considerably. He was wearing an open-necked denim shirt with rolled-up sleeves and a pair of bum-hugging jeans. I suddenly remembered that I was spending the evening with him. I'd been so distracted by my argument with Mum that I'd forgotten that gorgeous fact.

He locked up the shop and asked me if I was hungry, so I told him the truth, that I was starving, and thinking about the money issue again, I offered to buy him dinner.

I don't think Baruch's pride could even consider such a concept. 'There's a special restaurant,' he said. 'Not expensive at all. I'd be happy to take you if you like the idea?'

'Why is it special?' I asked. I was imagining the horror of a McDonald's lurking somewhere on the island.

'Only Greek people go there,' he said.

'But they'll let me in?'

Baruch laughed. 'Of course,' he said. 'You're with me.'

Virtually glowing at the thought that I was *with him*, I climbed onto the back of his bike and we roared off along the main road to Fira. Just before we reached the edge of town, he turned down a winding dirt road.

Baruch's special restaurant turned out to be in someone's house. It was a most peculiar set-up. The house was at the end of the dirt track and until you arrived in front of it, there were no indications that it was even there. From the front, other than the fact that there were ten cars parked along the side of the road, plus four or five scooters, there was nothing to show that this was anything other than a normal family home. But when you rounded the corner of the building, the rear terrace, which had been turned into a makeshift dining area, came into view. There were a dozen or so plastic tables and seating for thirty or forty people. Half of the tables were already occupied, as Baruch had predicted, by an exclusively Greek crowd, many of whom were about our age.

The 'restaurant' appeared to be run by a white-haired couple who both looked too old to be working.

'Can I speak?' I whispered once the husband had seated us.

Baruch laughed. 'Why do you think you can't speak?' he asked.

'Because they'll realise I'm not Greek,' I said.

'No, it's fine,' Baruch told me. 'They know already, believe me. And it's fine. You're here with me.' I wondered if I'd asked the question just to hear him say those words again.

'How come this place is so secret?' I asked. 'Why don't they want tourists?'

'Well, it's not, you know, very legal,' Baruch explained. 'With the crisis, everyone is a bit poor, yes?'

'Even here? Even in Santorini?'

Baruch nodded.

'It doesn't look poor. The place looks awash with tourist cash.'

'Well, these people,' Baruch said, nodding towards the house, 'are retired. And the money they get from the state . . . How do you call this?'

'Their pension?'

'Yes, their pension. It has gone down by half. More than half. And the bills, the electricity, the taxes, these have all gone up. So . . .'

'I see,' I said. 'So they've opened a secret restaurant.'

Baruch nodded. 'Their children are in Athens, too. So this way they can send them some money, I expect.'

'It's a great idea,' I said. 'But surely they'd make more money running a restaurant for tourists?'

'Yeah, but this is cash, you know?' Baruch said, raising an eyebrow. 'So no taxes. If they were taking business from the other places, people would complain. But those people have to eat somewhere too. The people in the hotels. The cleaners. The policemen . . . So this is a special place for them. Greek food at Greek prices.'

'For Greek people,' I said.

'Yes.'

'I feel very honoured to be able to come here then, so thank you.'

'You are welcome,' Baruch told me with a wink.

The restaurant had no menu and no set prices. There was a fixed three-course meal and a choice of red or white wine but that was it. On leaving, you left what you wanted to leave, a tax-free gift to the owners, but Baruch said that everyone knew the correct amount was ten euros a head. It was an absolute bargain.

Tentatively, not wanting to embarrass him, I asked Baruch how much the Greek minimum wage was. I needn't have worried because he chatted about it quite freely, explaining that it was about six hundred euros a month, while most people's pensions were less than five hundred. Because his uncle let him stay free of charge, Baruch was earning even less. His uncle paid him four hundred a month, he said.

I didn't dare try to work out what the miserly hourly rate might be, because as far as I could see Baruch was doing twelve-hour days, six days a week. But I certainly understood a little better why a fifteen-euro pina colada might seem out of reach.

Our first course arrived: two dishes, one of tzatziki and another of garlicky aubergine salad, served with little triangles of some kind of flatbread.

'So how was Akrotiri?' Baruch asked as he dished up. 'Did you go?'

I told him all about our trip to the museum. Trying to sound clever, I think, I explained about the other more ancient calendars too, but he seemed to know all about them already, and went on to tell me about various Greek philosophers who had been writing lengthy discourses on philosophy in around 400 BC.

'And your mother?' Baruch asked, once we had reached the logical end of that conversation. 'Where is she tonight?'

'I don't know,' I said, 'and I don't care that much.'

Baruch pulled a face and I became aware that to a Greek guy who clearly loved his family, that might have sounded particularly unattractive. So I reassured him that I loved my mother but admitted we had argued. 'It happens from time to time,' I said.

'Do you want to talk about this, or not?' he asked.

I nodded. 'Yeah,' I said. 'Yes, I think so.' And I proceeded, between occasional mouthfuls of our second course (a weird but delicious dish of spaghetti and aubergine, beans and feta cheese) to tell him the whole story.

When I reached the end, he was staring at me strangely. He had finished his dish long since and had his hands pressed together.

'What?' I asked, realising I was behind on the eating front and shovelling food into my mouth.

'I don't know,' he said.

'You don't know what?' I asked through a full mouth.

'I don't know what to say.'

I frowned and, when I could politely speak again, said, 'About what?'

Baruch cleared his throat. 'Look . . . you know I took my grandmother to the doctor yesterday, right?'

'Oh God, I'm sorry. Is she OK?' I asked, blushing at my own selfishness for not even having asked.

'Oh yes, she's fine. She just likes to go sometimes. It reassures her, you know? Old people . . .'

'Well, good. I . . . I'm glad she's OK.'

'But we had a long wait – it is always like this at the doctor – so I told her your story. And she remembers an accident. I'm thinking it might be the same one.'

'She does?' I ran my tongue across my teeth and leaned in closer. 'But that was years ago!'

'I know,' Baruch told me. 'I was surprised too. But Santorini's not such a big place. Not so much happens. And my mother was pregnant with me. It happened a few weeks before I was born. So that helped her remember too.'

My mouth had fallen open in shock. I could hardly believe what I was hearing. 'So, when was this? When is your birthday?' I asked.

'It's in two weeks, actually,' Baruch said. 'The fifteenth.'

'And what year?' I asked.

'Ninety-four,' Baruch said. 'Fifteenth of September, 1994.'

'God, that's incredible,' I said. 'The timing fits. I was born in 1995.'

Baruch counted on his fingers, then said, 'May?'

'Twenty-first of April,' I corrected. 'I was a bit early.'

'So, you see,' Baruch said. 'Who needs Google when you have a nosey grandmother?'

'Did she remember anything else?' I asked. I could feel the blood draining from my face. 'His name? His nationality? What exactly happened?'

Baruch shook his head slowly. 'It was just a story on the island. A gossip. But he was English, she said. He went off the cliff up near Oia.'

'Wow,' I said. 'That's amazing.'

'She said . . .' Baruch started. But then he visibly interrupted himself. 'No. That's about all, really.'

'Please,' I insisted. 'You were going to say something else. What were you going to say?'

'I don't know,' Baruch said, looking uncomfortable.

'*Please*,' I said again. 'I've been waiting twenty-three years for this and my mother won't tell me anything.'

Baruch pulled a pained expression and scratched his ear. 'Well, it may not be the same guy, of course.'

'The dates tally.'

The husband appeared from the house at that moment. He glanced at my plate and spoke to Baruch in Greek before returning indoors. I thought he sounded a bit annoyed.

'You need to eat,' Baruch told me. 'He thinks you don't like the food.'

While I wolfed down the rest of my pasta, Baruch told me what he knew, which was basically that my father had apparently been a bit of a lairy bastard. And that it had taken five people to remove him from a local taverna when he had got into a fight. He said no one had been surprised that he had crashed the car. He had been drunk most of the time and all the locals had thought he was trouble. And as he told me all of this, I thought back to Mum's comments on alcoholism, and once again, she suddenly seemed to make a little more sense to me.

But my father's sudden demotion from astronaut to drunken bar brawler had also left me feeling distinctly queasy.

Once the meal was over, Baruch insisted on paying. We walked back around to the front of the house where the bike was parked. It was almost dark and the only light came from a streetlamp whose feeble glow was partially obscured by the thousands of insects it had attracted.

'Do I get a kiss?' Baruch asked, as a bat swooped overhead, presumably to feast on the insects. 'For dinner?'

'Of course,' I said, stepping towards him. But though the kiss felt perfectly nice, the truth was that my mind was elsewhere. I was trying to think how to broach the subject of my father once again with my mother. I was trying, and failing, to come up with any kind of strategy that would not automatically lead to a fight.

Baruch had hooked one arm around me and was forcing his tongue into my mouth, and to my surprise I wasn't particularly keen on the sensation. When he slipped one hand up my T-shirt, my reflexes kicked in. 'Oi!' I said sharply, causing our 'moment' to judder to a halt.

'I'm sorry,' he said, sounding hurt. 'I thought you liked me.'

'I do,' I said. 'I really do.'

'Then what?' Baruch asked, pulling his keys from his pocket and jingling them.

'I don't know . . .' I said, trying to get a grip on what was really going on and deciding quickly that it was better to lie. 'Just not here,' I said, glancing back at the house. 'What if someone comes?'

'There's a room . . .' Baruch said. 'I don't want to be . . . you know . . . but there's a room.'

'A room?'

'In the hotel. There's an empty room. Actually there are a couple tonight. I could try to get the key. We could hang out there if you want? Take some beers from the shop . . . ?'

'Oh,' I said, trying to imagine the scene and feeling annoyed with myself because I was unable to do so. I'd been dreaming of spending the night with Baruch since I had set eyes on him, but now the opportunity presented itself I found myself almost entirely free of desire. All I wanted right now, the only thing I could really even think about, was getting back to my own unit so I could confront my mother with my newfound knowledge. Even if that turned out to be impossible, sitting quietly so I could think about it all seemed more appealing at that instant than a quickie with Baruch.

What a complex thing is desire! At least for me it is. Perhaps it's because we women multitask, so other thoughts can end up taking precedence. In my experience, as far as men are concerned, desire just stamps out every other available thought. I doubt any man in the history of the world ever struggled to concentrate on sex. 'I can't tonight,' I said, having decided once again to lie. 'I need to get back to Mum. Because of the argument.'

'OK,' Baruch said, climbing onto the bike and jumping on the kick-starter with even more vigour than usual.

'I'd really like to,' I shouted above the chugging of the motorbike. 'Just not tonight. I'm sorry.'

'Sure,' he said. 'It's fine.' But I could tell from the lack of eye contact, and I could tell from the speed at which we lurched off, that it wasn't fine at all.

◆ ◆ ◆

It was only eleven when he dropped me back, but Mum was already in bed.

I whisperingly asked her if she was asleep and she replied with a vague snoring sound that I suspected was thoroughly fake.

Once I was ready for bed, I peeped back in and tried again, but again she didn't reply and so, forced to acknowledge that the conversation would have to wait until the morning, I closed the door and sat on my bed.

I thought about Baruch for a moment and wondered what was wrong with me, wondered why my desire had evaporated at the exact moment he'd tried to seduce me. I managed to perform some complex mental operation whereby I regretted not having accepted his offer, even as I reassured myself that it would have been impossible to do so.

It was only when I pulled back the top sheet to climb into bed that I found Mum's note. It was written on the back of a prospectus for boat trips around the island and read, 'I'm sorry I've been such a grumpy so-and-so today. Ask me in the morning and I'll tell you. Love you to bits. Your Mumsy.'

I almost considered phoning Baruch then. Because the one thing I knew for sure was that I wasn't going to be able to sleep. But using him as a distraction, simply because I couldn't sleep, just felt too much like, well, using him, I suppose.

FOURTEEN

Laura

As soon as we had opened the door, Lena had informed us, mop in hand, that she needed us out right *now*, because she had guests arriving at twelve. So within ten minutes we were back at Leif's scooter, wondering what to do next.

'So,' Leif said, still grinning. We didn't seem to be able to stop smiling at each other that morning.

'So . . .' I repeated, taking the crash helmet from his outstretched hand.

'Are you ready to face Conor?' he asked. 'Or do you want to eat something first?'

'Eat,' I said without hesitation. The last twelve hours had been utterly magical and I simply couldn't bear for the moment to end. 'I really do need to change my things though. This T-shirt is getting a bit smelly.'

Leif nodded thoughtfully. 'We could have a picnic on the beach,' he said. 'This way we don't need any clotheses.'

I laughed at *clotheses*. 'Sure,' I said, 'let's do that. We can change our clotheses this evening.' I didn't need much convincing.

We rode to the outskirts of Oia, to the first little shop on the edge of town, but even this felt too close for comfort. I was floating in a bubble of joy and felt pleasantly spacey from lack of sleep. I knew instinctively that Conor, if and when I saw him, would surely pop my bubble.

But our visit to the shop went by without a hiccup and by twelve we were back on our beach. It looked completely different in the daylight, but no less beautiful. And best of all, we were again the only people there.

We ate cheese and bread and the sweetest tomatoes I have ever tasted, then we fooled around in the shallows. Later, we sat in the shade at one end of the beach where the rock face met the sea, and sighed with relief when a couple who had appeared on the path above us turned around and went back the way they had come.

The conversation flowed easily and as I talked about my school years and Abby, and Leif about his studies and life in general in Norway, that same sense of belonging came over me – that feeling of being in the right place at the right time. It somehow enveloped the day.

I had never realised it before, I don't think, but that afternoon I understood that I was a fairly highly strung person, that my default state was one of readiness. I had rarely felt completely comfortable in my skin or at ease with my surroundings. I was always in a state of alert, on the lookout for any kind of menace or danger, and events and people had often proved me right because, I suppose, my judgement simply wasn't that good. I suspect much of this came from my upbringing, which had rarely felt relaxed, or even happy. The fact that my mother had kept me to herself for as long as she could probably hadn't helped either. But it was only possible to realise this from the perspective provided by being in a different state, a place of utter, childlike relaxation. Of being with someone I trusted totally.

We swam together; we collected coloured stones and we explored both ends of the beach. We sat side by side and watched as tiny fish nibbled at our toes and felt, I think, like two innocents exploring the world together.

Two or three times we agreed that we needed to move. There was no doubt that recovering my passport was becoming urgent – that it was time to leave the beach and deal with it all. But each time, it simply didn't happen. 'Let's have one last swim,' one of us would say, and the swim would become a playful tussle, or a cuddle or a kiss, and that would lead to another sandy snooze on the beach.

It was gone six by the time we finally got it together to leave. We packed our wet things in Leif's backpack and, holding hands, crossed 'our' beach for the last time.

The ride back took us past Lena's Rooms and I wondered who was in the room now, and hoped it would be as wonderful for them as it had been for us. A little further on was the balcony taverna we had visited before and as we passed it, Leif slowed down, and pulled up at the roadside. 'We need to talk,' he said, solemnly. 'We need to agree what we say to Conor.'

I nodded. I'd been thinking the same thing but, because any discussion about Conor led to a discussion about everything else, just the thought of it made me feel nauseous. But I knew Leif was right.

The bar, once again, was empty. The same three people were there but this time only the waiter stood to greet us. The cook and the owner seemed far too engrossed in their game of backgammon.

'So, what do we tell him?' Leif asked.

I sipped at my drink. I was struggling to make my brain think about Conor or my passport or any of it. All I wanted to do was to lose myself in Leif's blue eyes. 'I ask him to give me my stuff back,' I said. 'If he's there.'

'If he's there,' Leif repeated. 'When is your flight home?'

The question hit me like a brick. I had been refusing to think about my flight home because the concept of this all ending had become unbearable.

'The fifth,' I told him. 'Which is the day after tomorrow, isn't it?'

Leif nodded. 'So it is quite urgent now. We need to fix this today. If he isn't there, I think we should go to the police.'

'The police?'

'They can maybe take his passport from the hotel. And give it back when we have yours.'

What Leif was saying made sense but getting the police involved shocked me all the same. 'Do you think there are police on Santorini?' I asked. 'I've never ever seen one.'

'Me either,' Leif said.

'Neither,' I corrected him, taking his hand in mine across the tabletop. Even the separation forced upon us by furniture seemed unbearable, let alone a flight home.

'Huh,' Leif laughed. 'I don't think I will ever be OK with this either/neither.'

'It doesn't matter,' I told him. 'Either is fine. Or you can just use neither.'

'And us?' Leif asked, either ignoring or missing my joke. 'Do we tell Conor about us?'

My heart fluttered at his acknowledgement that there was an 'us'. 'No,' I said, squeezing his hand. I did not want our magic to be sullied by Conor's opinion of it. 'No, it's none of his business.'

'No,' Leif said. 'Good.'

'How . . . ?' I started to ask. But I was too terrified at the thought that seeing Leif after we left Greece might turn out to be impossible to finish my question.

'How do we see each other after?' he asked, in tune as ever with my thoughts.

I nodded and bit my lip.

'We write,' Leif said. 'We phone. And we visit, I guess.'

'You think?'

'I don't think,' Leif said. 'I *know*. And I will show you Norway and you will show me England.'

I wondered for a second how I would ever square this with my mother, but pushed the thought away. Anything that complicated my future with Leif – and let's face it, it was all pretty complicated – seemed to hurt my brain that evening. It felt like one of those migraines which hovers over one eye, and the only way I could deal with it was to shut out whatever thought was causing the pain. 'I love it here,' I said, looking out at the sun, now arcing towards the horizon, delicately preparing the sky for this evening's light show.

'I know,' Leif said, taking my hand in both of his. 'I love it too. But we really have to go and do this.'

We walked slowly back to the scooter, pausing to look out at the seascape. The sun was now a huge red ball.

We stood side by side to stare. 'It moves so fast,' I commented. 'You can almost see it moving.'

'Do you think it will make a *pshhh* noise when it hits the sea?' Leif asked.

'It looks like it should,' I said. 'If it does, it's going to cook a lot of fish.'

'Mmm,' Leif said. 'Fish soup.'

We turned to face each other and kissed and by the time that kiss was over, the sun was missing a chunk from its base where it had begun to slip beneath the horizon.

As we approached Oia, a stunning palette of purples and reds streaked horizontally across the sky. One of the most amazing things about Santorini is its constant ability to better itself. Every time you think you have seen the most incredible view you could ever see, a better one is waiting around the corner.

As we reached the edge of town, I pointed out the sunset to Leif. I didn't want him to miss this. 'Have you seen?' I shouted.

'Yes,' he replied. 'It's beautiful.'

As we approached the next crossroads, Leif slowed to a halt. 'It's that way,' I said, pointing, stupidly thinking he was lost.

'I know,' he said. 'I'm just wondering . . . Do you think we have time to go north? I'm thinking I want a photo of this. A photo of you in this day.'

'Go for it,' I said. 'But be quick.' The day was nearly over and it seemed a shame to waste its final, most glorious moment.

Leif revved the scooter and we whizzed off around Oia and onwards towards the north.

When we neared the northernmost tip of the island, he stopped at a junction. To our left was a potholed dirt track. 'I think I'll leave the bike here,' he said. 'The road is too bad.'

I removed my crash helmet and Leif retrieved his camera from the top case and locked my helmet inside. 'Come,' he said. 'We need to walk fast.'

As I reached for his hand, a beach buggy squealed to a halt beside us on the main road. 'So, here you are!' a voice shouted, and I turned sharply to see Mike at the wheel. 'Conor's been looking for you everywhere.'

'Um, hi Mike,' I said, more to explain to Leif who this was than anything else. 'And no, he hasn't been looking for me everywhere. I haven't seen him for *days*.'

'He's been worried about you,' Mike said.

I laughed sourly at this. 'He's got a funny way of showing it.'

'Well, he has,' Mike insisted.

'Was he worried about Candy and Anthea or whatever her name is, too?' I asked.

The muscles around Mike's mouth twitched at this as if he had a sudden pain in his back teeth. 'Well, you look like you've found a way to pass the time, anyway,' he said, nodding in Leif's direction.

'This is Leif,' I told him. 'My friend.'

Leif stepped forward and offered his hand. But Mike just ignored its presence, and glanced down the road instead.

'I need to see him, Mike. He's got my passport. Do you know where he is?'

'Is that right?' Mike asked disinterestedly. 'Got your passport, has he? Well, he was at your hotel the last time I looked.'

'When?'

Mike shrugged. 'An hour ago. Maybe two.'

'If you see him, can you ask him to stay put?' I said. 'Tell him I'm on my way?'

Mike nodded. 'Yeah. I'll tell him I've seen you, all right.'

'Thanks.'

'Anyway, I'd better get my skates on,' Mike said. 'I need to get this buggy back. I've got a night boat to catch and if I miss it again, I won't have a missus at all.'

Once he was gone, we stood in silence for a moment. 'You want to go straight back?' Leif asked after a few seconds.

'No,' I said. 'Let's take the photo and then go back.' The fact that I knew Conor was at the hotel had suddenly made me afraid. It had made me even more reluctant to return there. Plus, not being able to leave Leif's side, because I didn't have my passport, had started to feel like a positive rather than a negative.

The track passed by two unfinished houses. The ground floors were entirely built, but without windows or doors. Steel spikes stuck up from the rooftops and Leif explained that these were so a second floor could be built at some point in the future. 'They don't pay the tax until it's finished,' he told me, 'so there's always another floor coming soon.'

The cliff edge was further than it had at first appeared, and we soon began to regret that we had walked, especially because, once the two buildings-in-progress had been passed, the gravel track improved significantly.

We walked in silence, our heads craned left so we could look at the incredible sky. 'Shall I go back and get the bike?' Leif offered. 'I think by the time we get there . . .'

'No, it's fine,' I said, squeezing his hand. 'It's nice.'

In fact it was far more than nice, but I was too scared to voice what I was feeling in case it spoilt the perfect equilibrium of the moment. Because what I was feeling, for the first time in my life, was pure, unadulterated hope. I felt submerged by the stuff.

My life up to that point had been pretty rotten, I suppose. These days, my mother would probably be diagnosed with some kind of mental illness – perhaps even treated for it – but her moods and ever-changing rules, her unpredictable explosions of anger, weren't something I had ever consciously labelled as abnormal, back then. I considered my upbringing as harsh, perhaps, but not really abusive. Being all I had ever known, it just seemed normal to me. But within that framework, my prospects for happiness had always felt few and far between. And until twenty-four hours earlier, I had found it pretty much impossible to picture any kind of escape for myself, to imagine any kind of desirable future.

Yet here I was, walking hand in hand with the loveliest man on Earth – a beautiful, gentle, sexy, protective man who, for no reason that I could fathom, also seemed to like little old me.

There was so much to look forward to suddenly, so much to hope for, that I wanted to scream out loud about it. I wanted to jump for joy. But I restrained myself. I simply gave his hand a squeeze and blinked back tears.

After another hundred yards or so, Leif said, 'Do you really have to go home on the fifth?' He sounded as if he was trying to sound relaxed about the prospect, but there was an urgency in his voice which gave him away.

'I think I do,' I said.

'You think?'

'I have stuff to get back to.'

'Your job?'

'Well, I don't go back to work till the ninth,' I admitted. 'But my flights and everything . . . I don't know how to change them. Or how much it would cost.'

'I could help you with that, maybe,' Leif said.

'And you?' I asked. 'When's your flight?'

'It's a boat,' Leif informed me. 'It's tomorrow.'

'Tomorrow!' I exclaimed, horrified at this revelation. 'What time?'

'In the morning,' Leif said. 'At ten. But I don't think I want to take this boat.'

'You don't?'

'No. I think I want to stay longer here.'

'Really?'

'I'm in love with you,' Leif said. 'So, yes. Really.'

I stopped walking, and took his hands in mine. I looked up at him in the dusky light and thought, for an instant, that I was going to weep. Because no one had ever said that to me before. Or at any rate, not that I could believe.

'So if I stayed . . .' Leif went on. 'Could you?'

'I don't know,' I said as, resisting the desire to skip, I started again to walk. 'I suppose I could, for a bit. If it's possible to change my flights.'

'For a bit?' Leif repeated.

'For a while.'

'Is a while more than a bit?' Leif asked.

'Yes,' I told him. 'Yes, I suppose it is.'

'Then that's good,' he said, turning to glance at me and grinning broadly.

He checked his watch and asked if this was all taking too long, if I wanted to turn around.

'No, I'm scared,' I admitted. 'I'm scared to go back. I'm scared of Conor. I'm scared of ending this moment. So anything that means we don't have to go back is good.'

'Well, you mustn't be scared of Conor,' Leif said. 'I will never let him hurt you, OK? I will never let anyone hurt you again.'

'Thank you,' I said. But I wondered, despite myself, if skinny Leif, as valiant as he might be, would really be a match for Conor's bull-like strength.

'Wow,' Leif said. We had reached the end of the path, where the gravel track faded into the scrappy undergrowth. Quite where the road had once led, Lord only knows, because wherever it had gone was now beneath the sea. The cliff edge had crumbled to meet the track.

Holding hands for safety, we moved to the very edge and looked down at the sea washing around the rocks below, before retreating a safe distance so Leif could take his photos. He took two or three of me with the sunset to my right and then I took a couple of him. Finally, we perched the camera on a rock and set the timer to take a funny selfie, and I remember wondering if that would be the photo we'd have on the mantelpiece, the photo that would slowly fade as we grew old together. It was the happiest thought I had ever had and yet it seemed, in that moment, as if it was actually possible. Everything seemed transformed.

The sun had all but vanished now, only the tip of it was still peeping over the horizon, but the sky was completely mad. It looked as if someone had pinned a colour chart up there, then hosed it down with solvent so the colours all merged together. Almost every conceivable colour seemed to be present, streaked horizontally across the skyline with each extremity fading into the indigo blue of the night sky.

'It reminds me of the fjords back home,' Leif commented, raising one hand and moving it like a wave to indicate the ins and outs of the coastline.

'It's beautiful,' I said. 'I love the coast when it's like this.'

'Then we will live overlooking a fjord,' Leif said. 'Maybe you would like a little house on the water's edge.'

I told him that I didn't know exactly what the word 'fjord' meant, and so he explained that the fjords were where the sea cut deeply, sometimes for hundreds of kilometres, into the crinkled Norwegian coastline. This created, he said, vast, open-ended saltwater lakes.

My heart was fluttering at the *we will live* of his phrasing, but it was almost too much for me, it was almost too much hope for me to bear, so, to make light of it, I replied with irony.

'Hmm, not sure about that,' I said. 'You told me it was cold. You said it rains all the time. I'm a bit of a sun lizard, me. I'm not sure that your fjords are going to do the trick.'

'Then we will live anywhere you want,' Leif said. He bumped his hip against mine, and I let myself fall into him, so that my head was resting on his chest. His arm came up to pull me in even more tightly.

'I want to stay here forever,' I told him as he rocked me gently in his arms.

'Then we will live right here,' Leif laughed. 'We will live looking over the fjords of Santorini.'

And though I knew it was impossible, though I knew it was only make-believe, I pointed to a house in the distance. 'There. I want to live *there*.'

'Then this is where we will live.'

'Right,' I said, trying to snap myself back to reality. 'It's getting dark.'

'Yes,' Leif said sadly.

'So we need to go.'

Once we had turned to leave, I glanced regretfully over my shoulder, but the sun was long gone and the colours were already fading. I was overcome by a sense of melancholy, and I thought with great sadness about the fact that I would never be able to relive that day again.

A flash of light caught my eye, shining across the scrubby landscape, and as I turned my head back to look, Leif squeezed my hand. I have no idea how, or why, but we both sensed that the car coming towards us down the gravel track was significant.

It was almost dark by this time, with only the remaining glow of the sunset to light the landscape, and as the car hurtled down the bumpy road, the headlights swept back and forth like a searchlight.

The resulting ambiance, perhaps because of all the connotations that searchlights have – none of them good – felt sinister.

'Mike?' I suggested.

'It's a car, not a buggy,' Leif said. We could hear the engine, revving as the car accelerated out of each bend.

'Joyriders, perhaps?' I offered.

'I don't know,' Leif replied, solemnly. 'But I am not thinking that I like this so much.'

'They're going really fast . . .' I commented. The car had already passed the unfinished houses and we could hear the sound of the tyres spitting gravel. 'Should we hide?' I asked, glancing around the barren landscape. The closest tree was thirty or forty yards away and even that was too weedy to hide behind.

'No,' Leif said. 'I don't think so. But I'm worried the car will . . .'

'Drive off the edge?' I exclaimed at the same time as Leif said, 'Drive into the sea.'

It was less than a hundred yards away and wasn't showing any sign of stopping, so I ran to the middle of the track and began to wave my arms. A second later, Leif joined me, hopping from side to side as he tried to position himself in the beam of the headlights.

The car was still coming at us. The driver had shown no sign of seeing either us or the cliff edge, so we started to shout, 'Stop! Stop! *Stop!*'

Finally, the driver noticed us. The car zigzagged wildly, then the wheels locked as it slid the final twenty yards.

Leif jerked me back out of the way and I clamped my hand to my mouth and watched in terror as the car slid towards the edge.

You know the way people always say that events take place in slow motion? Well, it's true. That is exactly how it seemed. I held my breath and watched as the car slithered towards the edge, and as it continued to slide I squinted, barely able to watch what was happening.

As it passed us – not that fast by then – I recognised it as Conor's hire car, and the driver as Conor himself.

The car stopped quite literally at the cliff edge. It was the final tuft of brush and bare rock that stopped it, I think – that enabled the wheels to grip. And despite everything I felt about Conor, I ran, gasping in relief, to the driver's door.

'Conor!' I said simply, as he clambered out of the car. I saw instantly that he was drunk.

'Jaysus!' Conor exclaimed, rubbing at his nose and sniffing as he looked out at the void in front of the car, before turning his gaze on me. 'What the *feck* are you doing out here?'

Leif, who had moved protectively to my side, said, 'You nearly went into the sea. We are scared you will not stop in time.'

'And who the fuck are you?' Conor asked, rolling his shoulders as he squared up to Leif. 'Are you the little friend that Mikey told me about?'

'I am Leif,' he said, offering his hand.

In a shocking gesture, Conor slapped Leif's hand away then glanced back at the car as if he had forgotten something there.

I followed his gaze – I think we both did – and saw the dirty interior of the car. It was littered with crisp packets and sandwich wrappers and there were empty beer cans everywhere. The inside light glowed warmly.

And then Conor punched him. Neither of us saw the punch coming, neither of us even imagined this was what Conor was going to do next, so incongruous was the gesture after having glanced back at the car. But that is what happened. He twisted his torso to look back at the car and as he straightened again he threw a punch. It landed squarely on Leif's cheek, sending him flying backwards onto the ground.

'Conor!' I gasped, but he had grabbed my hand and was dragging me around to the passenger door. 'You're coming with me,' he said menacingly. 'You little slut.'

'But—! *Conor!*' I protested, struggling to break free of his grip whilst trying to look back to see if Leif was OK – he was still struggling to clamber to his feet. 'What . . . are . . . you . . . doing?' I gasped as he manhandled me around the rear of the car. 'CONOR! Let . . . me . . . go . . . !' I shouted, as he fiddled with the door handle. In frustration, I slapped him across the side of the face, but it didn't even seem to register. It made about as much impact as a fly bumping into an elephant. I jumped and managed to kick the car door, which he was in the process of opening, so that it closed again, and in response, he jerked my arm, the way a parent jerks the arm of child who won't behave while crossing a road, only he did it so forcefully that I thought for an instant he had pulled my shoulder from its socket. I lost my footing and Conor pulled me upright once again, managing simultaneously to open the door. Desperate now, I landed a kick to his shin. I was briefly proud at the results of this, because he actually paused for a second, groaning and half doubling up. His mouth formed a snarl as he straightened. 'You fecking *hoor*!' he said quietly, relinquishing the door handle so he could take hold of my hair with his left hand. Just as he slapped me across the cheek, Leif reappeared behind him.

'Leave her alone,' he said, his Scandinavian accent making the order sound like a question.

Unexpectedly, Conor froze. He looked me straight in the eyes. His nostrils flared as he inhaled sharply, smiling sourly, before turning to Leif. 'Who. The *fuck*. Are you?' he asked.

'I am Leif,' he said again, sounding absolutely, totally, unreasonably reasonable. 'I am in love with Laura. She doesn't want you any more. So you can go home now. This is all over.'

Conor cracked up at this – he genuinely found it funny and his laughter was chilling. 'Oh, you're in love, are you?' he asked mockingly. 'You're in love with . . . with *this* . . .' He raised my wrist, as if to display the object they were discussing. 'Well, that's a *completely* different story, isn't it?'

Leif nodded. 'No one wants to fight here, Conor,' he said. 'We can talk about this like adults, yes?' He was stepping towards Conor now, looking strangely fearless, apparently convinced that thousands of years of human civilisation would obviously overcome this silly misunderstanding. He raised his palms like a negotiator approaching a gunman. 'So we are staying calm, OK?' he said.

'You know what?' Conor said. 'I would *love* to have a blather with you about this.' He pushed me sideways so hard that I fell to the ground.

'Just go, Conor,' I said, as I scrambled to get back up. 'Please. Just go.'

Once again, Conor's response was laughter.

'So, Leif, is it?' he asked, taking a step forward so he was face to face with him. 'What kind of a fecking name is that, anyway?' he asked, sounding vaguely conversational, jovial almost.

Leif shrugged. 'It is my name.'

Conor glanced back at me and smiled broadly enough that I caught a glimpse of his teeth shining in the moonlight. Then, using the same trick he'd used for that initial punch, as he turned back to face Leif he followed through with a sudden jerk of the head so that he nutted him squarely on the nose, sending him spiralling back. 'Is this true?' he asked, stepping forward so he was straddling Leif, who was now on the ground and clasping his nose, trying to stem the tide of blood. He bent over and gripped Leif by the collar of his T-shirt. He looked back at me again. 'Is this *true*?' he shouted.

'Is what true?' I asked feebly, struggling to speak through tears.

'That you two are an item now? With this eejit?'

'No,' I said, hoping this might save Leif. But Conor punched him on the side of the face anyway.

'Yes,' Leif said bravely, perhaps stupidly. 'Yes, it's true.'

Conor grimaced as if Leif's words hurt his jaw. 'What makes you think I'm talking to you?' he asked. He punched him again, sending Leif's head lolling sideways.

He looked at me and asked, with chilling calm. 'So, I ask you again. Is this true?'

'Yes,' I said, trying the opposite answer to last time, 'Yes, I love him. Please, leave him alone and just go before we call the police or something.'

'The police?' Conor asked, grimacing horribly. He glanced around the horizon as if to emphasise our complete lack of backup here, making a popping noise through his lips. 'The police,' he repeated. 'Of course. Be my guest.'

He turned back to face Leif and, as he raised his arm, I ran at him. I threw my arms around his neck and hung there, but it didn't even slow him down. He punched Leif again, only this time I felt the blow, transmitted through Conor's body to my own.

I tried kicking his legs, tried to repeat the success of my shin kick, but Conor continued as if I wasn't even there, or more precisely as if it was actually all quite fun, like some daddy character at a birthday party playing the giant while kids all hang from his neck.

Finding the process of punching Leif on the ground unsatisfactory, he yanked him to his feet, but as he pulled back to punch him again, I grabbed his arm instead and hung on it, yanking him off balance.

He stumbled, releasing Leif, before finding his footing and knocking me flying with a backhander.

I lost consciousness for a moment, I think. I had bashed the back of my head on the ground and when I looked up, Conor had hoisted Leif up by his collar again and was turning him, the better to see his face in the moonlight.

The sight of Leif was horrific and angry tears started to flow. Because Leif's features were a mess. Blood was flowing from his nose and he had a split cheek.

'I'm not afraid of you,' Leif said and, as he spoke, I saw that his teeth were bloodied, too.

To my surprise, Leif landed a punch on Conor's eye, but though he was a good ten inches taller than him, his punch was about as ineffectual as my own slaps had been. There was something beast-like about

Conor-on-the-rampage. It really did feel like you were trying to wrestle a rhinoceros.

'Leave him!' I said pleadingly. 'I'll come with you, Conor. I'm sorry. Whatever. Just . . . *stop*.'

But it was as if he was following a set process, as if he was on some kind of deadly autopilot. Because he simply jerked Leif upright as if he was as light as a rag doll, and landed another carefully calculated punch.

I was crying freely, sobbing really, and it was making me even more useless than usual. As Conor continued to land regular, well-spaced punches to Leif's stomach and face, I stumbled around looking for a weapon I could hit him with, glancing back up as each punch hit its mark.

'Conor . . . *please* . . .' I wept. 'Please. You're going to kill him if you carry on.'

Leif slipped from Conor's grasp at that point and slumped heavily to the ground. Conor stood over him and rolled his head to stretch his neck. And I thought for a minute that it was over. I thought that having seen Leif on the ground, he was satisfied. *Just stay there*, I thought. *Don't get up*.

But Leif had rolled to his side and gone up on all fours. He was starting to crawl away. And that's when Conor began kicking him, taking a few strides back and launching the toe of his shoe at Leif's stomach, or buttocks, or back, with all the precision and energy of a penalty kick.

I ran to them and began to ineffectually beat my fists against Conor's back. 'Stop,' I begged him. 'Please . . . please . . . *stop!*' And once again, Conor pushed me aside so hard that I stumbled and landed against the car.

Leif was on all fours, still desperately trying to escape, but Conor ran at him and kicked him to the side again.

Leif rolled into a ball. 'OK,' he said through tears. 'It's OK. You have win.'

This made Conor laugh some more. 'I have win, have I?' he asked, his mouth twisted in scorn.

Leif, who had raised his arms to protect his head, nodded feebly. 'You have win,' he said again. 'It's over.'

Conor snorted. 'I've barely got started, fella,' he said. Then, reaching between Leif's arms to grip his T-shirt, he pulled him to his feet all over again.

'You're going to kill him, Conor,' I cried.

'That,' Conor said, smiling at me, 'is the general idea.'

In that moment, I realised it was true. They had just been words up until then, but in that instant I understood that Conor really *was* going to kill Leif. Right here. Right now. Right before my eyes. And neither fighting, nor pleading, nor letting him win was going to change it. If I didn't do something, Leif would be gone. The only man I had ever truly been in love with would quite simply no longer exist.

A jolt of adrenalin flowed through me and my tears ceased. My brain seemed to shift into an unfamiliar mode of ultra-precise, triple-speed clarity, scanning the landscape once again for any kind of weapon and tugging my attention towards the car.

To the rhythm of Conor's metronomic punches, I quickly checked the interior, but there was nothing there I could use. I thought of driving at him but he had taken the keys. I tremblingly tried to check the boot, hoping to find a wheel brace or a jack, but it was locked.

I stood and looked analytically at the scene. I didn't have strength on my side. I didn't have a weapon, either. But I could, if I was clever, have the advantage of momentum and speed, and surprise.

FIFTEEN

Becky

Against all odds, Mum's promises of revelations did not stop me sleeping. I had distressing dreams involving Baruch and a smattering of car and motorbike accidents, but I slept deeply and far later than I had for days.

It was nine thirty when I finally stepped outside, and the day was already hot. There wasn't a hint of breeze.

I stood and, as every morning, stared out at the shocking blue of the horizon. I doubted that the view from Oia was one you could ever get tired of, or even used to. I honestly reckon that you could live there your whole life and still think *Wow!* every morning.

I pondered this for a while in that sleepy way you think about things when you've just got up and, deciding to ask Baruch about it later, I locked up the room and headed for the hotel restaurant.

Mum was seated at the back of the room sipping tea and reading a copy of the *Mirror*.

'Morning!' I said, on arriving at the table.

She looked startled at first, then smiled and folded the newspaper and laid her hands across it in an elegant, placid gesture. 'Morning,' she said. 'It's a beautiful day, isn't it? The first of September!'

'It is,' I said, reminding myself that I still needed to wrap the gift I had brought from home. 'Anything happening in the world?'

Mum looked puzzled for a second and glanced down at the newspaper. 'Oh,' she said. 'In the paper? I'm not sure. It's three days old, so . . . I found it on the table, that's all. Did you sleep OK?'

I told her that I had and headed off for a tour of the buffet, returning with toast, grilled tomatoes, and a slightly rubbery fried egg. In the meantime the waitress had filled my cup with coffee.

I ate in silence for a while and when that started to feel too uncomfortable, I began to speak. 'I found—'

At that precise moment, Mum spoke too. 'Did you find my note?' she asked.

'Yes. Yes, I did.'

'I *am* sorry,' Mum said, looking genuinely contrite. 'I . . . I don't know . . . It's such a difficult subject. For you. For me. For everyone, really. But I should be better at it by now. So I am sorry for yesterday.'

I nodded and smiled weakly at her as I continued to eat, expecting her to continue and say whatever she was going to tell me. Instead, she asked, 'Did you have a nice time last night? With Baruch?'

I nodded and, once I had swallowed, replied, 'Yes. It was lovely. He took me to a special restaurant only Greek people go to. The food was amazing and it was only ten euros a head.'

'Ten euros?' Mum said. 'Wow! Perhaps we should go there tonight?'

I shook my head. 'Like I said, it's for Greek people only, I'm afraid. I was OK because I was with him, but otherwise, I don't think I would even have got in.'

Mum pulled a face. 'That seems a bit unfair.'

'I think what's unfair is that the Greeks don't earn enough to eat in any of the normal restaurants.'

'Right,' Mum said. 'Yes, of course. Yes, I can see that. So you had a nice evening, anyway. That's good.'

'Yes, it was fine,' I told her. I didn't really want to talk about my evening with Baruch. I wanted her to cut to the chase. 'You said you had something to tell me,' I prompted. 'In your note?'

Mum nodded and blinked rapidly a few times. She cleared her throat and glanced around the room as if to check if anyone was listening, prompting me to follow suit. But we didn't seem to have caught anyone's interest.

She cleared her throat a second time. She chewed her bottom lip. 'I'm not sure where to start,' she finally said. 'I'm not really sure what you want to know.'

I shrugged and sighed deeply. I sipped at my coffee, trying to find the right words. 'I don't know, really . . .' I said. 'Just—'

'He was Norwegian,' Mum blurted out, speaking quickly as if the words were a train that could be missed if she didn't get there in time. 'That's what you wanted to know, wasn't it? His nationality? Well, he was Norwegian. He was tall and skinny and blond, like you. He was incredibly gentle and kind. And he was Norwegian.'

I put down my cutlery so that I could fiddle with my fingernails. I stared deeply into Mum's eyes while I tried to work out how I could possibly fit the two narratives – Mum's and Baruch's – together. Mum held my regard unblinkingly. Her eyes looked a little shiny and I wondered if she was going to cry.

Almost immediately I realised the stories couldn't be merged. Mum's gentle, blond Norwegian was not Baruch's English drunken thug and that was all there was to it. And when I tried to work out which of the two had the most reason to lie, I could only come up with one answer.

'Is that better?' Mum asked concernedly. 'I mean, does that help?' She seemed genuine enough, but then she had always been a pretty good actress.

My breath was quickening and I realised that I was starting to feel angry. I regretted having this conversation in such a public place because I was starting to feel *really* angry.

I was angry for all of the times she had shut down my attempts to discuss this in the past. Because it had never been easy for me to ask about my father. It had always taken days of trying to formulate a suitable question and then a couple more to pluck up the courage to ask it. And Mum had always closed the subject down with a short, sharp, often mean retort.

I felt angry for the wedge that I now realised she had driven between us, too. Because though I loved her, and though for much of my life she had represented pretty much my whole world, I understood that morning how, just like with Brian, she had always held something back from me.

Out of nowhere came a third wave of anger, an anger I had suppressed so effectively that I had barely been aware it existed. But I let myself feel it in that moment, and found I was quite furious that I didn't have a father – spitting mad that I was the only person amongst my school friends *not* to have had one. And for all my games, for all my fictitious astronaut or fireman fathers, I was incandescently angry about that, too.

Norwegian, I thought suddenly, remembering that my fake father had briefly been the president of Norway. Was that where Mum's lie had sprung from? Had she simply tried to think of a country and, remembering my fake president father, plumped for the first place to come to mind? It was shocking enough for her to still be lying to me. But to choose such a cheap, facile lie felt humiliating.

'Becky?' Mum prompted, wrinkling her brow and leaning in to attempt to take my hand. I snatched it out of her reach and only then realised that I was crying.

I wasn't sobbing. I wasn't even snivelling. I felt cold as ice as I sat there staring at my mother and hating her, really *hating* her, for the first time in my life. But I was, silently, against my will, crying.

I pulled a napkin from the dispenser on the table and dabbed at my cheeks, but the tears kept coming – there was nothing I could do to stop them. I felt like something had been definitively broken, as if something had snapped deep inside me.

'What's wrong, sweetheart?' Mum asked.

'I'm just tired of it,' I said quietly. 'I'm just so *tired* of it all.'

Mum looked confused, so I expounded. 'I'm exhausted by your lies. By all the pretence. By the constant . . . I don't know . . . the constant *obfuscation*, I suppose, is the word.'

'But I—' Mum said.

'I used to think you were protecting me,' I interrupted.

'I was. In a way, I am.'

'Only, you're not. You're protecting *you*, aren't you? And that's not fair, Mum.'

'But you wanted to know and—'

'It's not fair, Mum,' I said again. 'I'm twenty-three. I'm *twenty-three years old* and I'm the only person I know without a dad. And you can't even find it in you to tell me honestly who he *was*?'

My voice had risen at the end of my sentence, so we both glanced around the room once again, but no one, it seemed, had noticed.

'Maybe we should continue this conversation downstairs?' Mum offered, nodding towards the exterior.

'Carry on *what* conversation?' I asked mockingly. 'This isn't a conversation, Mum. It's just today's bullshit. It's just the latest batch of utter rubbish you've decided to chuck at me.'

Mum covered her mouth with one hand. She looked into my eyes for a moment and dabbed her little finger at a single tear, which had formed in the corner of her left eye. 'I don't know what you want from me,' she finally said.

I laughed sourly. 'Only you do,' I told her. 'You know perfectly well what I want. But you're just not prepared to give it.'

'But I told you,' Mum insisted. 'I know I've . . . Look, I know I've avoided it in the past. And maybe that was wrong. I mean, it's complicated, as a parent. Your child's too young to understand, and then too young to need to know. And then suddenly you're not too young any more, but it feels like it's already too late. There's never a right time for this sort of thing, but I have just told you.'

'*Norwegian?*' I said with disdain.

'Yes,' Mum said, nodding sincerely.

'Was he . . . I don't know . . . was he the president by any chance?'

Mum frowned. 'I'm sorry?'

'Was he the president? The president of Norway, maybe?'

'No!' Mum said. 'No, of course he wasn't. Now you're just being silly. He was a student. And his name was Leif.'

I gasped at this. My mouth actually fell open. I thought, *God, I don't know you at all.*

'What?' Mum asked, seemingly exasperated.

I pushed back my chair and began to stand but she leaned over the table and gently grabbed my wrist, and I don't know why – the contact with her skin, or just years of trained obedience – but I sat back down, albeit with my arms angrily crossed.

'What's wrong?' Mum asked. 'Talk to me.'

'I can't believe you,' I said. 'I can't believe you just did that.'

'Did what?'

'Invented a name for him. I mean, it's only taken you twenty-three years to come up with it. Is Leif even a Norwegian name? Do you actually know?'

'Of course it is,' Mum said. 'I'm not making anything up, sweetheart. He was Norwegian. Nothing to do with your make-believe president, but he was Norwegian. And his name was Leif. I'm not lying to you.'

'No,' I said. 'Because lying to your own daughter would be *so* shocking, wouldn't it?'

'It's the truth.'

'English, Mum!' I spat. 'He was *English*!'

Mum frowned and silently mouthed the word 'What?'

'He was English,' I said again, feeling proud and righteous and strangely pleased with myself. 'And he wasn't *gentle.* He was a drunk who got into bar brawls. Baruch's bloody grandmother remembers him only too well. She remembers it taking five men to pin him down and she remembers him driving off the cliff here in Oia. She even remembers the date, for God's sake, give or take a week. So you're lying. You're *still* lying to me after all these years.'

I looked her straight in the eye until she turned away. She sighed jaggedly and covered her eyes with one hand. She worked her mouth silently, and I thought, *Fuck you. This is enough! Twenty-three years of this bullshit is enough.*

I started again to stand, only this time I felt peculiarly calm. It felt like my relationship with my mother was ending, and I wanted to savour the moment, the way you savour pushing your tongue into a bad tooth. I wanted to feel the pain of it. I wanted to twist the knife, even if the knife was in me.

I leaned forward, grasping the table with both hands, and waited for her to look at me. I was going to tell her that I hated her. I was going to tell her that our cutesy little relationship, a relationship based on her lying and me pretending not to notice, was over. But I wanted her to look at me first.

When finally she slid her hand from her eyes to her mouth and turned to look at me, she spoke. 'That was Conor,' she said, speaking through her fingers.

The words made no sense to me so, still glaring at her, I simply shook my head a little.

'That was Conor,' Mum said, lowering her hand and speaking more loudly. 'And he wasn't English at all. He was Irish.'

'Great!' I said. Then, 'Who the fuck is Conor?'

'Conor?' Mum said.

But suddenly it was all too much for me – my emotions overflowed. I spun, almost knocking my chair over, and stormed out of the restaurant. Mum came running after me, trotting down the stairs.

'Go away!' I told her when we reached the unit. 'I'm just getting some stuff then I'll be gone for the day. But in the meantime, please, just leave me the fuck alone.'

Once I'd opened the door and headed inside, Mum, of course, followed. 'Look, I lied to you,' she said from my bedroom doorway. 'It's true.'

'I know you did!' I said, raising my voice now we were in privacy. 'I worked that much out for myself!'

'Becky, please sit down,' Mum said. 'What are you even looking for in there?'

I was rifling through my suitcase and in truth I'd forgotten what I was looking for. It had become nothing more than a way to avoid dealing with my mother.

'Becky,' she said, sitting on my bed and trying to touch my arm. 'Becky!'

'What?' I snapped, dropping the clothes I had in my hands and spinning around to face her. 'Would you like me to sit down, Mother, so you can tell me another fairy story? Is that what's on your agenda for today?'

'There *was* another man,' Mum said. 'His name was Conor. He was an Irish boxer. Not English. Irish. But he wasn't your father.'

'Because my father was a Norwegian called Leif?' I said sarcastically.

'Yes,' Mum said. 'That's what I'm trying to tell you. And it's the truth.'

I froze for a second as an internal battle raged, a battle between wanting to know more and wanting to hear nothing more from her hated, lying lips. It was the second option that won out, though. 'Can you please just leave me alone?' I said. 'I'm an adult and this is my room, and I'm asking you to leave. So just *leave*, will you?'

Mum chewed her bottom lip for a moment and then, shaking her head, she stood and left the room, gently pulling the door closed behind her.

I lay on my bed for almost an hour. I stared at the ceiling, at first too angry to think straight. Later, as I calmed down, I began to analyse, or at least try to analyse, what little information I had gleaned. But if she had been telling the truth, what she had told me created far more questions than it provided answers. Was Conor the same person as Baruch's drunken Englishman? Who had driven off the cliff? How did my mother know Conor, or Leif for that matter? And if my father was Leif, not Conor, how come he was dead as well? Could they have been in the car together?

I still wasn't sure I believed any of it, but I was regretting not having been calmer. I was regretting not having let her tell me more.

I was lying there trying to formulate a face-saving way to continue, something that didn't involve me apologising, when Mum rapped gently on the door.

'Becky?' she called out. 'Can I come in?'

My pride wouldn't let me answer, so I just waited for her to open the door as I knew, from experience, she would.

After a few seconds, the door creaked open and Mum's face appeared. She had panda eyes and I could see that she too had been crying. 'Are you sleeping?' she asked.

'Hardly!' I said.

'Then can I talk to you?'

I didn't say she could, but I didn't say 'no' either. And so she crept into the room and sat on the edge of the bed with one leg on the ground so that she could face me. 'You're right to be angry,' she said softly.

'I know I am.'

'I lied to you.'

'I know that too,' I said. On hearing my own voice, I suddenly felt ashamed. There's nothing like an argument with your mother to reduce you to the status of a sulking five-year-old, but at least at twenty-three I had begun to catch myself doing it.

'So, do you want me to tell you or not?' Mum asked.

I shrugged and tried to think up some word of encouragement I could use which wouldn't sound like I'd forgiven her completely.

'All right,' Mum said, starting to stand again. 'Maybe later on then.'

'I do,' I told her, reaching out for her arm to stop her leaving. 'But only if it's the truth, Mum. I don't think I can stand any more lies. I don't think our relationship can, either.'

'The truth,' Mum repeated, sitting down again. 'Of course.'

She fidgeted for a moment on the bed, then licked her lips and began to speak.

'So, I didn't go away with Aunt Abby. I told you that I went with her, but it's not true. I came away with Conor. I'm not proud of the fact, which is why I suppose . . . But I came away with Conor. I'd met him a few weeks earlier, and stupidly thought I was in love with him. Of course, I wasn't at all. I'd been infatuated, I suppose you'd call it. He could be quite charming when he wanted to be. And I had no idea what being in love was supposed to feel like. But anyway, once we got here I realised that he wasn't very nice. In fact he turned out to be bloody awful.'

'You're telling me you came to Greece with a guy you barely knew?' I asked.

Mum nodded. 'I was stupid. And immature. And inexperienced. And desperate to get away from your grandmother for a bit. And he seemed nice at first. He was generous – he paid for the whole trip – and I'd always wanted to come here. And I liked the idea of him, the idea of having a proper boyfriend, so I convinced myself, I suppose. I don't know, really. I can't explain it. Sometimes we do things that aren't logical. Sometimes we get things wrong. But I misjudged him.'

'OK . . .' I said slowly.

'He drank a lot,' Mum continued. 'He was an alcoholic, I think. It was the first time I'd ever met anyone with a really serious drink problem. And he got really nasty when he drank. He forced himself on me one time. He hit me a couple of times, too.'

I sat up in bed at this point and propped myself against the headboard, pulling my knees to my chest. 'He hit you?' I said. 'But that's awful.'

Mum nodded sadly. 'I know. It *was* awful. Anyway, one night he hit me in the face. We were in a taverna and I fell over. He wasn't sober. He was blind drunk, so . . . I mean, that's not an excuse of course. I don't know why I even . . . But anyway, he hit me and I fell over. I cut my elbow and I had a bruise on my cheek. And this Norwegian guy sort of . . . well . . . he saved me, really. He was so lovely, Becky. So kind and gentle. Everything Conor wasn't.'

'So you ended up sleeping with him too?'

Mum pulled a pained expression.

'I'm sorry, I didn't mean anything,' I said. 'It's just—'

'It just sounds a bit brutal, put like that,' Mum said. 'It happened quite slowly. He just . . . well, he looked after me really. Conor had taken my passport and my money, and Leif helped me get it back. And he gave me the loveliest birthday ever. I was having the most horrible time of it but Leif made everything OK.'

'And this Leif was my father?'

Mum nodded. 'You were conceived on my birthday. Well, the morning after.'

'But how do you know? I mean, are you sure? How do you know it wasn't this Conor guy?'

Mum shrugged. 'I didn't know. Not at first. But when you were born you looked so much like Leif. Blond and blue eyes. Those long limbs of yours. Conor was more of a . . . well, a bulldog shape, really. He was short and stocky and a redhead. Whereas Leif was like a gazelle, if you see what I mean. So as soon as I saw you, I never had any doubt.'

'And this Conor?' I said. 'Where did he come from? I mean, how did you meet him?'

'At a party,' Mum said matter-of-factly. 'At a big outdoor party in Northampton. I went with your Auntie Abby. She was dating a guy who knew the DJ back then and they dragged me along. And I met Conor there. I was drunk. And other stuff too. My judgement wasn't that good, I don't think.'

'You were *stoned*?' I asked, now wide-eyed. 'Is that what you're saying? You were stoned?'

'Not as such,' Mum said.

'Not as such?' I repeated.

'Look . . .' Mum sighed and rolled her eyes. 'OK, whatever. Your Aunt Abby made me take this pill, OK? Because I wasn't enjoying the music.'

I cupped one hand over my mouth and looked at my mother in amazement. 'Is this a *rave* party we're talking about?'

Mum nodded almost imperceptibly.

'And the pill . . . Are we talking ecstasy?'

Another nod. Mum looked as if her teeth were hurting.

I shook my head in disbelief. For this was by far the most outrageous story my mother had ever told me, and yet because of that outrageousness it felt as if it might be the most real, too. Despite myself I was finding it hard to not believe her.

'My mother took an E at a rave? And met a drunk called Conor? And came away with him to *Greece*?' I said, slowly summing up.

Mum nodded again.

'And this Leif guy saved you.'

'Yes, that's pretty much it.'

'So you slept with him?'

'No, I didn't sleep with him because . . . I slept with him because I'd fallen in love. Because he was gorgeous, inside and out. Because he was the best thing that had ever happened to me. Because he was the *only* good thing that had ever happened to me.'

'OK,' I said. 'I'm sorry. I didn't mean anything.'

'It's fine,' Mum said. 'I know how it sounds. That's why . . .'

'But who went over the cliff? Was it Leif? Or Conor? Or both of them?'

Mum looked away, towards the door. I waited a moment before prompting her. 'Mum?'

When she turned back to face me, I saw that she was crying. Her shoulders were shuddering as if she had hiccups.

'Mum,' I said softly, sliding to her side and putting one arm around her shoulders. 'I know this is all very . . . in fact, I can't even imagine how awful this must all have been. But I need to know what happened to these people. Who went over the cliff?'

'Conor,' she breathed, through her tears. '*Conor* went over the cliff.'

This revelation produced a fresh flurry of tears, which forced us to take a break and, to be honest, I didn't mind. I was feeling emotional and trembly, faint almost, at the thought of what was to come. I was happy to have a few minutes to calm myself.

But once Mum had removed her blurry make-up and made us each a cup of tea, we moved outside to the deckchairs to continue our conversation.

'I can't remember where I was up to,' Mum said, sipping her tea and glancing at me sideways before turning to look back out at the view.

'Conor went over the cliff,' I said, only hearing the brutality of my words once they were spoken. 'I'm sorry,' I added. 'But that's where we'd got to.'

'Yes,' Mum said in a strange, bright voice, as if she was telling me a children's story. It sounded as if she had done her best to select an appropriate voice but had made a mistake and got the wrong one. 'Yes, that's right!'

'Was it drink-driving?' I asked. 'Is that why he went off the cliff?'

Mum nodded. 'Yes, something like that,' she said.

'But Leif wasn't with him?'

'God, no!' Mum said, as if the suggestion outraged her. 'Why would Leif have been with him?'

I shrugged. 'I don't know,' I said. Then, 'Hang on, can you? I just need . . .' I jumped up and ran inside for my cigarettes and lighter. I guessed that, for once, Mum wasn't going to tell me off for smoking, and I was right.

Once I'd returned, I sat back down and lit up. 'So, what happened to Leif, Mum? What happened to my father?'

Mum sighed deeply. 'I've been so worried about telling you this,' she said. 'That's why . . . Well, that's why it's taken so long, I suppose.'

'You've been worried about telling me what?'

'The thing is . . . I don't know. I'm not sure how you'll react, that's my concern.'

'Just tell me, Mum,' I said. 'We've got this far. You might as well.'

'Yes. Yes, I suppose I'd better.'

I dragged on my cigarette and blew the smoke to my right. 'So, Leif, Mum. Come on. What happened?'

When she remained silent, I turned to study her features. She was running her tongue across her teeth and alternately sighing and swallowing. 'I lost him,' she finally said. 'I suppose you could say that I lost him.'

'Lost him to . . . ?'

'To . . . circumstance, really.'

A shiver ran down my spine because, stupidly, only now was it dawning on me that this was her biggest lie of all. 'He's not dead, is he?' I said tentatively, trying the sound of the words out on my tongue.

Mum shook her head slowly.

'Is that a "no"?'

'I don't know,' Mum said. 'That's the truth.'

'How can you not know?' I asked, struggling against a fresh flare-up of anger brewing on the horizon. 'Either he's dead or he isn't.'

'I lost track of him, sweetheart. That's what happened.'

I pinched the bridge of my nose between finger and thumb and repeated her words in a monotone voice. 'You lost track of him.'

'He . . . Everything went haywire, you see? After the accident. Conor had died. There were all sorts of arrangements to be made. I had to speak to the police. Leif's boat was a day before my flight. He lived in Norway. I lived in London . . .'

'You didn't get his address? Is that what you're telling me? That I don't have a father because you didn't bother to get his address?'

'No, I *did*,' Mum told me, swiping at a tear that was running down her cheek. 'I *did* get it. Of course I did. But they lost my suitcase on the way home. I had to transit in Athens and the case was supposed to follow. And it didn't. It never turned up. And his address . . . the piece of paper with his address . . . well, it was in the suitcase.'

'You're winding me up,' I said, my voice wobbling as I hesitated between fury and tears of my own.

Mum shook her head. 'I'm sorry,' she said.

'Then he's alive?'

'Somewhere, probably, he is.'

'Did you even *try* to find him?' I asked, my voice rising as the anger won out once again.

'You know I did, sweetheart. Why do you think we went to Bergen?'

'So he's in Bergen? We know this, do we?' My mind was racing ahead to Internet searches and Norwegian electoral rolls.

'He was. Twenty years ago . . . He probably isn't now.'

'And the Internet?' I said. 'Have you even googled him?'

'I can't,' Mum said.

'Of course you can. Well, *you* probably can't. But I can. What with Facebook and LinkedIn and Twitter and—'

'I'm sorry,' Mum interrupted. 'Please don't be angry with me.'

'I'm not,' I said. 'I'm just thinking about how—'

'I don't know his name,' Mum said. 'I'm sorry. But I never knew his surname.'

'Oh Jesus, Mum!' I exclaimed, covering my eyes with my hands.

I managed to glean a few more snippets of information from my mother before she retired to her bed for a snooze. But she didn't seem to know that much and if I'm honest, my heart was no longer in it.

I was feeling cheated and really quite depressed about the whole thing. I had been given, just for a few seconds, hope that the thing I'd always dreamed of, the thing I'd secretly fantasised about my whole childhood, was possible. But almost as soon as I'd grasped the possibility, Mum had snatched it away from me again. Because without a surname, she was right. It was almost certainly mission impossible.

For the simple reason that I needed some space to think, or – perhaps even more – the space to be miserable and wallow in self-pity, I took my swim things and the bike key and left Mum to have her snooze. Out of politeness I invited her to join me, but in such a way that it was virtually impossible for her to do anything but refuse.

I rode around the headlands of Oia wondering if Conor had crashed over here or over there, and when I came to a sign for a beach, I pulled up.

I rented a sunbed; I swam a few times; I even ordered a sandwich and a beer at a beach bar. But I did all of this without pleasure. I was feeling numb and isolated from my surroundings, as if I'd fallen asleep and woken up in a bubble. The sensation was strangely similar to the misery of a break-up. To the grief I felt when Brian left us, too.

I thought about Mum's relationship with Brian. Because if this Leif guy had been the great love of Mum's life, her half-hearted marriage to Brian suddenly made more sense.

At five, as I prepared to ride back, I received a text message from Baruch asking if I was free for dinner.

Thinking about Mum and how upset she'd be, I hesitated for a moment, but then I thought of her losing my father's address and used the anger that thought provoked to justify doing what I really wanted to do. I texted him back to say 'yes'.

His reply came almost immediately.

When I got back to the hotel, Mum was in a deckchair reading one of her novels. 'Hello stranger!' she said, using her fake, chipper voice again. 'Did you have a nice time?'

I told her it had been fine and that I had simply been to the beach.

'I went shopping,' Mum said. 'I thought we could picnic this evening for a change. I got some lovely ripe tomatoes and—'

'I said I'd have dinner with Baruch,' I interrupted before she could go any further. 'Is that OK with you?'

'Oh . . . sure.' Mum looked like she was being brave and wasn't thrilled about the news at all. 'Sure, that's absolutely fine.'

'You'll be OK? You're sure?'

Mum nodded. 'I'm really into this,' she said, flashing the cover of her novel at me. 'So I'll be fine. It's . . . you know . . . taking my mind off things.'

'But we'll eat together tomorrow, OK? We'll spend the whole day together for your birthday. Do something nice.'

'Sure, chicken,' Mum said. 'Of course. You can ask that Baruch of yours for recommendations.'

For an hour or so we read side by side until, I think embarrassed by the atmosphere, which remained awkward, Mum headed off down the Dreaded Steps for a swim.

◆ ◆ ◆

Baruch was talking to Damon outside the minimart when I got up to street level, so the three of us chatted and smoked cigarettes for a while until Baruch said something in Greek to Damon, something which instantly caused him to vanish.

'He's like a little brother,' Baruch told me. 'If you don't tell him to buzz away he never goes.'

'Buzz *off*,' I corrected him. 'Though "buzz away" is kind of cute.'

'Buzz off,' Baruch repeated. 'So . . . Fira?'

'Sure,' I said. I hadn't spent any time in Santorini's main town yet and was still obsessing about my father anyway. I didn't really care where we went. 'But only if you let me buy you dinner somewhere,' I added.

Baruch pulled a face. 'This is not the Greek way,' he said.

'Then it's lucky I'm not Greek,' I told him. 'Go on. It'll be nice.'

The ride along the coast was pleasant enough. Baruch rode at a leisurely pace, slowing to point things out to me, but I was still a bit lost inside my head – still churning over what little information I had about my father and finding it hard to live in the moment.

Once we had parked up, and as we wandered through the lanes of Fira, Baruch picked up on my strange mood. I think I must have been umming and aahing in the wrong places because I was struggling to listen to him. He asked me what was wrong.

And so I told him pretty much the whole story. I explained that I'd discovered my father wasn't dead, after all – that he hadn't gone off a cliff in Oia. I told him about the mysterious vanishing Leif, whose surname, Mum thought, might begin with the letter V, or perhaps even V-I-L, and who had once lived in Bergen, but about whom we knew nothing more.

The only detail I wilfully concealed was the fact that Conor had also been my mother's lover, albeit briefly. That was something I was struggling to deal with myself and there was no reason, I decided, to make it public.

As we arrived at the restaurant Baruch had chosen, a taverna overlooking the caldera called Volcano Blue, I reached the end of my sorry tale. It had been something of a monologue and I worried that I was sounding self-obsessed.

Baruch made a *hmm* sound and asked the million-dollar question. 'Do you believe her?'

I laughed at this and the laughter, my first that day, felt good – it felt like a form of release. 'Well, that's the thing, isn't it?' I said. 'She's given me so many versions.'

'It's just the suitcase that seems funny to me,' Baruch said. 'I've never heard of them losing a suitcase.'

'Really?' I said. 'Oh, that definitely happens. I've heard of it lots of times. Especially when there's a transfer from one flight to another.'

'Sure, but they always *find* the suitcase,' Baruch said. 'It always gets delivered later, right?'

'Unless you fail to put your address on it. Mum is famously dipsy.'

'Dipsy?' Baruch queried.

'Dizzy, disorganised. Actually, she's not that bad. But she could totally forget to attach a label to her suitcase. I didn't even do mine on the flight out, if I'm being honest.'

'Dipsy,' Baruch said again, apparently trying the word out for size. 'I like it. *Dipsy*.'

As we entered the restaurant, we were greeted by a waiter who apparently knew Baruch. He led us to the last remaining table, near the bannisters, overlooking the bay.

'Great view, huh?' Baruch asked once we were sitting down.

'Yes,' I agreed. And my question about the view came to mind so, because it was something to say, I asked him about it. His response was, I suppose, quite predictable in that he said that some days he noticed, and other days he didn't. That made perfect sense to me, because that very evening I'd been so preoccupied that I hadn't noticed the view myself until Baruch had pointed it out.

The other detail I hadn't noticed was that Baruch had chosen, horror of horrors, a seafood restaurant.

'Seafood,' I said, studying the menu in terror and wondering if I could fake knowing how to pull a prawn's legs off without screaming.

'Yes, I love seafood,' Baruch said. 'You?'

'Mmm,' I lied. 'Yes, some seafood. Not all.'

I managed to get through the ordering process without too much embarrassment by telling Baruch that I'd had seafood for lunch and wanted to try something new. I ordered tomato croquettes and fried feta instead.

It's a strange one really, because it's not like me to lie about these things. But there was something in his self-assurance that made me feel as if my own food phobias were a bit childish. I wanted to act like an adult. I wanted to impress him. I was still trying to seduce him, I suppose.

It all nearly fell apart when he held a peeled king prawn out to me on the end of his fork and said, 'Taste this. It's delicious. They cook it in ouzo.' I looked at his beautiful blue eyes then at the prawn, and I thought, *If you did this in Bergen for Mum, you can do it here*. And so I smiled and took the fork from his hand. I wasn't thrilled by the texture, I must say, and I struggled as I crunched into it not to gag. But the taste wasn't as bad as I remembered. In fact it was really quite sweet.

As we ate, we discussed how to hunt for a random person called Leif Vil-something-or-other. I pulled out my phone at one point to google Norwegian surnames and even convinced Baruch to put a call in to Granny. But Google, for once, came up empty, and Granny didn't seem to remember anything other than a car careering off a cliff.

Suddenly, unexpectedly, I became intensely bored with the subject, bored with myself really, and frustrated at my inability to think about anything else. And so I put all my efforts into getting Baruch to talk about himself. He was funny and self-deprecating and, in a pink-and-white-striped shirt and his usual bum-hugging jeans, was looking as sexy as ever. And he was visibly working a charm offensive, doing everything he could think of to seduce me, too. *If only I could concentrate on him instead*, I thought.

We got back to Oia about ten thirty and, once Baruch had locked up the bike, I shocked myself by asking if there were still empty rooms in the hotel. Was that slutty of me? Maybe. But everything happens for a reason and I honestly think that I was feeling desperate for some physical sensation to connect me to reality, to connect me to my body. I just so wanted to step outside my head for a moment.

We took beers from the minimart and Baruch got another friend in reception to give him a key. The room, number 12, was a good way from Mum's, which I was grateful for.

We drank our cans of beer on the little terrace before moving inside so that we could kiss. And it felt nice. Nothing revolutionary. Nothing earth-shattering. But it was nice. It felt *really* nice.

Baruch was gentle and polite and occasionally funny. After quite a lot of mucking around we shifted to the bed and things moved on quite naturally from there. After a fairly marathon performance on his part, he got me to climax too, which felt like an unexpected bonus. Because in that instant, just for a moment, I managed to forget about the rest, and be present with him in that bed, in that room, in Santorini, Greece, planet Earth. And considering the state my nerves were in, that was no mean achievement.

Once the deed had been done I had one of my usual bouts of self-doubt – self-hatred, even – about it. But then Baruch rolled onto his side and threw one heavy, hairy arm over me and I thought, *No. This is fine. No harm. No guilt. No shame.* It was the catchphrase of one of my girlfriends at college, and it had never seemed more appropriate.

◆ ◆ ◆

The next morning Baruch woke up and vanished before I'd even managed to yawn properly. The minimart, he reminded me, opened at seven thirty.

As I lay in bed trying to summon the energy to get up, I took inventory of my feelings and decided that, despite my doubts, my night of passion with Baruch had done me the world of good. I was feeling infinitely less insane than I had been, and the afterglow of sex was still with me, making me feel cosy and soft and a little stretchy, where only a few hours before I'd had the impression that I was built entirely out of right angles.

As I entered the minimart – with the aim of handing back the key – Baruch looked up at me and grinned, and I realised also that, despite my best efforts to avoid having feelings for him, I really rather liked the guy. There was something deliciously uncomplicated about him, about the situation and about us.

There were no clients in the shop, so I sat on the checkout counter and chatted to him with ease.

'I tried looking up that name again,' he said after a while, nodding towards his laptop. 'You said V-I-L, yes?'

'That's what Mum said.'

'I didn't find,' Baruch confirmed, reaching for the computer.

I squeezed in beside him to look and he reached around my waist and pulled me onto his knees, putting his arms around me to operate the keyboard.

'You see?' he said, once the listing was on-screen.

I studied the list, reading random names out. I pronounced Johansen, Olsen, Pedersen and Simonsen before pointing out, rather obviously, 'Most of them end in *sen*.'

'Vilsen?' Baruch suggested, opening a fresh window so he could google that.

'Villonsen? Vildersen? Vilolsen?' I offered. But none of our guesses came up with anything.

'Maybe it's one of these other endings,' Baruch said, pointing at the screen to Spillum and Storstrand and Tennfjord.

'Can you write those three down for me?' I asked, pointing at Vang, Vinter and Vollan. 'At least they begin with a V.'

'Hey, hey, hey! What is happening here?'

I jumped from Baruch's lap, almost knocking the laptop from the counter, and spun to see Damon leaning in the doorway looking smug. 'Nothing,' I said. I could sense my skin burning and guessed I was probably blushing.

'No, tell him,' Baruch said, and I thought, for one awful minute, that he wanted me to tell Damon we had slept together. But then he continued, 'He works in a hotel. He sees a million different names, right, Damon?'

Damon moved towards a display rack and selected a packet of chewing gum before crossing to the checkout and laying it and a one-euro coin on the counter. 'Tell me what?' he asked.

'Norwegian names beginning with V-I-L,' Baruch said. 'You'll see. We call him Mr Google,' he told me.

Damon grimaced. 'What?'

'Norwegian names beginning with V-I-L,' Baruch repeated more slowly.

Damon shrugged. 'How should I know? And why?'

'Becky's trying—'

'—to win a prize,' I completed. 'It's a quiz thing. And this is the only answer we can't find.'

'Google?' Damon suggested.

'We tried,' Baruch said. 'We found nothing.'

'You could ask the guys in my hotel,' Damon suggested. 'We've got a couple of Scandi guys staying. I'm not sure if they're Norwegian, but you could ask. Anyway, I've gotta go. I'm late.' And Mr Google, who was not Mr Google after all, scooped up his chewing gum and was gone.

'I'd better go and find Mum,' I told Baruch. 'It's her birthday today.'

'Sure,' he replied. 'But you should maybe do what he says. He might have some Norwegians staying. I bet they'd know the different names.'

I nodded. 'I guess,' I said. 'I might try later.'

'It's just up there,' Baruch said. 'The Blue Balconies. He's on reception.'

'Right,' I said. 'Can I see you tonight?'

Baruch smiled broadly. 'You can see me any time.'

'It's just, it's Mum's birthday, like I said, so it'll have to be late.'

'I'll check for spare rooms,' Baruch said with a wink.

I started towards the door but then hesitated. 'I don't suppose you sell wrapping paper, do you?'

'Wrapping paper?'

'You know, pretty paper. For gifts.'

'Oh, no . . .' Baruch said, glancing around. 'I have some brown paper from a delivery, I think . . .'

I wrinkled my nose.

'Down that way,' he said, pointing again. 'In the postcard shop. I think they might have some.'

I waved my fingertips at him and stepped back outside and started to make my way towards the postcard shop he'd indicated. But as I reached the point where the Dreaded Steps headed down to the tiny port, I noticed, for the first time, the name of the hotel where Mum said she'd stayed. It was the Blue Balconies.

I stopped walking and thought about this. For some reason I sensed a fluttering in my chest. I told myself I was being silly, but it seemed in that moment as if it was some kind of sign from the universe. And so I crossed the street and stepped, for the first time, into the ice-cool lobby.

Damon was already behind the desk, so I crossed the marble floor and leaned my elbows on the counter. When he looked up, he grinned at me salaciously. 'Hello, sexy lady,' he said. 'You bored with old Baruch? He's doesn't know how to satisfy the ladies. Not like I do.'

I rolled my eyes at him. 'Oh, perlease,' I laughed. 'How old are you anyway? Fourteen? Fifteen?'

'Sixteen,' Damon said. 'Old enough. You'll see.'

'Yeah, right. So, you said you could fix me up with some Norwegians?'

Damon sighed theatrically. 'Oh well,' he said. He nodded towards a group on the far right-hand side of the lobby, next to the entrance. There were three men and two women, all wearing sporty hiking gear. All but one were blond. 'Try them,' he said. 'I'm not sure if they're Swedish or something else. But they might know.'

I started to cross the lobby towards them and as I approached I could hear that they were talking in what was definitely some kind of Scandinavian language.

A shiver ran down my spine – I thought it was because of the powerful air conditioning – but then, when I was about six feet away, the tallest of the men turned his head to glance back towards the reception desk, and I froze.

He'd only glanced my way for an instant and had already turned back to continue the conversation with his friends, but my throat had gone dry and my heart was racing.

I moved to an empty chair against the wall – my legs had turned to jelly. I tried to reason with myself: I was being crazy. I wasn't thinking – or seeing – straight. But when, after a minute or so, he glanced my way again, I knew I was right.

SIXTEEN

Laura

She is in an airport, dragging her suitcase along a seemingly endless corridor, which leads, or so she hopes, to her boarding gate. She is late for her flight and has been alternating between trotting and walking rapidly. Her heels don't permit anything more, but even at that speed, she can hear her heartbeat pumping in her ear, and sweat is pearling on her brow.

They've been calling her name over the tannoy system, and she hears it ring out again now. '*Final boarding call for Laura Ryan. Laura Ryan! Please make your way to gate one-one-five immediately!*'

Thinking that it will be faster, she steps onto the moving walkway, but for some reason it feels as if it is slowing her down. When she runs on it she actually seems to be moving at walking pace, yet when she stops running she continues gliding forwards, albeit even more slowly – the sensation is like moving through treacle. She checks the gate she is passing – it is number eighteen – and thinks, *God, I'll never get there in time!* And so she bends down to remove her heels and, holding them in one hand while trundling her hated suitcase behind her with the other, she begins to jog. She runs and runs until she is breathless but at least the gate numbers begin to increase. Thirty-two . . . fifty-four . . .

When she finally gets to the gate, there is no queue. Everyone else has boarded.

The hostess looks up at her as she arrives and says, 'I hope you're Laura Ryan? We've been waiting for you.'

She pulls her printed boarding card from her pocket and the hostess unfolds it and feeds it into a machine, but instead of beeping and flashing green lights, the machine shreds it into tiny strips, which drift to the floor and immediately start to blow back down the corridor along which she arrived.

'I'm sorry,' the woman says. 'But that clearly wasn't your boarding pass.'

Perplexed and panicky, she checks her other pockets – she seems to have hundreds of them – and eventually finds another sheet of paper. 'Oh, here it is!' she says, handing it over.

This time the machine chirrups contentedly. 'You need to be quick,' the woman says. 'Otherwise you're going to miss your flight.'

She runs along the tunnel, only to be faced with a closed aircraft door, so she releases her suitcase and hammers on it with her fists until eventually it reopens. 'Laura Ryan?' the steward says. 'You're very late!'

No sooner has she buckled her seatbelt than the plane starts to move backwards from the gate. She wipes the sweat from her brow and turns to the man beside her. 'That was close!' she tells him. 'I thought I was going to miss it.'

'You gave them the wrong piece of paper,' he says.

'Yes. Yes, I did,' she replies, wondering how he could possibly know this.

As the plane changes directions and begins to taxi bumpily along the runway, the man adds, 'And now it's gone forever.'

His words puzzle her at first, but then a sense of panic washes over her and she starts to check her many pockets all over again. But the man is right. The piece of paper – she isn't sure what it was, but it was without doubt, the most important piece of paper in the world – is gone.

And as she imagines the strips blowing along the windy corridors of the airport, she realises that she's about to be sick.

I was sitting staring into the distance when Becky arrived. There were clouds on the horizon to the west, the first clouds we had seen in quantity since we'd arrived, and I was wondering if they would cancel out or enhance the sunset that evening, and then wondering how often it actually rained in Santorini.

I'd been up for almost two hours but, as often, the shadow of my nightmare was still hanging over me. I still felt vaguely nauseous and for this reason hadn't yet eaten breakfast.

She arrived, skipping down the stairs so fast I thought she would fall. Her face, despite the effort, was pale and her features looked tortured.

My first thought was that Baruch had done something to her so I jumped up to take her in my arms, but that wasn't what she wanted. 'You have to come, Mum,' she said, grabbing my hand and pulling on it. 'Come quickly.'

'Why?' I asked. 'What's happened?'

'Please!' Becky pleaded, jerking on my hand again. 'And be quick.'

I followed her far enough to see that whatever was going on, it wasn't happening on the staircase, and then I broke loose. 'My shoes,' I said. 'Wait! I need my shoes.'

All kinds of images were flashing through my mind as I pulled on my trainers and rapidly locked the door. Perhaps Baruch hadn't hurt her after all, but was hurt himself. Whatever was happening, it had Becky in a complete and utter panic. She was shaking her fists at her sides like a frustrated toddler as she urged me to get a move on.

I jogged up the stairs and the memory of jogging in the dream came back to me and I wondered if that hadn't foreshadowed this. But even jogging, I couldn't get up the stairs as fast as my daughter.

'What on earth?' I asked her, when I reached the top and she quite literally started dragging me down the street. 'Becky! Tell me what's happening,' I insisted.

'He's here,' she said. 'The Norwegian. My father. He's *here*!'

I froze on the spot and prised my hand loose. 'Just stop and tell me what you're talking about,' I said, feeling a little annoyed now at her urgency. Because no one was dying after all.

'He's in a hotel,' she said. 'Down here. I just saw him. Come *on*!'

I shook my head and started to walk behind Becky as she ran forwards a few paces then turned to walk backwards so she could urge me on. A few people had started to stare. 'This is exactly why I knew I shouldn't tell you,' I told her. 'I knew it would drive you mad.'

'I'm not mad, Mum. Trust me. He's here!'

'But he isn't, Becky,' I said. 'I don't know who you think you've seen . . .'

She had stopped in front of a hotel and as it was the same hotel I had stayed in all those years ago, albeit with the lobby rebuilt and with a different name and logo, I started to put a shape to Becky's madness. The components were evidently all of my making. It was me who had told her she'd been conceived in Santorini. I was the one who had lied to her for twenty years too, telling the poor thing that her father was dead. And now she knew that he wasn't, and I had told her this here, not a hundred yards from the place where I'd met him. How else could I have expected her to react other than with madness?

'In there,' she was saying. 'Go look. The tall, blond guy.'

I took her arm and tried to calm her down. 'Becky,' I said. 'Listen to me.' I wondered if she was having an actual breakdown and how I'd cope if she was. I wondered if there were mental health services in Santorini.

'Just go and *look*, will you, Mum?' she said. 'He looks exactly like me. It's freaky.'

'Becky, this is all my fault, but . . .'

'Just *look*!' she said again, and because she was actually crying with frustration at this point, I told her I would.

'I'm going to go in and I'm going to look,' I told her calmly. 'But you need to go and sit on that wall and calm yourself down, all right? Because I can assure you that it can't possibly be him.'

The doors slid open as someone stepped out, and Becky glanced indoors and said, 'Him! He's there. Look!' But by the time I had turned my head, the doors had closed again and all I saw was a reflection of the souvenir shop opposite.

'Just go!' Becky said, sounding really quite hysterical. 'Before he disappears or something.'

And so, thinking that the only way to deal with this was to do as she asked, to satisfy her need in that moment, I rolled my eyes, released her arm, and stepped towards the doors. As they slid open, I turned to ask her over my shoulder, 'Would you rather come with me?'

By way of reply, she simply shook her head.

I stepped into the lobby. It had been recently rebuilt and was far bigger than anything I remembered from my previous visit. The floor was a vast expanse of marble and the air conditioning, it crossed my mind, must have been unbearable to work in all day. It felt like stepping into the Arctic Circle.

I looked around the room at the various clusters of people before spotting the man Becky had surely meant. And though I could see why she had thought what she had, I knew immediately, even from behind, that it wasn't Leif. Of course it wasn't. How could it be?

My heart sank. In fact I had to gulp back a few tears, and I realised that even as I'd been insisting to Becky that it couldn't possibly be him, I'd been hoping that just perhaps it might be. All the dreams I'd had for my life with Leif, the dreams I'd held on to for years and had eventually been forced to relinquish, had briefly risen up in me anew.

I exhaled slowly and bit my lip, glancing back to look at Becky through the window. She was sitting on the wall opposite, alternating between smoking and biting her nails. I wondered how she was going to react when I broke the news.

I almost walked straight back out but then I became intrigued to see the man's face, this man that Becky had decided was her father. I wondered what image of him she had created. And so I crossed to the far wall and turned so I could look at him. He was tall and blond, and blue-eyed. That much she'd got right. He could even have been Norwegian, though for some reason my guess was that he was more likely German. But everything else about him was wrong. His shoulders were far broader than Leif's and his nose, where Leif's had one of those little blobs on the end, was incredibly pointy. I sighed again and started to return, heading for the door, but just as I reached it, a man's voice called out, 'Jens!' and something about his tone made me stop dead in my tracks. The door opened and closed, then opened again in front of me. I could see Becky opposite but she wasn't looking at me. She was busy lighting a fresh cigarette from the stub of the previous one. Over the sound of the crazed sliding doors opening and closing, I listened to the voices behind me. Tears started to flow: tears of hope mixed with tears born of the unspeakable terror that I was almost certainly wrong – that I was almost certainly being as mad as my daughter.

Swallowing with difficulty, I spun on one foot and looked back.

The blond man I'd seen before, who was apparently called Jens, was now facing me, while the man whose voice had rung out had his back to me and was slapping him on the arm as he spoke in a joyful, animated fashion. I went weak at the knees and had to step to the right so that I could steady myself by placing one hand on a column.

Jens apparently saw this, because he started to frown. In response, the man he was talking to turned to look at whatever it was that Jens had noticed. And what he saw when he turned was me.

He frowned at first, as if the image his retinas were feeding him didn't compute, then he opened his mouth to speak, only to close it again without having said a word. Finally, without averting his gaze for a second, he tapped his friend on the arm distractedly and crossed the lobby to join me.

'Is it you?' he asked simply.

But though I tried, I couldn't reply. Instead, I clasped one hand to my trembling lips and started, yet again, to cry.

He stepped even closer and, tentatively at first, he took me in his arms. 'Laura,' he said. 'Oh, *Laura.*'

His friend Jens and a blond woman came over to ask him something in Norwegian, presumably if everything was OK. Whatever Leif told them seemed to send them packing, smiling and apologising as they backed away.

I cried in his arms for a minute or so, making the most, between gasps, of the sensation of being held, of that warm, musky smell I remembered from all those years before.

I let him lead me to a love seat in the corner of the lobby, where we sat, side by side, but angled so we were half facing each other. When eventually I was able to speak, or at least croak, I asked, 'How can you be here, Leif?'

'Me?' Leif asked. He shrugged. 'We come quite a lot,' he said, matter-of-factly. 'Maybe ten times since . . . you know . . . And you? How come *you* are here?' He sounded businesslike, even a touch irritated. It wasn't the reunion I had so often dreamed of.

'I came for my fiftieth,' I told him. 'For old times' sake, really.'

Leif nodded. 'For old times' sake,' he repeated, stroking my back in a distracted manner. It felt friendly, but not passionate. In fact, even friendly would be pushing it. *Hesitantly* friendly, let's say.

'You stay here?' he asked. 'In the Blue Balconies?'

I shook my head. 'I wanted to,' I explained. 'But I couldn't find it when we were booking. They changed the name, so . . .'

'Yes,' Leif confirmed. 'Yes, they changed the name.'

It crossed my mind just how ridiculous it was to be discussing the name of the hotel. But everything else, everything I wanted to say, just seemed too complex, too vast somehow for words. And there didn't seem to be any way by which to get from here to there.

I suppose what I really wanted to know was whether Leif's regular returns to Santorini had anything to do with me. But it felt absurd and egotistical to even suggest such a thing. And there was something in his deadpan delivery that was warning me off – something in his wording, his *We come here quite a lot.*

We, I now thought. *Who's 'we'?*

It had been twenty-four years, after all. How could I possibly imagine that lovely Leif had stayed single? How could I think that I was still the reason he was here after so many years? We'd spent a couple of days together followed by twenty-four years apart.

'And you?' Leif asked, as if he was tuning into my thoughts. 'You are here alone?'

'No,' I said. 'No, I'm with . . . someone.' *I'm here with your daughter*, I thought. The words seemed simple enough, but like all the rest, they seemed insufficient for the task at hand.

'With a man?' Leif asked.

'Oh, no!' I said, glancing outside in an attempt at spotting Becky. But the place on the wall where she had been was now vacant. 'No, I'm . . . I'm with a woman. A friend.'

Leif nodded. 'This is good,' he said.

'Good?'

'It's not nice to travel alone.'

'No,' I agreed. 'No, it isn't.'

'So, I think I would be right if I wish you a happy birthday, yes?' Leif asked.

I nodded. I was fiddling with my fingernails, with a button on my top, basically doing anything to avoid looking Leif in the eye. Because I was terrified of what I might find there. Or perhaps it would be more honest to say that I was terrified of what I might find was missing. 'Yes,' I replied. 'Fifty today. *Fifty!* When did *that* happen?'

'It is hard to talk,' Leif said after a moment's silence. 'It's been so long.'

'Yes,' I agreed. 'Yes, you're right. Do you want to just go and join your friends or something?' It was madness to suggest it, really. I'd been praying for this moment pretty much constantly since I had last seen Leif, but now it was happening, I found I didn't know how to do it. I seemed to lack the strength, or the intelligence, or the courage to handle it properly. And as I made my suggestion that we effectively end this conversation here, I was both terrified that Leif would agree with me and also hopeful that in doing so, he would end the excruciating tension of the moment. Because it really was unbearable. I could hardly breathe.

In fact what happened was that Leif laughed. 'No,' he said. 'No I don't want to go and join my friends. Do *you* want me to?'

I shook my head gently and dared, because his laughter had made this possible, to look up at his face.

He'd put on a little weight over the years, but he still had the same basic physiognomy. His face was rounder and he had smile lines around his eyes which hadn't been there before. There was something icy about the blue of his eyes that was new, too, and I wondered if it was sadness or disappointment that had changed their hue. His nose was off-centre and I reached out to gently touch it.

'Conor,' Leif confirmed. 'I had to have it broken and reset afterwards at the hospital. But it was never quite right. So I always think of you. Whenever I look in the mirror.'

'I always think of you, too,' I said. 'I never stopped.'

Leif's eyes seemed to tint colder and I thought, *Oh, gosh, it's anger! It's anger that's made them this colour.*

'You didn't write,' he said, confirming my suspicions. 'You never called. Not once.'

Though in the early days I had often imagined Leif sitting by the phone, waiting for me to contact him, I'd forgotten over the years just how angry he might have felt, being more concerned with my own sorry lot – worrying more over my own loss and that of my daughter, who, because of fate, had grown up without a father. But of course, Leif had never known about the lost suitcase. Had he waited for my call? And if so, for how long? And how had that felt? How angry had that made him?

He had turned away from me and was looking out to the street, so I reached out to gently touch his arm. 'Leif,' I said, gently. 'It wasn't my fault. I know . . . I understand how it must have been for you, but I couldn't phone. I *couldn't* write.'

He sniffed and dried his eyes, which I only then saw were watery, on one sleeve. 'Not here,' he said, standing. 'We need to explain, but not here.' He stood, and I followed suit. 'Come,' he said, striding towards the sliding doors.

Outside the hotel, I looked left and right for Becky but she was nowhere to be seen. I checked my pocket for my phone – I was hoping to call her or at least send a text – but I hadn't brought it with me. And so, thinking that until I had spoken to Leif, I couldn't introduce them anyway, I followed him down the Dreaded Steps.

He stopped outside room 23, the same room he'd had all those years ago, and I thought he was going to comment on it; I thought he wanted to point it out to me. But instead he unlocked the door. He peered into the interior for a moment, then stepped back outside and gestured towards the deckchairs. 'We are better here, I think,' he said. I wondered if there were women's clothes lying on the bed. I wondered if the elegant woman I had seen in reception was his girlfriend, or even his wife. I checked his hands for a wedding ring. He wasn't wearing one.

We moved the chairs closer together and sat. 'You have the same room,' I commented.

'Yes,' Leif said. 'Always. I book very early and they save it for me.'

'Why?' I asked. 'I mean, why do you want the same room?'

'Because . . .' Leif started. But then he paused and sighed deeply. 'You know what?' he said. 'Let's talk about you, maybe? Let's talk about why you didn't call me. Why you *couldn't* call me?'

I covered my eyes for a moment with one hand then slid it down my face. 'I'm so sorry, Leif,' I said.

'Sorry,' he repeated. 'Yes. But why?'

'They lost my case,' I said with a shrug. 'They lost it on the way home. With everything in it. And it had your piece of paper. The piece of paper with your address on it. And without that . . .'

Leif screwed up his features strangely at this revelation and turned to look out to sea for a moment. When he finally turned back, his expression hadn't changed at all. He looked as if the sun was too bright and was making him squint. 'This is true?' he asked.

I nodded. 'I . . . I don't . . . Look . . .' I stammered. 'I don't want you to think I didn't try, that's all. I tried really hard. I phoned the embassy and everything. They couldn't help.'

'For your suitcase?'

I shook my head. 'No, I hassled the airlines for that. For over a year. I wrote to Aegean and BA and Athens' airport authority . . . And then I phoned the Norwegian Embassy. They couldn't help me, either. Or wouldn't. I wanted them to give me your name. I wrote to Bergen University, too. I even went there with . . . I went there. I tried so hard to find you, Leif. I dreamed about finding you. I *still* have dreams about finding, or losing, that damned piece of paper. I tried everything, really. But I just couldn't think how.'

Leif laughed sourly. 'And the phone book?' he said.

'I'm sorry?'

'The phone book. I'm in it. In Bergen.'

'But I don't know your name. I never knew your name.'

Leif lowered his head to his hands and breathed deeply, noisily, for a moment. 'Me neither,' he said finally. 'I never knew yours.'

'It's Ryan,' I told him and he gasped. 'Of course,' he said. 'Of course. I knew this, somewhere . . .' He pointed to his head and made a circular motion. 'I phoned the hotel, you know? I thought they might have it.'

'Me too,' I said. 'But it had closed.'

'Yes, but it reopened the next year. They found the old papers for me. And they told me your name was O'Leary.'

'That's Conor's name.'

'Yes,' Leif said. 'Yes, I know. The hotel had you down as Mrs O'Leary.'

'You tried to find me too?'

'Yes,' Leif said. 'I tried for years.'

'And your name,' I asked. 'What is it? Your surname?'

'Vilhjálmsson,' Leif said.

I asked him to spell it out. 'I knew it was *Vil*-something,' I said, once he'd done so. 'I asked at the library. There used to be this system where you could ask them a question. Any question. So I asked them for Norwegian surnames beginning with V-I-L. And then I looked online when that became possible, in 2000 or 2001, I googled it. But I could never find your name.'

'It's Icelandic,' Leif said. 'Not Norwegian. My parents were Icelandic.'

'God,' I said, shaking my head. 'Why didn't I know that?'

'We didn't talk of these things,' Leif said. 'We were quite busy. With Conor.'

'Yes. Yes, we were.'

'But you still thought about me?' Leif asked, sounding surprised.

'I never stopped,' I told him. 'Really, Leif. I never stopped. I've spent my entire life thinking about nothing else.'

Leif buried his head in his hands again, and I rested one arm across his back as occasional tears slipped down my own cheeks. *It's too late*, I was thinking. *I don't know what I was hoping for, but it's definitely too late*. I think only then, only once faced with the physical evidence provided by our transformed bodies, did I realise quite how many years had gone by. We'd had entirely different lives. We'd become entirely different people.

After a minute or so, I went indoors to wash my face. I was expecting to have panda eyes but when I looked in the mirror, I remembered I hadn't even put my make-up on that morning. It was probably just as well.

I washed and dried my face and, glancing over my shoulder, I checked the bathroom cabinet. But there were only men's things. And only a single toothbrush. This impression was confirmed as I walked back through the bedroom. Only one of the single beds had been slept in.

When I stepped back out into the sunshine, Leif was standing looking out to sea. 'Did you marry?' I asked quickly, speaking before my courage deserted me.

'Yes,' Leif said. 'And you?'

I nodded. 'It didn't work out though. Well, it did for a while . . .'

'Same here,' Leif said. He still hadn't turned to look at me. 'Five years.'

'Eight,' I said. 'I managed eight.'

'So, you win,' Leif said, and I wasn't sure if he was trying to be light-hearted or snide.

'Why did yours—?' I started to ask. I stopped myself. I didn't feel that I had the right to ask him that.

'Why did it go wrong?'

'Yes.'

He turned to face me. His eyes were red around the edges. 'I wanted children,' he said. 'Aslaug didn't. It caused a lot of problems. And . . .'

'And?'

Leif shrugged. 'That's the main thing, really,' he said. 'And you?'

'Me what?' I was scared that he was asking if I'd had children. Because I still couldn't work out how to tell him what I needed to say.

'Your marriage? Why did it stop?'

'Oh,' I said. 'I don't know really. Why do they ever?'

'You don't know?'

I shrugged. 'He was lovely. His name was Brian and he was friendly and funny and cute. So . . .'

'So?'

'I didn't . . . love him properly, I suppose. I was always . . . I don't know . . .'

'It's OK,' Leif said. 'You don't have to. I was just curious.'

'I was always comparing him with you. I suppose that's it, if I'm being honest. There was always this bit of me that was thinking about *you*. It made things . . . difficult.'

Leif smiled sadly. 'I'm not so special, you know?'

'No,' I said. 'Well, me neither.'

'But we . . .' Leif said, gesturing between myself and him. 'We were magic, weren't we? Back then?'

I nodded and chewed my bottom lip. I opened my mouth to speak, but found I couldn't make a sound. *Yes*, I thought. *We were magic.*

We returned to our chairs and Leif took my hands in his. 'So, tell me, Laura,' he said. 'Tell me the truth. Are you seeing someone now?'

I shook my head. 'There was no one else. No one before Brian, and no one else since. Even Brian, really. It wasn't . . . you know . . . And you?'

Leif shook his head. 'Not since Aslaug,' he said. 'I often think I should have stayed with her.'

'Really?'

'Well, I didn't have the children anyway. So it was kind of an argument about nothing.'

'Yes, yes I see,' I said. I tried again to formulate a sentence containing the name 'Becky', but once again couldn't seem to find the right words.

'I always hoped, you know,' Leif said. 'Every year that I come here. I'm thinking that this might happen. That I look around and I see you. Why didn't you come back?'

'I couldn't afford it,' I said. 'And I was scared, too. At the beginning I was, anyway. And I had a ch— The only holiday I ever took was to Bergen. And later on, I was married, so . . . I was hardly going to bring Brian here.'

'No,' Leif said. 'And now?'

'I'm sorry?'

'Why did you come here now?'

'Oh, I don't know really,' I said. 'I inherited a bit of money. And I lost my job, so I have the time. Plus I split up with Brian, of course. Perhaps I wanted to remember who I was before I met him. Something like that, anyway.'

'And you really came to Bergen. What year was that?'

'Two thousand, maybe? Two thousand and one? It took me years to save up.'

'Right,' Leif said.

'Were you there?'

He shook his head. 'I was working on the oil platforms. I was never anywhere, really. Always out at sea.'

I sighed. The fact that he hadn't been in Bergen provided a vague sense of comfort. Because I had always imagined that I had just missed him. I had often pictured us walking, just yards away, down parallel streets. I'd regularly had images of Becky and myself leaving a café only for Leif to take my still-warm seat just minutes later. But he hadn't been there after all. And that seemed better.

We sat like that for ten minutes, mostly staring into each other's eyes in silence.

Leif would occasionally exhale sharply and shake his head, as if the absurdity of it all was amusing. And I alternated between phases of tears and phases of not-tears. My mind had gone numb from the shock of it all, I think, and other than crying and not crying, there wasn't much going on.

The moment came upon me without me realising it. Suddenly it just happened. I broke free of Leif's grasp and stood. 'I need to check on someone,' I said, intending to fetch Becky to meet her father. 'Can you wait?'

Leif looked puzzled.

'Just trust me,' I said. 'And don't move. Whatever you do, don't move.'

'I'll stay right here,' Leif said.

As I stood to leave, however, he jumped up and made a grab for my hand. 'I'm scared,' he said. 'I'm scared you'll disappear again and never come back.'

'Then come,' I said after a moment's reflection. 'It's the same. Come with me.'

We climbed the steps to street level then walked back past the refrigerated lobby and on up to the minimart. I peeped inside to find Baruch busy ringing up a woman's purchases.

'Becky?' I asked, simply.

Baruch shrugged. Then he caught a glimpse of Leif behind me and his eyes bulged. 'Is that . . . ?' he asked.

I nodded. 'See you later,' I said.

When we got to our unit the door was open. 'Becky?' I called out.

'I'm in the bathroom,' she called back.

SEVENTEEN

Becky

I smoked a couple of cigarettes on the wall outside the hotel. My hands were trembling – like, *really* trembling. They were shaking so much that when I took a drag, my cigarette banged against my lips. My heart was racing too, and my mind seemed to be working at triple speed yet failing to produce a single coherent thought. My head felt like a washing machine on the spin cycle, producing an unrecognisable blur of colour.

Once I'd stubbed my third cigarette out, I decided it was time to see what was happening, but as I reached the entrance, a wave of fear swept over me – I just didn't have the nerve. So I turned towards town instead. Whether I'd been right or wrong, the stress of finding out suddenly seemed unbearable.

My mind was still a blur though; in fact, even my vision seemed out of kilter. And I found myself so unable to function that I bumped into a few people on the street. Even my navigational systems seemed to have packed up.

So I gave up and, almost sprinting as I passed by the minimart, headed back down to our unit. I sat and smoked for a while and then, hoping that this would calm me down where the cigarettes had failed to do so, I decided to take a cool shower.

The second Mum stepped into the room, I knew I had been right. Her eyes were red from crying but she had a peculiar glow about her, too. She looked – if this makes any sense to you – as if she'd found Jesus or Buddha or something. Her movements were languid, her features soft. Her voice sounded smoother than usual.

'Come,' she said, taking my hand and leading me out into the sunshine. The Buddha in question was standing there, looking out to sea.

'Leif,' she said. 'This is Becky.'

He turned to face me and there was a strange moment where we stared into each other's eyes, looking, I think, for resemblance. Not in the eyes themselves, but behind them, in our souls.

Leif wrinkled his brow. He looked puzzled. 'Hello Becky,' he said.

'Hello . . . *Dad*?' I offered dubiously.

He paled before my eyes and it was only then that I realised Mum hadn't forewarned him – she hadn't explained who I was. I felt suddenly embarrassed and a little nauseous on Leif's behalf, and furious, yet again, at my mother.

We stared at each other for a few more seconds, and it really was like looking in a mirror, albeit a deforming mirror at a funfair. Actually, I'll tell you what it was really like. You know those programs on the Internet that show you how you'd look as the opposite sex? Well it was like that. It was exactly like that. I was looking at me, but in the form of a fifty-year-old man.

Leif turned to Mum. 'Laura?' he said.

She nodded gently by way of reply and blinked slowly. Her eyes were moist and she still had that weird placid expression on her face and I toyed with the idea of slapping her out of it.

'Herregud!' Leif exclaimed, which sounded as if it might mean 'Oh my God!' or 'Jesus!' or maybe even 'Fuck me!'

'I . . . need to sit down,' he said, all wobbly-voiced, as he folded back into a deckchair.

I remained standing, watching his expression. I was still searching for similarities – there were many – but also desperately watching for any expression of pleasure on his part at having discovered a previously unknown daughter. But there was no such sign. He looked, if anything, as if he was going to throw up.

'You're twenty-three?' he asked, apparently trying to confirm that the impossible thing which seemed to be happening here really *was* happening.

I nodded. 'Made in Oia,' I said with a forced smile and a fake shrug.

'Yes,' Leif said weakly. 'Yes, of course. Please . . . sit down with me.' He gestured to a second deckchair, so I moved it to face him and sat. 'I'm sorry,' he said. 'It's a bit of a shock.'

'I know,' I said. 'Tell me about it.'

'I'll, um, make tea!' Mum said in that silly, bright voice of hers. 'Anyone want tea? Yes, I'll make a nice cup of tea.' As she vanished into the house, I wished I had thought of that first. Because the tension out here was mad. It seemed to have sucked all the oxygen out of the air and I was finding it increasingly difficult to breathe.

'I think . . .' Leif started. 'I think you are . . . Hmm. This is very hard, yes?'

'Very,' I confirmed.

'But we look very alike, you agree?'

'We do,' I said.

'Your hands,' Leif said, nodding in their direction. 'They are long, like mine. The fingers.'

I nodded and held out one hand to compare. 'My music teacher wanted me to do piano,' I said, looking at my shaky hand rather than at Leif. 'But I hated it. I could never read the music.'

'No,' he said. 'No, music is very hard.' He gestured towards my hand again and asked, 'Can I?'

I frowned for an instant because I didn't understand what he meant. But then I realised that he wanted to take my hand and tremblingly offered it. He enveloped it within his own two hands. They were the same temperature and his skin felt a little like my own, albeit rougher.

'I am surprised,' he said. 'You are very beautiful.'

I felt myself blush at this and prised my hand free. It was all just too embarrassing.

'Of course, your mother is beautiful too,' he said. 'It's just me . . .' He gestured at his own face and grimaced. 'So your name is Becky?'

I nodded. 'It's Rebecca,' I said. 'But everyone calls me Becky. Or Becks.'

'It's a lovely name,' Leif said.

'And your surname?' I asked. 'What is it?'

'Vilhjálmsson,' he said.

I hadn't really understood, but I nodded. 'Right,' I said.

'It's Icelandic. My parents were Icelandic. But I am Norwegian.'

'OK,' I said.

There was a moment's silence, during which I could hear Mum faffing around indoors with cups and teaspoons. 'Um, what do you do?' I asked, not only because the silence was unbearable but because my many and varied fantasies about my father had all revolved around his superhero career status.

'I am an engineer,' Leif said. 'I work on oil platforms. In the North Sea. You know, drilling?'

'Right,' I said, feeling vaguely disappointed.

'And you?'

'Me? I've, um, just finished college. I did humanities. I'm thinking about teacher training but I haven't decided yet.'

'You want to be a teacher?'

'Yes,' I said. 'Maybe. Or I might just look for a job. Any job. But there aren't many. Everything's a bit rubbish at the moment. What with the slowdown and Brexit and whatever . . .' My voice faded out. I had heard myself rambling about inanities in the midst of one of the most important moments of my life and hadn't liked it.

'No,' Leif said. 'Of course.'

Out of nowhere, a maelstrom of emotion began to swirl within me. It was made of a complex mixture of embarrassment for the tooth-achingly awkward conversation we were having, anger at Leif for not making this moment magical, and with Mum, too, for having left me to it, for not having managed the whole introduction thing better. And if I'm honest, I was feeling angry at her for having chosen someone so ordinary and ecologically unsound to be my father, as well. I mean, *oil drilling? Really?*

Before I even knew I was going to do it, I was standing, saying, 'I can't do this. I'm sorry, but I can't,' and storming off up the stairs.

I had run to the top, marched a hundred yards along the street and started to redescend the Dreaded Steps when Mum caught up with me.

'Becky!' she was shrieking. 'BECKY!'

I paused to let her catch up with me, then sat on a step when she arrived.

'What happened?' she asked breathlessly.

I shrugged and shook my head.

'Talk to me,' Mum said, sitting down beside me and resting one arm across my shoulders.

'It's not supposed to be like that,' I said feebly.

'What's not supposed to be like what?'

'Meeting your father,' I said, 'for the first time.' I was playing the images I had created over the years across the cinema-screen of my mind and comparing them with the lacklustre reality of what had just happened.

– Here we were, my father and I, hugging and crying in each other's arms.

– Here he was, appearing in a doorway, a god-like glow around his head, saying, 'You are my daughter and I love you.'

– Here he was again, pulling up outside in a big black car. 'Your father's outside waiting for you,' Mum would say, and as I ran out to meet him, a chauffeur would open the rear door of the car revealing my father, who was rich, suited, elegant, smiling . . .

Instead, the reality had been the kind of awkward conversation you're forced to have with a friend's father while you're waiting for them to get ready. You know – *How's school going? How's your mother doing?*

'It's like there's nothing,' I said as the tears started to flow. 'I expected to feel something, but there's nothing there, Mum. I've waited so long and there's just nothing there, you know?'

She took me in her arms and gently started to rock me. 'Oh, sweetheart,' she said. 'It takes time. You have to give it time.'

'He's just so ordinary,' I said, crying freely and hating the spoilt-brat words even as I was saying them.

'No, he isn't,' Mum said quietly. 'Come back and you'll see. He isn't ordinary at all.'

'It's not supposed to be like this,' I sobbed.

'Only, perhaps it is, chicken,' Mum said. 'Perhaps it's supposed to be exactly like this. How would we know?'

Eventually, I let Mum lead me back there because I suppose that's what I really wanted. I was already moving past my childish expectation that my father should be a superhero – I was understanding that he would, of course, be ordinary.

When we got back, Leif was indoors chopping tomatoes. 'I am thinking I can make some food,' he said to Mum. 'I hope you don't mind?'

Mum shook her head. 'Not at all,' she said. 'That's exactly what I was going to suggest. We have all this stuff I bought yesterday anyway, so . . .'

I was lingering in the doorway, doing my best not to glower like a teenager, but I think I must have looked fairly miserable all the same because Leif took one look at me and stopped what he was doing. He dried his hands on a tea towel and came and stood opposite me. 'If you want, I can go,' he said.

I shrugged. At that moment, it was the best I could manage.

'Of course we don't want you to go,' Mum said. 'Do we?'

'I'm sorry,' Leif continued. 'I'm not very good at this. They don't teach it in school, you know?'

I snorted. 'No,' I said. 'They didn't teach me either.'

'You know,' Leif said, 'I used to be terrible with either and neither.' He turned to my mother. 'Do you remember, Laura?'

'I do,' she said, reaching into the tiny refrigerator and pulling out a lettuce.

He turned back to face me. 'I know this is . . .' he started. 'I mean, if you don't want, you can say no, OK?'

'If I don't want what?' I asked.

'A hug,' Leif said. 'I am thinking maybe a hug would help?'

I swallowed and nodded nervously. Fresh tears were welling up even as he opened his arms. Because this was like something from one of those films I had imagined. This had been one of my fantasies. By the time his arms had closed around me, tears were running down my face.

Mum watched for a minute, her head tipped slightly to one side, then she set down the lettuce and, wiping her hands on the back of her shorts, she crossed the room to join us. 'May I?' she asked, enveloping both of us in her arms. 'I've waited so long for this.'

For the first time in my life I had something I had always dreamed of: not one but two parents to hold me. And they were doing it, right here, right now – it was happening, and I felt as if I might collapse at the sheer emotion of it all. But the moment didn't last long. I think embarrassment overcame all of us. So we separated and threw ourselves with vigour into the not particularly challenging task of putting lunch together.

Mum washed lettuce leaves and Leif and I carried the little table outside and laid it. I opened the tubs of hummus and tzatziki that Mum had bought and sliced the bread.

It was a strange feeling, doing something so ordinary. Because doing it together as a family was extraordinary. I felt like I was playing a part in a theatre piece, or working my way through one of the scenarios I'd spent my life building inside my head.

As we ate, we began to chat almost normally. Mum and Leif – I couldn't bring myself to call him Dad again – had a lot of catching up to do, and I felt honoured to be present, to be able to witness it all.

Leif explained how he'd been married to a university professor and arch-feminist, and how they had argued about having children, an act which bizarrely she had claimed demeaned women. He said he'd brought her to Santorini once but it had been awful. He'd been thinking about Mum the whole time, and his wife – her name was Aslaug – hadn't much liked the place.

Both Mum and I wondered out loud how such a thing was possible but Leif insisted that it was. 'Blue, blue, everywhere,' he said, apparently channelling his ex-wife's voice. 'It's just so boring, Leif.'

Mum explained a little about her own marriage to Brian, too. But it was a very sweetened version, presumably for my benefit. I think that by the end of it, Leif must have been as confused as I was as to why they had finally split up.

We talked a little about me, too. Mum ragged me about my 'thing' with Baruch, and Leif said that Santorini was a very romantic place and he wasn't surprised at all. He'd seen Baruch, too, and agreed that he was a 'very good-looking boy'.

'Just don't put his phone number in your suitcase,' Leif joked, a joke which fell rather flat. We all sat in silence for a moment, thinking, I reckon, about all the trauma and lost opportunities that simple error had caused.

'Can I ask a bit about Conor?' I said eventually. It was the only subject that hadn't been touched upon.

'Of course,' Mum said. 'Ask anything you want.' But her eyes seemed to say otherwise.

'It's just the accident, really,' I said. 'Can one of you tell me vaguely what happened?'

'Oh,' Mum said. 'We don't have to talk about that right now, do we?'

'You just said I could ask anything,' I reminded her. But seeing that she was already closing up like a clam, I turned to Leif instead. 'Did you actually see it?'

'Did I see what?'

'The accident. Conor's accident. Were you there when it happened?'

'Oh, yes . . .' Leif said. A shadow swept over his face. 'I mean, no,' he corrected himself, and I suspected that Mother had been giving him the evil eye behind my back.

'Do you think I could have a word with Leif?' Mum asked, confirming my suspicions.

'What, so you can get your stories straight?'

'No,' Mum said. 'No, that's not it. What are you like? It's just . . . just . . . Give us a minute, OK?' She stood and beckoned to Leif. He looked utterly confused. I don't think he had any idea what was going on.

'You're supposed to follow her,' I explained. 'So she can tell you what lies to tell me.'

I almost walked away at that point. I sat there imagining their hushed tones behind the closed door and thought about leaving them to it. I even tensed my legs to stand a couple of times, but in the end I stayed. Whatever they were going to tell me, I was intrigued. Plus for some reason, I suspected that Leif wasn't going to want to lie to me. I don't know why I thought that, but I did. He just had one of those faces, I suppose.

When they finally returned it seemed I was right. 'So, Becky,' Mum said, sounding businesslike. 'We've discussed this, Leif and I, and there's another bit of the story we need to tell you. But I need to know that I can trust you. Because it's . . . well . . . sensitive, I suppose you could say.'

'Trust me?' I repeated, outraged. Then, 'Sensitive? How?'

'It's not that I *don't* trust you,' Mum said. 'I do. That's why I want to tell you this . . . this thing. But you can't tell anyone. Really. Not ever. If we tell you the truth, and Leif thinks we should, then you have to promise me.'

'So I won't tell anyone,' I said. 'No worries.'

'Not even Baruch,' Mum said.

'Especially not Baruch,' Leif commented gravely.

'Yes, you're right,' Mum agreed. 'Especially not Baruch.'

'OK,' I said, solemnly. 'Not even Baruch.'

Mum sighed and she and Leif looked at each other, silently negotiating who should start.

'I don't know where to begin,' Mum said.

'At the beginning,' Leif said. 'On the night that Conor—'

'No,' Mum said, interrupting him. 'No, we need to go further back. Otherwise it doesn't make any sense. It'll sound terrible.'

'OK,' Leif said. 'Start where you want.'

Mum began telling me her story. She told me, again, about the rave where she'd met Conor. She told me how he had come to London to meet her and had decided, despite her protests, to buy the tickets to Santorini. She said that he'd been drunk at the airport when she'd arrived, and that she'd almost changed her mind.

Bits of the story were apparently new to Leif, too, because he seemed surprised at times. At others he asked questions like, 'But why did you get on the plane? Why didn't you just go home?'

Mum did her best to answer all of our questions, though sometimes she struggled to make us understand.

She told me about Conor forcing himself upon her in Mykonos, and it was my turn to ask her why she hadn't gone to the police. Again, she struggled to explain.

From the point in the story where she met Leif, they started to tell me together, sometimes speaking simultaneously, at others alternating. From time to time they good-naturedly contradicted each other, which was cute to see because, I suppose, it made them seem like a real couple struggling to agree on the past.

Mum explained how Conor had hit her and how she'd met Leif on the stairs again; Leif about Mum's passport and how they had hunted for Conor everywhere because they'd desperately needed to get it back.

Mum's birthday sounded crazily romantic and tears came to my eyes as I realised that, against all odds, they'd come together to tell me, to remember, on her birthday all over again. And then their tale took a darker turn, and the hairs on the back of my neck began to prickle.

It was like one of those moments in a horror film when the music changes and you just know something bad's going to happen. The protagonists park up at the side of the road and head down a dark track to the cliff's edge, and you want to scream, 'Don't! Don't go down that track!'

As I had guessed, Conor had rolled up and a fight had ensued.

'He was a boxer,' Mum reminded me. 'And as fit and solid as a bull. He was invincible, really.'

'And drunk,' Leif added. 'He was worse when he was drunk.'

'Yes, he had that drunken madness, you know? The strength of twenty men.'

'He tried to take your mother,' Leif explained. 'He tried to force her into the car. So I told him that it was over. I told him we were in love.'

'I could have killed you for saying that,' Mum said. She turned to me. 'Can you imagine? It was like a red flag to a bull. It was like lighting a very short fuse, and on the end of the fuse was Conor.'

'I thought he might be reasonable,' Leif said. 'I thought he needed to know.'

'Reasonable . . .' Mum said sarcastically.

'He went crazy, then?' I asked.

'More than,' Leif said.

'Yes, it was much worse than crazy,' Mum agreed. 'He was like a killer in a film or something. Cold, like Dexter, you know? He grabbed Leif—'

'By the collar,' Leif said, taking a fist of T-shirt in one hand to demonstrate.

'And then he punched him,' Mum continued. 'Over and over again. He wouldn't stop.'

'He broke it,' Leif said, indicating his wonky nose. 'And two teeth here, too.'

'You lost two teeth?' Mum asked.

Leif nodded. 'They were like this,' he said, gesturing to indicate that they'd been wobbly. 'They came out when I got home. These four are joined together.' He pointed at his front four teeth.

'You had to have a bridge,' Mum said.

'Yes, a bridge.'

'So what did you do? How did you stop him?' I asked. 'You didn't push him, did you? You didn't push him off the cliff?'

'I'm really not sure you want to hear this, sweetheart,' Mum said, glancing concernedly at Leif.

'You're joking,' I said. 'If you think you're stopping there, you're crazy!'

'It's just . . . it's a bit dark,' Mum said. 'I don't want it to haunt you.'

'It won't,' I told her. 'Tell me. I need to know.'

Mum glanced at Leif again, and he shrugged and said, 'I think we have to finish the story, Laura. I can tell her if you want.'

'No,' Mum said. 'No, it's fine.' She took a deep breath. 'So, I really tried everything I could think of to stop him. I tried hanging around his neck. I tried hammering my fists on his back. But nothing made any difference. It was like he didn't even notice I was there.'

'I gave in,' Leif admitted. 'I knew I couldn't beat him. I wasn't brave or anything. I was crying, begging him to stop.'

'You were *so* brave,' Mum told him. Then to me, tearfully, 'Don't listen to him. He was *so* brave. I was convinced Conor was going to kill him. He just kept punching him, over and over. Like a punching ball. Then when Leif was on the floor, he started kicking him. It was horrific.'

'I think that I am dying,' Leif said. 'I really did. I am starting to pray to God. I mean, I don't believe, you know? But just in case, I am starting to pray.'

◆ ◆ ◆

Leif, who had raised his arms to protect his head, nodded feebly. 'You have win,' he said again. 'It's over.'

Conor snorted. 'I've barely got started, fella,' he said. Then, reaching between Leif's arms to grip his T-shirt, he pulled him to his feet again.

'You're going to kill him, Conor,' Laura cried.

'That,' Conor said, smiling at her, 'is the general idea.'

In that moment she realised it was true. They had just been words up until then, but in that instant she understood that Conor really *was* going to kill Leif. Right there. Right then. Right before her eyes. And neither fighting, nor pleading, nor letting him win was going to change it. If she didn't do something, Leif would be gone. The only man she had ever truly been in love with would quite simply no longer exist.

A jolt of adrenalin flowed through her and her tears ceased. Her brain seemed to shift into an unfamiliar mode of ultra-precise, triple-speed clarity, scanning the landscape once again for any kind of weapon and tugging her attention towards the car.

To the rhythm of Conor's metronomic punches, she quickly checked the interior, but there was nothing there she could use. She thought of driving at him but he had taken the keys. She tremblingly tried to check the boot, hoping to find a wheel brace or a jack, but it was locked.

Laura stood and looked analytically at the scene. She didn't have strength on her side. She didn't have a weapon, either. But she could, if she was clever, have the advantage of momentum and speed, and surprise.

As Conor jerked Leif upright again, positioning him in order to maximise the pleasure of hitting him squarely, she ran in a wide circle and sprinted towards him as fast as she could. She quite literally flew through the air for the last few yards, before landing her shoulder in the exact centre of Conor's muscular back.

The result was more impressive than she could have dared hope for. She sent him flying past Leif, through the air, and into the distance, sprawling headlong onto the ground. Even then he almost managed to end up on his feet, only to trip at the last minute and fall back again.

Released, Leif sank to the ground and curled up again, desperate to protect his face from the next wave of blows, and as Laura folded to her knees and reached out, he cowered from her touch, making her cry all over again.

She enveloped him in her arms. She would protect him with her own body and, if need be, they'd die there together. Leif hadn't asked for any of this and it was enough, she thought. If Conor was going to kill him then he'd have to kill her first.

'I'm so sorry, Leif,' she said, sobbing at the thought that they were about to die. 'I love you. And I'm so, so sorry.'

A few seconds went by, maybe a minute, before she dared to look back towards the car. It was throwing a moonlight shadow where Conor had fallen, so it was difficult to see him precisely, but she could just about make out the soles of his brogues pointing sideways.

Leif, who was whimpering with fear, eventually peered through his fingers as well. 'Where is he?' he asked, his voice trembling. 'Why has he stopped?'

'I don't know,' she whispered, craning her head and looking back towards the car.

She hugged Leif more tightly for a moment, then, realising that Conor might be only stunned momentarily, said, 'I'd better look. Stay there.'

Leif tried to grab her hand to stop her leaving, but she gently peeled back his trembling fingers and crept over to where Conor was lying.

He looked peaceful. That was her first thought. He looked peaceful, as if he was asleep and having a rather pleasant dream. It was then that she saw the rock.

'He hit his head, I think, when he fell,' she called out, glancing back at Leif who was crouching, attempting, with difficulty, to stand. 'Should we tie him up or something?'

'Tie him up?' Leif repeated, as he slowly limped towards her. His face was so covered with blood, and he advanced with such difficulty, that he looked like an extra from a zombie movie.

'For when he comes around,' she said, her voice wobbling madly. 'What if he starts all over again?'

Leif sank to his knees beside her and peered at Conor. Blood dripped from his nose onto Conor's shirt. 'Is he breathing?' Leif asked.

'Of course he's breathing,' she said. 'He's not *dead*.' But as they knelt there in the cool night air, a chill came over her. 'What are you doing?' she asked.

In a strangely gentle gesture, Leif had taken Conor's hand. 'I'm checking for his heart,' he said, pressing a bloody finger to Conor's wrist. Laura braced herself. She was certain he was going to wake up and start all over again.

Conor moved then, and both Leif and Laura jumped back from his body. His legs had jerked suddenly as if he'd had an electric shock.

She looked nervously around for a weapon, but once again could see nothing of use.

But Conor did not stir, and after a minute or so the couple returned to his side. Leif took Conor's wrist once again, and leaned in to listen to his heart.

'He is dead,' Leif announced, his Norwegian intonation making this sound like an everyday announcement rather than the life-changing news that it surely was.

'What?' Laura asked. That information didn't seem to make any sense to her.

A trickle of blood oozed from the corner of Conor's mouth as Leif said again, 'He is dead. His heart has stopped.'

'I got hysterical,' Mum said. 'I went totally off the rails for a bit.'

'She really did,' Leif confirmed. 'I was wondering if I should slap her, you know?'

'It's hardly surprising,' I said. 'I mean, that's horrific. And was he dead? Was he actually dead?'

'Yes, he was gone,' Mum said. 'It was hitting his head on the rock, I think, that got him. It took me a while to believe it, but once I did, I got the shakes. My teeth were chattering and my hands were shaking. I couldn't do anything. I couldn't even think.

'We held each other for a while. Leif was worried I was cold, but I think it was just the shock. Leif was in a far worse state than me physically. He looked like *he'd* been in a car crash. But he was really calm and collected. It was me that was crying and shaking. Eventually, we started to walk back towards the bike, but halfway there I had this terrible idea.'

Leif hadn't wanted to do it at first. He'd wanted to go to the police.

But Laura was scared. She was really scared. They were in Greece, she reminded him, and who knew what Greek police were like?

Physically, they were in a terrible state, too. Any policeman would take one look at them and know they'd been in a fight.

'What if they think we *murdered* him?' she wept. 'What if they throw us in prison?'

Gradually Laura convinced him. And eventually Leif caved in.

But where Laura was hysterical, a strange calm of responsibility descended on Leif. If they were going to do this, they needed to do it perfectly, he thought. He'd read a lot of Swedish thrillers, and creating a convincing scene came surprisingly naturally to him.

While Laura sat shaking and weeping, Leif loped back down the track for the bike so they could use the headlights and his torch to see what they were doing.

Together, they dragged Conor to the car. He was so heavy that Leif momentarily doubted Laura's plan was even possible, but together, eventually, they managed to get him into the driver's seat.

Leif wiped their prints from the car with a rag he found in the boot and put the keys in the ignition and started the engine.

There were bloodstains on the ground, and so, on their hands and knees, they grovelled in the dust to brush them away, Laura's tears mixing with the blood and the dry earth as they worked. They had to dig up the bloody rock Conor had fallen on, too, and roll it over the edge.

Finally, they released the brake, shut the door and pushed the car to the very edge. It was only at the last possible moment that Leif remembered Laura's passport. And so they performed a gruesome final search of Conor's pockets, and then the car, before finally finding Laura's bum-bag in the boot.

Leif tried, for a while, to get the car to drive itself off the cliff. It would look more convincing that way, he reckoned. But without Conor's foot on the accelerator pedal, it stalled every time, and so eventually they put their backs against the boot and pushed with all their might.

Once the front wheels had gone off, the bottom of the car grounded on the rocks, and for a few panicky moments, they believed, once again, that they had failed. But then Leif had an idea to lift the rear end of the car rather than pushing it, and like a see-saw, the car tipped and slid eerily, almost silently, into the darkness.

Bracing themselves for the explosion, they ran to the bike. Laura feared that the whole town would turn up in seconds. But other than a vague crunching sound from below, nothing happened. It seemed that only in films did cars explode.

As they rode towards town, they argued about what to do next. Leif wanted to stay, but Laura argued over and over again he must leave. He looked like a wreck, she reminded him. He represented the most damning piece of evidence there was that Conor's accident wasn't quite as it seemed. Laura herself had only a few bruises, and they were nothing she couldn't cover up with make-up, but Leif, she insisted from the back of the scooter, had to vanish to save them both.

'So you left the next day?' I asked Leif.

'No. I left right then. I sneak to the room. Olav, my friend is there. He is so angry, he wants to kill Conor. So I had to tell him the truth. The only person I ever told this thing. I take a quick shower. And then he takes me to the port. We didn't want people to see me in the morning so Olav did checkout and everything and met me on the boat. He took the bike back, too.'

'Where did you sleep?' Mum asked.

'In the bushes, behind the port. I was very tired. When I got to Oslo, I went to the hospital. It hurt quite a lot. I have two broken ribs, and the nose of course. And the next day, the teeth. But the worst was my heart.' He reached out for Mum's hand at that point. 'She broke my heart,' he said. 'The call that never comes, you know?'

'Because you lost his address?'

Mum nodded. 'Well, Aegean did. Or BA.'

'And what happened then, Mum?' I asked. 'What happened with the police and everything?'

'Yes, please tell,' Leif said. 'I don't know this either.'

To avoid being seen together, he'd dropped her at the edge of town. But as soon as she stepped into the pool of light provided by a streetlamp, she realised this was a mistake. Her T-shirt was bloodstained, and the paranoid terror that someone would notice and remember her made her legs go wobbly as she walked.

Once the first group of tourists had passed, she ducked into an alleyway and turned the T-shirt inside out, but it was only a slight improvement. The stains had soaked right through. In the end, turning left and right to avoid oncoming tourists, it took her almost half an hour to get back to the room.

Once inside, she locked the door and moved to the bathroom. Her shorts were muddy, but it was the T-shirt that looked the worst. She was going to have to handwash everything, and quickly. Because if the police arrived, her clothes would be a dead giveaway.

It was only as she started to undress that she remembered her things in Leif's room. So she pulled her dirty clothes back on and strode to the door, actually relieved she would have an excuse to see Leif's face one last time before he left. But when she pulled the door open, she was startled. Because there, on the doorstep, his fist raised ready to knock, was Olav.

'Your case,' he said.

'Olav! Is he OK?'

'Yes. He's OK. I am taking him to the port right now,' Olav said, speaking quietly, urgently. 'But he asked me to give you this.' In his hand was a folded sheet of paper.

She dragged her case indoors, took the sheet of paper from Olav's grasp, thanked him, wished him goodbye, and relocked the door.

She fingered the sheet of paper for a moment, but then reminded herself that washing her clothes was urgent. So she set it down on her suitcase, and returned to the bathroom to undress.

Her shorts came up clean enough, but the stains wouldn't come out of the T-shirt, no matter how much she washed it. So after having stuffed it at the bottom of the rubbish bin, then, changing her mind, hiding it between the mattress and the bed, only to retrieve it again, she finally cut it to strips with a knife and, bit by bit, she flushed it down the toilet. The process seemed to take forever.

She tidied Conor's clothes into the wardrobe where they couldn't be seen – their presence was just too upsetting. Then, feeling numb and febrile, she sat cross-legged on the bed and unfolded the sheet of paper. It contained only four lines of Leif's spidery handwriting. Name, address, phone number, and six words, three in Norwegian and three in English. She guessed that they meant the same thing. *Jeg elsker deg.* I love you.

She felt numb as she looked at those words. Because the situation suddenly seemed hopeless to her. Even if the police didn't turn up to drag her away, surely whatever she'd had with Leif was now broken? Surely the horrific events of the day and their joint cover-up left no opening, no breathing space for love.

At the thought of Conor's body inside the cold, mangled car, she felt nauseous and returned to the bathroom believing that she was going to be sick. But nothing happened. There was no sickness; there were no more tears. Conor was dead. Leif was gone. She just felt cold and shaky and as alone as she ever had.

'Nothing happened that night, or the next morning,' Mum said. 'Nothing at all. I'm sure they must have found the car pretty fast; there were tourists everywhere. But perhaps it took a while to work out who he was, or to find out where he'd been staying. I don't know, really.

'I thought very carefully about what to do next. The people in the hotel knew there was no love lost between us, so I didn't make a fuss immediately. But in the evening I made myself look as pretty as possible and casually asked the desk clerk if Conor had booked a table for dinner. When he told me that he hadn't, I asked if he'd seen anything of him.

'He asked me about my passport. So I told him that I'd found it. I played the dipsy woman card and batted my eyelashes and apologised for troubling him with it. It had been in my handbag all along, I said. Something like that, anyway.

'The police arrived when I was eating dinner. I could see them from where I was sitting. They showed the guy on reception Conor's driving licence, and he pointed out where I was sitting. They crossed the restaurant to join me. Absolutely everyone was staring.'

'You must have been terrified, weren't you?' I asked.

Mum nodded. 'I was,' she said. 'But I felt numb, too, from the shock, I suppose. And from lack of sleep. But I was fully expecting them to accuse me of something and lead me away, so yes, I was scared. I was petrified.

'One of the policemen, the younger one, addressed me as Mrs O'Leary. So I told him that, no, my name was Ryan. I asked if something had happened to Conor. I was very aware that I needed to avoid overacting. I was terrified I'd over- or under-do it all, and he'd sniff out the lie like your grandmother always did when I lied to her.

'He asked me if he was my boyfriend, I think. And I answered vaguely. I said "sort of" or something like that. I told them it was a holiday romance. And I asked why they wanted to know. I asked if something had happened.

'"He's had an accident," the younger one said. "I'm very sorry but he is dead." I don't think his English was good enough to be subtle about it. I started to cry, which was perfect really. I didn't even have to force it. I cried from relief that they didn't seem to suspect me of anything, and I cried for Conor, too. The policeman's words had made the whole thing seem real. *It's my fault*, I kept thinking. *If I hadn't pushed him . . .* And so I sat there in the middle of a crowded restaurant with tears rolling down my face.'

'It's weird that they did it in public,' I commented. 'Telling you something like that.'

'Yes,' Mum said. 'Yes, I know. Eventually they led me to the room and I braced myself for some difficult questions. But there were none. They packed up all Conor's stuff in his suitcase, which felt weird. They were ever so polite, showing me each item and asking if they could take it all. They asked if I wanted to see his body, too, and I started to cry again just at the thought of how bashed up it must be after that fall. I think my tears made them feel embarrassed, because after a brief conversation in Greek, one of them told me that it wouldn't be necessary.

'They asked me if I wanted to deal with things, or something like that, and at first I didn't know what they meant. I'm not sure quite what words they used. Their English wasn't brilliant and I was crying a lot. It's all a bit blurry. But in the end I understood they meant the body, getting it home, all that stuff. They said they'd already been in contact with his brother – I had forgotten he even had one – and the thought of his poor brother brought on a fresh flood of tears. I asked if I could leave the next day – I had a flight booked, remember – and they said that of course I could, which was totally unexpected. They just asked if the hotel had my home address so they could contact me, and I lied and said that they had. It seemed a reasonable enough mistake to make under the circumstances. And then they left.'

'Just like that?' I said. 'No statement? No fingerprints? Nothing?'

'I don't think they were very good policemen, really,' Mum said, wrinkling her nose. 'Or at any rate, they certainly weren't very suspicious. I suppose from their point of view a known drunkard had driven off a cliff. Maybe it happens a lot.'

'And you flew home the next day?'

Mum nodded. 'I flew home.'

'And they never contacted you?' Leif asked.

Mum shook her head. 'Never. I mean, maybe they tried to, but no. The only person who ever contacted me was Conor's brother. He phoned about a week after I got back. He'd got my number from Conor's phone bill, or something. He wanted me to go to the funeral. Well, he wanted to invite me, at least. I'm not sure he cared if I actually went.'

'Did you go?'

Mum shook her head. 'No. I felt terrible, honestly – I felt sick about it. But I was too scared of getting tangled up in it all. Of having to explain things to people. It seemed safest just to lie low, you know? He didn't ask for my address or anything. And he never called again. So that was the end of that, really.'

'That must have been hard, though,' I said. 'His poor brother. He must have been really upset.'

'I think it must have been a lot of hassle for him. You know, getting the body back and everything. But I honestly got the feeling they weren't close. And he didn't seem surprised. He asked me if Conor had been drinking, actually. And when I said yes, he explained that he meant was he drinking in general, not just on the night of the accident. So I told him the truth, that yes, he'd been drunk pretty much all the time. And he said a strange thing. He said it was because of the home. Something like that, anyway.'

'The home?'

'Yeah. I asked him what he meant, and he said, "Oh nothing. Just shit that happened when he was a kid." That's the only phrase I remember clearly. *Shit that happened when he was a kid.* That's what he said. I remember Conor telling me that he'd grown up in care, and from the little his brother had said, it sounded like he'd maybe not had a very good time of it.'

'Maybe he got abused or something,' I said.

'Maybe,' Mum said. 'I can't say it didn't cross my mind.'

'And the letter?' Leif prompted. 'My address?'

'Well, that's like I said,' Mum told him. 'I'd tucked it into the lining of my suitcase. It seemed a bit . . . what's the word? *Incriminating*, that's it.'

'How so?' I asked.

'Well, it linked Leif to me, didn't it? And it sort of showed that I hadn't been in love with Conor, too. It provided a motive, as they say, for a fight. That's how I saw things, anyway. So I tucked it into the lining. There was a split in the satin at the back, and I hid it in there. Otherwise they probably would have delivered my suitcase to Leif in Norway. It was his address, after all.'

'Of course,' I said. 'I didn't think of that.'

'And you were pregnant,' Leif said. 'When did you know this?'

'Well, I had some . . . Tell me to stop if this is too much information, OK? But I had some spotting. Quite regularly, actually.'

'Spotting?' Leif repeated.

'It's when you bleed, just a bit,' I explained, because Mum was looking embarrassed. 'Like at the beginning of your period, only lighter.'

'So I thought I was OK, you see?' Mum continued. 'I thought my period was mucked up, which would hardly have been surprising, under the circumstances. But I thought I was safe.'

'You didn't want me?' I asked, feeling genuinely hurt.

'No, it wasn't that, sweetheart,' Mum said. 'But if I had been pregnant, which of course I was – only I didn't *think* I was – God, I'm not explaining this properly, am I?'

'I'm not sure,' I said. 'Keep going.'

'So, if I'd realised straight off that I was pregnant. Or if I hadn't believed that I had proof that I wasn't, then I would have definitely taken a pill to . . . you know . . .'

'Abort me,' I said brutally.

'But it wasn't you then, was it?' Mum said. 'It was just the beginning of a baby. The seed of a baby. Potentially *Conor's* baby. And I definitely didn't want that.'

'But you had spotting,' I said. 'So you didn't. Well, thank God for that.'

Mum sighed. 'Sweetheart,' she said gently. 'Try to understand.'

'I am trying,' I said. 'This is me trying. Carry on.'

'By the time I realised – because I had a couple of bouts of spotting a few weeks apart – I was more than eight weeks pregnant. And almost the second I realised, your grandmother worked it out too. I'd been weird ever since coming home, of course. My moods were all over the place because of what had happened. I was depressed, I think. And I kept bursting into tears. But then I got morning sickness, and it all just fell into place.'

'I remember you crying when I was little,' I said. 'Was that because of what had happened?'

'Sometimes it was. More often than not it was because I couldn't get in touch with Leif. I mean, I knew he was your father by then. So I was devastated. For both of us. He was the only good thing that had ever happened to me and he was out of reach. I was sick with it. But sometimes it was for Conor. Sometimes it was the horror of that night. I used to have nightmares about it. About the fight and about that damned sheet of paper.'

'And what about Gran?' I asked. 'She must have gone apeshit.'

'Apeshit?' Leif queried.

'It means mad. Angry. My gran was religious.'

'Yes, she was *very* religious,' Mum said. 'And a bit mad, really. And yes, she went batshit crazy. She kept slapping my face. And she locked me in my room for two days. I had to pee in a vase. She kept dragging me to confession, too. I just used to make stuff up. I wasn't telling *them* what had happened.'

'Did she want you to get an abortion?'

'No!' Mum said, laughing at the ridiculousness of the idea. 'No, you must be joking. That would have been the biggest sin of all. No, she wanted to send me to some awful place in Ireland to have the baby, like we were still in the fifties or something. She wanted me to hand the baby over for adoption as soon as it was born. I heard her discussing it with the parish priest. That's why I ran away.'

'To Margate.'

'Yes, to Margate. Your Aunt Abby had moved there to be with Winston, her boyfriend. They had this mouldy flat overlooking the telephone exchange where they put me up for a while. I stayed there a couple of months, I think. And then I slowly sorted myself out.'

'Did you ever think about adoption?' I asked. 'Did you ever consider it?' The idea that if my grandmother had had her way, I'd have been handed over to some random family, was terrifying to me.

'Look,' Mum said. 'I'm not going to lie to you. Not now. Not now you know everything else. So if I'm being honest, I'd have to admit that if I'd known I was pregnant, and because it might have been Conor's, I'd definitely have taken a pill. And if I'm telling the truth, I kept the adoption thing in the back of my mind as a bit of an escape route. I wasn't sure I'd be able to cope, you see. Not financially, or in any other way, really. I was still very immature. But when you were born, you looked so much like Leif. And it was just out of the question. I was still hoping to find him somehow, and I just couldn't imagine telling him I'd had his child and given it away. And I *wanted* you too. I loved you, almost immediately. I loved you like I've never loved anyone, sweetheart. You know that.'

'And now you did find me,' Leif said. 'And you made a good choice, because I will be very angry if you tell me I can't meet lovely Becky.'

'Yes,' Mum said, her mouth smiling while her eyes still looked sad. 'Yes, better late than never, I suppose.'

I asked then if we could go out there. I asked if they would show me where it happened. 'Or would that be too gruesome?'

Mum shrugged. 'I can't say I'm keen,' she said. 'But I suppose if you really want to. What do you think, Leif?'

Leif shook his head. 'I don't mind,' he said. 'I go there every time. I don't know quite why. For the memories, I think. For the bad ones and good ones. For Conor, too. To pay my respects.'

EIGHTEEN

Laura

It turned out that Leif, too, had rented a scooter, so we decided to ride out there together. He had to return to his room for the keys and then we all met up in the car park at street level.

Becky rode alone and, for old times' sake, I rode pillion behind Leif. I had a huge lump in my throat the whole way there.

We parked up next to an air-conditioning shop that had sprung up in the middle of nowhere, and locked our helmets in the top cases of the bikes and started to walk out towards the cliffs.

The narrow lane, which had been a dust track all those years ago, was now covered with smooth tarmac which shimmered in the heat, but even though it was hot, I kept getting the shivers. The two unfinished houses now had windows and people living in them, though even now, one of them still had metal spikes sticking skywards, ready for one-day-there'll-be-another-floor.

'These were still being built, back then,' I explained to Becky as we passed them. 'They didn't have windows or anything.'

'Your mother wanted us to live in one of them,' Leif said. 'Do you remember, Laura?'

I shook my head. 'No, it wasn't one of these. It was one right on the edge of the cliff. It was a house you could only see when you got right to the edge.'

The day was hot, but a breeze was blowing, a breeze that got stronger the further we walked. And the sky was deepest blue. It may be true, as Leif's ex-wife said, that Santorini is blue everywhere, blue every day. But the nature of that blue changes. On some days, particularly hot, windless days, it's a hazy, baby blue. But on windy days, like that day, it is deepest sapphire blue, sometimes almost a Klein blue. It seemed a sad, melancholy kind of blue to me that day.

It was a long walk to the cliff edge, even further than I remembered, and about halfway there Becky asked why we hadn't ridden. The road, after all, was perfectly smooth.

'I like to walk,' Leif told her. 'I like to use the time to remember.'

I think we all knew what he meant.

When we reached the cliff edge, I discovered that three huge concrete blocks had been placed there to mark the end of the road.

'So this is where it happened?' Becky asked.

'Yes,' I said, scanning the area for landmarks. 'These blocks weren't here, obviously.'

'No,' Leif said. 'They put these here just after. I came back the next summer and they were here.'

'You came back the very next summer?' I asked. 'Weren't you scared about the police?'

'Sure,' Leif said. 'But I was more scared of never seeing you again.'

I scanned the horizon once more and pointed to a house in the distance where it clung, as if by magic, to the cliff face. 'That's the one,' I said. 'That was the house I wanted to live in.'

'Maybe we still can,' Leif said. 'If it's for sale.'

I almost burst into tears at those words. But by pretending to myself that he'd been joking, I managed to keep it together. I just about kept my emotions in check.

'So run me through it,' Becky said, casting around. 'If it's not too hard for you, that is?'

'No,' I said. 'No, it's fine. You know most of it anyway. And it was so long ago. It feels a bit like a film I saw or a story someone told me, these days.'

'I know that feeling too,' Leif said. 'But it wasn't, was it?'

'No,' I agreed. 'No, it all really happened.'

Becky was looking at me expectantly, so I steeled myself and continued. 'So we were here, looking at the sunset. We stayed until it was dark.'

'Kissing,' Leif said. 'Good things happened here, too.'

'I'm sure Becky doesn't want to know about the kissing part,' I said.

'Only, I do,' Becky said. 'Because that's where I came from. Well, what came after the kissing.'

'No, you came from what happened *before* the kissing,' I told her. 'Before we got here. Nothing to do with this awful place. Anyway . . . we kissed. And then Leif told me that his boat was the next day. I was really upset about that.'

'Your flight was only one day after,' Leif pointed out.

'That's true. Mine was in two days' time. Just like now, in fact.'

'You are leaving the day after tomorrow?' Leif asked.

I nodded. 'I'm afraid so. Anyway, we had just agreed to stay in touch. I was going to visit Norway.'

'I wanted to show her the fjords,' Leif said.

'He wanted me to live on the fjords, but I said they'd be too cold and rainy. I wanted to live here in the sunshine.'

'The fjords of Santorini,' Leif said.

'Yes. Yes, I remember that . . .' I said wistfully. 'And I was going to show him London. You said you wanted to visit London, didn't you? And that's when Conor turned up and everything turned horrific.'

'The road was very bumpy,' Leif said. 'And very dark. We are worrying he will drive off the cliff. But he stops right there. Where the blocks are.'

Becky walked past the blocks to peer down at the sea. Because I was worried that she might slip, I asked her to come back. When, as ever, she ignored me, I joined her and took hold of her hand. Leif joined us, too, taking her other hand, and with the wind in our ears, and my hair blowing madly around, the three of us looked down at the sea below where it was crashing on the rocks.

'I wonder what happened to the car?' Becky asked. 'I mean, I wonder how they got rid of it.'

'A crane, I think,' Leif said. 'I can't see any other way.'

'Or maybe it just rusted away,' I said, another shudder rippling through my body as the image of Conor, dead in the car, forced its way into my mind.

'No,' Leif said. 'No, the next summer it was gone.'

We returned to the blocks and sat down in silence.

Leif pulled his wallet from one of the many pockets in his hiking trousers and produced a tatty colour snapshot. It was a photo of Leif and myself in this exact spot, the one I'd imagined on our joint mantelpiece. In it, we were laughing at the self-timer business and behind us the sun was setting in an extraordinary display of colour.

'My God, you kept it,' I said.

'I kept them all,' Leif said. 'The others are at home. In Norway.'

'You look so young,' Becky commented reverently. 'And so happy.'

I couldn't speak to reply. My throat had constricted and tears were pushing at my eyeballs. Because I was remembering just how happy I had been that day – how full of promise the world had seemed to me back then. And how a terrible moment in this terrible place had taken it all away.

Leif put his arm around me at that moment, and I began to cry properly, letting salty tears slide down my face. I think both Becky and Leif must have shed a tear as well.

'I just wish . . .' I managed to say, when the tears abated. 'I just wish things had been different. It's all such a waste.'

'They still can be different,' Leif said, giving me a squeeze around the shoulders. 'It's never too late.'

A wave of anger rolled over me at the cruel hand fate had dealt us. 'Only they can't,' I said, bitterly. 'It's all gone, isn't it? Becky's grown up, and you weren't there. You missed the whole damned thing. And we can't get that back no matter how hard we try. Conor . . . he stole our future.'

'No,' Leif said. 'No, we still have a future.'

'We have a *future*?' I repeated dismissively, and Leif looked exactly as you might expect him to in the face of such cruelty. He looked hurt.

I can't explain really, why I was so mean to him in that moment, except to say I was feeling angry, not with Leif, but with life. Poor Leif just happened to be the person who was next to me at the time.

He removed his arm from my shoulders and crossed to a patch of wildflowers. They had a crazy number of bees buzzing around them.

'Don't pick them,' Becky said, as he did just that. 'What about the poor bees?'

'I only take one,' Leif said, returning to the cliff edge, 'For Conor. The bees have enough other flowers.'

Becky followed him to the edge. 'I'm sorry,' she said. 'I didn't realise.'

I stood and joined them. 'For Conor?' I asked. 'Are you having me on?'

'Without Conor,' Leif said, 'we would never have met.'

And in an instant, my whole point of view shifted, and I saw that Leif was right. Because yes, without Conor, I would quite possibly never have visited Santorini. And I would certainly never have met Leif. Even Becky, my beloved daughter, was a direct result of the twists and ricochets that happened because of my time with Conor. That moment, on the cliff – the three of us. Even that couldn't have existed without Conor.

'Sometimes the worst things make the best things happen,' Leif said.

'Yes,' I agreed. 'Yes, I suppose you're right. Sometimes they do.'

Leif released the flower, and as it fell towards the sea, he said, 'To Conor.'

'To Conor,' I repeated. And then, as one, as a sort of family, I suppose, we turned and began to walk solemnly back towards the main road.

We were about halfway along the track before anyone spoke. 'Your flights,' Leif said. 'They're the day after tomorrow, yes?'

'Yes,' I said. 'Yes, I'm sorry about that. And yours?'

'I don't have one,' Leif said.

'You don't have one?'

'No, I'm retired. So I am thinking I will stay here for a while. I always wanted to see Santorini in winter, you know? To see what it is like.'

'You're retired?' I exclaimed. 'At fifty?'

'It's the oil business,' Leif said. 'It's very hard. But good money. And I never spend anything, so . . .'

'Wow,' I said. 'Well, good for you. That must feel wonderful.'

'It could,' Leif said. 'It could feel wonderful. If you'll stay.'

I glanced in embarrassment back at Becky, but she had paused to take a picture of a butterfly with her phone and was safely out of earshot.

'Do you have to go home so soon?' Leif asked, taking my hand.

'I don't know,' I said.

'When I come here, I'm always hoping I will see you,' Leif told me. 'Every year, I am hoping. And I always have this dream that we will just stay here, together. That we will rent that house you wanted.

Or another one, the same. That we will live the life we wanted. Do you think that's craysee?'

I smiled, because he had pronounced 'crazy' *craysee*, exactly as he had on this same day, twenty-four years earlier. And that memory linked the Leif I had known back then, the Leif I had been madly in love with, to this gentle, hopeful man standing beside me.

'No,' I said, speaking with difficulty. 'No, I don't think that's craysee at all.'

'But your life,' Leif said. 'You need to get home?'

'No,' I said, after a moment's thought. 'No, not really. Not immediately, anyway. I'm not working at the moment. I just lost my job, actually. I mean, there are bills to pay. I have to go to the job centre and stuff. But, no. There's no reason why I couldn't stay for a bit.'

'A while?' Leif said. 'Could you stay for a while?'

'Yes,' I told him. 'Yes I could.'

'Good,' Leif said. 'Because a while is longer than a bit, yes?'

'Yes,' I said, the strangest feeling of déjà vu washing over me. 'Yes, I suppose it is.'

When we got back to Oia, Baruch came rushing out to meet Becky. 'This is your father?' he asked, and when Becky nodded solemnly, he stroked her arm and asked, 'You want me to close the shop for an hour? You want to take time and we talk?'

'Yes,' Becky said, sounding close to tears. 'Yes, I'd really like that.'

'And us,' Leif said. 'Shall we go and get some food? I'm so hungry.'

'Me too,' I agreed, turning to Becky. 'I'll meet you back at our place later, OK? Have a nice time with your beau. But don't forget what we said.'

'Don't worry, Mum,' she said. 'My lips are sealed.' And then she vanished into the shadowed interior of the minimart, closing the door behind her. A hand appeared, to flip the sign over so that it read 'Closed'.

I wondered if Becky and Baruch would find a way to carry on their relationship. I hoped so, because I could tell from the way Baruch had understood Becky's mood, and from the way he had been worried about her, that there was a future in it if they'd just give it the space to blossom. And if fate would only decide to let them make their own way, of course.

'Up here?' Leif said, taking my hand and leading me gently towards the town centre.

'No,' I said, pulling back the other way. 'No, let's eat at the bottom of the Dreaded Steps.'

'I'm sorry?'

'At the little port. Where you swam that first time.'

'Oh,' Leif said. 'Yes, of course. OK.'

As we started to walk side by side towards the start of the staircase, I could feel my shoulders relaxing. Some tension I'd been holding for years, for as long as I could remember in fact, was draining away.

I'd been broken by what had happened – I'd always known it, even as I'd pretended that it wasn't the case. My hopes, my belief in hope, even, had been decimated and I had struggled for the longest time to even continue. Leif had been a brief island of hope in the middle of a vast, terrifying sea, and once he was gone I couldn't see anywhere on the horizon that I could even head for. I think, had I not had a daughter to look after, I might have ended my own life on more than one occasion.

But I suddenly felt stronger, as if things were back on track, as if someone had closed the brackets containing the last twenty-four years and the previous sentence had resumed. Could it really be that simple? Had the joyous, hopeful Laura of twenty-four years earlier been simply hiding in a corner, waiting for real life to start again?

As we passed by room 23, Leif paused. 'Can we just go in here for a minute?' he asked.

'To your room?' I said. 'Why, do you need something?'

'Yes, I need something,' Leif confirmed. 'I need to kiss you.'

I laughed embarrassedly at this but Leif insisted. 'Yes?' he said. 'It's OK? It is your birthday, after all. You can't have a birthday without a kiss.'

'OK,' I laughed. 'Why not? But just a kiss. And then we eat because I am way too hungry for anything else.'

I watched him as he slid his key into the door and felt overcome by an unexpected eruption of happiness. Out of nowhere, everything felt right in the world. Becky had met her father; she perhaps even had a boyfriend. I was in Santorini and the sky and the sea were deepest blue; the sun was shining but thanks to the gentle breeze it wasn't unbearably hot. There, smiling at me, was Leif. And maybe that meant there was a future, after all. Maybe there was a future for me that didn't involve the old age of cold, drizzle and loneliness I'd been increasingly imagining, but one of love, laughter and blue skies. I had that same feeling I'd had all those years before, a feeling I'd forgotten up until now, almost certainly because remembering it without being able to recreate it had been unbearable. But here it was again: that sense of belonging was back. Against all odds, I found myself in the right place at the right time with the right person, all over again.

Leif had opened the door and was bowing theatrically as he gestured towards the interior. 'Your palace, madam,' he said, grinning so broadly that his face looked split in two.

As I stepped into the room – that very same room – I half expected to find Olav there smoking a joint.

But it was just us. We were alone together, at last.

EPILOGUE

Becky

We travelled home, as planned, on the fourth of September.

Changing our flights had turned out to be not only a nightmare, but outrageously expensive, the equivalent in fact of three full return flights at the price we'd originally paid. Plus, Mum needed to sign on almost as soon as we got home, otherwise her benefits would get stopped. But I got to spend two gorgeous nights with Baruch and one full day with my father before we left.

On the final day, Mum and I joined his group for one of their hill-walks, a gentle amble from Akrotiri to the Red Beach, a route which I'm pretty sure had been downgraded due to our virgin status as hillwalkers. The six of us rode out to Akrotiri on our random collection of scooters, which was fun. Leif's friends seemed to be really young at heart and kept overtaking each other as we rode.

It was a sunny day with a hazy blue sky and a gentle breeze blowing, and initially Mum, Leif and I walked together, out front. But I soon got into conversation with a woman in the group and ended up dropping back, while Mum and Leif strode ahead. Her name was Anita, and she asked me all the usual questions – you know, how long we had been there, and what we'd been up to . . .

Out of the blue, because I was struggling to think about such ordinary things that day, I asked her what he was like.

'Who?' she asked. 'Oh, you mean Leif? Your father?'

I pulled a face. 'That seems weird, I suppose,' I said. 'Asking a complete stranger what my father's like.'

'It would be,' Anita said. 'But not in your case. Your case is kind of special, yes?'

'Yes,' I agreed. 'Yes, I'm a very special case. So, do you know him well, or is he just, like, a walking buddy?'

Anita laughed again. 'I've known Leif since I was five,' she said. 'But I'm not sure I can be . . . what's the word? Neutral?'

'Objective?' I offered.

'Yes, objective. Sorry, my English isn't great.'

'Your English is amazing!' I said. 'And neutral is fine too.'

'Well, thanks. But no, I'm not sure I can be objective. I think I love Leif more than almost anyone else in my life.'

I frowned. 'You're not . . . ?' I asked, wiggling a finger to indicate the two of them.

'God, no!' Anita said. 'No, I'm gay. I have a wife. She's in Oslo. But she's working, so she couldn't come this year.'

'Oh, cool,' I said.

'No, I've known Leif since I started school. He's an amazing person.'

'How?' I asked. 'How is he amazing?' I think that deep down I was still hoping to discover a Superman suit hidden beneath his hiking gear.

'He's just so nice,' Anita said. 'That sounds . . . it sounds like nothing, I suppose. But he's calm and generous. He's very helpful. He's the person you can call at midnight, yes? Because your car's broken or a pipe is burst, or just because your girlfriend's left you and you need a cup of hot chocolate and a cry. You know, I've never seen Leif say he's too busy to help someone. And I've only ever seen him get angry once, and that was against someone who was . . . *mistreating*? This is right? Yes, mistreating one of his friends. He's just the best, most reliable friend you could have. You can always count on Leif. Always.'

'Right,' I said. 'It must be nice. To have a friend like that.'

'Yes, it is,' Anita said. 'Having a friend like that changes your life. It really does.'

'So he's nice,' I said. 'He's *extra* nice.'

'I often think *nice* is underrated these days,' Anita said. 'Do you know what I mean? We value cleverness and intelligence and strength. Money, too. But nice is incredibly special. And it's not so easy to be this way all the time, you know? Other people are very difficult. It takes a lot of effort to understand them and stay nice despite everything.'

'Yes,' I agreed. 'Yes, I definitely know what you mean.'

'So, yes, Leif's very special to me. I think you'll really like him. I hope you get the chance to know him better, now.'

'I'll certainly try,' I said.

A man in the group, Jens, joined us, and after a few minutes both he and Anita began chatting in Norwegian, so I sped up until I caught up with Mum and Leif.

We were walking along a coastal path cut into the rock face. To our left the sea was sparkling in the sunlight like a million tiny jewels. It looked amazing. Mum and Leif were chatting easily, and he was making her laugh quite a lot.

Thanks to Anita, I began to think about Leif's niceness. Because it was true that he really did seem to ooze good humour. There was something incredibly open and honest about him that I'd picked up on the first time I'd met him, when I had suspected he'd never lie to me. And I got to wondering if being happy and helpful and nice wasn't perhaps my father's superpower. At any rate, it seemed a nice idea to hold about him.

We picnicked on the Red Beach – it was far less busy than the previous time we'd come, because it was now September, I suppose.

Mum and Leif splashed around in the shallows like kids. It was the most relaxed, by far, that I had ever seen her, and I couldn't help but feel a little sad as I imagined how different my childhood could have been if they'd only been able to be together.

On the flight home the next day, Mum began to shut down again. I could sense it happening almost as soon as the plane left the tarmac. And by the time we disembarked at Gatwick, where it was raining, she was the same friendly, efficient, but slightly brittle mother I had known all my life.

We hadn't had any kind of conversation about Leif, quite probably because we both felt talked-out about it all, and really a bit emotionally overwrought. But I was beginning to regret not having discussed the future with her while she was in open, relaxed mode. Because I could sense the walls going back up.

I thought about this all the way home, and then, back in Mum's flat in Margate, until the early hours of the morning, as the rain drummed on the roof.

Finally, over breakfast, I decided that one of us was going to have to make an effort to keep the channels of communication open, and that person would have to be me.

'Mum,' I said. She was sipping her tea. 'We need to talk.'

'Do we?' she asked. 'What about?'

'About Leif,' I said. 'About Leif and you, and what happens next.'

'OK, honey,' she said in her fake, upbeat voice. 'What do you want to say to me?'

There was something so false about her – it was as if she was a bad actress in a play. And yet this version of her was entirely familiar to me, and I realised that for much of my childhood she'd essentially been acting. She'd been playing a role – the role of a woman who, despite having lost the love of her life, despite having abandoned all hope, was holding it all together.

'Mum,' I said. 'Come back to me.' She looked puzzled, so I insisted. 'This isn't *you*, Mum. This is fake.'

She worked her mouth for a moment, then the confused expression faded. I could see she knew what I was talking about. Her eyes started to water and she formed a fist with one hand and raised it to her mouth. She stopped looking at me and her glistening eyes roved the ceiling and the corners of the room.

'You love him,' I said. 'He loves you. So what are you going to do about it?'

'I don't know,' she whispered, still avoiding eye contact. 'I don't know what to do.'

'You're going to spend a week putting things in order, then book a flight back out. That's what he thinks you're going to do, anyway.'

'But it's all so distant now,' Mum said, her voice wobbling. 'It's like a dream that can't really happen. And what about my life here? What do I do with that?'

'What life here?' I asked. 'This flat? The job centre? Boarded-up Margate High Street?'

'There's you,' Mum said. '*You're* here.'

'Me?' I laughed. 'I'll be fine. I'm all grown up, Mum. I need to find a job somewhere. And then I need to get on with my life. And I don't care where you are as long as you're happy. You were so *happy* out there, Mum. I've never seen you so happy.'

She started to cry properly, so I moved to her side and crouched down so I could take her in my arms. 'I'm scared, I think,' she breathed through her tears. 'It's silly, but I'm too scared to be that person again.'

'What person, Mum? Who are you scared to be?'

She shrugged. 'The one who believes in it all, I suppose,' she said through tears, her voice all over the place. 'The one who dares to hope.

Because it just hurts so much when that gets taken away. I don't think I could take it again.'

After a fair bit of pushing from my end, and a lot of pulling by Leif, Mum flew back out at the end of October.

Leif had rented a house for the two of them on the coast somewhere north of Oia, and he'd been sending photos to Mum's phone two or three times a day. They were always accompanied by the same sentence. 'Come!' he said every time. 'I'm waiting for you.'

And now, it's late November, and the rain's still drumming down.

Mum and I speak on the phone weekly. She's gone back to sounding normal again. Well, the new normal. The relaxed, funny, honest normal that had been missing for most of my childhood.

She sounds totally in love with Leif, and in love with Santorini too. She's even trying to learn Greek, if you can believe that.

As for me? Well, I've got a part-time job in a cupcake shop in the newly hipsterised centre of Margate. I'm not earning enough to live on, and am slowly eating into the money that Gran left me, but for now it's something, I suppose.

I've looked up a couple of old school friends and met a few new people too, so my evenings and weekends go by in a pleasant-enough way.

I've not yet found where I need to be in life, but I'm OK with that. As Mum has demonstrated, that can take quite some time.

It has been an emotional summer and I'm allowing myself time for the dust to settle before I decide what happens next, I think. That's how it feels, anyway.

I've had occasional WhatsApp messages from Baruch, and we're going to meet in December in Athens as I travel out to Santorini for Christmas. So who knows? Maybe he's *my* destiny. Perhaps that will still happen.

As for 'Dad'? Well, the word still feels strange to me, but I suppose it's starting to feel less so. And as it does, it seems as if the ground beneath my feet becomes less unstable, or maybe as if, having spent my childhood learning to stand perfectly adequately on one foot, I'm suddenly allowed to use both – maybe I can stand on both of their shoulders from here on in.

It's hard to explain, really, but it's made me feel a bit more solid – a tad surer of exactly who I am. And it's opened up fresh possibilities for how I see myself, too.

Maybe I don't have to become the brittle, nervous mother I grew up with, after all. Perhaps I can be relaxed and open, the way Mum is now. Perhaps, if I nurture it, I'll even find that I've inherited my father's superpower for being nice and calm and helpful to others, and I'll end up being a life-enhancing presence for all the friends I make along the way.

I think that would be a pretty good inheritance, don't you?

ACKNOWLEDGMENTS

Thanks to Carole for getting me thinking about romance while I was in Santorini. This novel came, if somewhat indirectly, from the conversation we had there!

Thanks to Rosemary – without your constant encouragement nothing would ever get finished and without your friendship this planet would be a much darker place.

Thanks to Lolo for being my touchstone and for talking these stories through with me long before they exist on paper.

Thanks to Apple for making such reliable work tools. Thanks to everyone at Amazon for all their hard work on this novel, and for turning writing back into something one can actually make a living at. Finally, a big thank you to all my readers for sticking with me and showing so much enthusiasm for every new project – you make it all worthwhile.

ABOUT THE AUTHOR

Photo © 2017 Rosey Aston-Snow

Nick Alexander was born in 1964 in the UK. He has travelled widely and has lived and worked in the UK, the USA and France, where he resides today. *You Then, Me Now* is his fifteenth fictional work. His 2015 novel *The Other Son* was named by Amazon as one of the best fiction titles of the year; *The Photographer's Wife*, published in 2014, was a number-one hit in both the UK and France; while *The Half-Life of Hannah* is the fourth-bestselling independently published Kindle title of all time. Nick's novels have been translated into French, German, Italian, Spanish, Norwegian, Turkish and Croatian. Nick lives in the South of France with his partner, three friendly cats (plus one mean one) and a few trout.

Printed in Great Britain
by Amazon